JAMES HOGG

A Queer Book

THE STIRLING / SOUTH CAROLINA RESEARCH EDITION OF
THE COLLECTED WORKS OF JAMES HOGG
GENERAL EDITOR—DOUGLAS S. MACK

THE STIRLING / SOUTH CAROLINA RESEARCH EDITION OF
THE COLLECTED WORKS OF JAMES HOGG
GENERAL EDITOR—DOUGLAS S. MACK

Volumes are numbered in the order of their publication in
the Stirling / South Carolina Research Edition

1. *The Shepherd's Calendar*, edited by Douglas S. Mack.

2. *The Three Perils of Woman*, edited by David Groves, Antony Hasler,
   and Douglas S. Mack.

3. *A Queer Book*, edited by P. D. Garside.

JAMES HOGG

A Queer Book

Edited by
P. D. Garside

EDINBURGH UNIVERSITY PRESS

1995

© Edinburgh University Press, 1995

Edinburgh University Press
22 George Square
Edinburgh
EH8 9LF

Typeset at the University of Stirling
Printed by The Alden Press, Oxford

ISBN 0 7486 0506 1

A CIP record for this book is available
from the British Library

The Stirling / South Carolina Research Edition of

The Collected Works of James Hogg

The Aims of the Edition

James Hogg lived from 1770 till 1835. He was regarded by his contemporaries as one of the leading writers of the day, but the nature of his fame was influenced by the fact that, as a young man, he had been a self-educated shepherd. The third edition (1814) of his poem *The Queen's Wake* contains an 'Advertisement' which begins as follows.

> The Publisher having been favoured with letters from gentlemen in various parts of the United Kingdom respecting the Author of the *Queen's Wake,* and most of them expressing doubts of his being a Scotch Shepherd, he takes this opportunity of assuring the public, that *The Queen's Wake* is really and truly the production of *James Hogg,* a common Shepherd, bred among the mountains of Ettrick Forest, who went to service when only seven years of age; and since that period has never received any education whatever.

The view of Hogg taken by his contemporaries is also reflected in the various early reviews of *The Private Memoirs and Confessions of a Justified Sinner*, which appeared anonymously in 1824. As Gillian Hughes has shown in the *Newsletter of the James Hogg Society* no. 1, many of these reviews identify Hogg as the author, and see the novel as presenting 'an incongruous mixture of the strongest powers with the strongest absurdities'. The Scotch Shepherd was regarded as a man of powerful and original talent, but it was felt that his lack of education caused his work to be marred by frequent failures in discretion, in expression, and in knowledge of the world. Worst of all was Hogg's lack of what was called 'delicacy', a failing which caused him to deal in his writings with subjects (such as prostitution) which were felt to be unsuitable for mention in polite literature. Hogg was regarded as a man of undoubted genius, but his genius was felt to be seriously flawed.

A posthumous collected edition of Hogg was published in the late 1830s. As was perhaps natural in the circumstances, the publishers (Blackie & Son of Glasgow) took pains to smooth away what they took to be the rough edges of Hogg's writing, and to remove his numerous 'indelicacies'. This process was taken even further in the 1860s, when the Rev. Thomas Thomson prepared a revised edition of Hogg's *Works* for publication by Blackie. These Blackie editions present a bland and lifeless version of Hogg's writings. It was in this version that Hogg was read by the Victorians. Unsurprisingly, he came to be regarded as a minor figure, of no great importance or interest.

The second half of the twentieth century has seen a substantial revival of Hogg's reputation; and he is now generally considered to be one of Scotland's major writers. This new reputation is based on a few works which have been republished in editions based on his original texts. Nevertheless, a number of Hogg's major works remain out of print. Indeed, some have been out of print for more than a century and a half, while others, still less fortunate, have never been published at all in their original, unbowdlerised condition.

Hogg is thus a major writer whose true stature was not recognised in his own lifetime because his social origins led to his being smothered in genteel condescension; and whose true stature has not been recognised since, because of a lack of adequate editions. The poet Douglas Dunn wrote of Hogg in the *Glasgow Herald* in September 1988: 'I can't help but think that in almost any other country of Europe a complete, modern edition of a comparable author would have been available long ago'. The Stirling / South Carolina Edition of James Hogg seeks to fill the gap identified by Douglas Dunn. When completed the edition will run to thirty-one volumes; and it will cover Hogg's prose, his poetry, and his plays.

Acknowledgements

The research for the first volumes of the Stirling / South Carolina Edition of James Hogg has been sustained by funding and other support generously made available by the University of Stirling and by the University of South Carolina. In addition, funding of crucial importance was received through the Glenfiddich Living Scotland Awards; this was particularly pleasant and appropriate, given Hogg's well-known delight in good malt whisky. Valuable grants or donations have also been received from the Carnegie Trust for the Universities of Scotland, from the Association for Scottish Literary Studies, and from the James Hogg Society. The work of the Edition could not have been carried on without the support of these bodies.

Douglas S. Mack
General Editor

Volume Editor's Acknowledgements

During the preparation of the present volume, many people and several institutions have provided help at crucial points. I am above all indebted to Douglas Mack and Gillian Hughes, whose interest in Hogg goes back much further than my own, and without whose guidance this edition would never have been possible. Particular thanks are also due to Ian Brown (Ettrick and Lauderdale Museums Service), John W. Cairns, J.B. Garside, David Groves, Alison Lumsden, Jean Moffat, Wilson Ogilvie, Phil Parr, Elaine Petrie, T.C. Smout, David Stevenson, and Damtew Teferra. I also wish to thank the Alexander Turnbull Library, Wellington, for permission to reproduce and cite manuscript materials in their possession—and, in particular, David C. Retter, who helped make my visit to New Zealand so pleasant and productive. Thanks are also due to the Curator of the James Marshall and Marie-Louise Osborn Collection, the Beinecke Rare Book and Manuscript Library, Yale University, for permission to reproduce the manuscript of 'Ringan and May'. Finally, I am again grateful to the staff and Trustees of the National Library of Scotland for help received and for permission to quote from the Hogg manuscripts in that library.

Peter Garside

Contents

Introduction xi

A Queer Book

The Wyffe of Edzel-more 1
Robyn Reidde 29
Elen of Reigh 45
The Goode Manne of Allowa 55
Jock Johnstone the Tinker 69
A Lay of the Martyrs 77
A Cameronian Ballad 84
The Carle of Invertime 90
The Lairde of Lonne 96
Ringan and May 106
The Grousome Caryl 110
Love's Jubilee 120
Ane Rychte Gude and Preytious Ballande . . . 125
Jocke Taittis Expeditioune till Hell 136
A Bard's Address to his Youngest Daughter . . 144
Johnne Graimis Eckspeditioun till Heuin . . . 147
St. Mary of the Lows 153
The Origin of the Fairies 157
A Highland Eclogue 170
Will and Sandy 175
The Last Stork 180
Superstition and Grace 189
The Witch of the Gray Thorn 193
A Greek Pastoral 197
A Sunday Pastoral 205
The Perilis of Wemyng 214

Notes 226

Glossary 272

Introduction

1. The Genesis of the Work.

On Wednesday 25 April 1832 a front-page advertisement in the *Edinburgh Weekly Journal* announced the publication, 'next week', of 'A QUEER BOOK, BY THE ETTRICK SHEPHERD', 'printed for William Blackwood, Edinburgh, and T. Cadell, London'. In London the book attracted the attention of a number of reviews, their interest no doubt stimulated by the recent visit of 'the Ettrick Shepherd' to the metropolis. Nearly all focused on the unusual nature of the title, invariably interpreting 'Queer' in its normal English (as opposed to Scottish) sense as connoting strangeness or oddness.[1] Typical in this respect is the *Literary Gazette* on Saturday, 5 May 1832: 'This is a queer book—queer in title, queer in plan, queer in execution, queer in beginning, in middle, and in end'. *The Athenaeum*, on the same date, considered eccentricity to be something of a redeeming feature: 'It is, nevertheless, a Queer Book—so wild, and yet so natural—so strange, and yet so true to popular belief, that we are inclined to rank many of its pages with the most successful of all the poet's attempts, saving always the incomparable "Kilmeny".' While, for the more formal and severe *Monthly Review*, Hogg was damned out of his own mouth: 'We suppose that the shepherd of Ettrick imagines that, in consequence of his late reception in London, he may publish any thing he pleases [...] Otherwise we could not have accounted for a [...] volume, which may be justly described not merely as a "Queer Book", but as a book filled with much rank nonsense and ridiculously bad writing.' Amongst all these voices, a more singular note was struck by a short notice in the *New Monthly Magazine*, which begged to differ in the following terms:

> The 'Queer Book' is by no means a queer book. It is simply a collection of poems which the worthy Shepherd of Ettrick has gathered from the north and from the south, from the east and from the west, or in other words, from a variety of periodical works in which they have been printed, and has here published them in a collected form, and in one of the most elegantly printed volumes we have seen. [...] With the greater number of them we are already well acquainted; but they will bear, and have borne, a second reading.[2]

Seen from one angle, the *New Monthly*'s assessment of the situation was entirely correct. Of the twenty-six poems anthologised in the *Queer Book* of 1832, all but two had appeared previously in contemporary periodical publications, during a fairly narrow span between 1825 to 1831, at least one item having been published more than once in this form. Each had been acknowledged by Hogg on their first publication, either under his own name or through well-known pseudonyms such as the Ettrick Shepherd, and more than half of the *Queer Book*'s poems had featured in *Blackwood's Edinburgh Magazine*, which enjoyed a wide readership, and where Hogg's own participation in a variety of guises was widely broadcast. When William Blackwood, publisher of both the Magazine and the *Queer Book*, fell out with Hogg at the end of 1831—a row precipitated by the author's accusation that publication was being deliberately delayed—his irritation more than once found expression in derogatory remarks about the project's credentials. As he wrote to Thomas Hamilton, on 25 April 1832, 'His Queer Book as he calls it is merely a republication of some of the humorous Ballads which appeared in Maga'.[3]

In one respect Blackwood was guilty of exaggerating for effect, since eight of the *Queer Book* poems had been originally sent by Hogg not to *Blackwood's* but to the literary 'annuals', which had sprung up as a major form of publication in the 1820s. This new outlet considerably extended Hogg's options in placing his poetry, while offering the challenge of writing in different contexts and for a new and extensive readership. So encouraged he was able to practise and develop a wide variety of styles, exhibiting the kind of virtuosity which had always characterised his more successful poetical works, notably *The Queen's Wake* (1813), with its seventeen 'bardic' performances, and the brilliantly parodic *Poetic Mirror* (1816). In this later period, too, Hogg continued to explore issues similar to those found in his major fiction—the nature of moral damnation, the relationship between sexual and spiritual love, the corrosive effect of aristocratical *mores*—sometimes employing the shorter form of the poem as a kind of 'sketch' in which new facets could be examined. While it would be wrong to deny a strong financial motivation behind the new project, Hogg must have relished the prospect of reassembling a body of material, self-confessedly eccentric but capable of revealing its own inner patterns, which otherwise seemed destined to drift into oblivion.

The earliest surviving evidence of Hogg's plan is found in a snippet of gossip in the *Edinburgh Literary Journal* for 25 December 1830: 'There is preparing for publication, in Edinburgh, "Ane

rychte queire and mervoullous buik, compilit be Maister Hougge"'.[4]
The project first surfaces in the Blackwood Papers in a letter from
William Blackwood to Hogg on 26 February 1831, which also
mentions Hogg's nephew, Robert Hogg, who worked as a corrector
of the press for the publisher, and Andrew Shortreed, who had
recently established himself in Edinburgh as a printer:

> Shortreed will print the volume, and you may I daresay leave
> the correction entirely to Robert. If therefore you send some
> more original ones with a list of the order in which those in
> Maga should be inserted, we will push on the printing as fast as
> possible. I am very anxious however you should give a few
> capital humourous ones to begin the volume with, before we
> take any of the Mag. ones. This is necessary for the sake of
> novelty & effect.
>
> Your Songs are liked by every body, and the sale is going on
> well.[5]

As the last sentence indicates, the planning of the *Queer Book* came in
the wake of the successful launching of *Songs, By the Ettrick Shepherd*
(1831). In this earlier project, Hogg had enjoyed an unusual amount
of autonomy, not only making the selection but also transcribing his
materials anew, with additional notes, and even making his own
suggestions for the layout and presentation of the volume.[6] The
'volume of Ballads'[7] now under consideration was clearly envisaged
as a companion-piece, bringing together a selection of longer poems
by Hogg. When finally published, the *Queer Book* was virtually iden-
tical in appearance to its predecessor, the embossed cloth binding
also resembling several of the literary annuals.

Owing to the more unwieldy nature of its materials, both in terms
of length and availability, Hogg's control of the second project was
more limited. As he wrote in his reply to Blackwood on 9 March
1831:

> Having no sets of Maga I cannot select the ballads but I have
> such a variety such a choice [...] that there is no occassion for
> adding any more save some very late ones in Maga and some
> very celebrated ones in the Annuals none of them will ever be
> recognised as having been printed before. [...] I leave Robert
> the selection with a reference to you when doubtful for without
> coming to Edinr I cannot select The best that strike me at this
> moment and I shall name as the[y] strike me in superiority
> "Ellen of Rey" (*the best I ever wrote*) "Superstition and Grace"

(see Bijou) "Some in the Amulet" "Ringan and May" "The Gudeman of Alloa" "Jock Johnstone the Tinkler" "The Lairde of Lonne" "The Gude greye Katte" But they are numberless and you will get them every where. There should likewise be a few of the *very best* of the Miscellanies for critics to quote from. It will be a grand book for thae Englishers for they winna understand a word of it. I mean such as Will and Sandy and all the best of a pastoral nature and in that case the title should be "*Romantic Ballads* and *Pastorals* of The Ettrick Shepherd" because in the selection we must keep the title in view.[8]

While apparently allowing Blackwood a free hand in the selection, Hogg noticeably manages to draw up his own list of items to include, at the same time shifting the emphasis away from a collection of ballads pure and simple. As well as nominating seven of the poems which later appeared in the *Queer Book*, he also invites the inclusion of 'A Lay of the Martyrs' and 'A Cameronian Ballad' from *The Amulet* (his only two poems to date in that annual); then, by implication, that of of 'A Sunday Pastoral' and 'A Greek Pastoral' from *Blackwood's Edinburgh Magazine*. The suggestion that 'some very late ones in Maga' be added is likewise interpretable as a recommendation of three further poems published in *Blackwood's*, 'The Last Stork' (February 1830), 'The Origin of the Fairies' (August 1830), and 'Jocke Taittis Expeditioune till Hell' (September 1830). To this list can be added 'Johnne Graimis Eckspeditioun till Heuin', which Hogg's next letter of 15 March offered as suitable for either the Magazine or the book (in the event it went into both!).

All but nine of the *Queer Book* poems with a periodical origin, according to this calculation, were tacitly proposed by Hogg at an early point and when he was supposedly incapacitated from checking past numbers himself. Indeed, one might suspect an element of manoeuvring on his part, with Blackwood being left with the impression of management while effectively being told what to do. A similar design could underlie the suggestion that Robert Hogg should make the 'selection', a significant shift from Blackwood's initial proposal, on 26 February, that the 'correction' be left 'entirely to Robert'. If a strategy was intended in this second instance, however, it was singularly ineffective. Blackwood's subsequent letter of 12 March left little doubt that still more radical changes were being contemplated:

I have given your Nephew a list of the Ballads and we will get on speedily with them. We had a long conversation the other

day on the subject. He thinks decidedly that the spelling you
have adopted, being neither genuine old Scotch nor English
would injure the book very much. He has however written you
at full length himself upon the subject and has altered a few
pages to show you what his idea is. I wish much you would leave
everything to him, as he will be most careful and understands it
much better than either you or me.[9]

The main target here was undoubtedly Hogg's 'ancient stile': a
combination of ballad phraseology, the rhetoric of the late medieval
Scottish 'makars', such as Robert Henryson, and more modern idio-
matic expression. Blackwood's impatience with its 'hybrid' qualities
was already known to Hogg. When 'The Grousome Caryl'—the
earliest of the poems, in terms of original date of publication, to
appear in the *Queer Book*—was first submitted to *Blackwood's*, he had
responded in the following terms: 'it is a capital production and will
strike every one. Your orthography however I have the same com-
plaint against as at no period whatever was the Scots language so
written.'[10] In this case, however, much of Hogg's orthography was
allowed to stand. Idiosyncrasies of this sort were not considered fatal
in a Magazine with a predominantly male and Scottish readership,
and where verbal games were allowed relatively free range. At the
very least, the foibles of 'the Shepherd' were to be tolerated. In a
published book, aimed at the general literary market, however, the
same licence could not be allowed. Hogg's jesting remark that
English readers 'winna understand a word of it' could hardly have
been worse calculated, since Blackwood would have been expecting
to offload at least half of the impression on his London partners. A
general distribution also implied a female as well as Southern reader-
ship, and some of the more rumbustious elements tolerated in *Black-
wood's* might also need toning down. Robert Hogg had been em-
ployed in just such a 'pruning' of indelicacies of style and matter in
Hogg's last full-scale prose publication, *The Shepherd's Calendar*
(1829).[11]

Blackwood's announcement must have come as a severe blow,
since up to this point Hogg had clearly viewed his 'ancient stile' as an
integral part of the *Queer Book* project. Increasingly in the 1820s
he had turned to this mode for self-expression, finding a major
outlet in *Blackwood's* in spite of its proprietor's reservations. Its
extended linguistic range and spontaneous rhythmic effects allowed
an escape from the stereotypical English lyricism of the journals, as
well too from an increasingly tired-looking form of Anglo-Scots

ballad which had proliferated in the wake of Scott's *Minstrelsy of the Scottish Border* (1802–03). Hogg also found freedom to mix different genres, combining pathos with dark humour, physical and spiritual levels of experience, the supernatural and the satirical, sometimes creating a kind of 'magic realism' not dissimilar to that now seen in postmodern fiction. Through word play, allegory, and the camouflage provided by 'antiquity', he could also be more daring in sexual terms than in any other contemporary public mode, and so discovered a means of circumventing, if only for brief moments, the incipient prudishness of the later 1820s.

In his next letter to Blackwood, on 15 March, Hogg conceded the issue with an air of good grace:

> On the consideration of all these things I give up my beloved ancient stile to you and Robert knowing that there *can be* nothing in the request but my fame and honour I cannot correct the sheets for it would take me to write them all over again but I beg to see the corrected copies before they are thrown finally off Perhaps there may be a few favourite terms that I cannot part with.[12]

The element of regret in 'my beloved ancient stile' is, nevertheless, palpable. Noticeably, too, the concession is positioned immediately after somewhat effusive thanks for sums of money received from Blackwood. One does not need to look hard to discover a fairly strong intimation that the concession belonged strictly to the material world.

There is nothing in Blackwood's reply of 17 March to indicate any sense of a resulting loss of quality: 'I am happy on all accounts that you allow Robert to exercise his own good taste in correcting your orthography. I am sure it will benefit the book much.'[13] Whether Hogg actually received proofs is a matter which will be discussed later. In all other respects, control of the text had effectively passed out of the author's hands. Such was by no means a novel experience for Hogg, whose social position made him vulnerable to the dictates of publishers. In fact, as the next section will argue, several of his poems had already suffered forms of censorship before their entry in the *Queer Book*.

2. The Periodical Context.

'I am perswaded that some things in Maga have operated singularly to my advantage for the applications for contributions from my *highly gifted pen* have of late increased to a most laughable and puzzling extent.'[14] Hogg's delight in the new outlets provided by the periodicals is unmistakable in his letter to Blackwood on 11 August 1827. In the following months, moreover, he was to receive applications from at least four more leading journals. This new prospect opened just as the opportunity for publishing full-length works was drying up. Hogg could also look forward to a series of prompt payments on receipt of material instead of the irregular and often mystifying shares of profits handed down by publishers. In this and other respects, however, his initial hopes were unfulfilled, and even before the publication of *A Queer Book* more than one 'editor' had been blacklisted by Hogg while relations with Blackwood were at breaking point.

Between 1825 and 1831 Hogg published more than forty poems in *Blackwood's Edinburgh Magazine*, of which sixteen of the longer pieces were selected for the *Queer Book*. There are several reasons why he should feel comfortable and well-placed in this journal. Since 1817 he had felt closely connected with its editors, J.G. Lockhart and John Wilson, playing a key part in the satirical 'Chaldee Manuscript' which arguably did more than anything to set the tone of the Magazine and fix its anti-Whig stance in Edinburgh.[15] The proximity of Hogg's two homes of this period, at Altrive Lake and Mount Benger, made communications relatively easy, a process bolstered by periodic visits to Edinburgh. William Blackwood was a regular correspondent, both as proprietor and friend, not only providing Hogg with fairly regular payments of up to £5 but also sending invaluable supplies of writing materials.[16]

Ideologically and culturally, *Blackwood's* could also seem welcoming from Hogg's vantage point. Based in Edinburgh, and with an audience concentrated in the northern areas of Britain, it represented an obvious receptacle for Scottish subjects and literature in Scots. As a monthly publication there was no obligation to cultivate the dignified air of establishment quarterlies, such as the *Edinburgh* and *Quarterly* reviews, while a primarily masculine readership obviated the need for absolute sexual propriety. Nor were the Tory politics of *Blackwood's* necessarily inimical to Hogg, whose persona as 'the Ettrick Shepherd' had a clear appeal in a Magazine directed at the landed interest. In the immediate pre-Reform years of 1829–31, there are some indications that Hogg felt uncomfortable with the High Tory, anti-Catholic stance struck by some of the Magazine's contributors.[17] Nevertheless the ferment of these years, and the Magazine's wholehearted engagement in controversy, provided a heady and exciting atmosphere, encouraging the submission of two topical poems, 'Will and Sandy' and 'The Last Stork', whose double-edged satire was perhaps not fully recognised by the original readers of the Magazine.

On the other hand, there is evidence of growing tension in Hogg's relationship with the *Blackwood's* circle in later years. Increasingly Hogg felt excluded from the inner sanctum, both patronised and disregarded by the classically educated and socially superior Wilson and Lockhart. In particular, his depiction as the buffoonish, bibulous 'Shepherd' in the 'Noctes Ambrosianae' series seemed to threaten his interests as a serious professional writer. An especially sore point was his failure to secure a grant from the Royal Society of Literature, which Hogg attributed to the pictures of dissipation in the 'Noctes'.[18] Outbursts against Blackwood himself are not infrequent in this period, and these can sometimes seem singularly unfair in view of the encouragement received. Yet it is noticeable the publisher generally reserved his praise for Hogg's more predictable contributions, especially the comic ballad. Indeed, as his contributions accelerated in 1830, Hogg probably felt caught in a dilemma, under pressure to vary his style but at the same time nervous of Blackwood's veto of his more innovative pieces.

Hogg was also subject to two forms of tacit censorship when making contributions to *Blackwood's*. While a certain degree of badinage and sexual innuendo was permissible—if only as a token of the Shepherd's uncouthness—explicit 'indelicacies', running counter to accepted standards of gentility, were vulnerable to editorial excision. Though there is no evidence of the texts later anthologised in the *Queer Book* having been altered for this reason, earlier manuscript drafts occasionally point to an element of self-censorship by Hogg before drawing up his final version. A more rigid barrier was presented by Blackwood's opposition to anything which risked offending orthodox Presbyterian opinion.[19] A clear example, directly relevant to the *Queer Book*, is found in the complex history of 'A Sunday Pastoral', where Blackwood's stated objection to the mixture of the 'ludicrous' with 'solemn and fine religious feeling' necessitated a complete redrafting by Hogg and the addition of an explicitly religious conclusion to the poem.[20]

After acceptance by Blackwood, Hogg's poems normally went straight to the compositors, who were often under pressure to meet printing deadlines. In the process of setting a number of changes were made to the text, which accumulatively can be seen to have had a deleterious effect on Hogg's writing. Invariably standard grammatical punctuation was supplied, even where Hogg had provided a full apparatus himself. Idiosyncratic spellings were normalised in English contexts; and, while much of Hogg's 'ancient' orthography was allowed to stand, comparison between the manuscript and printed versions sometimes reveals a shift to more recognisable forms (e.g., 'withinne' instead of 'wythinne'). Individual words could be misread in haste, especially those of a more arcane or personal nature, sometimes with serious consequences. A notable instance is the rendering of Hogg's 'maike' as 'snaike' in the third line of 'Ane Rychte Gude and Preytious Ballande', an error compounded by the survival of 'maike' later in the poem. Similarly in the 'The Witch of the Gray Thorn', no less than six key words were replaced by less satisfactory alternatives. In the light of these mistakes, it seems unlikely that Hogg saw proofs of any of the poems in the *Queer Book* before publication in *Blackwood's*.

The same pressures did not apply in the case of the literary annuals, which were usually published in time for Christmas, as a keepsake for the following year. The mould for this new form of publication was set by the *Forget Me Not*, subtitled 'A Christmas and New Year's Present', whose first number was offered for the year 1823. Another landmark was the foundation two years later of the *Literary Souvenir*, edited by Alaric A. Watts, and sales of these two publications had reached 10,000 copies annually by the later 1820s. The annuals were elegantly-produced miscellanies, assembling short literary pieces by contemporary writers of reputation, in lavishly bound and expensively illustrated single volumes. Hogg's first poetical contribution appeared in the *Literary Souvenir* for 1825, to which, early in 1825, he also sent 'Love's Jubilee'—the earliest of the annual poems later anthologised in the *Queer Book*.[21] By Spring 1827 Hogg had received a complimentary copy of the *Forget Me Not* from its publisher, and was sending material for the attention of Frederic Shoberl, its recently-appointed editor.[22] By the following Spring requests had arrived from three more London-based editors: Thomas Pringle, Allan Cunningham and Thomas Hood, editors (respectively) of *Friendship's Offering*, *The Anniversary*, and *The Gem*.[23] Another important contact was S.C. Hall, of *The Amulet*, who wrote on 8 April 1829 requesting 'a prose tale and a poem from you at your earliest convenience'.[24] Between the years 1825–30 Hogg was able to place more than twenty poems in the annuals, of which eight longer items, from seven of the more prominent titles, were reprinted in the *Queer Book*.

Seen as a group the annuals give the impression of having catered for a variety of tastes, from the relatively eclectic *Bijou* and *Gem*, which counted Southey, Keats and Coleridge among their contributors, to the more doctrinaire and evangelically-inclined *Amulet*. Yet all were essentially targeted at the same reading group: 'genteel', youthful, mainly southern, and with a large female component. Editorial prefaces tended to stress the propriety of the contributions and their suitability for the drawing-room. Thomas Pringle, introducing *Friendship's Offering* for 1829, drew attention to its 'uniform tone of pure morality'; while the first number of the *Amulet* (for 1826) vouched that 'Nothing [...] will occur, either to disturb the opinions, or to shock the prejudices of any Christian'. In the case of the latter, where the prohibitions were heavily signalled, Hogg appears to have selected his materials with circumspection, even offering S.C. Hall the option of making changes 'to suit the fastidious taste of the day'.[25] With *Friendship's Offering*, on the other hand, if Hogg had any expectations of extra licence they were quickly dashed. In a letter of 28 May 1828, Pringle rejected an (unidentified) poem in these terms:

> It is full of wild originality & bold striking imagery—but altogether it seems to me too strange & droll, & "high kilted" for the very "gentie" publication now under my charge. Were it for a Magazine or some such work I should not feel so particular but for these "douce" & delicate publications the annuals I think it rather inappropriate. [...] I think it ought to be a rule [...] to admit not a single expression which would call up a blush in the Cheek of the most delicate female if reading aloud to a mixt Company.[26]

Pringle was still resisting Hogg's 'broad' humour three years later, when he recommended Mrs Hogg (whose views, in actuality, were closer to her husband's) as a test of decorum, 'for without any disparagement to you, my friend, I opine that she knows better what will suit a lady's work Table'.[27] In varying degrees, all the poems from the annuals in the *Queer Book* were forced to run the gauntlet of the new propriety.

Another inhibiting factor was the annuals' preference for shortish 'set piece' poems—from Hogg, preferably in the 'Kilmeny' mode. Not untypical is Allan Cunningham's request on 9 October 1828 for 'some sweet delicious Fairy thing [...] in verse', no more than '4 or 5 pages long'.[28] Undeterred, Hogg continued to press longer pieces on some editors, even threatening Cunningham at one point with 'a poetical tale' capable of filling 'upwards of 35 pages'.[29] In the circumstances it is quite feasible that a few contributions, possibly including those later reproduced in the *Queer Book*, were cut edit-orially—an intervention, it should be added, almost half-invited by some of Hogg's letters. 'Your Poem is excellent—your tales capital —but too long for my space', Cunningham wrote on 26 May 1828, 'but this I can manage without injuring them in any little abridge-ment which I make.'[30] It is not impossible that the poem in question, 'The Carle of Invertime', was tailored down to size as a result, either by Hogg voluntarily or by Cunningham himself.

Just as debilitating could be the more venial intrusions of the London printers. Not surprisingly, no poem in Hogg's 'ancient stile' appeared in the annuals (perhaps none were submitted), but even the most orthodox Scots terms were capable of causing conster-nation. 'Superstition and Grace', which appeared in the *Bijou* for 1829, actually represented a diluted version of another item pub-lished by Hogg, 'The Gyre Caryl' (1822), where 'ancient' ortho-graphy had featured extensively. Even so, the compositor foundered on a number of surviving Scotticisms, misinterpreting 'fauldit' (folded) as 'faulelit' and 'asklent' (aslant) as the equally meaningless 'artlent'. Proper names could be equally confusing. In setting 'A Cameronian Ballad' the *Amulet* compositor misinterpreted Earlston (a historical figure) as 'Earlyton', misled no doubt by Hogg's long-tailed 's' in the manuscript.

By 1830 Hogg's relationship with a number of editors had become strained. One aggravation was their failure to return unwanted manuscripts, his stated reason for dropping Alaric Watts: 'If one M.S. of mine is lost I write no more for that editor as Mr A A Watts and several others can tell'.[31] Matters were made worse by the failure of Cunningham's *Anniversary* in 1829 and the unexpected prud-ishness shown by Pringle, and it is not impossible that some of the materials sent in this direction eventually tumbled back towards Blackwood. On 4 June 1831 Hogg told Frederic Shoberl, of the *Forget Me Not*, that 'you are likely to be the only editor this year who has aught from my pen'.[32] In this respect, the poems selected from the annuals scarcely represented an ongoing activity when the *Queer Book* finally appeared.

3. Production and Reception.

Production of the *Queer Book*, which began soon after the exchange of letters between Hogg and Blackwood in March 1831, appears to have been completed by early Summer that year.[33] 1000 copies were printed, 500 less than of *Songs, by the Ettrick Shepherd*, a reduction which suggests some caution on Blackwood's part. It is not entirely clear how Robert Hogg's 'correction' was implemented, but the probability is that a similar procedure was followed to that used to produce *The Shepherd's Calendar* (1829), with copies of the original magazines being marked up in preparation for the compositor.[34] In the case of the two lead poems, however, where no previously printed versions were available, the likelihood is that proofs were made up from Hogg's manuscript before any sizeable changes were made.

In the process of 'correction' the most sweeping changes were made to the ten *Queer Book* poems written in Hogg's full-flown 'ancient stile'. An idea of the pervasiveness of these alterations, and their effect on the tenor of Hogg's poetry, can be gathered by comparing the opening four lines of 'Ringan and May' in the *Blackwood's* version (itself, it is worth noting, already altered from Hogg's original manuscript) with the 'normalised' version found in the *Queer Book* of 1832:

Blackwood's
I hearit ane laveroke synging with gle,
And O but the burde sang cheirilye;
Then I axit at my true love Ringan,
Gif he kend quhat the bonnye burde wals syngan?

A Queer Book
I heard a laverock singing with glee,
And oh but the bird sang cheerilye;
Then I askit at my true love Ringan,
If he kend what the bonny bird was singing?

Here the changes are mainly orthographical—'If' for 'Gif', 'what' for 'quhat', 'bird' for 'burde'—though accumulatively this gives a flatter, more 'explicit' feel to the text. Elsewhere the search for English equivalents led to larger verbal shifts ('behind' for 'ahynde', 'swim' for 'soome'), while some replacements involved a fuller diminution of meaning: 'hackerit' in 'The Wyffe of Ezdel-more' (Fytte the Fourthe, line 45), denoting the cracked and wrinkled skin of the Laird's mother, is insufficiently represented by 'haggard', an etymologically distinct word. When replacements were not forthcoming, or proved too unsettling, 'ancient' words were left to stand, creating a new kind of 'hybrid' unimagined either by Hogg or Blackwood. This is particularly evident where rhyme schemes demanded the retention of a word (for example, 'dow' (dove) in line

13 of 'Ringan and May' was required to match 'you' immediately
below).

Additionally, the large-scale pruning of Hogg's suffixes ('is' and
'it', used normally for plural nouns and past tenses) has a noticeable
deadening effect on the open rhythm of these poems, leading to a
sense of hollowness which the *Queer Book* now and then attempted to
fill with the insertion of an entirely new word. The changes also
disrupted much of Hogg's verbal inventiveness, not least the playful
mixture of Henrysonian language and latter-day coinages, and it is
with a sense of disappointment that one finds 'haldockis' being
brought to ground as 'haddocks' and 'veetalis' returning to 'vitals'.
In such ways, Hogg's vibrant and liberating form was reconstructed
into a more orthodox kind of Anglo-Scots poetry, readily under-
stood on both sides of the Border, and grist to the mill for the
Edinburgh book trade at this period.

The *Queer Book* of 1832 also made a number of standard changes
through the text as a whole. Its punctuation is generally heavier than
the magazine originals, one noticeable feature being the large incur-
sion of commas and associated marks within lines. Initial capital
letters were also raised—for instance, 'tinkler' to 'Tinkler' in 'Jock
Johnstone', and 'heaven' to 'Heaven' in 'A Lay of the Martyrs'—
adding a more formal air to several poems. Apart from the disap-
pearance of the last stanza in 'St. Mary of the Lows'—itself probably
the result of an accident in production—there is no striking instance
of text being omitted. But five titles were substantially altered, gen-
erally to shorter and more explicit alternatives, partly perhaps to
detract attention away from their recent appearance in the journals.
Hogg's subtitles, with their various authorial descriptions, were also
removed; as too were his end inscriptions, giving date and place of
composition—with the exception of two items with a topical history.
Space was also opened up between verse paragraphs in some nar-
rative poems, no doubt in an effort to alleviate the cramped look of
the Magazine texts, though this sometimes has the effect of disrupting
Hogg's original design—lending, for example, an inappropriate
'lyric' air to 'Ringan and May'. Overall the *Queer Book* succeeds in
giving an impression of homogeneity, masking the different styles of
the poems and the various contexts in which they had first appeared.

It is not clear whether Hogg received proofs with his nephew's
corrections, as requested, though it is possible these are referred to in
a letter from Blackwood on 25 June 1831: 'I rec^d the proofs by the
Carrier just now but without even a line from you.'[35] Certainly, a
number of substantive changes in the *Queer Book* suggest an authorial

involvement of sorts. In 'A Cameronian Ballad', under its new title
'Bothwell Brigg', 'Earlyton' is corrected to 'Earlston'; while 'snaike'
in line three of 'Ane Rychte Gude and Preytious Ballande' (re-titled
'The Spirit of the Glen') is corrected back to Hogg's original 'maike'.
In a number of other poems, too, corrections of single words un-
cannily match Hogg's original intention: thus in 'Will and Sandy'
'rebellion's birr', as in *Blackwood's*, is changed in the *Queer Book* to
'rebellion's birn'—'birn' referring to the mark of ownership on an
animal, a term both familiar to Hogg and appropriate for his shep-
herd speaker. There is a faint possibility that these originated from
Robert Hogg consulting manuscripts held by Blackwood, but this
seems unlikely in light of the sporadic nature of the changes, and in
view of the fact that similar emendations are found in poems first
published in the annuals (e.g. 'asklent' is restored in 'Superstition
and Grace'). Especially telling, in this respect, is the addition of a
whole new paragraph to 'A Bard's Address to his Youngest
Daughter' which reproduces, without exactly replicating, a passage
from another version of the same poem then only known to Hogg's
family. Since it would have been highly disruptive to insert this at a
late proof stage, the most likely explanation is that it was added from
memory to a copy of the magazine text at an earlier point. This in
turn opens up the possibility that other poems in their magazine form
were marked up by Hogg before printing began. If corrected proofs
were eventually sent to Ettrick, they are unlikely to to have left much
leeway for the reintroduction of any of his 'favourite terms'.

At least Hogg could look forward to imminent publication, with
the prospect of payment from Blackwood. But even here he met
disappointment. In his letter of 25 June 1831, Blackwood noted a
slump in the book trade, due in his eyes to the current agitation for
Reform: 'It would be ruin therefore to attempt to publish your
Ballads till business gets into a more healthy state. [...] Maga is the
only thing that keeps us alive.'[36] By Autumn Hogg had begun
rebuilding his house at Altrive Lake, and was desperate for funds.
'The Ballads must be published the beginning of next month', he
protested on 1 October; and, again, in another letter on 24 October:
'Surely my new work should now be published. I wish it had come
out in the interregnum of Parliament.'[37] Blackwood nevertheless
continued to stall, writing on 29 October that he was unable to make
an advance, being out of pocket over the *Songs*, and that the times
were still not propitious for publication.[38] Presumably he knew his
own business—the book trade had suffered a series of bankruptcies in
1826, and the country was in turmoil after the House of Lords'

rejection of the second Reform Bill on 8 October 1831—but to Hogg it seemed beyond belief that the book should be printed and then not released. 'By all means let the Miscellanies be published. What signifies letting a thing lie over for a year after printing. Let it take its chance'. Undoubtedly Blackwood's refusal was a main factor in an open row which broke out before the end of the year. Writing on 6 December, shortly before leaving for London, Hogg demanded the return of all his literary manuscripts and stated his determination to find another publisher for the *Queer Book*:

> As to the trivial work which you have printed and dare not publish I will try to get some minor bookseller to pay you the expence and take it off your hand Were it in my power I would do it to morrow rather than have it published under your auspices.[39]

Encouraged by his reception in London, Hogg in the new year set about finding an alternative outlet. John Murray, having 'taken a fancy to the Title', wrote at the end of January for 'a copy of the sheets' for consideration;[40] and Hogg on 5 February urgently requested from Blackwood an account of printing expenses, adding somewhat cryptically that 'I have laid the whole of our transactions before the public'.[41] Here he was alluding to 'Reminiscences of Former Days', an extension to his 'Memoir of the Author's Life', which appeared shortly afterwards in *Altrive Tales* (1832). The relevant passage occurs after comments on the favourable reception of his *Songs*: 'the year before last, the baillie also ventured to *print* one thousand copies of a miscellaneous work of mine, which, for fear of that great bugbear, REFORM, he has never dared to publish, and I am convinced never will.'[42] On 13 February Blackwood duly presented his account: 'The impression of your Ballads is 1000 copies and the expences of the paper & printing is £92-16—on payment of which the whole will be shipped to your order.'[43] Hogg answered on 2 March with an urgent request for a copy to show Murray; but, as Blackwood observed on 7 March, one had already been dispatched to his partner Cadell for the author's express use. Hogg left London before the end of the month, without making an arrangement with Murray, and by then probably glad of Blackwood's proposal, in his letter of 7 March, that the work be 'completed and published' by him.[44]

The final preparations, including the printing of preliminaries, are likely to have taken place after Hogg's return, and the dedication to Christopher North and Timothy Tickler (two stalwarts in the

'Noctes') seems to signal a return to the *Blackwood's* fold. At the same time Hogg managed to preserve his chosen title for the work, in spite of evident misgivings on Blackwood's part.[45]

As previously indicated, *A Queer Book* received mixed reviews in London, while in Scotland it appears to have gone virtually unnoticed. The *Monthly Review*, in the longest and probably most influential notice, adopted a mocking attitude towards the remnants of Hogg's 'ancient stile':

> It contains a series of ballads and other poems, drawn up in what Mr. Hogg believes to be an 'old style'; but in what part of the country he found models for many of his strange and uncouth expressions [...] we are at a loss to conjecture.

The reviewer then proceeded to hold up some of the more risible examples in the first poem—'snoolit', 'deray', 'yuff' and 'fleg'—all of which in actuality were based on contemporary Scots usage (see Glossary). (It would be hard to find a better justification of Blackwood's fears for the fate of the volume in the South.) Among such 'base alloy', a few strands of gold could be distinguished, in the sentimental 'Elen of Reigh' ('a strange mixture of beautiful poetry with the most egregious silliness'), and in 'A Bard's Address', which was quoted in full.[46] Other reviewers were also inclined to pick out single items, from a collection generally held to be mixed in quality: the *Literary Gazette* quoting 'Will and Sandy' and 'Ringan and May' at length, the *Athenaeum* preferring 'Elen of Reigh' and 'A Sunday Pastoral'. Only the Scottish-based *Tait's Edinburgh Magazine* expressed unqualified enthusiasm for the more fanciful 'wild' poems: 'The stories most to our mind are, "Robin Reid", "Jock Johnstone, the Tinkler", "The Laird of Lun", and the "Origin of the Fairies".'[47] Interestingly both the *Athenaeum* and the *New Monthly Magazine* made a point of complimenting the 'getting up' of the volume (i.e. its physical characteristics), the latter declaring this to be 'highly creditable to the press of Scotland'.[48]

Sales of the work were unspectacular. On 27 June 1834 Hogg wrote asking Alexander Blackwood for 'a few copies of *the queer Book*', at the same time fishing for news of the edition:

> By the by I think that work has never been published as I never once saw it advertised but as I did not then get the Magazine it is probable it may have been advertised there. Published or not I request that you will change the title page into something like the following which your father will correct or alter as he lists

'The Shepherd's Ballads. Being a selection of all his best miscel-
laneous Pieces'.[49]

Earlier Hogg had written to a correspondent in America, hinting at
the possibility of an edition there, 'as all my best ballads, both
humorous and pathetic, are included'.[50] Hogg's poetry was popular
in America, but no edition at this period has been discovered, while
in Britain another impression was not called for. Sixteen of the *Queer
Book*'s twenty-six poems were reprinted (with some cuts), shortly
after Hogg's death, in the first two volumes of Blackie and Son's
Poetical Works of the Ettrick Shepherd [1838–40], but it is doubtful Hogg
had any part in the selection. These same items reappeared in
volume II of the Rev. Thomas Thomson's *Works of the Ettrick Shepherd*
(1865), further dispersed under two headings, 'Poetical Tales and
Ballads' and 'Poems Descriptive and Sentimental'. As collections
turned into selections, so did the *Queer Book* component diminish. By
the time of *The Poems of James Hogg, the Ettrick Shepherd (Selected), with
an Introduction by Mrs Garden* (1887) only the ballad 'Jock Johnstone'
and 'A Bard's Address' had survived.

    Recent developments in Hogg studies have led to a new awareness
of the complexity of the *Queer Book* poems, both from a critical and
editorial viewpoint. While showing scant attention to the collection
as a whole, several recent critical studies have highlighted individual
titles—notably 'Ringan and May', 'St. Mary of the Lows', and 'The
Perilis of Wemyng'—in illustration of the diversity of Hogg's output
as a poet in the 1820s. Noticeably, too, magazine versions of 'A
Cameronian Ballad' and 'The Goode Manne of Allowa' were pre-
ferred as the basis for annotated versions of these poems in two *Altrive
Chapbooks*, produced by the James Hogg Society in the 1980s—the
latter choice determined by a growing perception of the impor-
tance of Hogg's 'ancient stile' in releasing him from 'the mundane
sobriety of every-day English or Scots'.[51] A new sense of the validity
of Hogg's original manuscripts informs David Groves's edition of
Selected Poems and Songs (1986), where, for the first time, 'A Bard's
Address to his Youngest Daughter' is copied from a surviving
manuscript in the Alexander Turnbull Library in New Zealand.
Nevertheless, the effort to restore texts closer to Hogg's original in-
tentions has so far been conducted in a relatively sporadic fashion,
with the textual history of the *Queer Book* poems largely remaining
obscure.

4. The Present Edition.

The present edition follows two general principles which at first sight might seem contradictory. On the one hand, it accepts and repeats in the same order the collection of items brought together by the *Queer Book* of 1832. On the other hand, in establishing texts for individual poems it rejects on every occasion the version found in the first *Queer Book*, searching instead for earlier states of Hogg's text.

The reproduction of a volume comprising, in Edith C. Batho's words, 'a medley of ballads, serious and half-serious, descriptive and sentimental poems, and two or three political allegories',[52] might in itself seem a dubious activity. Financial motives played a large part in initiating the project, and Hogg's capacity to control the selection was limited. A lack of guiding purpose also seems to underlie the shifting titles found in Hogg's letters: from 'Romantic Ballads and Pastorals of the Ettrick Shepherd' (9 March 1831), through 'the Ballads' (1 October 1831) and 'the Miscellanies' (2 November 1831), to the post-publication suggestion of a change to 'The Shepherd's Ballads: Being a selection of his best miscellaneous Pieces'. Nevertheless, as previously argued, Hogg in some respects does appear to have manipulated the kind of selection he wanted—bringing together an assortment of longer poems, in different styles, which lay scattered in *Blackwood's Edinburgh Magazine* or were cast adrift in the annuals. The final title too was evidently present from the beginning, and held firm in Hogg's mind in the months immediately before publication. One of the possible connotations of 'queer' (as odd, quirky, eccentric) was reaffirmed in the dedication's reference to 'this motley work', though both epithets have a positive as well as negative application. Hogg's offering was, above all, a demonstration of his *versatility* as a contemporary author: a testimony to a varied output, written under several authorial personae, which had appealed to diverse literary audiences.

Equally by assembling a body of work, written in different styles and on different subjects, the *Queer Book* was a way of demonstrating its author's mastery as a latter-day 'makar'. Like some of his predecessors from the 'golden age' of James IV of Scotland, notably William Dunbar, Hogg covers the span of allegory, folk ballad, comic narrative, philosophical musing, and natural description. Mirroring Hogg's larger projects in the 1820s, such as the *Three Perils of Woman* (1823), his poems likewise cover a range of Scottish life in its different regions: not only Hogg's own Ettrick, but also in the North Highlands ('A Highland Eclogue'), on the banks of the Forth ('The Goode Manne of Allowa'), in Nithsdale and the South West

('A Lay of the Martyrs', 'A Cameronian Ballad'), in the South East ('The Lairde of Lonne', 'Superstition and Grace'), and on the Border with England ('Robyn Reidde'). Finally there is no sense of dissatisfaction on Hogg's part with the selection once it had been made. Even making allowance for his need to promote the work, there is no mistaking the genuine enthusiasm shown both at the beginning of the project ('it will be a grand book') and at its end—'all my best ballads, both humorous and pathetic, are included'.

If Hogg had reason to feel pleased with the 'selection' of the *Queer Book*, there is no evidence of anything more positive than stoical acceptance with regard to the 'correction' of his texts. The concession over his 'beloved ancient stile' was made regretfully and from a position of great weakness in dealing with Blackwood as publisher. Textual changes were implemented almost exclusively by Robert Hogg, under Blackwood's command, with any authorial involvement being limited to sporadic interventions made either on the original magazine copies or at a late proof stage. Furthermore, the texts used as a basis for the *Queer Book* were themselves often seriously flawed, either as a result of compositorial error or more direct editorial pressures. After the event, Hogg appears to have made no comment about the integrity of the texts created—to do so would have jeopardised a work he was eager to promote—though privately he must have sensed a disparity between the poems he had originally written and the form in which they were publicly presented.

A good sense of how Hogg originally presented his poems for publication can be gained from a volume in the Blackwood Papers, now held in the National Library of Scotland (MS 4805), containing the manuscripts of a number of longer poems published in *Blackwood's Edinburgh Magazine*. Five of the *Queer Book* poems previously published in *Blackwood's* are found in this form here: 'Ane Rychte Gude and Preytious Ballande' (fols 3–7); 'Will and Sandy' (fol. 8); 'A Greek Pastoral' (fols 9–13), 'A Sunday Pastoral' (fols 16–17); and 'Johnne Graimis Eckspeditioun till Heuin' (fol. 20). Hogg generally made no call for the return of his manuscripts after acceptance, and it seems likely that some of these were preserved by Blackwood as a token of copyright, though a sense of their value as literary mementos might also have played a part. All the manuscripts in question show signs of having been carefully prepared by Hogg as fair copies for the printer. All have formal headings, including authorial attributions; and in each instance the text is written almost entirely without alteration, in clear columns, down pages which are usually numbered in Hogg's hand. At the head of 'Ane Rychte

Gude and Preytious Ballande' Blackwood has written an instruction to the compositor, but apart from this there is no evidence of editorial interference before printing. Signs of the printer at work are found in the form of ink finger marks at various points, while four of the manuscripts bear the marks of having been cut into pieces— presumably so that more than one compositor could be setting at the same time—and then laminated together again. The loss of some of these pieces explains the absence of sections of text in 'Will and Sandy' and 'Johnne Graimis' (where, interestingly, the names of different compositors can be found written in pencil on the remaining sections). None of these manuscripts offers a full punctuational system, though Hogg normally provides a basic system of speech indicators, some question and exclamation marks, and a measure of other marks, especially at points where the reader might otherwise stumble.

A different perspective on Hogg's writing practices is provided by the large collection of his literary manuscripts held in the Alexander Turnbull Library, Wellington, New Zealand (catalogued as MS Papers 42). Whereas in the case of the Blackwood Papers, the surviving manuscripts clearly served as copy texts, the Hogg poems in the Turnbull library consist primarily of drafts and fragments. This collection, which derives from materials taken to New Zealand by Hogg's daughter Harriet and her husband Robert Gilkison in 1879, contains a heavy concentration of medium-sized items directed at the periodicals in the period 1825–31. In all no less than twenty items relating to poems which eventually appeared in the *Queer Book* can be found in the Turnbull papers, offering versions of fifteen out of the twenty-six poems anthologised there. Amongst these it possible to distinguish various types of draft: i) *early fragments*, in which Hogg can be seen experimenting with (say) the opening lines of a poem, perhaps on the remaining part of a booklet used for a completed poem; ii) *early drafts*, where a whole poem has been written out, evidently in a fairly spontaneous fashion, with Hogg often crowding extra text into the margins left by his main column; iii) *revised drafts*, in which the presence of corrections in different pens points to a more complex process of writing and revision; and iv) *recycled drafts*, where Hogg appears to have returned to an earlier draft (perhaps as the result of a first rejection) to begin a more substantial process of rewriting, preparatory to the writing out of a new version.

This variety of drafts helps contradict the notion, encouraged by a well-known passage in his 'Memoir of the Author's Life', that Hogg always wrote out his poetry spontaneously in one sitting.[53] Certainly by the 1820s his procedure was more complex; and, in all normal circumstances, it had become a rule to prepare final versions, often on larger paper and with formal headers and end inscriptions, specifically for submission to the journals. This final rewriting also allowed an opportunity to enhance rhyme schemes, improve phraseology, and (in the case of items written in his 'ancient stile') to further refine orthography.

The editorial practice of not returning accepted manuscripts best explains the paucity of manuscripts in a 'final' stage in the Turnbull collection, though in two clear instances poems connected with the *Queer Book* are found there in this form. Item 63 in MS Papers 42 is evidently the fair copy used for the *Amulet*'s version of 'A Lay of the Martyrs', and was probably returned by S.C. Hall because of the presence of another poem (by H.S. Riddell) on the same sheet.[54] Item 17, which contains a full version of 'The Witch of the Gray Thorn' with Blackwood's instruction to the printer at its head, was also presumably sent back to Hogg because of the rejection of another item in the same booklet.[55] Both these manuscript versions represent the end point of a sequence of drafts, and each therefore might be said to embody the author's final intentions. They also encourage the view that Hogg's punctuation was partly determined by the type of poem being prepared: 'The Witch of the Gray Thorn', written in a modern 'Gothic' style, has a full punctuational apparatus, while 'A Lay of the Martyrs', a traditional ballad, is virtually devoid of marks apart from basic speech indicators. Each manuscript is remarkably free of alteration, and offers a markedly less error-ridden text than its magazine counterpart.

Hogg's method of preparing final copy texts is further illustrated by the manuscript history of the two opening poems in the *Queer Book*, both of which were probably specially written for the project, in response to Blackwood's request for original materials to begin the volume. Early drafts of 'The Wyffe of Ezdel-more' and 'Robyn Reidde' survive, almost entire, in the Turnbull collection. In each case Hogg appears have been written his text without significant interruption, though different pen strokes suggest that a number of insertions and alterations were made at a later point, as if preparatory for another draft. Almost without fail, these changes are found incorporated in two later versions of the same poems which have been discovered in the Shortreed papers in the National Library of Scotland.[56] Though some sections are missing, the pagination of these later versions approximates that of the Turnbull drafts, indicating that Hogg was involved in a process of preparing fair copy (an additional advantage would have been that he retained a rough copy in case of loss). Comparison between the two states of texts also shows that in the act of transcribing Hogg continued to engage in local revisions, paying particular attention to his 'ancient' orthography. It is noteworthy that Hogg was still attending to this aspect virtually up to the moment that Blackwood declared his veto against the 'ancient stile' as a whole. The *Queer Book*'s subsequent butchery of these two poems offers a sharp reminder of the extent to which Hogg's wishes in this area were overridden. It also brings into clear relief the strong arguments that exist for basing a new text on Hogg's final manuscripts where available.

In all, the present edition uses Hogg's manuscript as the primary copy-text for eleven poems. Nine of these items, from the Blackwood, Turnbull, and Shortreed papers, have already been mentioned. Additionally, the present edition prefers manuscript versions in the case of both 'Ringan and May' and 'A Bard's Address to his Youngest Daughter'. The first of these, another fair copy, forms part of the Osborn Collection in the Beinecke Library at Yale University. As with 'The Witch of the Gray Thorn'—which appeared alongside 'Ringan and May' in the June 1825 number of *Blackwood's*—the Yale manuscript carries Blackwood's instruction to the printer at its head. It is also liberally punctuated, almost as if Hogg meant to invite a direct conversion into print. In the event, the compositor(s) imposed a more orthodox punctuation, with a deadening effect on the poem's rhetoric in key areas. The use of the sole surviving autograph version of 'A Bard's Address to his Youngest Daughter' in some respects runs counter to the general policy of accepting only Hogg's final copy texts. Item 62 in the Turnbull papers has a number of characteristics common in early draft poems—it shares a single sheet with another poem, and is written in both directions on the page—though the presence of a header and the almost complete lack of alteration are exceptional. One possibility is that the poem was written spontaneously in Hogg's earlier manner: another that the manuscript records a version intended only for private family consumption. Considering the likelihood that the poem which appeared in *Friendship's Offering* was subject to editorial pressure, and in view of Hogg's effort to restore part of this manuscript version to the *Queer Book*, it would seem pusillanimous to exclude such a delicate and exquisitely expressed example of Hogg writing in an intimate vein.

Though Hogg wrote his final manuscripts with care, inevitably a number of mistakes were made, sometimes it would seem as a direct result of transcribing an earlier draft. Occasionally words are left out, or unnecessarily repeated; single letters are transposed or omitted; or a homonym mistakenly replaces the word intended ('near' instead of 'neer'). In such cases the text has been editorially emended, guided whenever possible by a previous manuscript version or an early printed text. No attempt has been made to interfere with idiosyncrasies in Hogg's own orthography, even in standard 'English' contexts, especially as this can be a useful indication of pronunciation or emphasis. Hogg's punctuation has also been generally preserved, without any concerted effort to provide additional marks or to introduce the apparatus found in printed texts. However, where Hogg fails to complete his own punctuation—for example, by omitting closing quotation marks—the punctuation implicitly required is usually supplied. In a few instances, too, where the reader is in danger of losing the syntactical thread or missing important emphasis, guiding marks have been added.

Where the manuscript used as copy-text is incomplete, missing areas of text have been provided from the nearest or most appropriate source. In the case of 'Johnne Graimis Eckspeditioun till Heuin' two sections of text lost in the manuscript are supplied from Item 29 in the Turnbull collection, a penultimate draft which bears some of the marks of a final copy text. With 'Will and Sandy', where no other manuscript has been discovered, it has been necessary to provide the final paragraph from *Blackwood's Edinburgh Magazine*. In the first instance, readers are unlikely to note any significant difference; in the second, the transference to the Magazine's heavier punctuation and normalised spelling is more obtrusive.

Of the remaining poems, nine are reprinted from *Blackwood's Edinburgh Magazine* and six from the annuals. Where *Blackwood's* provides the copy-text every effort has been made to identify misreadings by the printer, an endeavour which has been aided by the evidence of surviving manuscript drafts and variants in the *Queer Book* which point to an authorial involvement. Usually the original Magazine punctuation has been allowed to stand, though in some local instances—as when inappropriate pointing distorts emphasis or meaning—editorial changes have been made. In the case of the six texts taken from the annuals, where normally no manuscript guidance is available, the existing punctuation is again largely accepted, except where Hogg's sense is deemed at risk. Special care, however, has been taken to locate and emend errors made by the London printers in interpreting Scots terms, idiomatic expressions, and proper names. Fuller accounts and listings of these emendations will be found under the 'Textual Notes' provided for each poem at the end of the volume.

The present edition also eschews much of the standardisation imposed by the *Queer Book* of 1832. Not only are Hogg's original titles restored, but the subsidiary titles and authorial descriptions which followed are also given in full in each case. The long sub-headings introducing poems in the 'ancient stile', which survived in the Magazine versions, played a key role in setting tone and introducing 'Maister Hougge' as a latter-day 'makar'. The authorial descriptions which introduced Hogg's other contributions, both in *Blackwood's* and the annuals, were likewise important signals: from the directness of 'James Hogg', through the familiarity of 'the Ettrick Shepherd', to the more formal and status-conscious 'by the author of The Queen's Wake'. In addition Hogg's end inscriptions, as a well-known hallmark, are preserved in all cases where found.

In following this policy, the present edition introduces a number of new challenges to the reader. Ten of the poems included are in Hogg's fully-fledged 'ancient stile', which at first sight can have an intimidating effect. Guidance about the meaning of individual terms will be found in the Glossary; although, in most cases, once the main rules in operation have been understood the difficulties are relatively few. Where the manuscript provides the copy-text, the reader will also face the unfamiliarity of verse virtually devoid of punctuation. However, the rhetorical flow of Hogg's poetry is usually easy to follow if attention is given to basic rhythmic patterns and to the conventions of the mode employed. Any difficulties encountered will be more than offset by the freedom gained through an absence of the often crippling punctuation supplied by magazine compositors. Above all, the present edition offers a more varied experience than its predecessor, restoring much of the original flavour of Hogg's work as a contributor to the periodicals in the later 1820s. The essential 'queerness' of the *Queer Book*—its humour, quirkiness, variety, and virtuosity—can thus be savoured in full for the first time.

Notes

1. The *Scottish National Dictionary* cites Hugh Mitchell's *Scotticisms* (Glasgow, 1799), p.69, in illustration of the dominant English and Scottish usages: '*Queer*, in English, means *odd, strange, singular*.—In Scotland, it is used in the sense of *witty, humorous, comical*.'
2. *Literary Gazette*, no. 798, Saturday, 5 May 1832, p.275; *The Athenaeum*, Saturday, 5 May 1832, p.284; *Monthly Review*, n.s. 2 (June 1832),

p.247; *New Monthly Magazine*, 36 (June 1832), p.247.

3. National Library of Scotland (hereafter NLS), MS 30312, pp.412–13.

4. *Edinburgh Literary Journal*, 25 December 1830, p.406.

5. NLS, MS 30312, pp.154–55.

6. See his letter to William Blackwood on 20 October 1830, NLS, MS 4027, fols 198–99.

7. The description is Blackwood's, in his letter of 26 February 1831 (NLS, MS 30312, p.154).

8. NLS, MS 4029, fol. 249. The appearance of quotation marks in the letter around "Some in the Amulet" probably stems from Hogg's habit of returning to add these to titles at a later point. 'The Gude Greye Katt' had originally appeared as a self-parody in Hogg's *Poetic Mirror* (1816), and represents one of the earliest and most successful examples of his 'ancient stile'. Its non-appearance in the *Queer Book* is perhaps attributable to copyright restrictions.

9. NLS, MS 2245, fol. 165.

10. NLS, MS 30308, p.43 (Blackwood to Hogg, 22 January 1825).

11. See Robert Hogg's letter to Blackwood on 9 February [1828], describing his way of proceeding (NLS, MS 4021, fol. 284).

12. NLS, MS 4029, fol. 251.

13. NLS, MS 30312, p.163.

14. NLS, MS 4019, fol. 195.

15. The Magazine had commenced publication in April 1817, originally under the title of the *Edinburgh Monthly Magazine*, with Blackwood bringing in Lockhart and Wilson after the sixth issue. The 'Chaldee Manuscript' appeared in October 1817.

16. For examples of Hogg requesting paper from Blackwood, see his letters of 4 January, 30 November 1830 (NLS, MS 4027, fols 178–79, 204). There is clear evidence that Hogg's literary work at this period was mostly written on the batches sent by Blackwood.

17. See, for example, his reference to the 'endless repetitions of political dogmas' in his letter to Blackwood on 6 December 1831 (NLS, MS 4029, fol. 268).

18. The term 'dissipation' is used in Hogg's letter to Blackwood, complaining about his unfair treatment, on 6 April 1830 (NLS, MS 4027, fol. 181).

19. An instance is provided by Blackwood's rejection of Hogg's prose tale, 'On the Separate Existence of the Soul', in a letter of 17 September 1831: 'I fear it would awfully shock the Orthodox if *I* were to publish it' (NLS, MS 30312, p.225).

20. Blackwood stated his objections in a letter to Hogg on 26 August 1830. For a fuller account of the redrafting of 'A Sunday Pastoral', see 'Textual Notes' to this poem at the end of the volume.

21. See Hogg's letter to Alaric Watts on 2 February 1825 (NLS, MS 1002, fols 102–03). Hogg's first contribution was his 'Invocation to the Queen of the Fairies', published in the *Literary Souvenir* for 1825, pp.122–26.

22. Hogg to R. Ackerman, 1 April 1827: 'I have written the romantic stories &c accompanying this solely for your work and request of you to show them to Mr Shoberl without loss of time' (NLS, MS 8887, fol. 36).

23. See letters to Hogg from: Pringle, 10 December 1827; Cunningham, 6 March 1828; and Hood, 22 April 1828 (NLS, MS 2245, fols 108–09, 114–15, 116–17).

24. NLS, MS 2245, fol. 144.

25. NLS, MS 1002, fol. 104 (Hogg to S.C. Hall, 17 April 1829).

26. NLS, MS 2245, fols 122–23.

27. Alexander Turnbull Library, Wellington, New Zealand, MS Papers 42, Item 81 (Pringle to Hogg, 1 June 1831).

28. NLS, MS 2245, fol. 128.

29. Yale University Library MS Vaults Shelves Hogg (Hogg to Allan Cunningham, 31 December 1828).

30. NLS, MS 2245, fol. 120. Hogg's prose story, 'The Cameronian Preacher's Tale', was consequently cut before its appearance in the *Anniversary* (see *James Hogg. Selected Stories and Sketches*, edited by Douglas S. Mack (Edinburgh: Scottish Academic Press, 1982), p.200). For possible cuts made to 'The Carle of Invertime', see 'Textual Notes' to this poem at the end of the volume.

31. Yale University Library MS Vaults Shelves Hogg (Hogg to Allan Cunningham, 31 December 1828).

32. Historical Society of Pennsylvania, Philadelphia (Hogg to Frederic Shoberl, [4 June 1831]).

33. In his letter to Thomas Hamilton on 25 April 1832, Blackwood refers to the *Queer Book* having been 'printed for nearly twelve months' (NLS, MS 30312, pp.412–13).

34. See Robert Hogg's letter to Blackwood concerning *The Shepherd's Calendar*, 9 February [1828]: 'I have also gone over a part of the articles, making such verbal alterations as appeared to improve the style, and striking out what was objectionable or superfluous.' (NLS, MS 4021, fol. 284).

35. NLS, MS 30312, p.200.

36. NLS, MS 30312, p.201.

37. NLS, MS 4029, fols 262, 264. Parliament had been dissolved on 22 April 1831; the second reform Bill was passed by the reassembled Commons on 21 September 1831.

38. NLS, MS 30312, pp.255–56.

39. NLS, MS 4029, fols 266, 268 (Hogg to Blackwood, 2 November, 6 December 1831).

40. NLS, MS 2245, fol. 186.

41. NLS, MS 4033, fols 123–24.

42. *Altrive Tales, by the Ettrick Shepherd* (London, 1832), pp.cv–cvi.

43. NLS, MS 30312, p.331.

44. NLS, MS 4033, fols 125–26; MS 30312, p.371. The copy had been sent at the same time as Alexander Blackwood's letter to Hogg on 25

January 1832, stating that his father had no objection to a new publisher being found (NLS, MS 30312, p.315). This same copy, which lacks title-page and dedication and is incomplete, is now owned by the University of Stirling Library (for additions by Hogg, see 'Textual Notes' on 'A Sunday Pastoral' at the end of this volume).

45. See, for example, Blackwood's disparaging reference to 'your Ballads or Queer Book as you call it' in his letter to Hogg of 7 March 1832 (NLS, MS 30312, p.371). Blackwood himself, as here, usually refers to the project as 'the Ballads'.

46. *Monthly Review*, n.s. 2 (June 1832), 247–53 (pp.247–48, 250).

47. *Tait's Edinburgh Magazine*, 1 (June 1832), 273–76 (p.276).

48. *New Monthly Magazine*, 36 (June 1832), p.247.

49. NLS, MS 4039, fol. 30.

50. Introduction to James Hogg, *The Domestic Manners and Private Life of Sir Walter Scott* (Glasgow, 1834), pp.53–54. The letter is printed with the date 7 March 1834, but internal evidence suggests that it was probably written a year earlier. Possibly Hogg's correspondent was Simeon De Witt Bloodgood, to whom he had sent the manuscript of his *Familiar Anecdotes of Sir Walter Scott* for publication in America—*The Domestic Manners and Private Life of Sir Walter Scott*, in which this letter appears, is a British piracy of this work.

51. 'A Cameronian Ballad' in *Altrive Chapbooks*, no. 1 (September 1984), 1–6; and 'The Goode Manne of Allowa' in *Altrive Chapbooks*, no. 3 (September 1986), 96–105. Both works were edited by Douglas S. Mack, whose comment (p.105) is quoted.

52. *The Ettrick Shepherd* (Cambridge: Cambridge University Press, 1927), p.140.

53. See James Hogg, *Memoir of the Author's Life* and *Familiar Anecdotes of Sir Walter Scott*, edited by Douglas S. Mack (Edinburgh and London: Scottish Academic Press, 1972), pp.10–11, 10n.

54. Riddell's poem, 'Ode to the Harp of Zloss' (of which three stanzas, in Hogg's hand, survive in Item 63) was rejected by S.C. Hall in his letter to Hogg of 25 June 1829 (NLS, MS 2245, fol. 148). It was then submitted successfully to *Blackwood's Edinburgh Magazine*.

55. 'The Anti-burgher in Love', later rewritten and published in *Fraser's Magazine* (March 1832) as 'The Elder in Love'.

56. Sections of both these poems can be found in MS 8997 (fols 11–20, 21–22).

This
MOTLEY WORK,
made up of all the fowls' feathers that fly in the air,
from the rook to the wild swan,
and from the kitty wren to the peacock,
as the Shepherd's *vade mecum*,
as the varied strains in which his soul delighteth,
he dedicates most respectfully to
CHRISTOPHER NORTH
and
TIMOTHY TICKLER,
Esquires.

The Wyffe of Ezdel-more

There dwallit ane wyffe in Ezdel-more
   Ane wonderous wyffe I wot wals she
Fore sho halde the wanyerthlye lore
   Of wytchcrafte and of glaumorye

And sho colde blenche the blomyng cheike   5
   And sho colde blynde the bauldest ee
For sho colde maike the wyndis to speike
   And the breizes laughe outower the le

And the lassies and the ladis gaed geyte
   Theye dauncit theye caperit and theye sung   10
Then laughit quhille teris ranne downe theyre cheikis
   Yet knowit not qhare the sporte had sprung

And sho colde bid the sternis stande stillè
   Als glowyng up the heuinlye lonis
And the sternyis blynkit with affrychte   15
   And stode als stille as they'd beine stonis

Sho brochte the egillis from the rockis
   And snoolit them in hir curset pennis
Sho turnit the shepherdis to morecockis
   And the prettye maydenis to morehennis   20

Then there wals blynking on the bente
   And flapperyng ower the purpil fellis
For the braif creturis were intente
   On toying mid the hadder bellis

At moultyng tymis there wals deraye   25
   Als the aulde damis haif taulde to me
For all that theye colde doo or saye
   The morecockis wolde not lette them bee

But yet there grewe soche raige for chainge
  That the wytche wyffe wals sore besette   30
For euery morne the men and maydis
  Were throngyng at hir synfulle yette

And the morehennis biggit theyre louesome nestis
  Amang the bellis of blomyng lyng
And theyre loferis skailit the mornyng mystis   35
  And crawit upon the wanton wyng

Quhille it felle about the Lammas tyde
  Quhan the moreland men doo wonne theyre haye
That the lairde of Gilbertoun hathe hyit
  To hount upon these mountanis graye   40

Als hee caime downe the Caldron brae
  He callit until his braif dog Colle
Quhais taille wals standyng out als straighte
  Als nedyl to the norlan polle

His ee wals sette and his fote wals up   45
  And his lippe wals clypping in the sloate
And his heidd wals on his sholder turnit
  It wals a sychte wals worthe ane groate

"Holde on braif boye" cryis Gilbertoun
  The dog helde on ane lyttil space   50
Then he begoude to yuff and barke
  And terrour strainge wals in his faice

"Hold on braif boye" cryis Gilbertoun
  "No maister braif be your's the pairt
There's somethyng in that hadder browne   55
  That frychtis mee to the very herte"

He toke his taille betwene his leggis
  And up the penne he ranne with speidde
And aye hee gaif the tidder yelpe
  Als one had smotte him on the heidde   60

"The doggis bewytchit" sayis Gilbertoun
  "Or els the deuil is in that denne

It maikis myne verye herte tille quaike
   Yet quhat to dreidde I lyttil kenne"

Hee raysit his doghedis brychte and keine   65
   And on he helde courageouslye
Yet there wals sumthyng in his eyne
   That haflins hynderit him to se

Then up there sprang ane goodlye braice
   Two fyner burdis neuir beatte the ayre   70
Thump! thump! went Gilbertounis two shottis
   And down caime bothe the cumlye payre

"Seike deidde seike deidde myne braif dog Colle
   Come downe heris gallante sporte for the"
"Thank youe sir Maister seike yourselle   75
   For deuil ane helpe you's gette from mee"

The lairde helde on his burdis to lyfte
   Soche grand begynnyng blythe to se
"Hold! Damme you sir!" sayis the morecocke
   "How darit you shotte your gunnis at mee?"   80

The lairde got neuir soche ane flegge
   Syn hee satte on his moderis kne
Hee flung his mosquette from his hande
   And lyke ane madmanne offe ranne hee

But at the fyrste bewylderit turne   85
   He caime unto the wytchis denne
For sho levit farre up in the Caldron burne
   Far from the walkis of chrystian menne

In half ane housse and half ane caife
   It wals ane firsum plaice to se   90
But in ranne the lairde of Gilbertoun
   Als frychtenit als ane manne colde bee

"Sir keipe your distance" cryit the wyffe
   "This daye I speike not withe youre kynde
So come not hydder for youre lyffe   95
   Go morder all quhom you canne fynde

You are soche baisse wanbrydlit knaife
    I am in payne quhille you depairt
There's youthful blode upon youre heidde
    And synne withynne youre verye herte"   100

Now this wytche wals not ane wydderit hagge
    Sho wals ane fayre and lordlye queinne
With maijestye in euery mofe
    And glamoure in hir colle blacke eyne

"Moste mervoullous and staitlye daime   105
    That you are here astoundethe mee
That you sholde liue in soche ane haime
    Fore passethe my capacitye

But heare and helpe mee if you maye
    I'll showe you sychtis you neuir sawe   110
Sumthyng hath fallen into myne waye
    That farre owerpasseth Naturis lawe"

"I knowe it all" cryit the wytch wyffe
    "Alace I knowe it all to weille
You haif shotte Tom Flemon of Blode-hope   115
    And bonny Maye of Phynglande-sheille

Och theye were loferis fonde and leille
    And of eiche oderis lofe so fayne
But theye wolde seye the moris a whyle
    And deirlye haif theye payit the cayne   120

Come lette us go to worke of woe
    And laye theyre hedis benethe the sode
That neuir manne theyre synne maye knowe
    Nor ferlye ower theyre laste abode"

Then sho toke oute ane wynding sheitte   125
    Wals quhyter nor the cheystist snow
And theye are awaye to the Caldron Brae
    To seike the loferis lying low

"Now keipe you backe" the wytche wyffe sayit
    "Keipe backe untille I calle youre naime   130

For it lyttil sutis the ee of manne
   To loke on vyrginis lyfelesse fraime"

Och quhan sho caime unto the spotte
   It wals ane scene of ruefulle skaithe
For Maye of Phynglande-sheille wals slayne   135
   And hir lofer weipyng faste to dethe

There neuir wals soche ane cumlye corpis
   Layit out so meiklye and so low
And hir bonnye skynne wals stryppit with blode
   Lyke raynbowis on ane wrethe of snow   140

They dyggit hir graife bee the wylde burne syde
   Far from the sychte of mortyl ee
"O maike it wyde" Tom Flemon sayit
   "That it maye holde bothe hir and mee"

They dyggit hir graife and lyit hir in   145
   And to diswadde hir lofer tryit
But Tom Flemon crepit into the graife
   And layit himselle downe bee hir syde

Hee foldit his deidd lofe in his armis
   And layit his heidde upon hir breste   150
"Now couer us up" Tom Flemon cryit
   "For this is the bedde I lyke the beste

I haif followit myne owne deire vyrginne lofe
   Through yirth and ayre alake to faste
But I neuer possessit hir quhille the graife   155
   Hath giuen hir to mee at the laste

Heire wille we lye in swete sounde sleippe
   Quhille the laste mornyng open hir ee
Then laye the greine sode on our heiddis
   For this is quhare I lofe to bee"   160

Theye shovellit the moulde upon theyre feitte
   And o'er theyre brestis theye shovellit it in
But lothe were theye to couer theyre hedis
   Whyle there wals anye lyffe withynne

Then Tom Flemon toke ane long laste kysse   165
   And hee lokit til heuin and wepit fulle sore
Then closyt his eyne and beddit his heidde
   Quhare it sholde lye for euirmore

Then theye couerit them up alyfe and deidde
   Theye couerit them up juste as theye laye   170
Then layit the greine sode on the heidde
   And sone the monyngis dyit awaye

And the lairde wepyt lyke ane verye chylde
   In sore distresse and grefe of mynde
But the weirde wyffe in passione wylde   175
   Pourit this wylde antheme on the wynde

The Wytchis Dirge

    Adieu—Adieu
    Sweet Spirits adieu
A kind farewell I send with you
    As fond and fair   180
    As ever you were
I see you pacing the fields of air
    Away—Away
    By the cloudlet gray
And the hues that mingle the night and the day   185
O'er valleys from which the dew descends
Where the glaring sunbeam never blends
But a gloaming dims the dell and river
And a holy stillness dwells for ever
    Where the ruffling breeze   190
    Never waves the trees
And the waters neither swell nor freeze
Where storms the soul can never harrow
Nor terrors of the lightening's arrow
Nor glances of delirious joy   195
Without illusion or alloy
But the lingering spirit's life is led
In a dreary hope and a holy dread
    Till the last day
    Shall pass away   200

Of hope of longing and dismay
When the doom is read that effaced is never
And the fates of spirits sealed for ever

    Adieu—Adieu
      Sweet spirits adieu   205
A kind farewell I send with you
To a land where I have lived approved
A land where I have sinned and loved
And thence was forced to earth's domain
To a body of flesh and blood again   210
For thrice as punishment condign
Has this unyielding soul of mine
Been driven away as being remiss
From verges of the fields of bliss
Downward away o'er fire and flood   215
To inherit mortal flesh and blood
But here above thy earthly shrine
I pray such fate be never thine
      May you love and kiss
        In dreamy bliss   220
In your home of slumbering quietness
And sometimes at the midnight noon
Climb the steep eyebrows of the moon
To watch her workings of commotion
That heave the tides of the earthly ocean   225
That torfel and roll her to and fro
Like surges of death in the world below
That call the mists to the fair moonshine
And the fresh sweet showers from the fields of brine
Then mark the workings of nature's strife   230
When the infant tempest springs to life
And how the bolts of burning levin.
Are moulded in the forge of heaven
And far in flaming vengeance hurled
Away to world beyond world   235

   O then how sweet your walks to renew
When the angels of night distil the dew
And sink to your sweet alcove again
In that benignant quiet reign
      Where roses twine   240

With the eglantine
In the fairy bowers that once were mine
    Adieu—Adieu
    Sweet spirits adieu
A kind farewell I send with you   245

But the beste of myne taille is yet to bee
For James Glendonnyng hath tould it mee
And the trothe of James can neuir faille
And so hath Tom Beattye of Meickyldaille
That ane ghostlye morecocke and morehenne   250
Stille haunte the wyldis of the Caldron glenne
At them no poynter wille turne his eye
But hangis his taille and passeth by
And nothyng avayleth the strongest shotte
For it passeth through them and hurteth notte   255
For both these blaidis mang oder crymis
Haif shotte at eiche ane thusande tymis
And euerilke yeirre at Lammas tydde
On a greine mounde by the wylde burn sydde
Maye these two bonnye burdis be seine   260
Sytting in sorrowe and in teine

FYTTE THE SECONDE

Now this wytche wyffe quhas yirdlye naime
Wals sayit to haif bein Raighel Graime
Hath wylit the lairde unto hir sheille
For sho sayit sho lofit his beiryng weille
Althoughe at firste he hadde some dreidde   5
That sho helde revenge intil hir heidde
Sho toke him in with queenlye graice
And sho set him in ane honourit plaice
And sho tould him ane taille to him so newe
That hee scaircely colde beliefe it trewe   10

"Now listen to mee thou sportesman goode
    Als thou waste listenyng for thyne lyffe
Thou shedder of young and guyltelesse blode
    Unto ane taille of storte and stryffe

And I moste telle it if I maye   15
   For it wolde stille lyffis stormye euin
If but ane man on yird sholde knowe
   The state that I stand in with heuin

About ane thusande yeris agone
   I wals ane ladye of renowne   20
I wals myne faderis darlyng bairne
   Myne moderis lofe wals alle myne own

But it wals in ane synnfulle lande
   That lyis beneathe the rysing sonne
Where the mychtie Aral rollis her tydde   25
   On shoris that freedome neuir wonne

And quhan I wonne myne youthfulle pryme
   And lofit with alle a vyrginis feiris
Myne fader sold mee for ane slaife
   Regairdlesse of myne cryis and teris   30

Hee solde me to ane mychtye kyng
   To live ane lyffe I colde not leidde
For somethyng whysperit mee withynne
   That for soche lyffe I wals not maide

There is nochte in lyffe so swete als lofe   35
   To lofe and bee belofit agayne
But to gif all to one we haite
   There wellis the soulis deadlyeste payne

So I let out myne lordis hertis blode
   Raither nor myne fre soule begryme   40
For I raither chusit to die ane mayde
   Than yielde myne lyffe to haitful cryme

I barrit the doris and windowis closse
   I barrit them alle myne selfe wythynne
And to his haram set ane cole   45
   And joyit mee of the deadlye synne

Then all his wyffis and weicked daimis
   Theye skirlit theye jompyt and they prayit

It wals ane awsum dance of deathe
  To all but one poore wrongit mayde   50

The wretches fledde before the flaime
  And to ane chamber roshit pell-melle
Where enek queene and wicked daime
  Were byrnit intill ane izel shelle

Myne bodye peryshit in that flaime   55
  But to myne wonder and delychte
I found I wals a being stille
  Pure als the snowis on Aralis heychte

A lychtsome lively lyving thyng
  A thyng without a form or naime   60
But alle myne energyis remaynit
  And all my feillyngis were the saime

I dancit me o'er Mamorais isle
  I dancit me o'er Mamora's sea
Then lychtit on ane guildit spyre   65
  To watch quhat the evente wolde be

And there I saw myne wratchit lorde
  Quha fayne wolde haif debasit me
Borne off by thre malyshous fiendis
  To euerlastyng slaiverye   70

And his wyffis and myngens passit in drovis
  Awaye awaye to plaice unknowne
And the enekis snoolit up behynde
  With wemyng stille to lose or wonne

Some of those damis were blacke als inke   75
  And some of hue without a naime
But not one soul wals quhyte but myne
  Of all quha peryshit in that flaime

I hied me awaye to the Aral shore
  Myne parentis and true lofe to see   80
And saw myne fader riche in store
  Of gayne he wonne be saille of me

And I cursit him in myne makeris naime
 And shoke myne hande before his ee
But myne hand wals viewless als myne fraime 85
 Myne soule he cold not hirre nor se

But my pore moderis herte wals broke
 Sho sat and pinit fro morn till euin
And als she namit myne naime sho prayit
 For blyssings on hir chylde from heuin 90

'But we haif giuin hir up till shaime
 And O quhat bliss can hir betyde
So I'll go wayling to myne graife
 That sho wals not ane virtuous bryde

Myne chylde myne lofe myne onlye joye 95
 Deirre to this herte als deirre can bee
O we shalle roulle in byrning fyre
 For skaith that we haif done to the'

I lokit intil myne parentis ee
 I sawe the teris rynne downe hir cheike 100
I sawe the sobbis that hevit hir breiste
 And then I thought myne herte wolde break

But spyrits haif no hertis of flesche
 Els myne had broke without remeide
I tryit hir ee I tryit hir eire 105
 But wals not known by worde or deide

I went unto myne own true lofe
 And found him at our trysting tre
And hee wals cronyng ower ane saung
 Of lofe that he had maide to mee 110

I kyssit his lyppis and comlye cheike
 And on his manlye bosome laye
And if ane spyrit colde haif wepit
 I wolde haif wepit myne lyfe awaye

But up there came an oder daime 115
 Quha's faice was rychte weille knowne to mee

And all his lofe wals laivishit there
  Efen undernethe our trysting tre

Then fondest dallyance passit betweinne
  Whyle I stode by and lokit on   120
I cursit them in the vyrginis naime
  And wyshit myne being turnit to stone

Och wolde the shaimeful sonnis of menne
  But thynke of friendis deidde and gone
And thynke in seckret dedis of synne   125
  That theye are standyng lokyng on

They durste not stope to dedis profaine
  If ponderyng on theyre frendis enshrynit
The eyes of spyritis lokyng on
  Is dreddful to the hoomyn mynde   130

I turnit myne faice unto the heuin
  And to myselfe sayit grefouslye
'I moste go seike ane oder home
  This is no restyng plaice for mee'

But ane spyrit helde me by the hande   135
  And did my boundyng flychte restrayne
'You moste forgiue you moste forgiue'
  Sayit hee 'or heuin you'll neuir gayne'

'The herte that solde ane chylde for golde
  The lofe that lastis but for ane daye   140
Though I in byrning flaimis bee rollit
  These curses I shalle ne'er unsaye'

The spyrit shoke his golden hayres
  And sayit out through aerial teris
'Och that unyieldyng soul of thyne   145
  Moste pennance doo ane thousande yeris'

Now I haif roamit o'er dismal spheris
  In darklyng plesure and in woe
Haif livit with fairyis and theyre feris
  Then dyvit into the depis belowe   150

Once to ane lychtsome lande I wonne
   Quhare plesure gan to maister payne
But there I lofit and there I synnit
   And wals expellit to yirth agayne

I haif livit in vyrgin wyffe and crone   155
   And stormit in ferce viragois mynde
Livit lyke unyirthlye being lone
   But neuir gaif byrthe to hoomyn kynde

I am not hoomyn nor dyvine
   But farre abofe frayle flesche and blode   160
For I haif elymental power
   That neuir canne bee understoode

For I can bydde the stormis raive loudde
   And straighte they raire alangis the heuin
And I can bryng the thonder cloudde   165
   And swath it rounde the fyerie leuin

And I can skaille the egellis neste
   And skaire him from his eyrie soone
And I can wryng his lordlye necke
   Betweine the quhyte cloudde and the moone   170

And I can stop the solanis flychte
   And barre him from his enterpryze
I with the raiven can converse
   And telle him where his quarrye lyis

I can turne ane manne intil ane beiste   175
   And gif him hornis of proper syze
Ane mayde into ane chermyng burde
   To frolycke through the summer skyis

Waike drousye slomberer! Waike in tyme
   Dare you myne wordis and workis despise   180
Who am ane mysterye sublyme
   Ane wonder underneathe the skyis"

For this strainge quene had foamit and ravit
   And wafit hir armis so feirfullye

Sho neuir noted that the lairde 185
  Wals sounde asleipe als manne colde bee

Until he gaif ane goodlye snore
  That soundyt lyke ane postmanis horne
Then the wytch gaif him soche ane flegge
  Als hee neuir gatte since hee wals borne 190

Sho gaif him ane skyffat on the cheike
  That maide him spryng to the bauke tre
"Hilloa—quhatis thys?" cryis out the lairde
  "Daime dare you playe youre prankis on mee?

I had gode mynde to aske youre lofe 195
  For you are ane lordlye louesome daime
But to let out your lordis hertis blode
  I trow it wals ane rychte greate shaime

Praye haif you nothyng heirre to drynke
  In that are joyis whiche neuir faille 200
I wolde raither haif some drynke and funne
  Than lyste to ane unyirthlye taille

Soche tailles als that I hope are fewe
  Theye maike a manne bothe sycke and sadde
And if one colde belife them trewe 205
  Theyre fytte to put ane body madde

Let us turn to yirthlye thyngis agayne
  And fyrste se quhatis to drynke or eitte
For quhat with trobil toylle and payne
  I haif great neidde of reste and meitte" 210

But quhat hee aitte or quhat hee dranke
  Or quhare he slepit that nychte his laine
In sothe wals neuir revealit to mee
  There fore I telle it not agayne

FYTTE THE THRYDDE

The bonnye graye ee of the daye
  Had scaircely hevit its drowzye lydde
Farre o'er the eistern hillis awaye
  Through blushes of vermyllion reidde

Quhan up gat many a braif more cocke   5
  Grand hoomyn gorcockis of renowne
And theye were nycheryng in the ayre
  Als if the worlde was all theyre owne

Whyle all that eiche hadde to the fore
  Wals ane swete maite of russet hewe   10
Sytting gledgyng in hir cozye neste
  Amang the bellis of purpil blewe

The blacke cocke lockeryt on the brae
  And spredde his taille lyke sylver fanne
His motelye maite in humbil graye   15
  Caime cowryng to hir proudde godemanne

And up gatte the wyffe of Ezdel-more
  And the lairde of Gilbertoun up gatte hee
For theye heryt some voycis at the yette
  Als swete als voycis welle colde bee   20

And quhan the lairde caime but the caive
  From out his darke and drowzye denne
The grandyst daime stode him before
  That euir wals seinne by eyne of menne

The lairde sanke downe upon his kne   25
  In perfecte wonder and dismaye
But sho raisyt him up rychte courteouslye
  And bade him neyther doo nor saye

Sayis sho "I'll showe to you ane sychte
  Wille sette youre tendir herte on flaime   30
And then I'll show ane oder sychte
  Wille maike you chainge your mortyl fraime"

"Confounde mee maddam if I wille
 And this I saye fulle certainlye
If euir I chainge myne mortyl frame   35
 That change it shalle be maidde for the"

But forth sho saylit unto the yette
 Lyke streimour of the rysing sonne
The radiante weathergalle bewet
 With dewis of heuin wals there outdonne   40

For there three lovelye vyrginis stode
 Waityng to chainge theyre mortyl fraime
For jealousye had them betrayit
 And forcit them intil mountain gaime

But quhan they saw ane gallante wychte   45
 Ane gentle hynde of hie respect
Had been in madamis denne all nychte
 Theye blushit until the very necke

Ane quhisperit "that moste be the deuil"
 Ane oder sayit rychte pawkilye   50
"Then he is moche better nor he's callit
 I haif seine waur lokyng chaps nor hee

But bee hee manne or be he more
 Or be hee worse than I can telle
This lustye wyffe of Ezdel-more   55
 Is littil bettir nor myselle

Myne herte it trembles me withynne
 Yet from my purpose I'll not fail
For I most haif myne lofe agayne
 In spyte of poulder and of haille"   60

Then sayit the wyffe of Ezdel-more
 "Come ane be ane myne bonnye thingis
But quhan the cloackyng tyme is o'er
 You'll rewe this langyng after wyngis"

The firste that caime wals Mary Roye   65
 With blushes of the roses hue

Hir cheikis were dymplit o'er with joye
    Hir eyne of heuinis owne awzer blewe

"Holde" cryit the lairde "This shalle not bee
    Against this chainge I maike a vowe   70
Though bonnyer burde mochte neuir flee
    Sho is ten tymis sweter als she's nowe

Gif up the moris myne prettye mayde
    And come and spende ane monthe with mee
And I'll cleide you from tope til toe   75
    In goude and sylken cramasye"

But sho threw him ane wytching smyle
    And sayit with wordis of languishyng
"The bonniest gowne in all our isle
    Is ane that is callit the morehenis wyng"   80

The wyffe toke hir ben to the caive
    And there were cries of mickle paine
But quat wals done or quhat wals sayit
    No mortal ewer toulde agayne

Then open flew the doore at last   85
    And out she sprang in nature new
And bounded for the Black-coom heighte
    The bonniest morehenne euir flewe

The lairde ranne on til ane knowe heidde
    To keip the bonny bird in syghte   90
For he helde it ane precious meidde
    To see quhare soche ane thyng wolde lychte

"Hah!" quod the lairde "I haif hir now
    I knowe hir very bosche and denne
I'll be ane moorecock als I vowe   95
    To cowre besyde yonne sweite morehenne"

The next fayre daime that toke the chainge
    Wals Jane Deyelle of Borrancleuch
Sho wals ane talle and sprychtelye lasse
    With waifyng lockis of raiven hewe   100

The lairde he lokyt intil hir eyne
  Quhille sho wals forcit to loke away
Thynkand he wolde them knowe agayne
  Quhan meityng on the mountaine graye

The thrydde that caime wals Barberry Blaike   105
  In robis of snowye quhitenesse cladde
And quhan the lairde lokit in hir faice
  Hir beautye almaste putte him madde

"Lorde!" cryit the lairde "but this excedis
  All thyngis that euir on yirthe befelle   110
This longing for the mountain heiddis
  And yirnyng for the hadder belle

Ah lofelye mayden if to mee
  So swete so fayre ane forme were giuen
I wolde not chainge its symmetrye   115
  Saife for ane angelis of the heuin

Swyth! raither staye at homme and breidde
  Fayre hoomyn thyngis with hoomyn soulis
Than nourysche yaupyng pouttis to feidde
  The greiddye gleddis and gairlye foulis"   120

"'Tis not for breidde 'tis not for feidde"
  Sayit the fayre maye "that I goe forthe
'Tis all for lofe! 'Tis all for lofe
  Bot that this worlde is lyttel worthe

For myne trewe lofe hathe taene the glennis   125
  And if he is als I dredde sore
Als greate ane deuil amang more-hennis
  Als wemyng I'll se him no more

So I moste chainge this mortyl fraime
  But not the soul withynne that dwellis   130
For that will gif mee joye and aime
  Als shymmeryng o'er the firthis and fellis"

The wyffe takis hir farre benne the caife
  The lairde hee chuckilis jumpis and flyngis

And tryit the poweris of his two armis   135
  Wauffyng them als theye had beine wyngis

For hee wals more nor half resolvit
  To haif ane chainge and wyng the ayre
And touzel with these lofelye thyngis
  Among the purpil blossomis rayre   140

And aye he wafit his armis aboute
  How theye wolde doo for wyngis to trye
And aye he gaif ane loudde gaffaw
  Thynkand the maydenis to outflye

Then out caime bonnye Barberry Blaike   145
  Ane sprecklit larke so swete to se
"Gode bye sir lairde" sho merrylye cryit
  "Now come and mounte the heuinis withe mee"

The lairde he ranne to the knowe heidde
  To se quhare that swete burde wolde fle   150
"Och chainge mee chainge me" quod the lairde
  "Or I for downrychte lofe moste dee"

The wyffe toke him far benne the caife
  And sore he rairit with tormente slowe
But alle that sho colde maike of him   155
  Wals ane unseimlye hoodye crowe

Then that gruesome burde wals sore in raige
  And cursit the wyffe bothe but and benne
For he wolde bee ane cocke laverocke
  To followe that bewytching henne   160

Then the wyffe sho toke the lairdis gode gunne
  And helde it at him glacheryng there
Lorde howe he skraichit and fledde for lyffe
  For that wals more than crowe colde beare

Then the lairde he toke his lonelye flychte   165
  Lamentyng sore his aspecke grimme
For neither laverocke rooke nor crowe
  Nor swete morehenne wolde melle with hymme

At his approach the hoodyis fledde
   The rooke but an the corbye crowe 170
The faulkon and the greiddye gledde
   Flewe half dementyd to and fro

The lordlye egill left the clyffe
   His herte gat neuir soche ane stounne
And yellit his terrour yont the lyfte 175
   For the blacke lairde of Gilbertoun

But hadde you seen the blewe herrounne
   Als sho satte caiperyng bee the streimme
You wolde haif lauchyt quhille you fallit down
   To haif seine hir loke and hearit hir screimme 180

Sho knottyt hir throppyl lyke ane purse
   And spredde hir yellow trammis behynde
And reardyng screwit the fyrmamente
   To the tap storyis of the wynde

I haif beine eiste I haif beine weste 185
   And o'er the border mountainis blewe
But I neuir sawe als dafte lyke beiste
   Als ane o'erfrychtenit herrounsheugh

But och that lofely sprecklit larke
   Wals teisit and perseceited so 190
That nychte and daye hee followit hir
   This vylde voluptuous hoodye crowe

And the sweite morehennis they jynkit and jeeryd
   And wolde not lette him once come neare
Quhille sore hee cursit and he sweirit 195
   And callit them naimis ane shaime til heare

Now this crowe he pruvit ane lonelye burde
   For hee hald no converse with his kynde
The morehennis lauchit him sore to scorne
   And theyre loferis dabbit him neirlye blynde 200

But the morehennis tirit of the moris
   And one bee one came hame theyre wayis

But they all had fedderis on theyre feitte
   And lymbis until theyre dying dayis

But the lairde remaynit though many a daye   205
   At the grande wytchis dore hee prayit
Sho only shuit the burde awaye
   And with the gunne his herte dismayit

"Bee gone" sho cryit "and taike the bente
   Tis meite ane crowe that you remayne   210
For euil wals your hertis intente
   And blacke myschefe youre whole desygne

And you shall rofe ane haitfulle burde
   And feidde on garbage ear' and laite
Until the larke of your deirre lofe   215
   Shalle syng you unto mannis estaite"

Then the pore crowis herte wals lyke to breake
   And the teris ranne ower his colle blacke chynne
And aye he cursit his amorit herte
   That ledde him on to deidlye synne   220

"O womanis lofe O womanis lofe
   Quhat greifis on manne it hathe brochte downe
But neuir wals blaide so harde bestaide
   Als the pore lairde of Gilbertoun

Now I to feidde myne lordlye gobe   225
   Moste daylye baigel through the wynde
To picke the eyne of pore deade lambis
   Or houke the haslet of the hynde

Or maybes of ane burstyn frogge
   To maike myne supper on the heathe   230
But the flesche or bonis of ane morecoke
   I'll neuir picke whyle I haif breathe

Now I haif loste myne forestis darke
   Myne hillis myne herdis and feildis of corne
And I haif loste myne lofely larke   235
   The bonnyeste burde that euir wals borne

But I will seike hir in the skye
  And ower the felle and by the se
And I will cower benethe hir eye
  And begge that sho wille pity mee"   240

Och quha colde haif thought that woeful burde
  Als whaiskyng over craig and lynne
Coulde haif hadde resounne at his herte
  But an ane hoomyn soule withynne

But there are thyngis of spelle and power   245
  That neuir wals knowne and neuir wille bee
Saife to the Wyffe of Ezdel-more
  The lairde of Gilbertoune and mee

FYTTE THE FOURTHE

There wals ane crow satte on ane stone
  Abone the yette of Gilbertoun
But it flewe awaye and there wals none
  Sure soche ane burde had neuir flowne

For that crow it spoke the wordis of menne   5
  It spoke the wordis that wemyng knewe
It sung ane sang of a morelande glenne
  Ane song that neuir colde bee trewe

And menne and wemyng fledd for frychte
  And crappe in holis and boris amayne   10
And messanis yowlit and lordlye grewis
  Glymit in amaize for lacke of brayne

Amd the horses snorkit at the stalle
  And the gainderis yellit ane pyteous waylle
But the loste lairdis braif poynter Colle   15
  Crepit to the yette and waggit his taylle

But the aulde laidye of Gilbertoun
  Caime loutyng twayfolde ower a rung
"Quhat burde is this" the laidye sayit
  "That syngis to mee with hoomyn tongue"   20

"Och I am ane sorryful synnful burde
   The curse of heuin is on myne heidde
For I bee guiltye thochtis wals lurit
   Myne Makeris image to degrade

Yit stille I lofe the hoomyn raice
   And I canne sorrowe for theyre synne
And I haif hopis of heuinis graice
   And ane immmortyl soule withynne

O moder deirre or I wals borne
   I haif hearit you telle with feire and woe
You dremyt you wals in chyldebedde layit
   And bure ane haitful hoody crowe

And so you did I am youre sonne
   Foredomyt to bee this creture lowe
I wyshit to bee ane tuneful larke
   But turnit ane pyteous hoodye crowe

Quhat shalle I saye quhat shalle I doo
   A moderis prayers maye moche availle
A moderis lofe maye yet subdue
   This synful spelle which I bewaille

Ane lofelye burde that farre hathe flowne
   And you moste fynde hir if you canne
Sho has the power and sho alone
   To turn me til ane mortyl manne"

The laidy raisit hir hackerit faice
   Hir senses all benumbit and gone
"Quhat sayis the beiste for be goddis graice
   Myne herte is turnit intil ane stone

This is some horryd thyng bewytchit
   Get all your gunnis and shotte it deidde
I wille gif that manne ane hundred merkis
   Quha bryngis to mee its illfaurd heidde"

Then the crowe hee thochte it tyme to flytte
   For gun shottis were his mortyl dreidde

25

30

35

40

45

50

But the greate bigge teris ranne downe his chekis   55
    Als rounde and cleire als draps of leidde

But wordis gone eiste and wordis gone weste
    That these darke deiddis of glaumourye
By the dredful wyffe of Ezdel-more
        Walde rewine all the southe countrye   60

Then prieste and peasaunte kyssit the roode
    And sayit theyre *aves* o'er and o'er
For all the lande wals in feirre and dredde
    For the pouerful wyffe of Ezdel-more

But it happenit on ane lofelye morne   65
    Quhan Maye had all hir blossomis sette
That there rayse ane laverocke from the corne
    And mounted to the mornyngis yette

And no one kennit quhence sho had flowne
    Quhille theye hearit its meltyng straynis abofe   70
And it saylit on the cloudis of eyder downe
    And it sang of heuinlye lofe

That bonnye burdis sang it wals so sweitte
    Als it melted from the skye
That the owssen lowit outower theyre meitte   75
    Charmit with the melodye

And the horses knelit withynne the stalle
    All quiveryng with delychte
The gaimsome lambis forgotte theyre playe
    And lokit to heuinis heychte   80

And all the burdis in the grene foreste
    Caime postyng through the ayre
It wals lyke ane brydal of boundlesse lofe
    For the layis of heuin were there

The bleyter caime bompyng from the mosse   85
    The stynte and the graye curlewe
And the plevir caime in his corslet blacke
    But he durste notte gif ane whewe

And the peaseweippe cockit hir creste of blewe
  Als highe als it wolde reirre   90
And the myresnyppe caime in his rokelaye newe
  To se quhat wals asteire

And the merlyn hang in the myddel ayre
  With his lyttil wyngis outspreadde
Als if let downe from the heuinis there   95
  By ane viewlesse sylken threadde

And Sandy the pyper lefte the brooke
  And the ouzel his glittye stone
And robyn lefte the grenewode nooke
  Though the boshe wals all his owne   100

From banke and brae and grenewode bushe
  All rounde fayre Gilbertoun
That morne there wals neither hish nor whush
  But the laiverockis sang alone

Och I wolde haif giuen quhat wolde I notte   105
  To haif hearit that heuinlye laye
For the strayne from seconde hand ygotte
  Is berefit of its magick swaye

But aye the burdyn of the sang
  If the trothe to me wals giuen   110
Wals of swete repentance on the yirth
  And foregivenesse from the heuin

But I maye not syng I dare not syng
  That strayne of heuinlye graice
For in ane auld wyffis taille lyke myne   115
  It wolde sore bee out of plaice

But amangis the burdis ane hoody crowe
  Satte hyche on the auld rown tre
Quha hang his heidde in doleful wyse
  And ane mournfulle burde wals hee   120

And aye hee turnit up his waterye eyne
  With hevye syche and grone

Als if the sang were maide for him
   And were maide for him alone

And the teris ranne downe his duffye chekis   125
   Aye als the bonny burde sung
And he shoke his dobye heidde and prayit
   Some wordis in hoomyn tongue

But thresher John he hearit these wordis
   And ane rychte blythe manne wals hee   130
For hee countyd on the hundred merkis
   That were offerit bee his ladye

And hee has gone up to the ende wyndowe
   That lokyt to the auld rown tre
And hee hathe let flie at the pore hoodye crowe   135
   Quhille downe to the grounde felle hee

"Faythe taike thou that!" quod thresher John
   "Thou creture of warlockrye
Thyne heidde is worthe an hundred merkis
   To myne auld wyffe and mee"   140

But quhan that crowe felle from the tre
   He gaif soche ane feirful crye
That rang from the grenewode to the cloudde
   And bobbyt agaynste the skye

And the lyttil wee seraph lefte the cloudde   145
   On the eebrow of the daye
And ane strayne of loudde lamente wals hearit
   Farre through the heuinis awaye

And all the burdis of the gode grene wode
   Of the more but an the daille   150
Theye followit awaye bee the selfsaime rode
   With ane deippe and pyteous waille

But thresher John caime downe the stayre
   Chauntyng this merrye song
"Myne laidye maye nowe drawe out hir purse   155
   For I'll maike its necke fulle long

And its hey for my gunne and my goode auld gunne
   Sho's the quene of the deeddlye playe
For ane hundred merkis bee ane aulde barne-manne
   Is not wonne everilke daye"   160

So Johnis awaye rounde to the auld rown tre
   His gallante preye to bryng
But the hoodye raysit two eyes to him
   Lyke ane wanyirthlye thyng

It wals ane loke John colde not thole   165
   And his preye hee darit notte taike
For it shoke him to the very soule
   And maide all his herte to quaike

"Goddis curse on you" quod the hoodye crowe
   "Do you know quhat you haif donne   170
You haif slayne ane soule and bodye bothe
   And youre sande of lyffe is ronne"

John ranne for lyffe he knowit not quhidder
   Through terrour and through payne
And hee neuir loote one scraughe byde anidder   175
   Quhille he felle on his owne herthe stayne

And hee hath tauld soche ane strainge mixit taille
   Of myrth and of mysterye
That all the menzie and theyre ould daime
   Ranne out this crowe to se   180

But quhan theye caime to the rown tre greinne
   With crosyer and with rode
There laye the lairde of Gilbertoun
   A welteryng in his blode

"Och quha has donne this rothelesse deidde   185
   Myne deirre sonne telle to mee"
"It wals thresher John" the lairde replyit
   And streikit him downe to dee

And hee neuir spoke ane oder worde
   But three tymis kyssit the rode   190

And turnit ane sorrowful ee til heuin
   Which wolde bee understode

And theye buryit him in the rown tre grene
   Beneathe the auld rown tre
For theye durste notte taike him to Maryis kyrke   195
   That martyr to wytcherye

So this is playne let wemyng or menne
   Through lyffe bee quhat theye maye
Deathe bryngis them to themsellis agayne
   To euil or gode for aye   200

Maye this bee ane wairnyng to all yong menne
   That sporte in the morelande fellis
To bee ware of the sleike and bonnye more-henne
   That lurkis in the hadder bellis

And O to bee ware of the swete swete burde   205
   Quhais notis gar the herte stryngis playe
And most of all quhan hir voyce is hearit
   Bee hir laine in the gloamyng graye

But quhat hathe become of pore thresher John
   O no thyng of moche availle   210
For theye hangit him on the auld rown tre
   Which endeth myne grefous taille

Robyn Reidde

Did you neuir heirre of Robyn Reidde
    Ane strainge unchancye boye
Quha from the daye that hee wals borne
    In mynde had some alloye

Yet hee was foremost at the leippe   5
    And foremost at the raice
And quhan ane boye contrairye profet
    He smotte him on the faice

Yes hee wolde go withoute one gleimme
    Of passione in his heidde   10
And beatte his haffatis black and blewe
    And maike his nose to bleidde

Then hee wolde turne and crone ane song
    Or putte ane muckil stonne
Or flye to ainy lychtsome playe   15
    Als nothyng had beine donne

And hee colde telle of Wallace wychte
    And Robyn Brusse the goode
Of Will Skarlette and lyttil Johne
    And of bold Robyn Hoode   20

Of Adam Belle and Clyme of the Cleuch
    And William of Cloudesslee
Quha were thre aircheris gode eneuch
    The best in the sothe countrye

Then hee with everye boye wolde fychte   25
    With staff but an with steille
And those quha helde not fayre defence
    He maide theyre crownis to feille

And hee colde bende ane rychte strong bowe
  And aime with ane steadye eye   30
And bryng ane crow downe from the lyfte
  Quhan mainye crowis wente by

Yet at the tryste or weapanshawe
  So symple wals his meinne
That all menne toke him for ane foole   35
  The graitest euir wals seinne

But lord Douglasse has raisit the Jedde forest
  And the laddis of Liddiesdaille
To meitte lord Scrope on the Dyrdan waiste
  To settle the Border maille   40

And Robyn Reidde amongis the reste
  Wente forthe als ane behoulder
With gode strong bowe acrosse his backe
  And sorde out ower his shoulder

His doublette wals the gode buckis hyde   45
  Ane goodlye frocke to se
And his brekis from the back of the gode black oxe
  Als strong als theye colde bee

He had no buskynis on his feitte
  Nor bonnette on his heidde   50
And all the troperis helde theyre sydis
  And lauchit at Robyn Reidde

But aye hee loutchit and trodgit alang
  Skyppyng ower hagg and heugh
And sometymis hee wolde crone ane sang   55
  Or quhistle ane whilly-whewe

And the English caime to the Dyrdan waiste
  All mairchyng ranke and fylle
The Tynedaille laddis and the Bewcastil laddis
  And the gentilis of merrye Carlysle   60

Then there wals bouzyng on the bente
  And aye the myrthe grewe loudder

For they drank to the helthe of James Stewarde
   And eke of Harry Toudder

And all wals aimetye and pece   65
   No solderyng there to maike
But the Englysh laughit at Robyn Reidde
   Quhille theyre fat sydis did sheike

Then there wals jouste and tournamente
   But the Scottis wonne euerye ploye   70
Whyle Robyn stode and lookit onne
   And clappit his handis for joye

But quhan the bowmenne toke theyre turne
   The Scottis were sorre outdonne
At euerye flychte theye were o'ershotte   75
   Yet the botte wals neuir wonne

Then Robyn bente his gode oulde bowe
   Ane better wals neuir strung
And he drewe ane arrowe from his belte
   And awaye his sorde he flung   80

But quhan he baitte his beardless lyppe
   And 'gan his strength to strayne
And the winde blew up his bowzelly heidde
   The Englysh roarit amayne

"Restrayne youre myrthe" sayis lord John Scrope   85
   "An't were but for courtesye
If that clownne can not his shafte dyrecte
   Hee sore deceiveth mee"

Then Robyn sette his leggis asperre
   And hee wynkit with his ee   90
And drew the bowstryng til his eirre
   And ane steaddye ayme toke hee

The bow playit twang lyke smythye clang
   Soche yerke ne'er stunnit the eirre
It maide the Englysh lounis to sterte   95
   With wonder and with feirre

The arrowe toke ane gentil ryse
　　The airche of moste availle
Lyke raynbowe at the houre of none
　　When the showir is in the daille　　　　　　　100

And through the bullockis ee it wente
　　Wythinne the outer ryng
And piercit the solyd masse behynde
　　Downe to the greye gose wyng

The watcher twyrlit his cappe on hee　　　　　　105
　　And catchit it als it felle
"Welle donne yong hynde" sayis lord John Scrope
　　"Thine bowe becomis the welle

I'll backe thyne skille—seye it agayne
　　With arrowe of the saimme　　　　　　　　　110
Leiste menne sholde saye it wals but chaunce
　　And not thyne goodlye aymme"

He shotte agayne the arrow flewe
　　With swyftnesse manyfolde
But of its pathe alongis the ayre　　　　　　　115
　　The eye colde not keippe holde

The watcher twyrlit his cappe on hee
　　And catchit it tymis thre
"The Lord forbydde" sayit lord Jhonne Scrope
　　"That thou sholdest shotte at mee"　　　　　120

He knowit the sygne it toulde him playne
　　Als playne als tongue colde saye
That rychte out through the bullockis eye
　　The arrow founde its waye

Then euerye bowe wals sore unbente　　　　　125
　　To yielde it all were fayne
And straighte unto the butte they wente
　　For nonne would shotte agayne

"Now my goode lordis" the watcher sayit
　　"I haif beinne watcher heirre　　　　　　　130

And at the target stode the judge
   For thre and thretty yeirre

But soche two shottis als these two last
   Myne eyis did neuir se
If he wals not the deuil quha sente the shaftis   135
   Ane maister hande is hee"

Then everilke ee on Robyn Reidde
   Wals turnit with wondir blynde
They thochte the deuil had comme indeidd
   In lykenesse of ane hynde   140

For there the two braif arrowis stucke
   Sunke to the graye gose wyng
And the laste had splette the fyrste in twayne
   Ane moste unyirthlye thyng

"Tell mee thyne naime" sayis lord Jhonne Scrope   145
   "Thou moste uncourtlye hynde
For with myne gode lord Douglas' leive
   To the I haif ane mynde"

"Myne naime" sayit hee "is Robyn Reidde
   I thynke no shaime to telle   150
Myne fader wals dafte myne moder wals keude
   And I'm hardlye rychte myselle

But quhat's withhelde from mee in wytte
   In strengthe of airm is giuen
For I will not yielde to anye wychte   155
   That braithis benethe the heuin"

"Quhatis this I hear!" sayit lord Jhonne Scrope
   "May I myne senses trowe
That such ane lowne als that hath leirre
   And matchless vygour to   160

Then Reidde it is an Englyshe naime
   Of braif Northumberlande
Therefore I clayme the hynde als myne
   And joyne him to myne bande"

"Taike him" myne lord the Douglas sayit   165
    "On that wee shall agre
Hee is lyker to ane beggirlye foole
    Than warriour meitte for mee"

Then Robyn Reidde he hang his heidde
    And the teirre wals in his ee   170
Sayis hee "lord Douglasse thou shalte rue
    The pairtyng thus with mee

But if there's one in all your trayne
    Daris trye mee at one thyng
I throwe myne gaige chose hee the gaime   175
    And turne him to the ryng"

Out steppit Jocke Dickson of Haugh-sheille
    Ane wrestler bolde and vayne
"If thou throwis me" Jocke Dickson sayit
    "I neuir shalle rysse agayne"   180

Jocke sette his boudlye leggis fulle wydde
    "Stande fayre you burlye lounne
Lorde I'm ashaimit to claspe youre waiste
    Or laye soche lomber downne!"

The strypplyng seizit him bee the necke   185
    His rychte hande swynging outte
Then broughte his heidde before his breiste
    And fouldit him lyke ane cloutte

"Damn you!" sayis Jocke "that wals not fayre
    Ane quirke befytting you   190
Stande als I stande thus breiste to breiste
    And grippe als I grippe to"

Pore Robyn didde als he wals bidde
    He no objectiounis maide
But set his feitte als Jocke sette his   195
    And for the onsette staide

Jocke maide ane broostle and ane tryppe
    With mychte and maijistye

But Robyn brochte his backe to beirre
    Then hevit him up on hee   200

And awaye he ranne from out the ryng
    With baisse and wycked speidde
And in ane greate and firsome pole
    He jawit him owre the heidde

"Now taike thou that!" sayit Robyn Reidde   205
    "To cole thyne corage trewe"
Then put his handis behynde his backe
    And whystled ane whilly-whewe

Jocke Dickson then wals sorely snoolit
    The playe wals ower with him   210
Hee wrang his duddis and shoke his luggis
    And shyverit everilke lymbe

Now Robyn Reidde the sporte had spyllit
    Not one wolde taike the ryng
Nor trye that wylde unyirthly chylde   215
    For ainy yirthlye thyng

So he is gone awaye with lord Jhonne Scrope
    His motelye foole to bee
And quhan nexte you heirre of Robyn Reidde
    You will wonder more than mee   220

FYTTE THE SECONDE

The graite St Edmundis fayre comis on
    And Englandis all on styrre
For all are there from ladye fayre
    To vyldest pilfererre

And prestis and prelatis wyffis and bairnis   5
    And captainis of renownne
And cowlit monkis and troperis sterne
    All crowdyng rounde the townne

Into ane splendid tente there satte
   Two youthis and maydenis fyne   10
Chattyng and wooing plesauntlye
   And quaffyng blode reidde wyne

In caime ane champyon troper sterne
   With ladye of that townne
"Maike rome!" hee cryit "Get hence you trashe!"   15
   And dang theyre tabil downne

The wyne wals spillit the glasses broke
   The maydenis skremyt outrychte
"Syr quhat menis this?" the youthis replyit
   "Wee did you no despychte"   20

Hee cursit the youthis and hee kickit the youthis
   Quhille all theyre bonis were sore
And then hee toke them bee the neckis
   And flang them from the dore

And then the madamme of the townne   25
   Sho gygglit and sho mumblit
Sho wals so proudde of hir braif knychte
   Quha had two bumpkinnis pummilit

The champyoune spoke in lofty phraise
   And caiperit mychtilye   30
That no manne colde compaire with him
   Wals playne als playne colde bee

But there satte ane grousye monke behynde
   With quaiffe upon his heidde
And hee wals smackyng at the sacke   35
   And knollyng up the breidde

The troper poppit the bedismanis cowlle
   Backe ower his burlye necke
"Some manneris monke! If not for mee
   For ladyis haif respecke"   40

The monke caime sloutchyng rounde aboutte
   To the champyoune and his deirre

"Maike rome!" cryit hee "Get hence you trashe!
   Quhat garbage haif we heirre?"

Then with the staffe into his hande   45
   Hee sweepit the tabil cleinne
And strak the troper cross the necke
   Till fire flewe from his einne

"Monke I'll gif the soche chastysemente
   Als monke gat ne'er before   50
Thy sackclothe frocke and motelye cowlle
   Shall the protecke no more"

"I know it welle" the monke replyit
   "But bee Sant George's heidde
I am resolvit with soche ane knaife   55
   To fychte quhille I bee deidde"

Then he pullit off his scallopit cowlle
   And rollit it round his hande
Then brandyshit his unseimlye kente
   Againste the troperis brande   60

Then all the fayre they gatherit rounde
   In thousandis to the fraye
And the foremost man wals lord John Scrope
   To se fayre rome and playe

And there were the yuthis and maydenis to   65
   That from the tente were dreuin
And that the monke mychte maulle the knaiffe
   They sente theyre prayeris to heuin

The fychte beganne with deidlye feidde
   With florysh and with knelle   70
And aye the monkis unfarrante staffe
   Made all the falchione yelle

"Welle done braif monke! laye on braif monke!"
   Ane thousande shoutis combyne
"Syrr saif youre heidde!" the monke replyit   75
   "Or maike ane slappe at myne"

The troper gaif ane horryd slashe
　　To clefe the bedesman downe
Quha parryit it withoutte dismaye
　　And crackit him ower the crowne　　　　　　　80

The troper jumpit from the grene
　　With ane convulsife strayne
Then droppyt his sorde and downe he felle
　　His skull wals splette in twayne

And there he laye and spurrit the gerse　　　　　85
　　Chackyng his tethe fulle sore
But neuir closit his dymme sette eyne
　　Nor worde spoke euirmore

Then sholder hee theye hevit the monke
　　And bure him through the towne　　　　　　　90
Shoutyng and laudyng als they wente
　　The monkis supreme renowne

Some sayit he wals ane lorde disguysit
　　One faimit for nobil deidde
But oderis sayit he wals the deuil　　　　　　　95
　　Or els daft Robyn Reidde

Lord Scrope hee toke him by the hande
　　And ledde him from the fraye
Saying he sholde be ane captayne soone
　　And caste the coulle awaye　　　　　　　　100

About that braif and manly monke
　　Ane mychtye stirre wals maidde
But theye neuir colde heirre of him agayne
　　Either alyve or deidde

FYTTE THE THRYDDE

Next yeirre there caime to Newcastle
　　Ane Frenchmanne of renowne
Quha techit lordis and knychtis to fense
　　His lyke wals neuir knowne

For hee had jynkis and quhelis and ayeris 5
   That daizzyllit all mennis sychte
And hee colde twirle theyre foylis on hee
   So wonderous wals his slychte

But all his quirkis and slychtye dedis
   Unto this lande were newe 10
For he colde spryng out ower folkis hedis
   And felle them als hee flewe

Then there wals publyshit through the realme
   Ane greate appoyntit day
Quhan hee and all his pupilis grande 15
   Theyre valour shoulde displaye

And thousandis caime from farre and neirre
   This wonderous playe to se
Bothe nobyl knychtis and ladyis fayre
   And hyndis of lowe degre 20

Och it wals rairre! soche dedis of weare
   Neuir entrancit the view
So laidyis sayit and nobylis swaire
   So it most haif bene trewe

Then wals ane nobyl challenge giuen 25
   Daryng all Brytanis isle
And seuin tymis it wals proclaimit
   At crosse and at kyrke style

But good lord Piercy got a hynt
   From one that knowit full well 30
Sayis hee "Syrr mayster I held mynde
   To haif tryit your skille myselle

But that I thynke it tryfling playe
   Which common mychte may stande
Therefore the lowest hynde I haif 35
   Shalle fychte you hand to hande"

"I haif thrown my gaige" the maister sayit
   "To playe with lord or knychte

I dare all Brytanis nobyl blode
     With hinde I will not fychte"   40

"Nay you haif braifit all Brytain brode
     And shalle not now recedde
So with the lowest we'll begynne
     And ryse als wee see neidde

Get up you greate and awkward cooffe   45
     And fychte that foreigne manne
Holde up your heidde and take the foylle
     And beatte him if you canne"

Then up theyre steppit upon the staige
     Ane moste uncourtlye wychte   50
The shoutis rang to the very skyis
     At soche ane gloryous sychte

Hee had not sandalis on his feitte
     Nor hatte upon his heidde
And duddye wals his doublette greinne   55
     And his bluff chekys were reidde

And aye he hang his muckil faice
     And girnit lyke any thyng
And then pullit up his duddye brekis
     And tyit them with ane stryng   60

"Myne nobyl lorde this is to badde"
     The maister hee did saye
"But if this mockerye is youre wille
     It is meitte that I obeye

But canne I beatte that sillye loutte   65
     Als I wold foyle ane knychte
Or is there anye sport to playe
     In nobyl ladyis sychte?"

"Nay knabbe him welle" lord Piercye sayit
     "Lay on with hevye hande   70
There is not one wille lesse be missit
     In all Northumberlande

Come my braif nolt-herde take the foylle
  Thou stupydyst of menne
If that French manne sholde be thyne deidde   75
  Quhat will myne stottis do thenne"

The maister quhelit and quhelit agayne
  That ladyis mychte adore
Rounde also quhelit the awkwarde hynde
  Which sporte gaif ten tymis more   80

But quhan they mette on myddil staige
  Hee sette his fraime so tychte
That all the thousandis helde their braith
  Marvellyng at soche any sychte

One, two, three hits were counted straighte   85
  Againste the Frenchmannis skille
But not one hit his airte coulde gette
  Though aymit with rychte gode wille

The arm it wals so long and strong
  Of this unsychtelye clowne   90
He drofe the maister to the raillis
  And then hee knockit him downe

Then all the lystes with shoutis were fyllit
  Quhille the brode skye did rende
The clowne drewe up his brekis and trodgit   95
  Unto the other ende

The maister rose but staggerit sore
  And to the rayling clung
The clowne hang down his nether lyppe
  And to himself hee sung   100

"Some sayis you are possissit Robyn
  Some sayis you are the deille
But clinkum clankum is the sporte
  That Robyn louis fulle weille"

The Maister came up to the clowne   105
  With faice rychte paille and wanne

"I yield you up my foylle" said hee
  "Which I ne'er did to manne

If you are not the deuille himselle
  In which caisse I resygne   110
I pray thee yielde mee up thy name
  In fayre exchainge for myne"

"Myne naime" sayit hee "is Robyn Reidde
  I thynke no shaime to telle
Myne fader wals daft myne moder was keude   115
  And I'm hardly rychte myselle

But quhat is wythhelde from mee in wytte
  In mychte of airm is giuen
For I will not yielde to ainy wychte
  That braithis aneathe the heuin   120

For I haif ane knolege at myne herte
  From quhare I cannot telle
That I am double—I'm Rob Reidde
  And I'm besyde myselle"

The Maister spredd out his handes to heuin   125
  Sygning the cross with speidde
"Heauinis! haif I darit the dreddfulle deidde
  To fychte dafte Robyn Reidde

Then I am gone! for it wals known
  Before I saw the lychte   130
That ane madde wychte of fayre Scotland
  Should beatte mee in the fychte

And all myne honoris and my lyffe
  Reive at ane syngle blow
Och! I am gone" And down he felle   135
  And rollit him to and fro

Then laye he streitchit upon his backe
  Trying to guairde his heidde
And with passado lunge and fense
  Hee foughte quhille hee wals deidde   140

There wals no tournamente or sporte
   Through Englande at that daye
In which some strainge outlandysh wychte
   Bare not the pryze awaye

Ane miller wonne at Shrewsburye   145
   The pryze in gallante style
Ane tailor with his elwand gode
   The jouste at merrye Carlysle

Ane blacksmythe with his apron on
   With ganne all blacke and brownne   150
Enterit the lystis before kyng James
   At his graite Langhame townne

Lord Douglasse wals the champyone there
   And everye knychte bore downne
But the blacksmythe met him hand to hande   155
   And crackit him ower the crownne

Kyng James he lauchit till from his steidde
   Upon the grounde felle hee
For welle he lofit hombylit to yirth
   His nobilis pryde to se   160

Then hee sente for the burlye smyth
   To maike him a propyne
Sayis hee "ane earldome I wold gif
   An that bolde lowne were myne"

But some one whysperit him to spaire   165
   His proffer and his meidde
For that he wals ane knaife possessit
   Quham menne callit Robyn Reidde

That euerye manne hee tryit he beatte
   That euerye pryze he wonne   170
And euerye manne he foughte he kyllit
   Als hee that daye had donne

"I'll gif him worke" kyng James replyit
   "To kylle myne nobilis all

For they're so proudde that they will fychte   175
    And fychting theye will fall

Och it wolde joye myne herte to see
    Ane hero in disguise
Laye euery one of them als lowe
    Als proudde lord Douglasse lyis   180

For they are tyrantis voyde of ruthe
    Of loyaltye and faithe
And oft haif grefit myne very herte
    For my pore pepylis skaithe

Bryng mee the wychte I'll chainge his naime   185
    And haif some gloryous gle
For if these knaifis not hombylit are
    The deuil maye reygne for mee"

So Robyn Reidde is gone with speidde
    Ane Royalle paige to bee   190
And quhan you next heirre of his tryckis
    You will wonder more than mee

Elen of Reigh

By the Ettrick Shepherd

Have you never heard of Elen of Reigh,
The fairest flower of the north countrie?
The maid that left all maidens behind
In all that was lovely, sweet, and kind:
As sweet as the breeze o'er beds of balm,   5
As happy and gay as the gamesome lamb,
As light as the feather that dances on high,
As blithe as the lark in the breast of the sky,
As modest as young rose that blossoms too soon,
As mild as the breeze on a morning of June;   10
Her voice was the music's softest key,
And her form the comeliest symmetry.

But let bard describe her smile who can,
For that is beyond the power of man;
There never was pen that hand could frame,   15
Nor tongue that falter'd at maiden's name,
Could once a distant tint convey
Of its lovely and benignant ray.
You have seen the morning's folding vest
Hang dense and pale upon the east,   20
As if an angel's hand had strewn
The dawning's couch with the eider down,
And shrouded with a curtain gray
The cradle of the infant day?
And 'mid this orient dense and pale,   25
Through one small window of the veil
You have seen the sun's first radiant hue
Lightening the dells and vales of dew,
With smile that seem'd through glory's rim
From dwellings of the cherubim;   30
And you have thought, with holy awe,
A lovelier sight you never saw,
Scorning the heart who dared to doubt it;
Alas! you little knew about it!

At beauty's shrine you ne'er have knelt,   35
Nor felt the flame that I have felt;
Nor chanced the virgin smile to see
Of beauty's model, Elen of Reigh!

When sunbeams on the river blaze,
You on its glory scarce can gaze;   40
But when the moon's delirious beam,
In giddy splendour woos the stream,
Its mellow'd light is so refined,
'Tis like a gleam of soul and mind;
Its gentle ripple glittering by,   45
Like twinkle of a maiden's eye;
While all amazed at Heaven's steepness,
You gaze into its liquid deepness,
And see some beauties that excel—
Visions to dream of, not to tell—   50
A downward soul of living hue,
So mild, so modest, and so blue!

What am I raving of just now?
Forsooth, I scarce can say to you—
A moonlight river beaming by,   55
Or holy depth of virgin's eye;
Unconscious bard! What perilous dreaming!
Is nought on earth to thee beseeming,
Will nothing serve, but beauteous women?—
No, nothing else. But 'tis strange to me,   60
If you never heard aught of Elen of Reigh.

But whenever you breathe the breeze of balm,
Or smile at the frolics of the lamb,
Or watch the stream by the light of the moon,
Or weep for the rosebud that opes too soon,   65
Or when any beauty of this creation
Moves your delight or admiration,
You then may try, whatever it be,
That to compare with Elen of Reigh:
But never presume that lovely creature   70
Once to compare with aught in nature;
For earth has neither form nor face
Which heart can ween or eye can trace,

That once comparison can stand
With Elen the flower of fair Scotland.   75

   'Tis said that angels are passing fair
And lovely beings;—I hope they are:
But for all their beauty of form and wing,
If lovelier than the maid I sing,
They needs must be—I cannot tell—   80
Something beyond all parallel;
Something admitted, not believed,
Which heart of man hath ne'er conceived;
But these are beings of mental bliss,
Not things to love, and soothe, and kiss.—   85
There is something dear, say as we will,
In winsome human nature still.

   Elen of Reigh was the flower of our wild,
Elen of Reigh was an only child,
A motherless lamb, in childhood thrown   90
On bounteous Nature, and her alone;
But who can mould like that mighty dame
The mind of fervour and mounting flame,
The mind that beams with a glow intense
For fair and virtuous excellence!   95
Not one! though many a mighty name,
High margin'd on the lists of fame,
Has blazon'd her ripe tuition high.
The world has own'd it, and well may I!
But most of all that right had she,   100
The flower of our mountains, fair Elen of Reigh.

   But human life is like a river—
Its brightness lasts not on for ever—
That dances from its native braes,
As pure as maidhood's early days;   105
But soon, with dark and sullen motion,
It rolls into its funeral ocean,
And those whose currents are the slightest,
And shortest run, are aye the brightest:
So is our life—its latest wave   110
Rolls dark and solemn to the grave;

And soon o'ercast was Elen's day,
And changed, as must my sportive lay.

When beauty is in its rosy prime,
There is something sacred and sublime,   115
To see all living worth combined
In such a lovely being's mind;
Each thing for which we would wish to live,
Each grace, each virtue Heaven can give.
Such being was Elen, if such can be;   120
A faith unstain'd, a conscience free,
Pure Christian love and charity,
All breathed in such a holy strain,
The hearts of men could not refrain
From wonder at what they heard and saw;   125
Even greatest sinners stood in awe
At seeing a form and soul unshadow'd—
A model for the walks of maidhood.

You will feel a trembling wish to know,
If such a being could e'er forego   130
Her onward path of heavenly aim,
To love a thing of mortal frame.
Ah! never did heart in bosom dwell,
That loved as warmly and as well,
Or with such ligaments profound   135
Was twined another's heart around;
But blush not—dread not, I entreat,
Nor tremble for a thing so sweet.

Not comely youth with downy chin,
Nor manhood's goodliest form, could win   140
One wistful look, or dew-drop sheen,
From eye so heavenly and serene.
Her love, that with her life began,
Was set on thing more pure than man—
'Twas on a virgin of like mind,   145
As pure, as gentle, as refined;
They in one cradle slept when young—
Were taught by the same blessed tongue;
Aye smiled each other's face to see—
Were nursed upon the self-same knee;   150

And the first word each tongue could frame
Was a loved playmate's cheering name.

Like two young poplars of the vale,
Like two young twin roes of the dale,
They grew; and life had no alloy,—   155
Their fairy path was all of joy.
They danced, they sung, they play'd, they roved,
And O how dearly as they loved!
While in that love, with reverence due,
Their God and their Redeemer too   160
Were twined, which made it the sincerer,
And still the holier and the dearer.

Each morning, when they woke from sleep,
They kneel'd, and pray'd with reverence deep;
Then raised their sightly forms so trim,   165
And sung their little morning hymn.
Then tripping joyfully and bland,
They to the school went hand in hand;
Came home as blithesome and as bright,
And slept in other's arms each night.   170

Sure in such sacred bonds to live,
Nature has nothing more to give.
So loved they on, and still more dear,
From day to day, from year to year;
And when their flexile forms began   175
To take the mould so loved by man,
They blush'd—embraced each other less,
And wept at their own loveliness,
As if their bliss was overcast,
And days of feelings pure were past.   180

But who can fathom or reprove
The counsels of the God of love,
Or stay the mighty hand of Him
Who dwells between the cherubim?
No man nor angel—All must be   185
Submiss to his supreme decree.
And so it hap'd that this fair maid,
In all her virgin charms array'd,

Just when upon the verge she stood
Of bright and seemly womanhood,   190
From this fair world was call'd away,
In mildest and in gentlest way.
Fair world indeed; but still akin
To much of sorrow and of sin.

Poor Elen watch'd the parting strife   195
Of her she loved far more than life;
The placid smile that strove to tell
To her beloved that all was well.
O many a holy thing they said,
And many a prayer together pray'd,   200
And many a hymn, both morn and even,
Was breathed upon the breeze of heaven,
Which Hope, on wings of sacred love,
Presented at the gates above.

The last words into ether melt,   205
The last squeeze of the hand is felt,
And the last breathings, long apart,
Like aspirations of the heart,
Told Elen that she now was left,
A thing of love and joy bereft—   210
A sapling from its parent torn,
A rose upon a widow'd thorn,
A twin roe, or bewilder'd lamb,
Reft both of sister and of dam—
How could she weather out the strife   215
And sorrows of this mortal life!

The last rites of funereal gloom,
The pageant heralds of the tomb,
That more in form than feeling tell
The sorrows of the last farewell,   220
Are all observed with decent care,
And but one soul of grief was there.
The virgin mould, so mild and meet,
Is roll'd up in its winding sheet;
Affection's yearnings form'd the rest,   225
The dead rose rustles on the breast,
The wrists are bound with bracelet bands,

The pallid gloves are on the hands,
And all the flowers the maid held dear
Are strew'd within her gilded bier;   230
A hundred sleeves with lawn are pale,
A hundred crapes wave in the gale,
And in a motley mix'd array
The funeral train winds down Glen-Reigh.
Alack! how shortly thoughts were lasting   235
Of the grave to which they all were hasting!

    The grave is open; the mourners gaze
On bones and skulls of former days;
The pall's withdrawn—in letters sheen,
"Maria Gray Aged eighteen"   240
Is read by all with heaving sighs,
And ready hands to moisten'd eyes.
Solemn and slow the bier is laid
Into its deep and narrow bed,
And the mould rattles o'er the dead!   245

    What sound like that can be conceived?
That thunder to a soul bereaved!
When crumbling bones grate on the bier
Of all the bosom's core held dear;
'Tis like a growl of hideous wrath—   250
The last derisive laugh of death
Over his victim that lies under;
The heart's last bands then rent asunder,
And no communion more to be
Till Time melt in Eternity!   255

    From that dread moment Elen's soul
Seem'd to outfly its earthly goal;
And her refined and subtile frame,
Uplifted by unearthly flame,
Seem'd soul alone—in likelihood,   260
A spirit made of flesh and blood—
A thing whose being and whose bliss
Were bound to better world than this.

    Her face, that with new lustre beam'd,
Like features of a seraph seem'd;   265

A meekness, mix'd with a degree
Of fervid, wild sublimity,
Mark'd all her actions and her moods.
She sought the loneliest solitudes,
By the dingly dell or the silver spring,   270
Her holy hymns of the dead to sing;
For all her songs and language bland
Were of a loved and heavenly land—
A land of saints and angels fair,
And of a late dear dweller there;   275
But, watch'd full often, ears profane
Once heard the following solemn strain:—

Maria Gray. A Song.

1.
Who says that Maria Gray is dead,
    And that I in this world can see her never?
Who says she is laid in her cold death-bed,   280
    The prey of the grave and of death for ever?
Ah! they know little of my dear maid,
    Or kindness of her spirit's giver!
For every night she is by my side,
    By the morning bower, or the moonlight river.   285

2.
Maria was bonny when she was here,
    When flesh and blood was her mortal dwelling;
Her smile was sweet, and her mind was clear,
    And her form all human forms excelling.
But O! if they saw Maria now,   290
    With her looks of pathos and of feeling,
They would see a cherub's radiant brow,
    To ravish'd mortal eyes unveiling.

3.
The rose is the fairest of earthly flowers—
    It is all of beauty and of sweetness—   295
So my dear maid, in the heavenly bowers,
    Excels in beauty and in meetness.
She has kiss'd my cheek, she has kemb'd my hair,

And made a breast of heaven my pillow,
And promised her God to take me there,   300
  Before the leaf falls from the willow.

4.

Farewell, ye homes of living men!
  I have no relish for your pleasures—
In the human face I nothing ken
  That with my spirit's yearning measures.   305
I long for onward bliss to be,
  A day of joy, a brighter morrow;
And from this bondage to be free—
  Farewell, thou world of sin and sorrow!

O great was the wonder, and great was the dread,   310
Of the friends of the living, and friends of the dead;
For every evening and morning were seen
Two maidens, where only one should have been!
Still hand in hand they moved, and sung
Their hymns, on the walks they trode when young;   315
And one night some of the watcher train
Were said to have heard this holy strain
Wafted upon the trembling air.
It was sung by one, although two were there:—

Hymn Over A Dying Virgin.

1.

O Thou whom once thy redeeming love   320
Brought'st down to earth from the throne above,
Stretch forth thy cup of salvation free
To a thirsty soul that longs for thee!
O Thou who left'st the realms of day,
Whose blessed head in a manger lay,   325
See her here prostrate before thy throne,
Who trusts in thee, and in thee alone!

2.

O Thou, who once, as thy earthly rest,
Wast cradled on a virgin's breast,

For the sake of one who held thee dear, 330
Extend thy love to this virgin here!
Thou Holy One, whose blood was spilt
Upon the Cross, for human guilt,
This humbled virgin's longings see,
And take her soul in peace to thee! 335

———————————

That very night the mysterious dame
Not home to her father's dwelling came;
Though her maidens sat in chill dismay,
And watch'd, and call'd, till the break of day.
But in the dawning, with fond regard, 340
They sought the bower where the song was heard,
And found her form stretch'd on the green,
The loveliest corpse that ever was seen.
She lay as in balmy sleep reposed,
While her lips and eyes were sweetly closed, 345
As if about to awake and speak;
For a dimpling smile was on her cheek,
And the pale rose there had a gentle glow,
Like the morning's tint on a wreath of snow.

All was so seemly and serene, 350
As she lay composed upon the green,
It was plain to all that no human aid,
But an angel's hand, had the body laid;
For from her form there seem'd to rise,
The sweetest odours of Paradise. 355
Around her temples and brow so fair,
White roses were twined in her auburn hair;
All bound with a birch and holly band,
And the book of God was in her right hand.

Farewell, ye flow'rets of sainted fame, 360
Ye sweetest maidens of mortal frame;
A sacred love o'er your lives presided,
And in your deaths you were not divided!
O, blessed are they who bid adieu
To this erring nature as pure as you! 365

Mount Benger
July 27th, 1829

The Goode Manne of Allowa

Ane most strainge and treuthfulle Ballande
Made be Mr Hougge

Did you never heire of ane queere ould manne,
  Ane verry strainge manne wals hee,
Quha dwallit on the bonnye bankes of Forthe,
  In ane towne full deire to mee?

But if all bee true als I herit telle,   5
  And als I shall telle to the,
There wals neuir soche ane thyng befelle
  To a man in this countrye.

One daye hee satte on ane lonely brae,
  And sorely he maide his mone,   10
For his yuthfulle days had passit awaye,
  And ronkilit aige came on;

And hee thoughte of the lychtsome dayis of lufe,
  And joifulle happy soulis,
Quhille the teris ran ower the oulde manis chekis,   15
  And downe on his button holis.

"Ochone, ochone!" quod the poore oulde manne,
  "Quhare shall I goe laye myne heide?
For I am wearie of this worlde,
  And I wish that I were deide;   20

"That I were deide, and in myne graif,
  Quhare caris colde not annoye,
And myne soule saiflye in ane lande
  Of ryches and of joie.

"Yet wolde I lyke ane cozye bedde   25
  To meite the strok of deth,
With ane holie sawme sung ower myne heide,
  And swoofit with my last brethe;

"With ane kynde hande to close myne een,
　And shedde ane teire for mee;
But, alaike, for povertye and eilde,
　Sickan joies I can neuir se!　　　　　　　　　　30

"For though I haif toylit these seuentye yeris,
　Waisting bothe blode and bone,
Stryffing for rychis als for lyffe,
　Yet rychis I haif none.　　　　　　　　　　　35

"For though I sezit them be the taylle,
　With proude and joifulle mynde,
Yet did theye taike them wyngis and flye,
　And leive mee there behynde.　　　　　　　　40

"They left me there to rante and raire,
　Mockying myne raifing tung,
Though skraighing lyke ane gainder gose,
　That is refit of his yung.

"Och! woe is mee, for all myne toylle,　　　　　45
　And all myne deire-boughte gainis,
Yet most I die ane cauldryffe dethe,
　In pouertye and painis!

"Och! where are all myne ryches gone,
　Where, or to what countrye?　　　　　　　　50
There is golde enough into this worlde,
　But none of it made for mee.

"Yet Provydence wals sore misledde,
　Myne ryches to destroye,
Else many a poore and vertuous herte　　　　55
　Sholde haif had cause of joie."

Then the poore aulde manne layit down his heide,
　And rairit for verye greef,
And streikit out his lymbis to die;
　For he knowit of no relief.　　　　　　　　60

But bye there came ane lovely dame,
　Upon ane palfraye graye,

And sho listenit unto the auld mannis tale,
  And all he had to saye

Of all his grefis, and sore regraitte   65
  For thyngis that him befelle,
And because he colde not feide the poore,
  Which thyng he lofit so welle.

"It is greate pity," quod the daime,
  "That one so verie kynde,   70
So fulle of cherityis and lofe,
  And of such vertuous mynde,

"Sholde lie and perish on ane brae
  Of pouvertye and eilde,
Without one singel hande to prufe   75
  His solace and his sheelde."

She toke the oulde manne hir behynde
  Upon hir palfreye graye,
And swifter nor the sothelande wynde
  They scourit the velvet brae.   80

And the palfreyis taille behynde did saille
  Ower locker and ower lee;
Quhille the teris stode in the oulde mann's eyne,
  With swiftness and with glee.

For the comelye daime had promysit him   85
  Of rychis mighty store,
That his kynde herte might haif fulle scope
  For feeding of the poore.

"Now Graice me saife!" sayit the goode oulde manne;
  "Quhare beris theyne brydel hande?   90
Art thou going to breake the Grenoke Banke?
  Or the Bank of fair Scotlande?

"Myne conscience hardlye this maye bruike;
  But on this you maye depende,
Quhateuir is giuen unto mee,   95
  Is to ane rychteous ende."

"Keipe thou thyne seate," sayit the comelye daime,
  "And conscience cleire and stenne;
There is plentye of golde in the seais boddam
  To enryche ten thousand menne.   100

"Rydde on with mee, and thou shalt se
  Quhat tressuris there do lie;
For I can gallop the emeralde waife,
  And along its channelis, drie."

"If thou canst doo that," sayit the goode ould manne, 105
  "Thou shalt ryde thy lane for mee;
For I can nouther soome, nor dyve,
  Nor walke the raigyng se.

"For the salte water walde blynde myne eyne,
  And what sholde I se there?   110
And buller buller downe myne throte;
  Which thyng I colde not beare."

But awaye and awaye flewe the comlye daime
  Ower moorelande and ower felle;
But whether they went northe or southe,   115
  The aulde manne colde not telle.

And the palfreyis taille behynde did saille,
  Ane comelye sychte to se,
Lyke littil wee comet of the daille
  Gawn skimmeryng ower the le.   120

Quhan the aulde manne came to the salt se's brynke,
  He quakit at the ocean faeme;
But the palfrey splashit into the saime,
  Als it were its naityffe haeme.

"Now Chryste us saiffe!" cryit the goode oulde manne; 125
  "Hath madnesse sezit thyne heide?
For wee shall sinke in the ocean waiffe,
  And bluther quhille wee be deide."

But the palfrey dashit o'er the boundyng waiffe,
  With snyfter and with stenne;   130

It wals fyrmer nor the fyrmest swairde
   In all the Deffane glenne.

But the goode aulde manne he helde als dethe
   Holdis by ane synneris taille,
Or als ane craiffan clyngis to lyffe, 135
   Quhan dethe doth him assaille.

And the littil wee palfrey shotte awaye,
   Lyke dragonis fyerie trainne,
And up the waiffe, and downe the waiffe,
   Like meteor of the mainne. 140

And its stremyng taille behynde did saille
   With shimmer and with sheine;
And quhanever it strak the maene of the waiffe,
   The flashes of fyer were seine.

"Ochone! ochone!" saide the goode oulde manne, 145
   "It is awsome to bee heire!
I feire these ryches for which I greine
   Shall coste mee very deire.

"For wee are runnyng soche perylous raice
   Als mortals nevir ranne; 150
And the deuil is in that littil beiste,
   If euir he wals in manne."

"Hurraye! hurraye! myne bonnye graye!"
   Cryit the Maydin of the Se:
"Ha! thou canst sweipe the emerant deipe 155
   Swifter nor birde can fle.

"For thou wast bredde in ane coral bedde,
   Benethe ane sylver sonne,
Quhare the brode daylichte, or the mone by nychte,
   Colde neuir neuir wonne; 160

"Quhare the burdlye whayle colde neuir sayle,
   Nor the laizy walrosse rowe;
And the littil wee thyng that gaife the socke,
   Wals ane thyng of the caiffis belowe.

"And thou shalt ronne till the laste sonne   165
    Synke ower the westlande hille;
And thou shalt rydde the ocean tydde,
    Till all its waiffis lie stille.

"Awaye! awaye! myne bonnye graye!
    Quhare billowis rocke the deide,   170
And quhare the rychest pryze lyes lowe
    In all the ocean's bedde."

The palfrey scraipit with his fote,
    And snorkyt feirsumlye;
Then lokit ower his left sholder,   175
    To se quhat he colde se.

And als evir you sawe ane moudiwort
    Bore into ane foggye le,
So did this littil deuilish beiste
    Dive downe into the se.   180

The goode oulde manne he gaif ane raire
    Als loude als hee colde straine:
But the wateris closit abone his heide,
    And downe he went amaine.

But hee nouther blutherit with his braith,   185
    Nor gaspit with his ganne,
And not one drop of salt watere
    Adowne his throppil ranne.

But he rode als faire, and he rode als fre,
    Als if all swaithit and furlit   190
In Mackintoshis patent wairre,
    The merval of this worlde.

At length they caime to ane gallante shyppe,
    In the channellis of the se,
That lenit hir sholder to ane rocke,   195
    With hir mastis full sore aglee.

And there laye many a gallante manne,
    Rockit by the mofyng mainne;

And soundlye soundlye did they sleipe,
  Nevir to waike againne.   200

The shippis mighte sayle, and friendis mighte wayle
  On mairgen of the se,
But newis of them theye walde nevir heire
  Till the dayis of eternitye;

For it wals plaine, als plaine colde bee,   205
  From all theye saw arounde,
That the shippe had gone downe to the deipe
  Without one warnyng sounde—

Without one prayer pourit to heuin—
  Without one pairtyng sighe,   210
Lyke se-burde sailling on the waiffe,
  That dyves wee knowe not whye.

It wals ane wofulle sighte to se,
  In bowellis of the deepe,
Loferis and lemanis lying claspit   215
  In everlasting sleipe.

So caulmlye theye laye on their glittye beddis,
  And in their hammockis swung,
And the billowis rockit their drouzye formis,
  And ower their creddilis sung.   220

And there wals laide ane royall maide,
  Als caulme as if in heuin,
Who hald thre golde ryngis on eiche fyngir,
  On hir mydde fyngir seuin.

And sho hald jewillis in hir eiris,   225
  And braicelettis braif to se;
The golde that wals arounde hir heid
  Wold haif boughte erldomis thre.

And jewylis glowit on hir whyte hass-bane,
  And rounde hir hollande serke;   230
But ane mossell held hir by the nose,
  Als harde als hee colde yerke.

Then the goode oulde manne pullit out his knyffe,
 It wals both sharpe and cleire,
And he cut off the maydenis fyngeris small,   235
 And the jewellis from ilkan eire.

"O shaime, O shaime!" sayit the comelye daime,
 "Wo worth thyne rothlesse hande!
How daurest thou mangil ane royall corpse,
 Once flower of many a lande?   240

"And all for the saike of trynkets vaine,
 Mid soche ane storre als this."
"Ohone, alaike!" quod the goode aulde manne,
 "You judge fulle fare amiss;

"It is better they feide the rychteousse poore,   245
 That on their God depende,
Than to lye slobberyng in the deipe
 For nouther use nor ende,

"Unlesse to graice ane partanis lymbe
 With costlye, shyning orre,   250
Or decke ane lobsteris burlye snoutte,—
 Ane beeste whiche I abhorre!"

Then the Se Maide smyllit ane doubtfulle smylle,
 And sayit, with liftit ee,—
"Fulle many a rychteousse manne I haif seine;   255
 But neuir a one lyke the!

"But thou shalt haif thyne hertis desyre,
 In feidyng the uprychte;
And all the goode shalle blisse the daye
 That first thou saw the lycht."   260

Then sho loaded him with gemis and golde,
 On channel of the maine;
Yet the goode manne wals not contente,
 But turnit him backe againe.

And eviry handfulle he put in,   265
 Hee sayit rycht wistfullye,

"Och, this will ane wholle fortune profe
  For ane poore familye."

And he neifuit in, and he neifuit in,
  And neuir colde refraine,   270
Quhille the littil wee horse he colde not mofe,
  Nor mount the waife againe;

But he snorkit with his littil nose,
  Till he made the se rockis ryng,
And waggit his taille acrosse the waiffe   275
  With many an angry swyng.

"Come awaye, come awaye, myne littil bonnye graye,
  Thynke of the goode before;
There is als moch golde upon thyne backe
  Als will feide ten thousande poore."   280

Then the littil wee horse he strauchlit on,
  Through darkling scenis sublyme—
Ower sholis, and stonis, and deide mennis bonis;
  But the waiffe he colde not clymbe.

But along, along, he sped along   285
  The floris of the sylente se,
With a worlde of wateris ower his heide,
  And grofis of the coral tre.

And the tydde streime flowit, and the billowis rowit
  Ane hundred faddomis high;   290
And the lychte that lychted the floris below
  Semit from some oder skie;

For it stremit and tremblit on its waye
  Of bemis and splendour shorne,
And flowit with an awful holynesse   295
  Als on ane journeye borne.

Till at length they saw the gloryous sonne,
  Far in the weste that glowit,
Flashyng like fyer-flaughts up and downe
  With every waiffe that rowit.   300

Then the oulde manne laughit ane hertsome laughe,
   And ane hertsome laughe laugh'd he,
To se the sonne in soche ane trymme
   Dauncyng so fooriouslye.

For he thought the angelis of the evin   305
   Had taken the blissit sonne,
To tosse in the blue blankit of heuin,
   To make them gloryous fonne.

But at length the Maye, and her palfreye graye,
   And the goode ould manne besyde,   310
Set their thre hedis abone the waiffe,
   And came in with the flowyng tydde.

Then all the folkis on the shoris of Fyffe
   Ane terrour flychte beganne,
And the borghesse men of oulde Kilrose   315
   They lefte their hamis and ranne.

For they kend the Se Maydis glossy ee,
   Lyke the blue of hevin that shone;
And the littil wee horse of the coral caiffe,
   That nouther had blode nor bone.   320

And they sayit quhan sho came unto their coaste,
   Sho neuir came there for goode,
But wairnyng to giffe of stormis and wrackis,
   And the sheddyng of chrystian bloode.

Alaik for the goode men of Kilrose,   325
   For their wyttis were neuir ryffe!
For now sho came with ane myghtie store,
   For the saifyng of poore mennis lyffe.

Quhan the littil wee horse he found his foote
   On the fyrme grounde and the drie,   330
He shoke his maene, and gaife ane grane,
   And threwe his helis on hie,

Quhille the golde playit jyngille on the shore,
   That eisit him of his paine;

Then he turnit and kickit it quhare it laye,   335
    In very great disdaine.

And he hatte the oulde manne rychte behynde
    With soche unspairyng mychte,
That he made him jompe seuin ellis and more,
    And on his face to lychte.   340

"Now, wo bee to the for ane wicked beiste!
    For since euir thyne liffe beganne,
I neuir sawe the lift thyne fote
    Againste ane rychteousse manne.

"But fare thee welle, thou goode oulde manne,   345
    Thyne promysse keip in mynde;
Let this greate welthe I haif giuen to the
    Be a blessing to thy kynde.

"So as thou stryffe so shalt thou thryffe,
    And bee it understoode   350
That I moste vyssit the againe,
    For evil or for goode."

Then the bonnye Maye sho rode her waye
    Along the se-waiffe greine,
And awaye and awaye on her palfreye graye,   355
    Lyke the oceanis comelye Queene.

Als sho farit up the Firthe of Forthe
    The fysches fledde all before,
And ane thousande coddis and haldockis braif
    Ranne swatteryng richte ashore.   360

Ane hundred and threttye bordlye whailis
    Went snoryng up the tydde,
And wyde on Allowais fertylle holmis
    The gallopit ashore and died.*

* As this is likely to be the only part of my *Treuthfulle Ballande* the ver-
acity of which may be disputed, I assure the reader that it is a literal
fact; and that, with one tide in the month of March, one year lately,
there were no fewer than 130 whales left ashore in the vicinity of

But it greifith myne herte to telle to you,   365
    What I neuir haif tould before,
Of that manne so rychteousse and so goode,
    So long als he wals poore.

But quhaneuir he gotte more store of golde
    Than euir his wyttis coulde telle,   370
He neuir wolde giffe ane mite for goode,
    Nouther for heuin nor helle.

But he broded ower that mychtie store
    With sordyd herte of synne,
And the housselesse wychte, or the poore by nychte,   375
    His gate wanne neuir withynne.

And the last accountis I had of him
    Are verye strainge to telle:
He wals seene with the Maye and the palfrey graye
    Rydding feircelye out through helle.   380

For the Mynister of Allowa he wals there,
    With some of his freinds in towe,
Puttyng them up in that cozey hame,
    Quhair hee toulde them they sholde goe.

And the Mynister knowis the place full welle,   385
    And greate delychte hath hee
For to descryve it out and in,
    In patente geographye.

Alloa. The men of Alloa called them young ones; but to me they appeared
to have been immense fishes. Their skeletons at a distance were like those
of large horses. There were two old ones ran up as far as the mill-dam of
Cambus, on the Devon, where the retreating tide left them, and where,
after a day's severe exercise and excellent sport to a great multitude,
they were both slain, alongst with a young one, which one of the old
ones used every effort to defend, and when she saw it attacked she bel-
lowed most fearfully. But, moreover, on testifying my wonder one day to
the men of Cambus why the whales should all have betaken them to the
dry land, I was answered by a sly fellow, "that a mermaid had been
seen driving them up the Frith, which had frighted them so much, it
had put them all out of their judgments."

                                                  J.H.

And hee sayit hee sawe the poore oulde manne,
  With the Maiden of the Se,   390
Boundyng awaye to the hottest place
  Of all that hotte countrye.

And aye she cryit, "Hurraye, hurraye!
  Make roome for mee and myne!
I bryng you the Manne of Allowaye   395
  To his poonyshmente condyne.

"His Maker tryit him in the fyre,
  To make his herte contrytte;
But, quhan he gat his hertis desyre,
  He profit any hyppocrytte."   400

And quhan the Mynister hee came hame,
  Hee hearit with wonderyng mynd,
That the myser had gane, and left this worlde
  And his ryches alle behynde.

Then all you poore and contrytte ones,   405
  In deipe afflictiounis hurled,
O, neuir grieue or vex your hertis
  For the ryches of this worlde;

For they bring nouther helthe nor pece
  Unto thy spyritis frame;   410
And there is ane tressure better farre,
  Which mynstrelle daris not name.

Hast thou not herit ane oulden saye,
  By one who colde not lee?—
It is somethyng of ane greate bygge beiste   415
  Ganging through ane nedilis ee.

Then thynke of that, and bee contente;
  For lyffe is but ane daye,
And the nychte of dethe is gatheryng faste
  To close upon your waye.   420

I haif ane prayer I ofte haif prayit,
  And ofte wolde praye it againe—

Maye the beste blessyngs heuin can giffe
  On Allowa long remaine!

I neuir aske ane blessynge meite,   425
  Outher on kythe or kynne,
But the kynde hertis of Allowa
  That asking comis withynne.

Then maye thaye lairne, from their Shepherdis taile,
  To truste in Heuin alone,   430
And they'll neuir be mette by their Mynister
  In soche ane place als yonne.

MOUNT BENGER
10th October, 1828

Jock Johnstone the Tinkler

By the Ettrick Shepherd

"O came ye ower by the Yoke-burn Ford,
  Or down the king's road of the cleuch?
Or saw ye a knight and a lady bright,
  Wha hae gane the gate they baith shall rue?"

"I saw a knight and a lady bright,   5
  Ride up the cleuch at the break of day;
The knight upon a coal-black steed,
  And the dame on one of the silver grey.

"And the lady's palfrey flew the first,
  With many a clang of silver bell;   10
Swift as the raven's morning flight,
  The two went scouring ower the fell.

"By this time they are man and wife,
  And standing in St Mary's fane;
And the lady in the grass-green silk   15
  A maid you will never see again."

"But I can kill, thou saucy wight,
  And that the run-aways shall prove;
Revenge to a Douglas is as sweet
  As maiden charms or maiden's love."   20

"Since thou say'st that, my Lord Douglas,
  Good faith some clinking there will be;
Beshrew my heart, but an my sword,
  If I winna turn and ride wi' thee!"

They whipped out ower the Shepherd cleuch,   25
  And down the links o' the Corsecleuch burn;
And aye the Douglas swore by his sword
  To win his love, or never return.

"First fight your rival, Lord Douglas,
And then brag after, if you may;
For the Earl of Ross is as brave a lord
As ever gave good weapon sway.   30

"But I for ae poor siller merk,
Or thirteen pennies an' a bawbee,
Will tak in hand to fight you baith,
Or beat the winner whiche'er it be."   35

The Douglas turned him on his steed,
And I wat a loud laughter leuch he;—
"Of all the fools I have ever met,
Man, I hae never met ane like thee.   40

"Art thou akin to lord or knight,
Or courtly squire or warrior leel?"
"I am a tinkler," quo' the wight,
"But I like crown-cracking unco weel."

When they came to St Mary's kirk,   45
The chaplain shook for very fear;
And aye he kissed the cross, and said,
"What deevil has sent that Douglas here!

"He neither values book nor ban,
But curses all without demur;   50
And cares nae mair for a holy man,
Than I do for a worthless cur."

"Come here, thou bland and brittle priest,
And tell to me without delay,
Where you have hid the Lord of Ross,   55
And the lady that came at the break of day?"

"No knight or lady, good Lord Douglas,
Have I beheld since break of morn;
And I never saw the Lord of Ross,
Since the woful day that I was born."   60

Lord Douglas turn'd him round about,
And lookit the tinkler in the face;

Where he beheld a lurking smile,
  And a deevil of a dour grimace.

"How's this, how's this, thou tinkler loun?   65
  Hast thou presumed to lie to me?"
"Faith, that I have!" the tinkler said,
  "And a right good turn I have done to thee.

"For the Lord of Ross, and thy own true love,
  The beauteous Harriet of Thirlestane,   70
Rade west away, ere the break of day;
  And you'll never see that dear maid again.

"So I thought it best to bring you here,
  On a wrang scent, of my own accord;
For had you met the Johnstone clan,   75
  They wad hae made mince-meat of a lord."

At this the Douglas was so wroth,
  He wist not what to say or do;
But he strak the tinkler o'er the croun,
  Till the blood came dreeping ower his brow.   80

"Beshrew thy heart," quo' the tinkler lad,
  "Thou bear'st thee most ungallantly!
If these are the manners of a lord,
  They are manners that winna gang down wi' me."

"Hold up thy hand," the Douglas cried,   85
  And keep thy distance, tinkler loun!"—
"That will I not," the tinkler said,
  "Though I and my mare should both go down."

"I have armour on," cried the Lord Douglas,
  "Cuirass and helm, as you may see."—   90
"The deil may care," quo' the tinkler lad,
  "I shall have a skelp at them and thee."

"You are not horsed," quoth the Lord Douglas,
  "And no remorse this weapon brooks."—
"Mine's a right good yaud," quo' the tinkler lad,   95
  "And a great deal better nor she looks.

"So stand to thy weapons, thou haughty lord,
　　What I have taken I needs must give;
Thou shalt never strike a tinkler again,
　　For the langest day thou hast to live."   100

Then to it they fell, both sharp and snell,
　　Till the fire from both their weapons flew;
But the very first shock that they met with,
　　The Douglas his rashness 'gan to rue.

For though he had on a sark of mail,   105
　　And a cuirass on his breast wore he,
With a good steel bonnet on his head,
　　Yet the blood ran prinkling to his knee.

The Douglas sat upright and firm,
　　Aye as together their horses ran;   110
But the tinkler laid on like a very deil,—
　　Siccan strokes were never laid on by man.

"Hold up thy hand, thou tinkler loun,"
　　Cried the poor priest, with whining din;
"If thou hurt the brave Lord James Douglas,   115
　　A curse be on thee and all thy kin!"

"I care no more for Lord James Douglas,
　　Than Lord James Douglas cares for me;
But I want to let his proud heart know,
　　That a tinkler's a man as well as he."   120

So they fought on, and they fought on,
　　Till good Lord Douglas' breath was gone,
And the tinkler bore him to the ground,
　　With rush, with rattle, and with groan.

"Ohon! ohon!" cried the proud Douglas,   125
　　"That I this day should have lived to see!
For sure my honour I have lost,
　　And a leader again I can never be.

"But tell me of thy kith and kin,
　　And where was bred thy weapon hand?   130

For thou art the wale of tinkler louns
    That ever were born in fair Scotland."

"My name's Jock Johnstone," quoth the wight,—
    "I winna keep in my name frae thee;
And here, take thou thy sword again,   135
    And better friends we two shall be."

But the Douglas swore a solemn oath,
    That was a debt he could never owe;
He would rather die at the back of the dike,
    Than owe his sword to a man so low.   140

"But if thou wilt ride under my banner,
    And bear my livery and my name,
My right-hand warrior thou shalt be,
    And I'll knight thee on the field of fame."

"Wo worth thy wit, good Lord Douglas,   145
    To think I'd change my trade for thine;
Far better and wiser would you be,
    To live as journeyman of mine.

"To mend a kettle or a casque,
    Or clout a goodwife's yettlin pan;   150
Upon my life, good Lord Douglas,
    You'd make a noble tinkler man!

"I would give you drammock twice a-day,
    And sunkets on a Sunday morn;
And you should be a rare adept   155
    ·In steel and copper, brass and horn.

"I'll fight you every day you rise,
    Till you can act the hero's part;—
Therefore, I pray you, think of this,
    And lay it seriously to heart."   160

The Douglas writhed beneath the lash,
    Answering with an inward curse,—
Like salmon wriggling on a spear,
    That makes his deadly wound the worse.

But up there came two squires renown'd;   165
   In search of Lord Douglas they came;
And when they saw their master down,
   Their spirits mounted in a flame.

And they flew upon the tinkler wight,
   Like perfect tigers on their prey;   170
But the tinkler heaved his trusty sword,
   And made him ready for the fray.

"Come one to one, ye coward knaves,—
   Come hand to hand, and steed to steed,
I would that ye were better men,   175
   For this is glorious fun indeed!"

Before you could have counted twelve,
   The tinkler's wondrous chivalrye
Had both the squires upon the swaird,
   And their horses galloping o'er the lea.   180

The tinkler tied them neck and heel,
   And mony a biting jest gave he:
"O fie, for shame!" said the tinkler lad,
   "Siccan fighters I did never see!"

He slit one of their bridle reins,—   185
   O what disgrace the conquer'd feels;
And he skelpit the squires with that good tawse,
   Till the blood ran off at baith their heels.

The Douglas he was forced to laugh,
   Till down his cheek the salt tears ran;   190
"I think the deevil be come here
   In the likeness of a tinkler man."

Then he is to Lord Douglas gone,
   And he raised him kindly by the hand,
And he set him on his gallant steed,   195
   And bore him away to Henderland.

"Be not cast down, my Lord Douglas,
   Nor writhe beneath a broken bane,

For the leech's art will mend the part,
    And your honour lost will spring again.   200

"'Tis true, Jock Johnstone is my name,
    I'm a right good tinkler, as you see;
For I can crack a casque betimes,
    Or clout one, as my need may be.

"Jock Johnstone is my name, 'tis true,—   205
    But noble hearts are allied to me,
For I am the Lord of Annandale,
    And a knight and earl as well as thee."

Then Douglas strain'd the hero's hand,
    And took from it his sword again;   210
"Since thou art the Lord of Annandale,
    Thou hast eased my heart of muckle pain.

"I might have known thy noble form,
    In that disguise thou'rt pleased to wear;
All Scotland knows thy matchless arm,   215
    And England by experience dear.

"We have been foes as well as friends,
    And jealous of each other's sway;
But little can I comprehend
    Thy motive for these pranks to-day."   220

"Sooth, my good Lord, the truth to tell,
    'Twas I that stole your love away,
And gave her to the Lord of Ross
    An hour before the break of day:

"For the Lord of Ross is my brother,   225
    By all the laws of chivalrye;
And I brought with me a thousand men,
    To guard him to my own countrye.

"But I thought meet to stay behind,
    And try your Lordship to waylay;   230
Resolved to breed some noble sport,
    By leading you so far astray.

"Judging it better some lives to spare,
  Which fancy takes me now and then,
And settle our quarrel hand to hand,   235
  Than each with our ten thousand men.

"God send you soon, my Lord Douglas,
  To Border foray sound and haill;
But never strike a tinkler again,
  If he be a Johnstone of Annandale."   240

Mount Benger
Jan. 8th, 1829

A Lay of the Martyrs

By the Ettrick Shepherd

"O where hae you been bonny Marley Reid
   For mony a lang night and day
I have missed ye sair at the Wanlock-head
   And the cave o' the Louther brae

Our friends are waning fast away   5
   Baith frae the cliff and the wood
They are tearing them frae us ilka day
   For there's naething will please but blood

And O bonny Marley I maun now
   Gie your heart muckle pain   10
For your bridegroom is a missing too
   And 'tis feared that he is ta'en

We have sought the caves o' the Enterkin
   And the dens o' the Ballybough
And a' the howes o' the Ganna linn   15
   And we wot not what to do"

"Dispel your fears good Marjory Laing
   And hope all for the best
For the servants of God will find a place
   Their weary heads to rest   20

There are better places that we ken o'
   And seemlier to be in
Than all the dens of the Ballybough
   Or howes o' the Ganna linn

But sit thee down good Marjory Laing   25
   And listen a while to me
For I have a tale to tell to you
   That will bring you to your knee

I went to seek my own dear James
   In the cave o' the Louther brae   30
For I had some things that of a' the world
   He best deserved to hae

I had a kebbuck in my lap
   And a fadge o' the flower sae sma'
And a sark I had made for his boardly back   35
   As white as the new dri'en snaw

I sought him over hill and dale
   Shouting by cave and tree
But only the dell with its eiry yell
   An answer returned to me   40

I sought him up and I sought him down
   And echos returned his name
Till the gloffs o' dread shot to my heart
   And dirled through a' my frame

I sat me down by the Enterkin   45
   And saw in a fearfu' line
The red dragoons come up the path
   Wi' prisoners eight or nine

And one of them was my dear dear James
   The flower of a' his kin   50
He was wounded behind and wounded before
   And the blood ran frae his chin

He was bound upon a weary hack
   Lashed both by hough and heel
And his hands were bound behind his back   55
   Wi' the thumbikins of steel

I kneeled before that popish band
   In the fervor of inward strife
And I spread to heaven my trembling hands
   And begged my husband's life   60

But all the troop laughed me to scorn
   Making my grief their game

And the captain said some words to me
   Which I cannot tell you for shame

And then he cursed our whiggish race   65
   With a proud and a scornful brow
And bade me look at my husband's face
   And say how I liked him now?

O I like him weel thou proud Captain
   Though the blood runs to his knee   70
And all the better for the grievious wrongs
   He has suffered this day frae thee

But can you feel within your heart
   That comely youth to slay
For the hope you have in heaven Captain   75
   Let him gang wi' me away

Then the captain swore a fearfu' oath
   With loathsome jest and mock
That he thought no more of a whigamore's life
   Than the life of a noisome brock   80

Then my poor James to the captain called
   And he beg'd baith hard and sair
To have one kiss of his bonny bride
   Ere we parted for evermair

I'll do that for you said the proud captain   85
   And save you the toil to day
And moreover I'll take her little store
   To support you by the way

He took my bountith from my lap
   And I saw with sorrow dumb   90
That he parted it all among his men
   And gave not my love one crumb

Now fare you well my very bonny bride
   Cried the captain with disdain
When I come back to the banks of Nith   95
   I shall kiss you sweetly then

Your heartiest thanks must sure be given
    For what I have done to day
I am taking him straight on the road to heaven
    And short will be the way   100

My love he gave me a parting look
    And blessed me ferventlye
And the tears they mixed wi' his purple blood
    And ran down to his knee"

"What's this I hear bonny Marley Reid?   105
    How could these woes betide?
For blither you could not look this day
    Were your husband by your side

One of two things alone is left
    And dreadful one to me   110
For either your fair wits are reft
    Or else your husband's free"

"Allay your fears good Marjory Laing
    And hear me out the rest
You little ken what a bride will do   115
    For the youth she likes the best

I hied me hame to my father's ha'
    And through a' my friends I ran
And I gathered me up a purse o' goud
    To redeem my young goodman   120

For I kend the papish lowns would well
    My fair intent approve
For they'll do far mair for the good red goud
    Than they'll do for heaven above

And away I ran to Edinburgh town   125
    Of my shining treasure vain
To buy my James from the prison strang
    Or there with him remain

I sought through a' the city jails
    I sought baith lang and sair   130

But the guardsmen turned me frae their doors
    And swore that he was not there

I went away to the popish duke
    Who was my love's judge to be
And I proffered him a' my yellow store   135
    If he'd grant his life to me

He counted the red goud slowly o'er
    By twenties and by tens
And said I had taken the only means
    To attain my hopeful ends   140

And now said he your husband's safe
    You may take this pledge of me
And I'll tell you, fair one, where you'll go
    To gain this certaintye

Gang west the street and down the bow   145
    And through the market place
And there you will meet with a gentleman
    Of a tall and courteous grace

He is clad in a livery of the green
    With a plume aboon his bree   150
And armed with a halbert glittering sheen
    Your love he will let you see

O Marjory never flew blithesome bird
    So light out through the sky
As I flew up that stately street   155
    Weeping for very joy

O never flew lamb out o'er the lea
    When the sun gangs o'er the hill
Wi' lighter blither step than me
    Or skipped wi' sic good will   160

And ay I blessed the precious ore
    My husband's life that wan
And I even blessed the popish duke
    For a kind good-hearted man

The officer I soon found out   165
    For he could not be mistook
But in all my life I never beheld
    Sic a grim and a gruesome look

I asked him for my dear dear James
    With throbs of wild delight   170
And begged him in his master's name
    To take me to his sight

He asked me for his true address
    With a voice at which I shook
For I saw that he was a popish knave   175
    By the terror of his look

I named the name with a buoyant voice
    That trembled with extacye
But the savage brayed a hideous laugh
    Then turned and grinned at me   180

He pointed up to the city wall
    One look benumbed my soul
For there I saw my husband's head
    Fixed high upon a pole

His yellow hair waved in the wind   185
    And far behind did flee
And his right hand hang beside his cheek
    A waesome sight to see

His chin hang down on open space
    Yet comely was his brow   190
And his een were open to the breeze
    There was nane to close them now

What think you of your true love now?
    The hideous porter said
Is not that a comely sight to see   195
    And sweet to a whiggish maid?

O haud your tongue ye popish slave
    For I downae answer you

He was dear dear to my heart before
   But never sae dear as now   200

I see a sight you cannot see
   Which man can not efface
I see a ray of heavenly love
   Beaming on that dear face

And weel I ken yon bonny brent brow   205
   Will smile in the walks on high
And yon yellow hair all blood-stained now
   Maun wave aboon the sky

But can you trow me Marjory dear
   In the might of heavenly grace   210
There was never a sigh burst frae my heart
   Nor a tear ran o'er my face

But I blessed my God who had thus seen meet
   To take him from my side
To call him home to the courts above   215
   And leave me a virgin bride"

"Alak alak bonny Marley Reid
   That sic days we hae lived to see
For sickan a cruel and waefu' tale
   Was never yet heard by me   220

And all this time I have trembling weened
   That your dear wits were gone
For there is a joy in your countenance
   Which I never saw beam thereon

Then let us kneel with humble hearts   225
   To the God whom we revere
Who never yet laid that burden on
   Which he gave not strength to bear"

A Cameronian Ballad

By James Hogg

"O what is become o' your leel goodman,
  That now you are a' your lane?
If he has joined wi' the rebel gang,
  You will never see him again."

"O say nae 'the rebel gang,' ladye,   5
  It's a term nae heart can thole,
For they wha rebel against their God,
  It is justice to control.

When rank oppression rends the heart,
  An' rules wi' stroke o' death,   10
Wha wadna spend their dear heart's blood
  For the tenets o' their faith?

Then say nae 'the rebel gang,' ladye,
  For it gi'es me muckle pain;
My John went away with Earlston,   15
  And I'll never see either again."

"O wae is my heart for thee, Janet,
  O sair is my heart for thee!
These covenant men were ill advised,
  They are fools, you may credit me.   20

Where's a' their boastfu' preaching now,
  Against their king and law,
When mony a head in death lies low,
  An' mony mae maun fa'?"

"Ay, but death lasts no for aye, ladye,   25
  For the grave maun yield its prey;
And when we meet on the verge of heaven,
  We'll see wha are fools that day:

We'll see wha looks in their Saviour's face
    With holiest joy and pride,   30
Whether they who shed his servants' blood,
    Or those that for him died.

I wadna be the highest dame
    That ever this country knew,
And take my chance to share the doom   35
    Of that persecuting crew.

Then ca' us nae rebel gang, ladye,
    Nor take us fools to be,
For there is nae ane of a' that gang,
    Wad change his state wi' thee."   40

"O weel may you be, my poor Janet,
    May blessings on you combine!
The better you are in either state,
    The less shall I repine.

But wi' your fightings an' your faith,   45
    Your ravings an' your rage,
There you have lost a leel helpmate,
    In the blossom of his age.

An' what's to come o' ye, my poor Janet,
    Wi' these twa babies sweet?   50
Ye hae naebody now to work for them,
    Or bring you a meal o' meat;

It is that which makes my heart sae wae,
    An' gars me, while scarce aware,
Whiles say the things I wadna say,   55
    Of them that can err nae mair."

Poor Janet kissed her youngest babe,
    And the tears fell on his cheek,
And they fell upon his swaddling bands,
    For her heart was like to break.   60

"O little do I ken, my dear, dear babes,
    What misery's to be thine!

But for the cause we hae espoused,
  I will yield thy life and mine.

O had I a friend, as I hae nane,   65
  For nane dare own me now,
That I might send to Bothwell brigg,
  If the killers wad but allow,

To lift the corpse of my brave John,
  I ken where they will him find,   70
He wad meet his God's foes face to face,
  And he'll hae nae wound behind."

"But I went to Bothwell brigg, Janet,
  There was nane durst hinder me,
For I wantit to hear a' I could hear,   75
  An' to see what I could see;

And there I found your brave husband,
  As viewing the dead my lane,
He was lying in the very foremost rank,
  In the midst of a heap o' slain."   80

Then Janet held up her hands to heaven,
  An' she grat, an' she tore her hair,
"O sweet ladye, O dear ladye,
  Dinna tell me ony mair!

There is a hope will linger within,   85
  When earthly hope is vain,
But when ane kens the very worst,
  It turns the heart to stane!"

"O wae is my heart, John Carr, said I,
  That I this sight should see!   90
And when I said these waefu' words,
  He liftit his een to me.

'O art thou there, my kind ladye,
  The best o' this warld's breed,
And are you gangin' your liefu' lane,   95
  Amang the hapless dead?'

I hae servants within my ca', John Carr,
   And a chariot in the dell,
An' if there is ony hope o' life,
   I will carry you hame mysel'.   100

'O lady, there is nae hope o' life—
   And what were life to me!
Wad ye save me frae the death of a man,
   To hang on a gallows tree?

I hae nae hame to fly to now,   105
   Nae country an' nae kin,
There is not a door in fair Scotland
   Durst open to let me in.

But I hae a loving wife at hame,
   An' twa babies dear to me;   110
They hae naebody now that dares favour them,
   An' of hunger they a' maun dee.

Oh, for the sake of thy Saviour dear,
   Whose mercy thou hopest to share,
Dear lady take the sackless things   115
   A wee beneath thy care!

A long fareweel, my kind ladye,
   O'er weel I ken thy worth;
Gae send me a drink o' the water o' Clyde,
   For my last drink on earth.'"   120

"O dinna tell ony mair, ladye,
   For my heart is cauld as clay;
There is a spear that pierces here,
   Frae every word ye say."

"He was nae feared to dee, Janet,   125
   For he gloried in his death,
And wished to be laid with those who had bled
   For the same enduring faith.

There were three wounds in his boardly breast,
   And his limb was broke in twain,   130

An' the sweat ran down wi' his red heart's blood,
    Wrung out by the deadly pain.

I rowed my apron round his head,
    For fear my men should tell,
And I hid him in my lord's castle,   135
    An' I nursed him there mysel'.

An' the best leeches in a' the land
    Have tended him as he lay,
And he never has lacked my helping hand,
    By night nor yet by day.   140

I durstna tell you before, Janet,
    For I feared his life was gane,
But now he's sae well, ye may visit him,
    An' ye's meet by yoursels alane."

Then Janet she fell at her lady's feet,   145
    And she claspit them ferventlye,
And she steepit them a' wi' the tears o' joy,
    Till the good lady wept to see.

"Oh, ye are an angel sent frae heaven,
    To lighten calamitye!   150
For in distress, a friend or foe
    Is a' the same to thee.

If good deeds count in heaven, ladye,
    Eternal bliss to share,
Ye hae done a deed will save your soul,   155
    Though ye should never do mair."

"Get up, get up, my kind Janet,
    But never trow tongue or pen,
That a' the warld are lost to good,
    Except the covenant men."   160

Wha wadna hae shared that lady's joy,
    When watching the wounded hind,
Rather than those of the feast and the dance,
    Which her kind heart resigned?

Wha wadna rather share that lady's fate,   165
   When the stars shall melt away,
Than that of the sternest anchorite,
   That can naething but graen an' pray?

The Carle of Invertime

By the Author of The Queen's Wake

Who has not heard of a Carle uncouth,
The terror of age, and the scorn of youth;
Well known in this and every clime
As the grim Gudeman of Invertime;
A stern old porter who carries the key   5
That opens the gate to a strange countree?

   The Carle's old heart with joy is dancing
When down the valley he sees advancing
The lovely, the brave, the good, or the great,
To pay the sad toll of his darksome gate.   10
'Tis said nought gives such joy to him
As the freezing blood and the stiffening limb;
It has never been mine his house to scan,
So I scarce trow this of our grim Gudeman.

   Wise men believe, yet I scarce know why,   15
That he grimly smiles as he shoves them by;
And cares not whither to isles of bliss
They go—or to sorrow's dark wilderness;
Or driven afar, their fate should be
To toss on the waves of a shoreless sea;   20
Or sunk in lakes of surging flame,
Burning and boiling and ever the same:
Where groups of mortals toss amain
On the sultry billow and down again.
Time from the sky shall blot out the sun,   25
Yet ne'er with this den of dool have done.
It makes me shake and it makes me shiver,
His presence forbid it should last for ever!

   Sad, wise, or witty—all find to their cost
That the grim old Carle is still at his post.   30
He sits and he sees, with joy elate,
In myriads, men pour in at his gate.
Some come in gladness and joy, to close

Account with Time and sink to repose;
Some come in sorrow, they think in sooth   35
It hard to be summoned in strength and youth.
There lady and losel,—peasant and lord,
Men of the pen, the sermon, the sword;
The counsellor, leach, and the monarch sublime,
All come to the Carle of Invertime.   40

   Amongst the others, one morning came
An aged and a venerable Dame,
Stooping and palsied and pained to boot,
Moaning, and shaking from head to foot.
Slow in her pace, yet steady of mind,   45
She turned not once, nor looked behind;
Nor dreading nor daring her future fate,
She tottered along to the dismal gate.

   A gleam of light glanced in the eye
Of the grim Gudeman as the dame drew nigh;   50
Little cared he for an old gray wife,
Who hung like a link 'tween death and life;
But by the side of the eldern dame,
A Form so pure and so lovely came,
That the Carle's cold veinless heart heaved high, 55
A tear like an ice-drop came to his eye;
He vowed through his gate she should not win,
She seemed no child of sorrow and sin.
As thus he stood in his porch to mark,
His looks now light and his looks now dark,   60
He marvelled to hear so lovely a thing
Lift up her voice and gently sing
A strain, too holy, too sweet, and wild
And charming to come from an earthborn child;
It glowed with love and fervour and faith,   65
And seemed to triumph o'er time and death.

   "Great Fountain of Light, and Spirit of Might,
To work thy will has been my delight;
And here at my knee, from guiltiness free,
I bring a mild meek spirit to thee.   70
When first I went to guide her to truth,
She was in the opening blossom of youth;

When scarce on her leaf, so spotless and new,
Ripe reason had come with her dropping dew.
Where life's pure river is but a rill   75
She grew and scarce knew good from ill;
But my sisters three came soon to me,
Pure Love, true Faith, sweet Charity.
Through doubts and fears, these eighty years,
We have showed her the way to the heavenly spheres. 80
Our first stage down life's infant stream
Was all a maze and a childish dream;
And nought was there of sin or sense
But dawning beauty and innocence:
A fairy dance of sweet delight,   85
Through flowers and bowers and visions bright.
Sometimes a hymn and sometimes a prayer,
Was poured to Thee with a fervent air;
'Twas sung or said, and straight was seen
The sweet child gamboling on the green;   90
While the pure hymn, late poured to thee,
Was chanted light as a song of glee.

    "As we went down the vale of life,
With flowers the road became less rife.
By pitfall, precipice, and pool,   95
Our way was shaped by line and rule.
'Mid hours of joy and days of mirth,
And hopes and fears, high thoughts had birth,
And natural yearnings of the mind,
Of something onward undefined—   100
Which scarce the trembling soul durst scan,
Of God's most wondrous love to man—
And some far forward state of bliss,
Of beauty and of holiness;
But to all woes and evils blinded,   105
Or thoughts of death, unless reminded.
O! happy age, remembered well,
Where neither sin nor shame can dwell.
Even then thine eye, from heaven high,
Saw that her monitor was nigh;   110
At morn and even, to turn to heaven
The grateful eye, for blessings given.
And from the first prevailing tide

Of sin, and vanity and pride,
To save her, and to lead her on   115
To glories unrevealed, unknown.

"Onward we came; life's streamlet then
Entered a green and odorous glen;
Increased, and through fair flowerets rolling,
And shady bowers, seemed past controlling;   120
Flowing, 'mid roses, fast and free—
This was a trying stage for me;
The maiden's youthful heart began
To dance through scenes elysian.
To breathe in Love's ambrosial dew,   125
Moved by sensations sweet and new;
For without look or word of blame,
Her radiant blushes went and came;
Her eye, of heaven's own azure blue,
In glance and lustre brighter grew: 130
Showing fond feelings all akin
To that pure soul which lived within.

"With heart so soft and soul sincere,
Love found his way by eye and ear.
Then how I laboured, day and night,   135
To watch her ways and guide her right.
I brought cool airs from paradise
To purify her melting sighs.
I steeped my veil in heaven's own spring
And o'er her watched on silent wing;   140
And when she laid her down to rest,
I spread the veil o'er her virgin breast:
All earthly passions far did flee,
And heart and soul she turned to thee.
Throughout her life of wedded wife,   145
I weaned her soul from passion's strife;
But Oh! what fears and frequent tears
For the peril of childhood's tender years!
And when her firstborn's feeble moan
Was hushed by the soul's departing groan;   150
In that hour of maternal grief,
I pointed her way to the sole relief.
Another sweet babe there came and went—

Her gushing eyes she fixed and bent
Upon that mansion bright and sweet, 155
Where severed and kindred spirits meet.

"She has wept for the living, and wept for the dead,
Laid low in the grave her husband's head.
She has toiled for bread with the hands of age,
And through her useful pilgrimage, 160
Has seen her race sink one by one—
All, all she loved—yet left and lone,
With cheer unchanged, with heart unshook,
On God she fixed her steadfast look.
And now with the eye of purest faith, 165
She sees beyond the vale of death,
A day that has no cloud or shower—
She has less dread of her parting hour,
Than ever had babe of its mother's breast,
When it lays its innocent head to rest. 170
Oh! Maker of Earth, dread Ruler above,
Receive her spirit, her faith approve—
A tenderer mother, a nobler wife,
Ne'er waged, 'gainst earth and its sorrows, strife;
I never can bid a form arise 175
With purer heart than her's to the skies."

The Carle was moved with holy fear,
That lovely seraph's sweet song to hear;
He turned away and he covered his head,
For over him fell a visible dread. 180
While she gave her form to the breeze away,
That came from the vales of immortal day;
And sung her hymns far over the same,
And heavenly HOPE was the seraph's name:
The guide to a land of rest and bliss, 185
To a sinless world—how unlike this.

To earth's blest pilgrim, old and gray,
The gate dissolved like a cloud away;
And the grim old Carle he veiled his face,
As she passed him by with a holy pace; 190
With a touch of his hand and a whisper mild,
He soothed her heart as one stills a child.

The song of faith she faintly sung,
And God's dread name was last on her tongue.

  Now from the pall, bright and sublime,   195
That hangs o'er the uttermost skirts of Time,
Came righteous souls and shapes more bright,
Clothed in glory and walking in light;
Majestic beings of earthly frame,
And of heavenly radiance over the same,   200
To welcome the Pilgrim of this gross clime,
They had come from Eternity back to Time—
And they sung, while they wafted her on the road,
"Come, righteous creature, and dwell with God."

The Lairde of Lonne

Ane Rychte Breiffe and Wyttie Ballande
Compilit by Maister Hougge

There wals ane manne of muckil mychte,
  His naime wals Lowrie of the Lonne,
Quha helde the loudeste bragge of weir,
  Of manne that evir battylle wonne.

He beatte M'Killum lance to lance,   5
  He beat Gilfillane of the daille;
And at the tiltis and tourneymentis,
  He downit our gallantis all and haille.

His falshown wals the fire-flaughtis glyme,
  His speire the streimer of the sonne,   10
So that the championis stode alofe,
  And quailit before the Lairde of Lonne.

Then he rade este and he rade weste,
  Braiffing eche baulde upsettying manne;
There nevir wals ane knichte so proudde,   15
  Since this proudde warlde at first beganne.

But there livit ane mayden in the Mers,
  Sho wals the flouir of fayre Scotland,
And sho hald manye landis and rentis,
  And ane erildome at hir command.   20

But yet sho wolde not yelde to wedde,
  Nor trust hir herytage to manne;
And quhan the lordis came syching sadde,
  Sho lynkit at hir quheele and spanne.

And on them passit hir mirry jokis,   25
  Pitying their caisse rychte wofullye;
But bade them seik ane odir sposse,
  For ane marryit wyffe sho wolde not bee.

But downe came Lowrie of the Lonne,
  To carrye the mayden, landis, and alle,   30
He knowit sho nevir colde dysclaime
  Ane lover so gallant, braiffe, and talle.

His armour wals so daizzling brychte,
  That eyne colde hardlye loke thereonne;
He semit cladde in burnishit golde;   35
  But alle wals nevir golde that shonne.

His saddyl clothe wauffit in the wynde,
  With golden tassillis coverit o'er;
His steide he caperit lyke ane hynde,
  And rerit with his brodeside before.   40

And quhan he rappit at Landale gaite,
  No porter sterne wals to be seine;
But ane prettye May came to the yette,
  And the blynke of gle wals in hir eyne.

Then the Lairde he made his horse to rere,   45
  And the beiste he snortit awsomelye;
"If maydin Mariote is withynne,
  Go bid hir speike ane worde with mee.

"For I am the mychtie Lairde of Lonne,
  The hero of the Scottish lande;   50
And I am comit in cortesye,
  To claim your winsum ladyis hande."

And then he maide his horse to spang,
  Als though he wolde not renit bee,
Quhille the graivell flewe lyke bullet shouris—   55
  It wals ane gallante sychte to se!

The mayden squelit and keikit bye,—
  "Och, sir! myne leddye is at her quheele,
And sho moste spynne her daylie tasque,
  Else sho and I can ne'er doo wele.   60

"Sho is ane pore but thryftie daime,
  Quha workethe out her daylie breidde,

And hath no tyme to jaulke with ane
    That cairryeth so hie ane heidde.

"Quhan you can worke with spaidde and shole,   65
    Or dryffe ane trade of honeste faime,
Then come and woo myne ladye deire,
    Till then speide back the gaite you caime."

Then the Lairde of Lonne, he thochte it goode,
    To take this connyng May's avyse,   70
For ane womyn workyng for her breidde
    For him to wedde would not be wyse.

So he turnit his horsis heidde about,
    Quha neither spangit nor caperit nowe,
But the plomis upon the Lairdis helmette,   75
    They noddit dourlye ower his browe.

Then hee has gone to the Lorde of Marche,
    And hee has toulde him all his taille;
And that goode lorde hee laughit at him,
    Quhile bothe his sydis were lyke to faille.   80

Quod hee, "It wals the May herselle,
    I know it by her saucye saye;
But go you back and courte her welle,
    She may notte, can notte saye you naye.

"And scho has Landale touir and toune,   85
    Whitfielde, and Kelle, and Halsyngtonne;
Her very tythe of yearly rentis
    Wolde purchesse all the landis of Lonne."

The Lairde he mountit his gallant steidde,
    And staitlye on his saddyll sette,   90
He nevir styntit the lycht galloppe
    Untille he came to the Landale yette.

He gaif his steidde untill ane manne,
    And staitely strade into the halle,
Resolvit to win that ladye fayre,   95
    And her brode landis the best of alle.

And there he stode, and there he strode,
    And often sent he benne his naime;
But all that hee could saye or doo,
    They wolde not bidde him to the daime.   100

For the mirrye May she jinkit and jeerit,
    And the oulde foteman gyrnit amaine,
But the Lairde hee wolde not mofe one fote,
    But manfullye hee did remaine.

At length May Mariote she caime downe,   105
    Lyke ane brychte aingelle comit fro hevin,
And askit howe he daurit intrude
    Into a maydenis bower at evin?

Quod he, "Myne deire and comelye daime,
    I hidder come to maike demande   110
Of quhat is welle myne rychte to aske,
    Youre maydene herte but and your hande.

"For I am the hero of fayre Scotlande,
    No knychte can stande before myne armis,
And welle it suittes the fayreste daime   115
    To yielde the hero up hir charmis."

"If you be the hero of fair Scotlande,
    Then woe to Scotlande and to mee!
There is not ane manne on all myne lande
    But wald thwacke youre hyde most hertilye.   120

"You haif caipperit at the tourneymentis,
    And broken ane speire in ladyis sychte;
But there is not ane knychte of nobyl blode
    With gladdyautter bowis to fycht.

"To mete our meaneste Borderer's mychte,   125
    The menne whose daylie worke is stryffe,
Walde let you knowe quhat fychting is,
    And plie youre helis for dethe or lyffe."

The Lairde he trampit with his footte,
    Quhill all the hallis of Landale rung;   130

"Madame," quod he, "were you ane manne,
    You sholde repente youre wyckede tongue.

"There is myne pledge, now taike it up
    Als franklye als you se it throwne,
And if you haif ane hero in fayre Scotlande,   135
    I pledge myne lyff to bryng him downe!"

"I lift the gauntlet," said the dame,
    "To-morrowe come to thyne dejeune,
And pass you furthe to este or weste,
    Or northe or southe, als sutis thyne tune,   140

"And the firste manne thou meitest with,
    Give him ane challenge manfullye,
And fycht him on the very spotte,
    Then come and tell the news to me.

"If thou canst bryng the first two downe,   145
    Either on horsbacke or on footte,
I pledge myne mayden courtesye
    To listen to thyne honeste suitte.

"You lyttil knowe the Mers-mennis mychte,
    Bredde unto battyllis deadlyest blee;   150
There is not ane manne on all myne lande
    Quha will not bryng you to your kne."

Then the Lairde pullit off his fedderit cappe,
    And thryce he wafit it rounde his heidde,
And he utterit soche ane lordlye shoutte   155
    Als neirlye strak that ladye deidde.

"Hurrah!" cryit hee, "for lucky mee!
    Now let the skaithe go with the skorne;
The fayrest May in all the Southe,
    And hir braid landis, are myne the morne!"   160

The Lairde he came to his dejeune,
    And loudde he braggit of his weire;
But soche ane bleze of wycked wytte
    The herte of manne did nevir beire.

The Lairde then mountyd his gallante steidde,   165
   And forth unto the weste rode hee,
Quhere he wals aware of ane beggir manne
   Comyng slowlye slodgyng ower the le.

Then the Lairde he thochtis unto himselle,
   "This is the warke will nevir doo,   170
If I sholde fycht ane beggir manne,
   For lyffe I shall haif cause to rooe.

"But yet it wals hir stricke beheste,
   And myssing him I losse myne ple,
Bot to bryng downe ane leille aulde manne   175
   Befyttis not herois courtysye."

The beggir hee came loutchyng on,
   His heidde it shoke, his steppe wals fraille,
His sholderis bendyt lyke ane bowe,
   His berde wals lyke ane quhyte meris taille.   180

He had wallettis behynde, and wallettis before,
   That waggit about him wondyr welle,
But quhat wals in his clouttit bonnette
   There wals no bodye knawit but the beggir himselle.

He pullit off his bonnette unto the Lairde,   185
   And speirit ane aumousse churlishlye,
Then the Lairde gave him ane twalpennye piece
   With ane aire of mycht and maijestye.

And then he turnit him rounde aboutte,
   Saying, "Tell to mee, thou beggir knaiffe,   190
Didst thou evir fychte in felde of blode,
   Or battyll ane foemanne hande to glaiffe?"

"Yes, I haif fouchte in syngill fychte,
   And in the fronte of battyll keinne,
And I haif stode on felde of blode,   195
   Quhere gossyp like thee durste not be seinne."

"Quhat wolde you thynke, then, beggir knaiffe,
   With me to trie your mettyll here?"

"Deil taik the hindmoste," the beggir sayit,
   "If I had borrowit the mylleris mere."   200

Then the beggir hee gotte the mylleris mere,
   Als goode ane beiste als beggir colde hae,
His bryddle wals the hayre helterre,
   His saddyll wals the sonke of strae.

But soche ane bordlye warriour maike   205
   Ne'er dashyt forthe to dedis of weire;
He semyt to wax in size and shaippe
   Quhan mountit on the mylleris mere.

He had walletis behynde, and walletis before,
   And walletis out ower his sholderis had hee;   210
You mychte als welle perce ane packe of wole,
   Als trie to perce his fayre bodye.

He heifit his pykit staffe on hie,
   And gallopit on, and cryit "Wellhee!"
And his walletis waifit like twentye wyngis,   215
   That evin ane feirsome sychte wals hee;

But the Lairdis horse colde not stande the sychte,
   His very soulle did quaike for dreidde,
For he reirit and snortit lyke ane quhale,
   And neirlye fellit his maister deidde.   220

And or the beggir rechit the grounde,
   Be fortye ellis, als I herit saye,
The horse, in spytte of bytte and spurre,
   Quhelit off, and fledde lyke fire awaye.

But the mylleris mere wals ane mere of breide,   225
   And better mere nor myller behofit;
For all the warre-steidis horryd dreidde,
   Ane fleiter better yaude sho provit:

For the beggir pursuit, shoutyng "Wellhee!"
   And harde came on the battyll steidde,   230
Then he wanne the Lairde ane sturdye thwacke,
   That dang his helmette off his heidde.

And rounde and rounde the Landale touir
   They gallopit on with mychte and mayne,
Quhille May Mariote and all hir maydis   235
   Lauchit als they nevir lauchit agayne.

And rounde and rounde the Landale touir
   The Lairde and his pursuer flewe;
And the walletis daddit rounde and rounde,
   And raisit the stoure at every hewe.   240

And many a hard and hevvye knolle
   Felle on the rumpe of the warre steidde,
Whilom the braiffe hors gronit and ranne,
   Holdyng out his taille, and eke his heidde.

Then wolde the beggir quhele aboutte,   245
   To meite the Lairdis horse faice to faice;
But the horse no sooner the beggir sawe,
   Than spite of dethe he turnit the chaice,

And rounde and rounde the Landale touir,
   For the outter gatis were barrit amayne;   250
And soche ane chaice in soche ane plaice,
   Ladye shall nevir behoulde againe.

Till the Lairde, in black despaire and rage,
   Flung himselle fercely fro his steidde,
Then threwe the bryddle fro his graspe,   255
   Swearyng to bee the beggiris deidde.

But footte to footte, and hande to hande,
   The beggir mette him gallantlye;
At the first buffe the beggir gatte,
   The stoure lyke ane snowe-dryfte did flee,   260
And it flewe intille the Lairdis two eyne,
   Till feinte ane styme the Lairde colde se.

But whidder it came fro pepper pocke,
   Or beggiris pouche, hee colde not telle,
But it wals als hotte and sharpe to beir,   265
   Als asches fro the graitte of helle.

Then the beggir he lauchit ane wycked lauche,
    Als the Lairde he jumpit lyke ane possessit,
And the beggir had nothyng more to doo
    But to ¹aye on als lykit him best.   270

Hee thwackit the Lairde, and hee daddit the Lairde,
    And hee clouttit him quhille in wofull plychte.
"You gaif me ane aumouss," the beggir sayit,
    "So I'll not taike thyne lyffe outrychte.

"But betydde mee weille, betydde mee wo,   275
    Thyne glyttering garbe shalle go with mee,
To teche thee challynge ane hombil beggir,
    Quha wals not trobyling thyne nor thee."

He tyrelit the Lairde unto the boffe,
    And buskit himselle in his fynerye,   280
Then beltyd on his nobyl brande,
    And wow but ane jollye beggir wals hee!

But he lefte the Lairde his pykit kente,
    His powlderit duddis, and pockis of meille—
Och! nevir wals wooir so harde bestedde,   285
    Or ane hauchtye herte broughte downe so weille!

He hathe clothit himselle in the beggiris duddis,
    No oder remede had hee the whylle,
But his horse wold not lette him come neirre—
    No, not wythin ane half a mylle.   290

But quherre he fledde, or quherre he spedde,
    I nevir colde lerne with all myne lore,
But hee nevir sette uppe his faice agayne,
    And nevir wals seine in Scotlande more.

But wo be to that May Mariote!   295
    Quhatis to be wonne at womanis hande!
For sho has wedded that beggir knaiffe,
    And maide him lorde of alle hir lande!

For quha wals hee but the Knychte of Home,
    The dreade of all the Border boundis,   300

Quham that connyng May had warnyt weille
  To watche the Lairde in alle his roundis.

And the pretendit mylleris mere
  Wals the ae best beste that evir wals born;
Oft had sho broke the English rankis,   305
  And laid theyre leideris all forlorne.

May nevir ane braggarde bruike the glaive
  That beste befyttis ane nobyll hande—
And everye lovir losse the daime
  Who goes hir favour to commande!   310

*** The hero of this legend seems to have been Sir Alexander, the tenth
knight of Home; for, on consulting the registers of that family, I find that he
was married to Mariote, or Mariotta, sole daughter and heiress of Landale
of Landale, in the county of Berwick.

J.H.

Mount-Benger
March 12, 1830

Ringan and May

Ane rychte murnfulle dittye
Maide be Mr Hougge

I hearit ane laveroke synging with gle,
And O but the burde sang cheirilye;
Then I axit at my true love Ringan
Gif he kend quhat the bonnye burde wals syngan?
  Now my love Ringan is blithe and yongue,   5
But he hethe ane fayre and flatteryng tongue;
And Och I'm fearit I like ower weille
His talis of lufe, though kynde and leille.
So I sayis to him in scornfulle wayis;
"You ken no worde that burdye sayis."   10
  Then my love he turnit aboute to mee,
And there wals ane smyle in his pawkye ee;
And he sayis, "My May, my dawtyit dowe,
I ken that straine farre better nor you;
For that littil fairye that liltis so loude,   15
And hingis on the freenge of the sonnye cloude,
Is tellyng the taille in chantis and chymis,
I haif tellit to thee ane thusande tymis.
I will lette thee heire our straynis accorde,
And the laverokis sweite sang worde for worde.   20

Interpretation of the larfis song

'O my love is bonnye, and mylde to se,
Als sweitlye sho sittis on hir dewye le,
And turnis up hir cheike and cleire greye eye,
To liste quhatis saying withinne the sky;
For sho thynkis my mornyng hymne so sweite,   25
With the streimmers of hevin anethe my feite,
Quhare the proude Goss-hawke colde nefer wonne
Atweene the greye cloude and the sonne,
And sho thynkis her love ane thyng of the skyis
Sent downe fro the holye Paradyse   30

To syng to the worild at morne and evin
The sweite lufe sangis in the bowris of hevin.
  'O my love is bonnye, and yongue, and cheste,
Als sweitly sho syttis in hir mossy este!
And sho demis the burdis on boshe and tre   35
Als nothyng but duste and droulle to mee.
Tho the Robyn wairbel his waesum chirle;
And the Merle gar all the greinwode dirle;
And the Storm-cock toutis on his touryng pyne,
Sho trowis their sangis ane mocke to myne;   40
The Lintyis cheipe ane dittye tame;
And the Shillphais everlestyng rhame;
The Pliveris whew ane soloch dreire,
And the Whilly-Whaupis ane shaime to heire;
And quhanevir ane lufer comis in viewe,   45
Sho cowris anethe her skreine of dewe.
  'O my love is bonnye! Her virgyn breste
Is sweiter to me nor the dawnyng eiste,
And weille do I lyke at the gloamyng stille,
To dreip fro the lyfte or the louryng hille,   50
And presse her este as quhyte als mylke,
And her breste as soft als the downye sylke.'"

                *   *   *   *   *   *   *

  Now quhen my love had warbelit awaye
To this baisse parte of the laverokis laye,
Myne herte wals lyke to burste in twaine,   55
And the teris flowit fro myne eyne lyke raine.
At lengthe he sayit, with ane syche fulle lang,
"Quhat ailis my love at the laverokis sang?"
  Sayis I, "He is ane baisse and wycked birde
Als ever rase fro the dewye yirde;   60
It's a shaime to mounte on his mornyng wyng
At the yettis of hevin sikan sangis to syng;
And all to win with his awmerous dynne
Ane sweite littil virgyn birde to synne,
And wrecke with flatterye and song combynde   65
His deire lyttil maydenis pece of mynde.
O were I hir, I wolde let him se
His sangis sholde all be loste on mee!"
  Then my love toke me in his armis,

And gan to laude my leifu charmis;   70
But I wolde not so moche als let him speike,
Nor stroke my chynne, nor kisse my cheike,
For I feirit myne herte wals going wrang,
It wals so movit at the laverokis sang.

    Yet stille I laye withe ane upcaste ee,   75
And stille he wals syngin so bonnilye,
That, tho withe my mynde I had grit stryffe,
I colde not forbeire it for my lyffe,
But als he hang on the hevinis browe,
I saide, I kenit not why, nor howe,   80
"Quhatis that lyttil deuil sayand nowe?"

    Then my love Ringan he wals so gladde
He leughe tille his follye pat me madde;
And he said, "My love, I will tell you true,
He semis to syng that strayne to you,   85
For it sayis, 'I will rainge the yirde and ayre
To feide my love with the finest fare;
And quhen she lukis fro her bedde to mee
Withe the yearnyng lufe of a moderis ee,
O then I will come, and drawe her neirer,   90
And watche her closer, and lufe her deirer,
And wee never shalle pairte till our dying day,
But lufe and lufe on for ever and ay!'"

    Then myne herte it bled with a thrylling pleasure,
Quhen it lernit the laverokis closyng measure,   95
And it rase and rase and wolde not reste,
And wolde hardly bide wythinne my breste.
Then up I rase, and away I sprongue,
And saide to my love with scornfulle tongue,
That it wals ane baisse and byrning shaime;   100
That hee and the larke were bothe to blaime;
For there were some layis so softe and blande
That breste of mayden colde not stande;
And if he laye in the wode his laine,
Quhille I came backe to list the straine   105
Of ane awmerous birde amang the brome,
Then he mochte lye quhille the daye of dome!

    But for all the storte and stryffe I maide,
For all I did, and all I saide,
Alas! I feire it will be lang   110
Or I forgette that wee burdis sang!

And langer stille or I can flee
The lad that tellit that sang to me!

ALTRIVE LAKE
March 14*th,* 1825

The Grousome Caryl

Ane most Treuthful Ballant
Compilit be Mr Hougge

There wals ane man came out of the weste,
    And ane uncouth caryl wals hee,
For the bouzely hayre upon his hede
    Wals pirlit with his derke eebree.

And the feint ane browe had this caryl ava,   5
    That mortyl man cold see,
For all from his noz to his sholder blaide
    Wals dufflit rychte fearsomelye.

And hee nouther hald bonnet, hoze, nor shone,
    Nor sarke nor trewis hald hee,   10
But ane short buffe jerking rounde his waiste,
    That hardlye reechyt his knee.

And hee hald a belt of the gude bullis hyde,
    And ane buckil of irone hald hee,
And he buir ane pole on his sholder,   15
    Wals ten lang feite and three.

Als hee came up by the Craigyeburn,
    With stalwarde steppe and free,
Hee lokit up to the Saddil-Yoke,
    Als hee wolde take wingis and flee.   20

And aye hee keuste his burlye heede
    To flyng the hayre from his ee;
And hee hemmit and snockerit so awsome loude,
    That the levis shoke on the tree.

And the lyttel wee burdis helde up their neckis,   25
    And maide their croppis full sma',
And till that caryl wals out of sychte,
    Ane breath they durste not drawe.

And the wodeman grypit to his long bille,
   Thynking his lyffe wals gone,   30
And ranne behynde the hezil bushe,
   Tille the stalwarde caryl passit on.

And the deeris toke to their heelis and ranne,
   With their nozes fro the wynde,
And till they wonne to Carryfron Gans,   35
   They nefer lokit them behynde.

And the verrye doggis of the sheepherd ladis
   Were seizit with burninge dreide,
For they toke their tailes betweine their houghis,
   And made to the braies with speide: 40

And they eshotte out their crookyt tungis,
   In lenthe more than ane spanne,
And laid their luggis backe to their neckis,
   And whynkit als theye ranne.

And the oussen cockyt their stupid heedis,   45
   And swatchyt theire tailis full longe,
And aye they caiperit rounde and rounde,
   And wiste not quhat wals wronge.

And aye quhan the caryl gave a yowte,
   Or snockerit with belsche and braye,   50
Then all the rockis playit clatter agayne,
   And nicherit for mylis awaye.

And the welderis started on the steipe,
   Or scowrit alongis the lee,
And the lyttil wee kiddis rose from their layris,   55
   And blette most eldrischlye.

But iffe this caryl wals fleshe and blude,
   Or ane monstoure comit fro helle,
Or risen out of the deepis of the se,
   No manne in the londe colde telle.   60

But sickan ane daye and sickan ane fraye,
   Or sickan ane frightesome tale,

Nevir pat that contraye in dismaye,
   Since God maide Annerdaille.

For it wals saide ane horryde trayne   65
   Had passit at the braike of daye,
Of monstouris haisting out of the weste,
   And bounde for the fellis away.

The caryl he came to the Greye-Meris Linne,
   Benethe the rorynge steipe,   70
And he howckyt ane holle lyke bendyd bowe,
   Ane trenche bothe longe and deipe.

And he pullit the braiken fro the slacke,
   The hedder fro the hille,
The rown-tree fro the Straung-Cleuche Linne,   75
   And the birke of the Raken Guille.

And seven Scottis ellis of that deipe holle,
   He coverit up cairfullye,
And there he laye with his horrid crewe,
   Unseine be mortyl ee;   80
For no manne dorst come nie that houffe,
   For the lyffe of his bodye.

But the oussen sancted fro the houmis,
   The welderis fro the brae;
Quhille the herdis gromblit throu the londe,   85
   And wist not quhat til saye.

Young maidis were missyng fro their beddis,
   Before the brikke of the daye,
And moderis rockyd their tome credlis,
   For the bairnis had elyit awaye.   90

But worde is gone easte, and worde is gone weste,
   From Yarrawe unto the Ae;
And came to the Lord of Annerdaille,
   At Lochess quhare he laye.

That Lorde he leuche at his vasselmenis tale,   95
   And he sayde full jocundlye,

I will wende to the Grey-Meris Linne the morne,
   This grousome caryl to see.

Lord Annerdaille rose at the skreigh of the daye,
   And mounted his berry-browne steide,   100
With foure-and-twentye wale wychte menne,
   To guairde him in tymme of neide,

And thre stainche blode-hundis at his heile,
   Of the terrouble border brude,
That weille cold tracke the mydnichte theiffe,   105
   Or the sheddour of Chrystean blude.

And quhen hee comit to the Hunter-Heck,
   Och there wals a greeveous maene,
For somethynge wals myssing over nychte,
   That colde not be tolde againe.   110

But hee lousit the leishes of his blode-hundis,
   That lokit bothe doure and droye,
For they nouthir rowit them on the swairde,
   Nor scamperit runde for joye.

But they snokyd the dewe, and snokyd the dewe,   115
   And snokit it ouer againe;
And the byrsis raise uponne their backis,
   Broschit lyke ane wyld boris maine.

Then Jowler hee begoude to youffe,
   With a shorte and ane aungrie tone,   120
And German's ee begoude to glent,
   With a blode-reide glaire thereonne.

But Harper turnit his flewe to the hevinis,
   And hee gaif ane tout so longe,
That all the wodis in Moffat-daille,   125
   With moulesse echois ronge.

That wals the true and the wairnynge note,
   Awaye wente the hundis amaine,
And awaye wente the horsmen them behynde,
   With spurre and with steddye reine.   130

But the fordis were deippe, and the bankis were steippe,
   And paithwaye there wals none,
And or they wonne to the Selcothe Burne,
   The braif blode-hundis were gone.

But they hearit the echois dynnling on,   135
   Alonge the cludis so caulme,
Als gin the spyritis of the fellis
   Were synging their mornyng psaulme.

And the egill lefte his mistye haime,
   Amiddis the cliffe so grimme,   140
And he belted the mornyngis ruddye browe,
   And joinit in the blodye hymme.

"Spur on, spur on," cryit Annerdaille,
   "Leiste evil mine hundis betydde,
Gin the reiveris hydde were maide of irne,   145
   Ane ryving it moste bydde."—

Quhan they came up to the Greye-Meris Linne,
   To the trenche bothe deippe and longe,
Lord Annerdaille's steide turnit runde his heide,
   No farther he dochte gange: 150

But aye he scraipyd, and he snorit,
   And lukyd with wylde dismaye,
And fain wald haif spoken to his maister;
   But colde not get worde to saye.

"Who holdis this holle," cryit Annerdaille,   155
   "This denne of dreide and doubte?
Gin yee bee creaturis of mortyl byrthe,
   I soummont you to come oute."—

He hearit ane snockir, and than ane laughe,
   And than ane smotherit screime,   160
Als gin the devil hald been asleipe
   And wakenit oute of ane dreime.

And the three blode-hundis youlit aloude,
   Quhan theye hearit their maisteris voyce;

For theye were chainit withyne the cave;   165
  And frightesome grewe the noise.

But oute then came the grousome caryl,
  And up on his trenche stode hee,
And his towzlye hede it kythit als hiche
  Als the hill of Turnberrye.   170

Lord Annerdaille hald not worde to saye,
  For his herte it beatte so faste;
And thoche he put grette couryge on,
  He stode full sore aghaste.

And aye hee lokit at the carylis maike,   175
  And then at his pygmye mennis;—
They were no more before his faice
  Than ane scrowe of cockis and hennis.

"Chryste be mine shielde!" said Lord Annerdaille,
  "For als mine faithe shall thryve,   180
If ten such carylis were in the londe,
  They wold swallowe it up alyve."—

"Quhat seike you heire?" quod the gyant caryl,
  "Or quhat is your wille with mee?"—
"We seike for oussen, sheipe, and kye,   185
  And eke for ane faire ladye!"—

"You shall haif their bonis then," said the caryl;
  "You shall haif them with righte gode wille,
Quhan mine gude demis and nobil sonnis
  Haif gnawit at them their fille."—   190

"Lorde be myne shielde!" quod Annerdaille,
  "And saife me from skaithe and scorne!
For the lykis of that I nefer hearit,
  From the daye that I wals borne.

"Louse forthe myne hundis, thou baisse reiver!   195
  If rackle thou woldest not bee."—
"Lothe wold I bee," the caryl replyit,
  "For outhir youre golde or fee.

"Theye will brynge downe the stott but and the steire,
  The welder and the fleite hynde;   200
Or be dejune to myne gude demis,
  Quhan better they may not fynde."—

Lord Annerdaille he waxed wrothe,
  Such thochtis he colde not thole,
And he vowit to shede the carylis blode,   205
  And burrye him in his holle.

"Art thou for battil?" the caryl replyit,
  "That thynge rejoysethe mee;
For it will pleisse our stomackis to feiste
  On thyne fatte men and thee."—   210

Hee bore ane polle on his sholder
  Wals ten large feite and three,
And out of that hee throste ane speire,
  Moste dreadfulle for to see.

Lord Annerdaille's men drew out their brandis,   215
  And flewe on the caryl amaine;
But in five twynkillyngis of an ee,
  Ane thirde of them lay slaine.

The reste whelit runde their steedis and fledde,
  Swifte als the westlande wynde;   220
But some they quakit and stode agaste,
  Quhan lokinge them behynde:

For there they saw bothe wyffis and barnis,
  Of frychtsome gyant brode,
Come runnyng out of the horryde holle,   225
  And drynke their kinsmenis blode.

And aye they quaffit the reide warme tyde,
  Their greide it wals so ryffe,
Then trailit the bodies into the holle,
  Though fleckeryng still with lyffe.   230

Lord Annerdaillis men they rode and ranne
  O'er all the Border bounne,

Till they founde out Johne of Littledeane,
  Ane aircher of gritte renounne.

He came to the Gray-Meris Linne ouernighte,   235
  And dernit him dexterouslye,
And there hee watchit for the grousome caryl,
  To walke on his blodye lee.

Quhan hee had tokyn his horryde meale,
  Too baisse quhereon to thynke,   240
Then strode hee downe unto the streime
  To taike his mornyng drynke.

And Johne hee lokit out ouer his denne,
  And sawe the monstour lye;
And the littil fisches swatteryng awaye,   245
  For they thochte the streime gone drye.

The caryl hee rose up lyke ane tree,
  And toke his steidfaste stande,
For hee behelde our gode yeomanne
  With bent bowe in his hande.   250

Hee dorste not turne him runde to flye,
  Though moche hee hald ane mynde,
For hee knewe the fleite and flying shafte
  Wolde pierce his herte behynde.

Our yeomanne sent ane airrowe fleite,   255
  From bowe of the good yew-tree;
But the caryl keppyt it in his teethe,
  Als easily als ane flee.

Another and another flewe,
  With als moche mychte and speide,   260
But stille hee keppyt them in his teethe,
  And chewit them for ane meide.

But Johne hee wals ane cunnyng manne,
  Hee seyis his skille againe—
Hee put two arrowis to his bowe,   265
  And drewe with mychte and maine:

The caryl deftly caught the ane
  Full fiercelye als it flewe;
But the other piercit him throw the breiste,
  And clave his herte in two.   270

Hee gaif ane growle—hee gaif but ane,
  It maide all the hillis to rore;
Then down hee fell on the Peele-Knowe side,
  And wordis spoke nefer more.

Then up rose the Lord of Annerdaille   275
  From ambosche quhair hee laye,
And hee sackit the carylis grousome holle,
  And herryit it for ane preye.

But, och! the sychte wals there displayit
  Of horrour and of paine,   280
Lorde graunt that the men of Annerdaille
  May nefer beholde againe!

For soche ane wylde and salvage schene
  By barde hald never beine sunge,
It wolde not syng, it wolde not saye,   285
  Be anye Chrystean tunge.

They toke the carylis menzie brode,
  His sonnis and his wyffis three;
And they haunkit towis abote their neckis,
  And hangit them on ane tree;   290

Then toke them to their grousome holle,
  For their last horryde roome;
And the Gyantis Trensche and the Gyantis Grave
  Will kythe till the daye of doome.

Now, long live Jamis, our nobil Kyng,   295
  And Lord Annerdaille, long live hee,
And long live John of Littledeane,
  Quha set this countrye free.

Some saide those gyantis were brotal bestis,
  And soulis they colde haif none,   300

Some saide they had, but shoke their hedis,
   And wonderit quhare they were gone.

Till Peter of Bodisbecke hee came forthe,
   With prufis of the verye beste,
That put ane end to the dispute,   305
   And set the lande at reste:

For Peter wals out at eventyde,
   Upon his heightis, I wotte,
And Peteris eyne colde see full weille
   Quhat other mennis colde notte.   310

So Peter behelde ane flocke of deilis,
   Lyke greifous hoddye-crawis,
And ilk ane hald ane gyantis soule
   A-writhing in its clawis.

They flewe als they were bounne to helle,   315
   Swyfte als the fyerie flaime,
But they drappit the fiendis in Gallowaye,
   The place fro whence theye caime;

They flewe ouer bonny Annerdaille,
   And ouer the Nythe they flewe;   320
But they drappit the soulis in Gallowaye,
   Als the worste helle they knewe.

Maye the Lorde preserve bothe manne and beiste
   That treade this yirde belowe,
And littil bairnis, and maydenis fayre,   325
   And graunt them graice to growe;

And may never ane reude uncouthlye gueste
   Come their blessit bowris withynne;
And neuer ane caryl be seine againe
   Lyke him of the Greye-Meris Linne.   330

Love's Jubilee

By James Hogg

FIRST SPIRIT

Lovely Spirit, where dost thou fly
With such impatience in thine eye?—
Behold the hues of the closing day
Are mingled still with the gloaming gray;
And thine own sweet star of the welkin sheen,   5
The star of love, is but faintly seen!
See how she hangs like a diamond dim
By the walks of the holy Seraphim,
While the fays in the middle vales of blue
Have but half distilled their freight of dew.   10
It is too early in the night
For a spirit so lovely and so bright
To be tracing the walks of this world beneath,
Unhallowed by sin, and mildewed by death;
Where madness and folly are ever rife,   15
And snares that beleaguer mortal life.—
I know thee well, sweet Spirit of Love,
And I know thy mission from above;
Thou comest with every grace refined
To endow the earthly virgin's mind;   20
A record of her virtues to keep,
And all her thoughts awake and asleep.
Bright Spirit, thou hast a charge of care!
Come tarry with me in this woodland fair,
I will teach thee more in one hour of joy   25
Than all thou hast learned since thou left'st the sky.
Come tarry with me, let the maidens be,
'Till the hour of dreaming and phantasy;
And then will I seek with thee to share
The task of fanning their foreheads fair,   30
And scaring the little fays of sin
That tickle the downy dimpling chin;
That prank with the damask vein of the cheek,
And whisper words it were wrong to speak.
From all these foes thy wards shall be free,   35

If thou wilt go woo in the wood with me;
Till yon twin stars hang balanced even,
Like ear-rings on the cheeks of heaven!

SECOND SPIRIT
And who art thou, that with shameless brow,
Darest here such license to avow?   40
If aright I judge from what I've heard,
This courtesy might well be spared;
For of all the spirits beneath the sun
Thou art the one that I most would shun!
Art thou not he of guardian fame,   45
That watchest over the sex supreme?
Say, Spirit, was the charge not given
To thee, before the throne of heaven,
To guard the youth of this vale from sin,
From follies without and foibles within?   50
If so, thou hast honour of thy trade!
A glorious guardian hast thou made!
To the dole and the danger of mine and me,—
My malison light on it and thee!
Go woo with thee!—by this heavenly mind   55
I had rather go woo with a mortal hind!

FIRST SPIRIT
Sweet Spirit, sure thou could'st never opine
That my charge could be as pure as thine?
Something for sex thou should'st allow;
Yet have I done what spirit might do,   60
And more will I still, if thou wilt go rest
With me on the wild thyme's fragrant breast,
By form of an angel never prest!
I will spread thee a couch of the violet blue,
Of our own heaven's cerulean hue;   65
The sweetest flowers shall round thee be strewed,
And I'll pillow thy head on the gossamer's shroud;
And there, 'neath the green leaves closely furled,
I will cool thy cheek with the dew of the world;
I will bind thy locks with the sweet wood-reef,   70
And fan thy brow with the wabron leaf;
I will press thy heaving heart to mine,
And try to mix with our love divine

An earthly joy, a mortal bliss;
I will woo thee and woo thee for a kiss,   75
As a thing above all gifts to prize,
And I'll swear 'tis the odour of Paradise!
In earthly love, when ardent and chaste,
There's a joy which angels scarce may taste;
Then come to the bower I have framed for thee;   80
We'll let the youth of the vale go free,
And this eve shall be Love's Jubilee!

Second Spirit

I will not, I dare not such hazard run,
My virgin race may be all undone.
The breeze is chill,—it is wearing late,   85
Away thou guardian profligate!

First Spirit

Sweet spirit, why that quivering lip,
Which an angel of light might love to sip?
And why doth thy radiance come and go,
Like the hues of thine own celestial bow?   90
And why dost thou look to the ground and sigh,
And away from the green-wood turn thine eye?
Are these the symptoms, may I divine,
Of an earthly love, and is it mine?

Second Spirit

Ah, no! it is something about my head,   95
Some qualm of languour or of dread.
That breeze is surely in a glow,
And yet it is chill—what shall I do?
Wilt thou not go?—ah! haste away
Unto thy charge; thou art worse than they.   100

First Spirit

I will not, cannot leave thee so;
I must woo thee whether thou wilt or no;
Let us hide from the star-beam and the gale,—
Why dost thou tremble and look so pale?

Second Spirit

Oh, my dear maidens of beauty so bright,   105

What will become of you all to-night!
For I fear me this eve of wizard spell
May be, by shade, by bower, and dell,
An eve to dream of—not to tell!

First Spirit
I will charge the little elves of sin   110
To keep their silken cells within,—
In the night-flower's breast, the witch-bell blue,
Or wrapt in the daisy's silver flue;
And not to warp, on any pretence,
The thoughts or the dreams of innocence.   115
There shall not one of them dare to sip
The dew of love from the fervid lip,
Till the sleeping virgin, pale and wan,
Shrink back, as if from the kiss of man.
There shall no elfin, unreproved,   120
Take the dear form of the youth beloved;
Or whisper of love within the ear
A word for maiden unmeet to hear.
From man's deep wiles thy sex I'll guard,
If a smile from thine eye be my reward;   125
For all beside we must let them be,
And this eve shall be Love's Jubilee!

The guardian angel of virgin fame,
In one sweet dale which I may not name,
Was won for that dear eve, to prove   130
The thrilling enjoyments of earthly love:
And if by matron the truth was said,
There was ne'er such an eve since the stars were made,
For young delight, and for moments bright,
And all that could virtuous love requite;   135
For all was holy, and pure, and chaste,
As the angels that wooed in their home of rest.
The welkin glowed with a rosy blue,
And its star of love had a brighter hue;
The green wood strains with joy were rife,   140
And its breeze was a balm of heavenly life.
Ay, 'twas an eve—by bower and dell—
An eve to dream of—not to tell:

For ever hallowed may it be,
That eve of LOVE's HIGH JUBILEE!

ALTRIVE LAKE
Candlemas-day, 1825

Ane Rychte
Gude and Preytious Ballande

Compylit be Mr Hougge

"O dearest Marjorie staye at home
    For derkis the gaite you haif to goe
And theris ane maike adowne the glenne
    Hath frichtenit mee and many moe

His leggis are lyke two pillaris talle   5
    And stille and stalwarde is his stryde
His faice is rounder nor the mone
    And Och his muthe is awsum wyde

I saw him stande the oder nychte
    Yclothed in his gryzely shroude   10
With ane fote on ane shadowe plaicit
    The oder on a misty cloude

Als far asunder were his limbis
    On the firste storye of the ayre
Ane shippe colde haif sailit thru betweine   15
    With all hir coloris flying fayre

He noddit his heide againste the heuin
    Als if in referende mockerye
Then fauldit his armis upon his breste
    And ay he shoke his berde at mee   20

And he poynted to my Marjory's cotte
    And be his motione semit to saye
'In yon swete home gae seike thy lotte
    For there thyne yirthlye lotte I lay'

Myne very herte it quaikit for dredde   25
    And turnit als colde als beryl stone
And the moudyis cheipit belowe the swairde
    For feire their littil soulis were gone

The cushat and the corbye craw
    Fledde to the highest mountayne heichte   30
And the littil burdyis tryit the saime
    But felle downe on the yirthe with frychte

But there wals ane shaimfulle Heronshu
    Wals sytting be the plashy shore
With meager eyne watchyng powhoodis   35
    And oder fyshis lesse or more

But quhan sho sawe that gryzelye sychte
    Stande on the billowe of the wynde
Graice als sho flapperit and sho flewe
    And lefte ane stremorye tracke behynde   40

And ay sho rairit als sho were wode
    For outter terror and dismaye
And lefte ane skelloche on the cloude
    I toke it for the milkye waye

Had I not seine that heydeous sychte   45
    Quhat I had done I colde not saye
But at that Heronis horryde frychte
    I'll lauche until myne dying daye

Then deirest Marjorie staye at home
    And raither courte ane blynke with mee   50
For gin you se that awsome sychte
    Yourselfe againe you will neuir bee"

"But I haif maide ane tryste this nychte
    I may not brikke if take myne lyffe
So I will runne myne riske and goe   55
    With mayden spyritis haif no stryffe

Haif you not hearit sir domonye
    That faice of vyrgin beris ane charme
And neither ghaiste nor manne nor beaste
    Haif any power to doe hir harme?"   60

"Yes, there is ane, sweite Marjorie
    Will stande thy frende in derksum euin

For vyrgin beautie is on yirthe
  The brychtest teipe wee haif of heuin

The collie couris upon the swairde   65
  To kisse hir feite with kindlye eye
The maskis will not moofe his tung
  But wag his taylle if sho passe bye

The ether hathe not power to stang
  The slae-wormis harmlesse als ane eile   70
The burlye taed the eske and snaike
  Can not soe moche als wounde hir heile

The angelis lofe to se hir goode
  And watche her wayis in bowre and halle
The deuillis paye her sum respeck   75
  And Gode lofis hir that is beste of alle"

"Then sothe I'll taike myne chance and wende
  To keipe myne tryste quhateuir maye bee
Quhy sholde ane virtuous mayden dredde
  The tale of ane craizit domonye?"   80

"Ochon ochon deire Marjorie
  But of your virtue you are vaine!
Yet you are in ane wonderous haiste
  In runnyng into toyle and payne

For maydenis virtue, at the beste,   85
  (May hee that maide her kynde, forgive hir!)
Is lyke the blewe belle of the waiste
  Swete swete a whyle and gone for ever

It is lyke quhat mayden moche admyris
  Ane bruckle sette of cheenye store   90
But one fals stumbil sterte or steppe
  And downe it fallis for evermore

It is lyke the floryde Eden rose
  That peryshethe withoute recallyng
And ay the lovelyer that it growis   95
  It weris the neirer to the fallyng

It is lyke the flauntyng mornyng skie
　　That spreddis its blushes farre before
But plashe there comis ane storme of raine
　　And all its glorye then is ouir   100

Then bee not proude swete Marjorie
　　Of that whiche haithe no sure abode
Man littil knowis quhat lurkis withynne
　　The herte is onlye knowne to Gode."

But Marjorie smylit ane willsum smyle   105
　　And drewe her frocke up to hir kne
And lychtlye downe the glenne sho flewe
　　Though the teire stode in the domonyis ee

Sho had not gone ane myle but one
　　Quhille up there stertis ane droichel manne   110
And hee lokit rewfulle in hir faice
　　And sayis "Fayre mayde quhare be you gaunne?"

"I am gaunne to meite myne owne true lofe
　　So maister Brownie saye youre reide
I know you haif not power to hurte   115
　　One syngil hayre of vyrginis heide"

The Brownie gaif ane goustye laughe
　　And saide "Quhat wysdome you doo lacke!
For if you reche your owne trewe lofe
　　I maye haif power quhan you come backe"   120

Then nexte sho mette ane eldron daime
　　Ane weirdly wytche I wot wals shee
For though sho wore ane human faice
　　It wals ane gruesum sychte to se

"Staye prettye mayde quhat is youre haiste?   125
　　Come speike with mee before you goe
For I haif newis to telle to you
　　Will maike youre very herte to glowe

You deime that vyrginis haif ane charme
　　That holdes the universe at baye   130

Alas poore foole to snare and harme
    There is none so lyabil als theye

It is lofe that lyftis up womanis soule
    And gifs hir eyis ane heuinlye sway
Then wolde you bee ane blessit thyng   135
    Indulge in lofe without delaye

You goe to meite youre owne true lofe
    I knowe it welle als well can bee
But or you passe ane bowshotte on
    You wille meite one thryce als goode als hee   140

And hee wille presse youre lillye hande
    And hee wille kisse your cheike and chynne
And you moste goe to bower with him
    For he is the youthe youre lofe moste wynne

And you moste doo quhat he desyris   145
    And greate goode fortune you shall fynde
But quhen you reche youre owne true lofe
    Keipe closse your secret in youre mynde"

Awaye wente Marjorie and awaye
    With lychter steppe and blyther smyle   150
That nychte to meite hir owne true lofe
    Sho wolde haif gone ane thousande myle

Sho had not passit ane bowshotte on
    Until ane youthe in manlye trim
Came up and pressit the comelye maye   155
    To turne into ane bower withe him

He promysit hir ane gowne of sylke
    Ane mantil of the cramasye
And cheyne of golde aboute hir necke
    For ane hour of hir companye   160

He tooke hir lillye hande in his
    And kissit it with soch fervencye
That the poore maye began to blushe
    And durste not lifte hir modeste ee

Hir littil herte began to beatte   165
    And flutter moste disquyetlye
Sho lokit eiste sho lokit weste
    And alle to se quhat sho colde se

Sho lokit up to heuin abone
    Though scaircelye knowyng how or why   170
Sho hevit ane syghe—The day wals wonne
    And brychte resolf bemit in hir eye

The first sterne that sho lokit upon
    Ane teire stode on its browe for shaime
It drappit it on the flore of heuin   175
    And ay its blushes wente and caime

Then Marjorie in one momente thochte
    That blessit engelis mighte hir se
And often sayit withynne hir herte
    Doth Godis owne plennitis blushe for mee?   180

That they shall neuir doo againe
    Leille virtue still shall bee myne guyde
"Thou stranger youthe passe on thy waye
    With the I will not turne asyde

The angel of the glenne is wrothe   185
    And quhare shall mayden fynde remeide?
Se quhat ane heydeous canopye
    He is spreddyng high abofe our heide"

"Take thou no dredde swete Marjorie
    It is lofis owne courtaine spredde on highe   190
Ane timeous vaile for maydenis blushe
    Yon littil crombe-clothe of the skie

All the goode angelis take delichte
    Swete womanis happinesse to se
And quhare colde thyne be soe complete
    Als in the bower this nychte with mee?"   195

Poor Marjorie durste no answer maike
    But stode als meike als captif dofe

Her truste fyxit on hir maker kynde
   Her eyis upon the heuin abofe 200

That wyckede wychte (for sure no youthe
   But demon of the glenne wals hee)
Had no more power but spedde awaye
   And left the mayden on hir kne

Then alle you virginis swete and yongue 205
   Quhan the firste whisperyngis of synne
Begynne to hanker on youre myndis
   Or steile into the soule withynne

Keipe ay the eyis on heuin abone
   Bothe of youre bodye and youre mynde 210
For in the strengthe of Gode alone
   Ane womanis weaknesse strengthe shalle fynde

And quhan you goe to bowir or delle
   And knowis noe human eye can se
Thynke of ane eye that neuir slepis 215
   And angelis weipyng over the

For manne is but ane selfyshe maike
   And littil reckis of maydenis woe
And alle his pryde is to advyse
   The gaite sho is farre ower app to goe 220

Awaye wente bonnye Marjorie
   With alle her blossomis in the blychte
Sho had not gone ane bowshotte on
   Before sho saw ane awesum sychte

It wals ane maike of monsterous mychte 225
   The terror of the sonnis of menne
That by sir domonye wals hychte
   The gyaunt spyrit of the glenne

His maike wals lyke ane moneshyne cloudde
   That fillit the glenne with human forme 230
With his greye lockis he brushit the heuin
   And shoke them farre abone the storme

And gurly gurly wals his loke
    From eyne that semit two borrelis blue
And shaggy wals his syluer berde   235
    That down the ayre in stremoris flewe

Och but that mayde wals harde bestedde
    And mazit and modderit in dismaye
For bothe the guestis of heuin and helle
    Semyt hir fonde passage to belaye   240

Quhan the greate spyrit sawe her dredde
    And that sho wiste not quhat to saye
His faice assumit ane mylder shaidde
    Lyke midnychte meltyng into daye

"Poore waywarde airtlesse aymlesse thyng   245
    Quhare art thou goyng canst thou telle?"
The Spyrit saide "Is it thyne wille
    To rinne with open eyne to helle?

I am the guardianne of this glenne
    And it is myne sovereygne joie to se   250
The wycked manne runne on in synne
    Rank ruthless gaunte and gredilye

But stille to gairde the virtuous herte
    From pathis of dainger and of woe
Shalle bee myne earneste deireste parte   255
    Then telle me daime quhare dost thou goe?"

"I go to meite myne owne deire lofe
    True happynesse with him to seike
The comelyest and the kyndest youthe
    That euir kissit ane maydenis cheike"   260

The Spyrit shoke his sylver hayre
    That stremit lyke sunne-beime thru the rayne
But there wals pitye in his ayre
    Though mynglit with ane mylde disdayne

He whuppit the mayde up in his armis   265
    Als I wolde lyfte ane tryveal toye

Quod hee "The upshotte thou shalte se
    Of this moste pure and virtuous joie"

Hee toke two strydis he toke but two
    Although ane myle it semyt to bee   270
And showit the maye hir owne true lofe
    With mayden wepyng at his kne

And Och that maydenis herte wals sore
    For stille with teris sho wet his feite
But then he mocked and jeerit the more   275
    With thretis and language moste unmeite

Sho cryit "O deire and cruelle youthe
    Thynk of the lofe you vowit to mee
And alle the jois that wee haif prewit
    Benethe the beilde of birken tre   280

Synce neuir mayde hathe lofit lyke mee
    Leafe mee not to the worldis scorne
Be youre deire hande I wille raither dee
    Than liue forsaiken and forlorne"

"Als thou haste sayde soe shalt thou dre"   285
    Sayde this moste cursit and cruelle hynde
"For I moste meite ane maye this nychte
    Quham I lofe beste of womankynde

So I'll let forth thyne wycked blode
    And neither daunte nor rewe the deide   290
For thou art loste to graice and goode
    And ruinit beyonde alle remeide"

Sho openit up her snowye breste
    And ay the teire blyndit hir ee
"Now taike now taike myne harmlesse lyffe   295
    All guiltlesse but for lofing the"

Then he toke oute ane deidlye blade
    And drewe it from its blodye shethe
Then laid his hande upon hir eyis
    To blynde them from the stroke of dethe   300

Then straight to perse hir broken herte
    He raisit his ruthlesse hande on high
But Marjorie utterit shriek so loude
    It made the monster sterte and flye

"Now mayden" sayde the mightye shaide   305
    "Thou seest quhat daingeris waited the
Thou seest quhat snaris for the were laide
    Alle underneathe the grenewode tre

Yet straighte on rewyng woldest thou runne!
    Quhat thynkest thou of thyne louir meike   310
The comelyest and the kyndest youthe
    That euir kyssit ane maydenis cheike?"

Then sore sore did poore Marjorye weipe
    And cryit "This worlde is ane worlde of woe
Ane plaice of synne of snaire and gynne   315
    Alace quhat shalle poore woman doe!"

"Let woman truste in heuin highe
    And bee alle venturis rashe abjured
And neuir truste hirself with man
    Tille of his virtue welle assured"   320

The Spyrit turnit him rounde aboute
    And up the glenne he strod amayne
Quhille his whyte hayre alangis the heuin
    Stremyt lyke the cometis fyerie trayne

Highe als the egillis mornyng flighte   325
    And swifte als is his cloudye waye
He bore that maydene throughe the nyghte
    Enswathit in wonder and dismaye

And he flang hir in the domonyis bedde
    Ane goode softe bedde als bedde colde bee   330
And quhan the domonie hee came home
    Ane rychte astoundit man wals hee

Quod hee "Myne deire swete Marjorie
    Myne beste belouit and dawtyit daime

You are wellcome to myne bedde and borde   335
   And this braif housse to bee thyne haime

But not quhille wee in holye churche
   Bee bounde neuir to loose againe
And then I wille lofe you als myne lyffe
   And long als lyffe and brethe remaine"   340

Then the domonie toke hir to holie churche
   And wedde hir with ane gowden ryng
And he wals that daye ane joifulle man
   And happyer nor ane crownit kyng

And more unsmirchit happynesse   345
   Neer to ane yirthlye paire wals giuen
And alle the dayis they spente on yirthe
   They spente in thankfullnesse to heuin

Now maydenis deire; in grenewode shawe
   Ere you maike trystis with flatteryng menne   350
Thynk of the sychtis poore Marjorie sawe
   And the GREAT SPYRIT of the glenne

MOUNT-BENGER
July 9th, 1828

Jocke Taittis Expeditioune till Hell

Compilit bee Maister Hougge

Jocke Taitte hee satte on yonne hille syde,
   And wow but his herte wals sore,
For he hadde weiped so long and loudde,
   That hee cold weipe no more.

The scaldyng teris his chekis did smerte,   5
   Quhille bothe his eene ranne drie;
The sobbis were bobbyng at his herte,
   And his mouthe was sore awrie.

He toke his bonnette off his heide
   And threwe it on the greine,   10
And aye he clawit his burlye powe,
   And gaif ane raire betweine:

"Och, woe is me," sayit the grefous youth,
   "That evir I once wals borne,
For I haif lost my owne true lofe,   15
   And myne herte is lefte forlorne!

"I lofit hir better nor my breidde,
   Far better than myne lyffe;
I would haif given this bullet heide
   To haif halde hir for myne wyffe!   20

"Sho wals the sonne-blink on the brae,
   Als sweite and als deire to mee;
Far sweiter nor the lychte of daye
   To the weirye waikryffe ee.

"Sho wals the raynbow among the cluddis,   25
   The lyllye among the dewe,
The bonnye moorehenne amang the menne,
   Of all the burdis that flewe.

"Ane roz-budde grewe withynne her mouthe,
    Which manne colde nevir espye;   30
But the breize out of the vernalle southe
    Wals sweite quhan sho wals nighe.

"Sho wals the roz among the flouris,
    The cherrye amang the hawis,
The starre of lofe among the starris,   35
    The sea-mawe 'mang the crawis.

"It wals hir power, it wals hir parte,
    The soulis of men to thralle,
But, och! she halde ane wycked herte,
    And that was worst of alle!   40

"Sho garrit me waire myne pennye fee,
    And nevir thochte it synne,
On sylken cloke of cramasie
    To rowe her beautye in.

"Sho garrit me selle myne collye true,   45
    My last lamb on the le,
To decke her all in the skarlette hue,
    Ane comelie sight to see;

"And nowe the ende of all myne geire,
    It grefeth mee to telle;   50
It hathe sente my bonnye lasse to the deille;
    I woulde raither haif gone myselle!"

With that Jocke Taitte hee heerit ane lauche,
    Some quhair abone his heide,
And hee lokit eiste, and hee lokit weste,   55
    For his herte wals fillit with dreide;

Hee lokit ower his leite sholdere
    To se quhat hee colde se;
There he behelde the muckil deille
    Comyng stendyng ower the le!   60

He wore ane boustrous shepherdis plaidde,
    That wauffit als hee were wudde;

And the blue bonnette on his heide
   Wals lyke ane thonder cludde.

His lockis were lyke the hedder cowe,   65
   And swarthye wals his hue,—
It wals of that derke and feirsum tinte,
   Betwine the blacke and blue.

In sothe he wals ane goustye gaiste
   Als anie eye colde se,   70
And jollye mischieffe on his face
   Wals prentit stamphishlye.

The shepherde wals astoundit sore,
   And he courit him downe for feare:
"O quha are you, ye boustrous kairle,   75
   Or quhatte are you seiking heire?"

"I am Gil-Moullis, the shepherdis deille,
   And ane heavye chairge haif I,
For they are the moste rampaugent raice
   That braithes benethe the skie.   80

"They thynke of wemyng nychte and daye,
   And nothyng els thaye mynde,
Quhille theyre verrye soulis doe falle ane preye
   To the lofe of womankynde.

"I wille not clayme the comelye daime   85
   Which you gaif owre to mee;
For ane lychte recklesse deidde of shaime,
   Myne scho wille nevir bee.

"But your kynde offir in hir plaice,
   I taik with herte and hande,   90
For wee lyke to se ane shepherdis faice
   Better nor alle the lande.

"I haif wemyng enewe, of rozie hue,
   Alle rathe and rubycounde;
I cannot stirre myne fote at home,   95
   Theyre numberis so abounde.

"But ane shepherde is theyre greate delychte,
  Theyre is none they lyke soe weille,
For he touzilis them bothe daye and nychte,
  And garris them lauch and squeille. 100

"And hee syngis them queire and funnie sangis,
  Which maike theyre hertis fulle gladde,
And tellis them melting tailes of lofe,
  Which almaist puttis them madde."

Then the shepherde clawit his burlye hede, 105
  And girnit and leuche amayne,
And he pullit the fogge up fro the hille,
  For he coulde not refrayne.

Quod he, "You are ane funnye deille,
  Be more quhate'er you maye; 110
Faythe I wolde lyke to se the jaddis,
  And heire what theye walde saye!"

"I trowit als moche," sayit the muckelle deille,
  "That garrit me come with speiede;
For it is ane haime will suite you weille, 115
  In all youre tymis of neidde.

"It wals maide for you, and you for it,
  And monie more besyde;
There is nathyng happenis in nature brade,
  That wysdome can deryde." 120

Hee rowit the shepherde in his plaidde,
  And hee toke him on his backe
Als I wolde do ane poore blynde whalpe,
  The lyttellest of the packe.

And awaye and awaye went the muckle deille, 125
  Stryding ower hille and daille;
It wals soche ane awsum sychte to se,
  That the shepherdis herte did faille.

The mountains were his stepping stonis,
  While far ower firthe and floode, 130

His bonnette bobbit yont the skie,
   Ane derke and trobilit clude.

He walked lyke columne sterke and stoure
   On toppis of mountainis greinne;
For aye he spangit frae hille to hille,   135
   Though twentye mylis betwinne.

And the frychtenit morefoulis fledde amayne
   All shymmering on the wynde;
And the ptarmigandis theye lefte the heighte,
   And nevir lokit behynde.   140

And ower the mountayne and the mayne
   He helde his mychtie waye,
Quhille they lefte the daylychte far behynde,
   And enterit ane twilychte graye.

And the sonne went downe into the Eiste,   145
   And the mone into the mayne;
And the lyttil byrning lampis of hevin,
   Theye vainishit ane bee ane.

At length theye caime to the deillis halle yette,
   And tirlyt at the pynne,   150
And ane jollye porter openit the dore,
   And smudgit als theye came in.

"Maistere Gill-Moullis," then sayit Jocke Taitte,
   "Is this youre lustie haime?
I will thanke you then to taike mee backe,   155
   To the plaice fro whence I caime.

"For heire I cannot se ane styme,
   And darre not gang for feirre;
But I heire the yelpe of womannis tungis,
   Which I lyke welle tille heirre."   160

"Och!" sayit the deille, "the lychte is goode
   Quhan heire a quhile you dwelle;
It is rather sombere at the fyrste,
   But sutis exceedyng welle.

"For it is the bagnio of helle,   165
   Ane braif and gallante plaice,
The grandiste gaime that evir wals fraimit
   For synneris of human raice.

"For wee haif kyngis, and dukis, and lordis,
   That daylie come in pairis;   170
But the jollye shepherdis and the prestis
   Are our best customeris.

"'Tis strainge wee haif no ladyis heire,
   Scairce one our hallis withynne;
Thes are alle pryncessis and quenis,   175
   And lymmeris of vulgar kynne.

"But you shalle find them lofyng and kynde,
   Rychte blythesum, franke, and fre,
And aye the longer you lofe them,
   The madder in lofe you'll bee."   180

"Coulde I but se," the shepherde sayit,
   "To maike myne choyce arycht,
This is the very plaice for mee,
   In which I wolde delychte."

Then the deille he flung the shepherde downe   185
   Als hee were ane deidde sheippe,
And hee lychtit on ane feddir bedde,
   Betweine two queanis asleippe.

But hee colde not se quhat they were lyke,
   So up he sprang withe speidde;   190
But he hearit them gigglyng, als he ranne
   In darknesse and in dreidde.

Hee spyit the Lord of F—— suppyng
   His kaille out throughe the reike,
And the doughtye chieftaine of M,Nab   195
   Wals playing at hydde-and-seike.

And he sawe the lordis and lemanis gaye
   Syttand bebbyng at the wyne,

And aye theye dronke theyre merrye tostis
   With oggylle and with sygne.   200

And everilke draughte they swallowit downe
   More greidillye nor the fyrste;
For aye the langer that theye dronke,
   The hotter grewe theyre thyrste.

Enjoymente there brought no allaye,   205
   Desyre stille waikyt anewe;
The more that theye indulgit in synne,
   The madder on synne theye grewe.

The fyrste lemanne our shepherde chose
   Wals lyke ane roze newe blowne;   210
But ane jollye preste came them behynde,
   And knockit the shepherde downe.

The next lemanne our shepherde chose
   Downe in his armis sho laye;
But sho turnit ane awsome ugly snaike,   215
   That frychtenit his wittis awaye.

For mony a yeirre and mony a daye
   Our shepherde did remayne;
But nought of pleissure caime his waye
   But quhat grewe byttere payne.   220

For he wals fairlye stawit of lofe—
   Of routte and revelrye;
Hee haitit the wemyng from his soull,
   Yet colde not let them bee.

And hee thocht upon his owne firste lofe   225
   With alle his earlye flaime,
Who though she had fallen in ane snaire,
   Hir herte wals nevir to blaime.

And ofte he sayit unto himselle,
   Withe the teirre blynding his ee,   230
"Och had I hir on the greine hille syde,
   And nevir ane eye to se!

"'Tis sweitte to se the lasse we lyke
    Come lynking ower the le;
'Tis sweite to se the earlye budde   235
    First nodding fro the tre;

"'Tis sweite to se the mornyng beime
    Kyssing the sylver dewe;
But forgivenesse is the sweeteste thyng
    That evir ane kynde herte knewe.   240

"Yes, I wolde kysse her blushyng cheike,
    And grante forgivenesse free;
For if I dinna forgive myne lofe,
    Then quha can pardon mee?

"But heirre may I in shaime and synne   245
    For evir more remayne,
For I'll nevir se the greine hille syde,
    Nor my true lofe agayne!

"Bay-hay! bay-hay!" quod the shepherde lad,
    Als loude als he coulde raire;   250
And "Bouff!—bouff!" quod his colley dogge,
    For it wonderit quhat wals there.

The shepherde started to his feitte
    In terrour and in teene;
For hee laye upon the greine hille syde,   255
    Nor farder had evir beine.

He soughte his lofe that verye nychte,
    And at his calle sho caime,
And hee toulde hir of his dreidful dreime
    Of sorrow, synne, and shaime.   260

And hir wee errour with the lairde
    Wals alle forgiven fre;
And I wals at theyre weddyng yestreinne,
    And ane merrye nycht hald wee!

ALTRIVE LAKE
18th August, 1830

A Bard's
Address to his Youngest Daughter

Come to my arms my wee wee pet
My mild my blithesome Harriet
The sweetest babe art thou to me
That ever sat on parent's knee
Thou hast that eye was mine erewhile   5
Thy mother's blithe and grateful smile
And such a playful merry vein
That greybeards smile at pranks of thine

And if aright I read thy mind
The child of nature thou'rt designed   10
For even while yet upon the breast
Thou mimic'st child and bird and beast
Can'st cry like Maggy o'er her book
And crow like cock and caw like rook
Boo like a bull and blare like ram   15
And bark like dog and bleat like lamb
And when abroad in pleasant weather
Thou minglest all these sounds together
Then who can say thou happy creature
Thou'rt not the very child of nature   20

Child of my age and dearest love
As precious gift from God above
I take thy pure and gentle frame
And tiny mind of mounting flame
And hope that through life's chequered glade   25
That weary path which all must tread
Some credit from thy name will flow
To the old bard who loved thee so
At least thou shalt not lack as meed
His blessing on thy beauteous head   30
And prayers to him whose sacred breath
Lightened the shades of life and death

And said with sweet benignity
Let little children come to me

'Tis very strange my little dove   35
That all I ever loved or love
Come o'er my mind in visions bright
While gazing on thee with delight
Thy very name brings to my mind
One whose high birth and soul refined   40
Withheld her not from naming me
Even in life's last extremitye
Sweet babe thou art memorial dear
Of all I honour and revere

Come look not sad—though sorrow now   45
Broods on thy father's cloudy brow
Thy prattle soon will that remove
Although the sorrow's sweet to prove
One kiss I crave for grandam's sake
Who never saw thy tiny make   50
And one for her who left thee late
Laid low but not forgotten yet
One for thy sweet mamma's dear claims
And one for Jessy and for James
One for wee Maggy next and dearest   55
And one for her whose name thou bearest
And now again I say thou art
A strange memorial to my heart

How dar'st thou frown thou freakish fay
And pout and look another way   60
Why turn thy chubby cheeks athraw
And skelp the beard of thy papa
I know full well thy deep design
'Tis to turn back thine eye on mine
With triple burst of joyful glee   65
And fifty strains at mimicry
What wealth from nature may'st thou won
With pupilage so soon begun
Well hope is all, thou art unproved,
The bard's and nature's best beloved   70
And now above thy brow so fair

And flowing films of flaxen hair
I lay my hand once more and frame
A blessing in the holy name
Of that supreme divinity   75
Who breathed a living soul in thee

Johnne Graimis
Eckspeditioun till Heuin

Compilit be Mr Hougge

There wals ane carle rychte worldlye wyce
   Quha dyit without remeidde
Yet foughte his waie tille Parradyce
   Eftir that he wals deidde
And the first soulle that hee met there   5
Wals of ane mayden mylde and fayre
Quha once hadde fallen into ane snayre
   Whilke led tille euil deidde

"Och Mrs madam!" cryit Johnne Graime
   "I wondir mychtilye   10
How leddye of soche euil faime
   Gatte into this countrye
If soche als you get fotynge heirre
Then ould John Graime hath cause tille feirre
He hath the wrong sowe be the eirre   15
   And sorre dismayit is hee

Is this ane plaice of blissitnesse
   Or is it ane plaice of woe?
Or is it ane plaice of myddil spaice
   That lyis betweine the two?   20
For there's ane myldnesse in your meinne
And blithenesse in your brychte blue einne
Whilke sertis sennil solde be seinne
   Quhare wychit demis do goe"

"Ocho Johnne Graime! Are you but there?   25
   Did you nere heirre of this
That everilke plaice quhare spyritis fare
   To them is plaice of bliss?
That menne and wemyng be Goddis mychte
Were fraimit with spyritis bemyng brychte   30
Rysing from darknesse into lychte
   Though sunke in synnis abyss

Ane thousande yeris or thousandis tenne
    Notte reckonit once can bee
The immortyl spyrit rysis onne   35
    To all Eternitye
It rysis on or morre or lesse
In knowledge and in happynesse
Progressyng stille to purer blisse
    That ende can neuir se"   40

Johnne shoke his heidde and primmyt his mou
    And clawit his lugge amayne
And sayis "Fayre daime if this be true
    How comis it menne haif layne
In darknesse to theyre spyritis fraime   45
Theyre Makeris manage and his ayme
Quhille lychtenit be ane synnful daime
    Quhan lychte canne profe no gayne?

Sothe it is ane plesaunt doctoryne
    For wychit hertis I trowe   50
And sutis the lordly lybberdyne
    And leddyis soche als you—"
Then the fair daime with wytching wylle
Upraisit hir eye withoutten guille
Flung backe hir lockis and smyllit ane smylle   55
    And sayit "How judgest thou?

Is it for symperyng sordid sotte
    Ane heipocrytick craiven
To saie quhais wycked and quhais not
    And wythershynne with heaven?   60
Do you not knowe in herte full welle
If there had beinne ane byrning helle
That you deservit the plaisse yourselle
    Als welle als any leiving?

You judge lyke menne and judge amysse   65
    Of sympil maydenis cryme
But through temptationis faddomlesse
    You cannot see ane styme
Through darke and hyddin snairis of synne
And warryngis of the soulle withynne   70

The einne of mortyl may not wynne
   Within the boundis of tyme

But wolde you knowe quhat brochte mee heirre
   To this caulm worlde of thochte
It wals the sadde and sylente teirre   75
   That sweite repentance brochte
Of all the thyngis on earthe that bee
Whilke Godde and angelis lofe to se
It is the hertis deippe agonye
   For soulle so deirlye bochte   80

'Tis that whilke bryngis the heuenlye blisse
   Downe lyke the mornyng dewe
On lost sheippe of the wyldernesse
   Its longyngis to renewe
Till the poore lambe that went astraye   85
In vice's wydde and weitlesse waye
Is ledde als be ane heuinly raye
   The lychte of lyffe to viewe

And let mee telle you oulde Johnne Graime
   Though heirre you seimme to bee   90
You haif through darknesse floode and flaime
   Ane weirye weirde to dree
Unlesse you do at Goddis commande
Repente of all your synnis offe hande
Whilke in your haiteful natife lande   95
   Haif griefous beine to se

Ane gritter synner wals not borne
   In daille of fayre Scotlande
You knowe you stole Jock Laidleyis corne
   And broke his herte and hande   100
And though menne knowit you were forsworne
Yet quhan his family felle forlorne
You treatted theyre complaynte with scorne
   And broke them from the lande

Och fie Johnne Graime! You sordid slaife!   105
   It settis you welle to cracke
You cheittyng lying scurfye knaife

Your herte is raiven blacke
Insteidde of ane progressife paice
In vertue knowledge and in graice   110
Thou art laggyng everilke daye ane spaice
   And feirfullye gone backe

And there's ane thraldome wayting the
   Thyne herte cannot concieve
Worryit ane thousande yeiris to bee   115
   Without the leist reprieve
Tyme was, tyme is; but wille not bee
For when I pass from wairnyng the
Ane aingel with thyne dethis decre
   The yettis of heuin shall leive"   120

"Alake" sayis Johne "it grefis mee sorre
   Shorte mercye I shalle fynde
I thought I had beine dead beforre
   But how I can notte mynde
Moche to repentance I incline   125
And I colde praye and I coulde whyne
But to gif backe quhat nowe is myne
   To that I shalle not bynde"

Then Johnne knelit downe in hombil waye
   Upon the swairde of heaven   130
And prayit als loude als manne colde praye
   That hee mochte bee forgiven
"Johnne!" cryit his wyffe, quha laie awaike
"Quhat horryd dynne is this you maike?
Get uppe oulde braying brocke and take   135
   Some braith to ende this stevin"

"Whisht wyffe!" sayis Johnne "for I am deidde
   And praying on the skie.
Quhatis this? I knowe myne soulle is fledde
   Or very soone moste flie;   140
For there is ane aingel on the waye,
How long hee taikis I cannot saye,
But or to morrowe or to daye
   Poore auld Johnne Graime moste die

And wyffe we moste repente for lyffe   145
   And alle mennis goodis restorre"
"The fiende be there then!" quod the wyffe
   "Though theye were ten tymis morre
Tis goode to keipe the grip one heth
Either for lyffe or yit for dethe   150
Repente and praye while you haif braith
   And all your synnis gif o'er

And taike your chaunce lyke mony a shippe
   And mony a better manne"
Johnne rose and sworre hee wolde restorre   155
   And syne begoude to banne
All wychit wyffis of bad intente
Quha wolde not lette theyre menne repente
Without theyre frowarde cursit consente
   That helle mochte them trapanne   160

Johnne lokit at alle his yowes and kie
   Och theye were fayre to se
His golde he countit thre tymis bye
   The teirre blyndit his ee
But still hee sworre hee wolde restorre   165
And blamit the wyffe and wepit fulle sorre
Countyng his treassure o'er and o'er
   And grainyng grefouslye

They yermit and flaitte ane sommeris daye
   Of quhat wals to bee donne   170
And juste als spredde the glomyng graye
   Behynde the settyng sonne
The aingel with the warrande caime
Johnne felit his veetalis in ane flaime
Ghastlye hee stairit upon his daime   175
   But language hee had nonne

Hee gaif ane shiver and but one
   And still his golde hee eyit
Hee poyntit to it—gaif ane grone—
   And als hee livit hee dyit   180
The slaiffe of that o'erpoweryng vyce
That deiddenyng craifyng AVARYCE

That turnis the humain herte tille ice
　Unblissit unsatisfyit

This carle was haited whylle he levit　　　　　　185
　Unwept quhan hee wals gone
But quhaire he wente or how recievit
　To me wals notte maide knowne
But on this truth I can reclyne
That he's quhare mercyis rayis combyne　　　　190
In better handis nor his or myne
　Whilke menne wille notte disowne

St. Mary of the Lows

By James Hogg, the Ettrick Shepherd

O lone St. Mary of the waves,
   In ruin lies thine ancient aisle,
While o'er thy green and lowly graves
   The moorcocks bay and plovers wail;
   But mountain-spirits on the gale   5
Oft o'er thee sound the requiem dread,
   And warrior shades and spectres pale
Still linger by the quiet dead.

Yes, many a chief of ancient days
   Sleeps in thy cold and hallow'd soil,   10
Hearts that would thread the forest maze
   Alike for spousal or for spoil,
   That wist not, ween'd not, to recoil
Before the might of mortal foe,
   But thirsted for the border-broil,   15
The shout, the clang, the overthrow.

Here lie those who, o'er flood and field,
   Were hunted as the osprey's brood,
Who braved the power of man, and seal'd
   Their testimonies with their blood: 20
   But long as waves that wilder'd flood
Their sacred memory shall be dear,
   And all the virtuous and the good
O'er their low graves shall drop the tear.

Here sleeps the last of all the race   25
   Of these old heroes of the hill,
Stern as the storm in heart and face;
   Gainsay'd in faith or principle,
   Then would the fire of heaven fill
The orbit of his faded eye,   30
   Yet all within was kindness still,
Benevolence and simplicity.

GRIEVE, thou shalt hold a sacred cell
   In hearts with sin and sorrow tost,
While thousands, with their funeral-knell,   35
   Roll down the tide of darkness lost;
   For thou wert Truth's and Honour's boast,
Firm champion of Religion's sway—
   Who knew thee best revered thee most,
Thou emblem of a former day!   40

Here lie old forest bowmen good;
   Ranger and stalker sleep together,
Who for the red-deer's stately brood
   Watch'd, in despite of want and weather,
   Beneath the hoary hills of heather: 45
Even Scotts, and Kerrs, and Pringles, blended
   In peaceful slumbers, rest together,
Whose fathers there to death contended!

Here lie the peaceful, simple race,
   The first old tenants of the wild,   50
Who stored the mountains of the chace
   With flocks and herds—whose manners mild
   Changed the baronial castles, piled
In every glen, into the cot,
   And the rude mountaineer beguiled,   55
Indignant, to his peaceful lot.

Here rural beauty low reposes,
   The blushing cheek and beaming eye,
The dimpling smile, the lip of roses,
   Attractors of the burning sigh,   60
   And love's delicious pangs that lie
Enswathed in pleasure's mellow mine:
   Maid, lover, parent, low and high,
Are mingled in thy lonely shrine.

And here lies one—here I must turn   65
   From all the noble and sublime,
And o'er thy new but sacred urn
   Shed the heath-flower and mountain-thyme,
   And floods of sorrow, while I chime
Above thy dust one requiem.   70

Love was thine error, not thy crime,
Thou mildest, sweetest, mortal gem!

For ever hallowed be thy bed,
  Beneath the dark and hoary steep;
Thy breast may flowerets overspread,   75
  And angels of the morning weep
  In sighs of heaven above thy sleep,
And tear-drops of embalming dew;
  Thy vesper-hymn be from the deep,
Thy matin from the æther blue!   80

I dare not of that holy shade
  That's pass'd away one thought allow,
Not even a dream that might degrade
  The mercy before which I bow:
  Eternal God, what is it now?   85
Thus asks my heart, but the reply
  I aim not, wish not, to foreknow;
'Tis veiled within eternity.

But O, this earthly flesh and heart
  Still cling to the dear form beneath,   90
As when I saw its soul depart,
  As when I saw it calm in death:
  The dead rose and funereal wreath
Above the breast of virgin snow,
  Far lovelier than in life and breath,   95
I saw it then and see it now.

That her fair form shall e'er decay
  One thought I may not entertain;
As she was on her dying day,
  To me she ever will remain: 100
  When Time's last shiver o'er his reign
Shall close this scene of sin and sorrow,
  How calm, how lovely, how serene,
That form shall rise upon the morrow!

Frail man! of all the arrows wounding   105
  Thy mortal heart, there is but one
Whose poisoned dart is so astounding

That bear it, cure it, there can none.
　It is the thought of beauty won
To love in most supreme degree,　　　　　　　110
　And by the hapless flame undone,
Cut off from nature and from thee.

Farewell, dear shade! this heart is broke
　By pang which no allayment knows;
Uprending feelings have awoke　　　　　　　115
　Which never more can know repose.
　O, lone St. Mary of the Lows,
Thou hold'st a treasure in thy breast,
　That, where unfading beauty glows,
Must smile in everlasting rest.　　　　　　　120

The Origin of the Fairies

By the Ettrick Shepherd

I have heard a wondrous old relation,
How the Fairies first came to our nation;
A tale of glamour, and yet of glee,
Of fervour, of love, and of mystery.
I do not vouch for its certain truth,   5
But I know I believed it in my youth;
And envied much the enchanted Knight,
Who enjoy'd such beauty and pure delight.
I will tell it now, and interlard it
With thoughts with which I still regard it,   10
And feelings with which first I heard it.

The Knight of Dumblane is a hunting gone,
   With his *hey!* and his *ho!* and *hallo!*
And he met a merry maid alone,
   In the light green and the yellow.   15
That maiden's eyes were the pearls of dew,
And her cheek the moss-rose opening new;
Her smile was the sun-blink on the brae,
When the shower is past, and the cloud away.
And then her form was so light and fair,   20
That it seem'd to lean on the ambient air;
So very blithesome and so boon,
That the Knight was afraid it would fade too soon;
Mount on the ether from human ken,
Or melt away in the breeze of the glen.   25
   His frame thrill'd to the very core
When he saw that beauty stand him before,
With the gleam of joy on her brow so meek,
And the dimple on her damask cheek.
And then so ripe was her honey lip,   30
That the wild-bee, lingering, long'd to sip;
And the merl came by with an eye of guile,
For he hover'd and lighted down a while
On the snowy veil in which she was dress'd,
To pick the strawberries from her breast.   35

O was there aught below the heaven
I would not have done, or would not have given,
To have been the Knight of Dumblane that day!—
But 'twas better for me that I was away.
   The Knight came nigh, and essay'd to speak,   40
But the glamour of love was on his cheek;
And a single word he could not say,
For his tongue in thirsty silence lay.
But he doff'd his cap from his manly brow,
And he bow'd as low as a knight could bow,   45
Then stood with his velvet cap in hand,
As waiting for the maiden's command.
   Sure this was witless as could have been,
I cannot conceive what the Knight could mean;
For had I been there, in right or wrong,   50
As sure as I sing you this song,
I would, as the most due respect,
Have twined my arms around her neck;
And sure as man e'er woo'd a maid,
Have row'd her in my shepherd plaid,   55
And in token of my high regard,
Have set her down on the flowery sward;
And if some discourse had not begun,
Either in quarrel or in fun,
Take never a shepherd's word again,   60
And count my skill in wooing vain;
All this I would have done with speed—
But for ever would have rued the deed.
   Oh, never was knight so far o'ercome
As he who now stood blushing and dumb   65
Before this maid of the moorland brake,
With the cherub eye and the angel make.
At first no higher his glance was thrown
Than the flowery heath that her foot stood on;
When by degrees it embraced her toe,   70
But over the ankle durst not go;
Till at length he stammer'd out modestly,
"Pray—madam—have you—any commands for me?"
   Shame fa' the Knight! I do declare
I have no patience with him to bear;   75
For I would have look'd, as a man should do,
From the shoe-tie to the glancing brow;

Nay, from the toe's bewitching station
Even to the organ of veneration.
For what avails the loveliest face,   80
Or form of the most bewitching grace,
Which on earth are made for man alone,
If they are not to be look'd upon?
Yes, I would have look'd till my sight had rack'd,
And the very organs of vision crack'd,   85
And I would have sworn, as a man should swear,
That I never saw virgin half so fair:
This I had done, despite all pain,
But, ah! I never had done it again!
  But the maid was delighted beyond expression   90
To mark the young Knight's prepossession,
And with a smile that might have given
Some pangs even to a thing of heaven,
She took so moving a position
That set his soul in full ignition: 95
One limb alone scarce press'd the ground,
The other twined her ankle round;
Her lovely face was upward cast;
Her sunny locks waved in the blast;
And really she appear'd to be   100
A being divine—about to flee
Away from this world of self and sin,
A lovelier, holier clime to win.
No posture with that can ever compare—
What a mercy that I was not there!   105
  But he raised his eyes as hers withdrew,
And of her form got one full view:
The taper limb, and the slender waist,
The modest mould of her virgin breast,
The lips just opening with a smile,   110
And that eye upraised to heaven the while;
The purple tides were seen to entwine
In a thousand veins all crystalline!
Enough! The sequence is too true:
For though the Knight got but one view,   115
One full intoxicating look,
It was more than his fond heart could brook;
For on the ground he fell as dead
As he had been shot out through the head.

Now this was rather a sad o'erthrow;   120
I don't think I would have fallen so;
For though a lovely virgin face
Has sometimes put me in piteous case,
Has made me shed salt tears outright,
And sob like the wind on a winter night,   125
Nay, thrown me into a burning fever,
Yet I never just went off altogether;
But I have reason, without a flam,
Thankful to be—and so I am—
That I was spared the illusive sight   130
That was seen by that enchanted Knight.
    Now it seems that the maiden to fear began
For the life of that young and comely man;
And every art essay'd to try
To make him uplift his amorous eye.   135
But in reality, or in mime,
The swoon continued a weary time.
And better had it been if he had never
Re-open'd his eyes, but slept for ever;
For when next they awoke on the light of day,   140
His cheek on the maiden's bosom lay.
He felt its warmth new life impart,
And the gentle throbs of her beating heart;
He felt, beneath his aching head,
The enchanting mould that had laid him dead;   145
He felt her hand his temples chafing,
And every tenderness vouchsafing;
He lifted his head—he hid his face—
And stole his cheek from that witching place;
Yet still he cast, though disinclined,   150
A longing, lingering glance behind,
Where he saw—but I dare not describe the view,
For if you are a man it will kill you too;
If you are a woman, and lovely beside,
You will turn up your nose in disdain and pride.   155
If you are not, without a frown,
You will laugh at the Knight till you fall down;
For true it is, when the Knight had seen
The beauteous bed where his cheek had been,
The blush, and the smile, and the lucid vein,   160
He gave one shriek, with might and main,

Then shiver'd a space—and died again!
  From that time forth, if I durst tell,
Unto that Knight such hap befell,
As never was own'd by mortal man,   165
And never was told since tales began.
He got his wish—It proved a dear one,
It is an old story, and a queer one;
But free of fear, and free of fetter,
I'll tell it out even to the letter—   170
The wilder 'tis I love it the better.
  We all have heard the maxim old,
That a tale of truth should aye be told;
For nothing in nature happen can,
That may not a lesson prove to man: 175
Now this is true:—Yet things, we ken,
Oft happen between the women and men,
So wild, romantic, and precarious,
So complicated, and contrarious;
So full of passion and of pain,   180
They scarcely can bear to be told again.
Then think of love 'twixt a mortal creature,
And a being of another nature!
  The Knight was lost—that very morn
Rung the last peal of his hunting horn;   185
His comrades range the mountain reign,
And call his name, but call in vain;
From his hawks and his hounds he is borne away,
And lost for a twelvemonth and a day;
And all that time, he lived but to prove   190
The new delights and the joys of love—
His mistress, a pattern of sweetness and duty,
And her home a palace of splendour and beauty.
But whether it was in the sinful clime
That bounds mortality and time,   195
In a land below, or a land above,
In a bower of the moon, or the star of love,
He never could fathom or invent,
Or the way that he came, or the way that he went;
But he ween'd, from his love's aerial nature,   200
That she barely could be a mortal creature.
  And every night in his ears there rung
The accents sweet of the female tongue;

Light sounds of joy through the dome were ringing—
There was laughing, dancing, harping, singing;   205
But foot of man in the halls was none,
Nor sound of voice but his own alone:
While every night his beloved dame
In new array to his chamber came;
And, save herself, by day or night,   210
No other form ever met his sight.
So ween'd the Knight; but his mind was shaken,
And, alas! how far he was mistaken!
For love's full overwhelming tide
O'er the mind of man is hard to bide.   215
Yet this full fraught of delirious joy,
Without reverse and without alloy,
I would once have liked to have essay'd,
But at last—how I had been dismay'd!
    The times soon changed, for by slow decay,   220
The sounds of joy were melted away
To a tremulous strain of tender wailing
Of sufferings for a former failing;
While something was sung, in a plaintive key,
Of a most mysterious tendency,   225
Of beings, who were not of the earth,
To human creatures giving birth;
Of seven pure beings of purity shorn,
Of seven babies that might be born,
The nurslings of another clime,   230
By creatures of immortal prime,
Of the mother's thrilling fears, and more
Of the dark uncertainty before!
    The Knight then dreaded, as well might he,
That things were not as things should be,   235
And a hearty wish rose in his mind,
That he were at the home he left behind.
To wish, and to have, in the charmed ring
Of that sweet dome, was the self-same thing;
For the Knight awaken'd, as from a dream,   240
And he stood by the wild and mossy stream,
Where first he felt the bewitching power
Of the beauteous maid at the morning hour,
Where he fell a victim to beauty's charms,
And died of love in a virgin's arms!   245

He sought his halls and his stately bower,
But a solemn stillness seem'd to lour
Around his towers and turrets high:
His favourite hound would not come nigh,
But kept aloof with a murmuring growl,   250
And a terror his heart could not control;
For he prick'd up his ears, and snuff'd the wind,
Though he heard his master's voice behind,
Then fled with his bristles of dread unfurl'd,
As from a thing of another world.   255
And every maiden, and every man,
Away from their master in terror ran;
While his aged mother, in weeds of wo,
Conjured him solemnly to go
Back to his grave, and his place of rest!   260
For her mind with terror was sore oppress'd.
But there he remain'd, and once again
Was hail'd as the true Knight of Dumblane.
    But, oh! how changed in every feature,
And all the vehemencies of his nature,   265
As if an eagle from cliffs above
Had been changed into a plaintive dove;
From a knight of courage and of glee,
He was grown a thing of perplexity,
Absent and moping, puling, panting,   270
A vacant gaze, and the heart awanting:
Earth had no pleasures for his eye,
When he thought of the joys that were gone by.
This to some natures may be genial,
Or, as a failing, counted venial;   275
For me, I judge the prudent way,
Let past time have been what it may,
Is to make the most, with thankful mind,
Of that which still remains behind.
    The Knight lived on as scarce aware,   280
How long I neither know nor care,
Till at the last, one lovely morn,
The fairest lady that ever was born
Came into his bower with courtesy bland,
And a lovely boy was in either hand;   285
Two tiny elves alike, not less
Than twin flowers of the wilderness.

"Thou art my lord, my own true knight,
Whose love was once my sole delight.
Oh, I recall—how can I not?—   290
That morning never to be forgot,
When I met thee first with horn and hound
Upon the moor to the hunting bound,
When thy steed like lightning fled away,
And thy staghound howl'd and would not stay;   295
Thou stolest the heart that never had birth,
The heart of a being not of this earth:
And what is more, that heart to wring,
The virtue of an immortal thing.
Dost thou own these babes in the gold and green,   300
The loveliest twins that the world has seen;
Wilt thou here acknowledge us as thine own,
Or bear the brunt of our malison?"
    Then the Knight shed tears of joy apace
At seeing again that lovely face;   305
And his heart with love was sore oppress'd
As he folded the fair dame to his breast:
"Thou art my lady love," said he,
"And I never loved another but thee!"
    "Alas, how blind are earthly eyes   310
To those that are lighted by other skies,
By other breezes, untainted by sin,
And by other spirits that dwell within!
Well might thy raptures of pleasures be
Sublimed by creatures such as we:"   315
The lady said with an eye of shame,
When enter'd another most comely dame,
As like to the first as she could be,
As like as cherries on the same tree;
While hanging on either hand were seen   320
Two lovely babies in gold and green.
    "Thou art my own true lord and love,"
The second said, "and thou wilt approve
This dear love-token, I changed with thee,
When sitting in the bower upon thy knee."   325
The Knight acknowledged the token rare,
And flew to embrace his lady fair;
But remembrance came with a thrilling pain,

That instead of a lady he now had twain,
And instead of two babies of beauty and grace,   330
There were four all looking him in the face.
He stood like a statue, of sense bereft,—
He look'd to the right and then to the left,
But one from the other he could not know,
They were both the same, and yet there were two.   335
While thus he stood prepared for shrift,
In came a third—a fourth—a fifth—
A sixth—a seventh! All round they stand,
And each had a baby in either hand,—
And each had her love-tokens to display,   340
Which the Knight acknowledged without delay.
But how that maid he met on the hill,
And loved so dearly, and loved her still,
Had thus the powers of nature outdone,
And multiplied into twenty and one—   345
Why, that was more than he could believe,
Than his head could frame, or his heart conceive;
And still he cast his eye to the door,
Distrustful that there were not more.
    His lady mother at length attended,   350
And her courtesies were with wonder blended,
To see such beauty in such array,
Seven dames all lovely as morns of May,
With fourteen babies in a ring,
And all like the children of a king;   355
And she laid on her son her quick behests,
To tell her the quality of their guests.
    "Why, mother, 'tis strange as strange can be,
And yet it is truth I tell to thee,
That all these dames of beauty so bright,   360
Claim me for their own true lord and knight;
Nay, and I may not deny it neither,
And all these children call me father.
But I swear by my vows of morn and even,
And I swear before the throne of Heaven,   365
That I never knew of daughter nor son,
Nor of a love save only one;
There is glamour abroad in moor and glen,
And enchantment in all the walks of men."

"Why, son, it has often been told to me,   370
That you never could learn to multiply.
Your bold advancement now I greet;
It is practice that makes the man complete."
This said the dame with a sullen smile,
And a gloom upon her brow the while;   375
For she soon perceived by dint of lore,
That the seven weird sisters stood her before,
Who had dwelt in enchanted bower sublime,
From the ages of an early time,
Condemn'd for an unhallow'd love   380
Endless virginity to prove,
And endless longings for bliss to be,
In their palace of painful luxury,
Unless a mortal knight should fall
In their love-snares, and wed them all.   385
And for all this numerous comely birth,
She knew that her son was lost to earth,
And perchance would be caught in enchantment's thrall,
And lost to heaven—the worst of all.
"My son," she said, "since so it be   390
That all this comely progeny
Are here acknowledged to be thine,
Before they can be received as mine,
I have lock'd the doors, the gates, and all,
And here within this stately hall   395
They shall kneel before a sacred sign,
And be christen'd by a name divine."
Then a shriek arose from the lovely train,
Was never heard such a yell of pain,
Till the gorgeous cieling that glow'd o'erhead   400
Was shiver'd like an autumn reed,
And the images all prostrate lay,
And the casements of the tower gave way,
And the lovely train, all three by three,
Walk'd forth in beauty and in glee;   405
While many a glance they cast behind,
As they trode the billows of the wind;
For they danced as lightly through the air
As if heaved on the gilded gossamer,
That play'd, with a soft and silent motion,   410
Like the gentlest swell that woos the ocean;

And many an eye beheld them fly,
And heard this plaintive melody:

"Now we are free, now we are free,
We seven sisters now are free,   415
To fly where we long have wish'd to be;
And here we leave these babies of ours,
To dwell within our shady bowers,
And play their pranks in the moonlight dell,
With the human beings they love so well;   420
For O, they are babies of marvellous birth,
They are neither of heaven nor yet of earth;
And whether they will live till time be done,
Or fade away in a beam of the sun,
Or mount on the polar heights sublime,   425
And to worlds of unknown splendour climb,
Is a mystery which no eye can pierce
But His, the Lord of the universe:
But this we know, that above or below,
By the doors of death they shall never go.   430
    "Adieu, our sweet little babies, for ever!
Blithe be your lives, and sinful never;
You may play your pranks on the wicked and wild,
But wrong not virtue's sacred child,—
So shall your frolics be lightsome and boon   435
On the bridge of the rainbow or beam of the moon;
And so shall your loves in the bridal bowers
Be sweeter still than your father's and ours,
And the breezes shall rock you to soft repose
In the lap of the lily or breast of the rose,   440
And your beauty every eve renew
As you bathe your forms in the fragrant dew,
That stands a heavenly crystal bell
In the little dew-cup's lovely well;
Your drink be the haze on the moonlight rill,   445
And your food the odour which flowers distil,
And never let robes your forms adorn
That are not from the web of the rainbow shorn,
Or the purple and green that shines afar
In the breast of the eastern harvest star;   450
And then shall you ride o'er land and o'er tide,

O'er cloud, and o'er foam of the firmament wide,
O'er tree and o'er torrent, o'er flood and o'er flame,
And THE FAIRIES shall be your earthly name:
In joy and in glee your revels shall be,   455
Till a day shall arrive that we darkly foresee;
But note you well when these times commence,
And prepare for your departure hence.
   "When the psalms and the prayers are nightly heard
From the mossy cave or the lonely sward;   460
When the hunters of men rise with the sun,
And pursue their game till the day be done;
And the mountain burns have a purple stain
With the blood of men in the moorland slain;
And the raven croaks in the darksome cloud,   465
And the eagle yells in the heavens aloud,
We you command, with heart and hand,
To leave the links of fair Scotland.
Away! dismiss! and seek for bliss
In a happier, holier sphere than this!   470
   "Sweet babies, adieu! and may you never rue
The mingled existence we leave to you.
There is part of virtue and part of blame,
Part of spirit and part of flame,
Part of body and passion fell,   475
Part of heaven and part of hell.
You are babies of beauty and babies of wonder,
But fly from the cloud of the lightning and thunder,
And keep by the moonbeam or twilight grey,
For you never were made for the light of day.   480
Long may you amid your offspring dwell,—
Babies of beauty, kiss and farewell!"

   The Knight of Dumblane from that day forth
Never utter'd word upon the earth;
But moved about like a spirit in pain   485
For certain days, then vanish'd again,
And was chosen, as my old legend says,
The patriarch King of the Scottish Fays,
With full command o'er these beings strange;
But his human nature never would change,   490

Till, at the end of a thousand moons,
All deck'd with garlands and gay festoons,
He was borne away with lament and yell,
And paid as kane to the Prince of Hell!

   From such unhallow'd love as this,   495
With all its splendour and all its bliss,
Its end of terror and its bane,
The Lord preserve us all!—Amen.

ALTRIVE LAKE
July 10, 1830

A Highland Eclogue

By the Ettrick Shepherd

At the dawning of morn, on a sweet summer-day,
Young Mary of Moy went out to pray,—
To pray, as her guileless heart befitted,
For the pardon of sins that were never committed;
A grateful homage to render Heaven   5
For all its gifts and favours given,—
For a heart that dreaded the paths of sin;
For a soul of life and light within;
And a form, withal, so passing fair
That the rays of love seem'd centering there.   10

Mary felt that her eye was beaming bright,
For her bosom glow'd with a pure delight:
As over the green-wood sward she bounded,
A halo of sweets her form surrounded;
For the breezes that kiss'd her cheek grew rare,   15
Her breathing perfumed the morning air;
And scarce did her foot, as she onward flew,
From the fringe of the daisy wring out the dew.

She went to her bower, by the water-side,
Which the woodbine and wild-rose canopied: 20
And she kneeled beneath its fragrant bough,
And waved her locks back from her brow;
But just as she lifted her eye so meek,
A hand from behind her touch'd her cheek:
She turn'd her around with a visage pale,   25
And there stood Allan of Borlan-dale!

ALLAN

Sweet Mary of Moy, is it so with thee?
Have I caught thee on thy bended knee,
Beginning thy rath orisons here,
In the bower to the breathings of love so dear?   30
Oh tell me, Mary, what this can mean!
Hast thou such a great transgressor been?

Is the loveliest model of mortal kind
A thing of an erring, tainted mind,
That thus she must kneel and heave the sigh, 35
With the tear-drop dimming her azure eye?
To whom wert thou going thy vows to pay?
Or for what, or for whom, wert thou going to pray?

MARY

I was going to pray in the name divine
Of Him that died for me and for mine; 40
I was going to pray for them and me,
And haply, Allan, for thine and thee.
And now I have answer'd as well as I may
Your questions thus put in so strange a way:
But I deem it behaviour most unmeet, 45
Thus to follow a maid to her lone retreat,
To hear her her heart of its sins unload,
And all the secrets 'twixt her and her God.
For shame, that my kindred should hear such a tale
Of the gallant young Allan of Borlan-dale! 50

ALLAN

Sweet Mary of Moy, I must be plain:
I have told you once and tell you again,
Though in love I am deeper than woman can be,
You must either part with your faith or me.

MARY

What! part with my faith? You may as well demand 55
That I should part with my own right hand!
Than part with that faith I would sooner incline
To part with my heart from its mortal shrine.

ALLAN

Ah! Mary! dear Mary! how can you thus frown,
And propose to part with what's not your own? 60
For that heart now is mine; and you must, my sweet dove,
Renounce that same faith on the altar of Love.

Then Mary's sweet voice took its sharpest key,
And rose somewhat higher than maiden's should be;
But ere the vehement sentence was said, 65

A gentle hand on her lips was laid,
And a voice to her that was ever dear,
Thus whisper'd softly in her ear:—

LADY OF MOY
Hush, Mary! dear Mary! what madness is this?
These dreams of the morning, my darling, dismiss: 70
Awake from this torpor of slumber so deep;
You are raving and clamouring through your sleep:
Up, up, and array you in scarlet and blue;
For Allan of Dale is come here to woo.

MARY
Tell Allan of Dale straight home to hie,   75
And court Helen Kay, or his darling of Sky:
This positive message deliver from me,
For I list not his heretic face to see.

LADY
My Mary! dear Mary! what am I to deem?
Arouse you, my love; you are still in your dream: 80
Your lover's views of things divine
May differ in some degree from thine;
But I think he is one who will not pother
Betwixt the one faith and the other.

MARY
That is worse and worse; for my lover must be   85
Attach'd to my faith as well as to me:
We must kneel at one beloved shrine,
And the mode of his worship must be mine.
For why should a wedded pair devout,
By different paths seek heaven out?   90
Or in that dwelling happy be,
Who of the road could never agree?
O mother! this day, without all fail,
I had given my hand to young Borlan-dale;
But I've had such a hint from the throne on high,   95
Or some good angel hovering nigh,
That tongue of mortal should never prevail
On me to be bride to this Allan of Dale,

Unless he sign over a bond, for me
In the path of religion his guide to be.   100

Young Allan to all his companions was known
As a sceptic of bold and most dissolute tone,
Who jeer'd at the cross, at the altar, and priest,
And made our most holy communions his jest;
Yet Mary of this had of knowledge no gleam,   105
Till warn'd of her danger that morn in her dream.
He loved his Mary for lands and for gold,
For beauty of feature and beauty of mould,
As well as a cold-hearted sceptic could love
Who held no belief in the blessings above;   110
And whene'er of his faith or his soul she spoke,
He answer'd her always with jeer and with joke.

The frowns of the maiden, and sighs of the lover,
With poutings and nay-says, were all gotten over;
And nothing remain'd but the schedule-deed gerent,   115
The bonds and the forms of the final agreement,—
A thing called a contract, that long-galling fetter!
Which parents love dearly, and lawyers love better.
In this was set down, at the maiden's inditement,
One part, to devotion a powerful incitement,   120
That her lover should forfeit, without diminution,
Her fortune redoubled, (a sore retribution!)
If ever his words or his actions should jostle
With the creed she revered, of the holy apostle.
The terms were severe, but resource there was none;   125
So he sign'd, seal'd, and swore, and the bridal went on.

Well was it for Mary! for scarce were got over
The honey-moon joys, ere her profligate lover
Began his old jibes, when in frolicksome mood,
At all that the Christian holds sacred and good;   130
But still, lest the terms might be proven in law,
The bond and the forfeiture kept him in awe;
Which caused him to ponder and often think of it,—
This thing that he jeer'd at, and where lay the profit?
Till at last, though by men it will scarce be believed,   135
A year had not pass'd, ere he daily perceived
The truths of the Gospel rise bright and more bright,

Like the dawning of day o'er the darkness of night,
Or the sun of eternity rising to save
From the thraldom of death, and the gloom of the grave. 140

Then Mary's fond heart was with gratitude moved
To her God, for the peace of the man that she loved;
And her mild face would glow with the radiance of beauty,
As he urged her along on her Christian duty;
For, of the two, his soul throughout   145
Grew the most sincere and the most devout.

Then their life pass'd on like an autumn day,
That rises with red portentous ray,
Threatening its pathway to deform
With the wasting flood and the rolling storm;   150
But, long ere the arch of the day is won,
A halo of promise is round the sun,
And the settled sky, though all serene,
Is ray'd with the dark and the bright between;
With the ruddy glow and the streamer wan,   155
Like the evil and good in the life of man;
And, at last, when it sinks on the cradle of day,
More holy and mild is its sapphire ray.
O why should blind mortals e'er turn into mirth
The strange intercourse betwixt heaven and earth,   160
Or deem that their Maker cannot impart,
By a thousand ways, to the human heart,
In shadows portentous of what is to be,
His warnings, His will, and His final decree?

This tale is a fact—I pledge for't in token,   165
The troth of a poet, which may not be broken;
And, had it not been for this dream of the morn,
This vision of prayer, intrusion, and scorn,
Which Heaven at the last hour thus deign'd to deliver,
The peace of the twain had been ruin'd for ever.   170

MOUNT BENGER
July 6, 1829

Will and Sandy

A Scots Pastoral
By the Ettrick Shepherd

It happened once upon a day
In the most pleasant month of May
Upon a year foretold langsyne
The Eighteen Hundred Twenty Nine
Of which enlightened martyrs said   5
'Twould see the dire foundation laid
In kingdom or in isle adjacent
Of Scotland's ruin and debasement
Alak for my old native land
Of the bold heart and ready hand   10
Of the wild mountain, moor, and braken
I hope these prophets were mistaken
    Man cannot tell—chance as it may—
A simple tale I only say
Of two young blithesome shepherd blades   15
With their good collies and grey plaids
Who chanced to meet near fall of night
Upon Mount-Benger's lofty height
The sun lay swathed in vapours pale
Beyond the moors of Meggat-dale   20
And the mild gloaming's lovely hue
Her shades of purple and of blue
And radiance of her cherub breast
From golden window of the west
Told to the shepherd's practiced eye   25
That they were harbingers of joy
Angels of love sent forth to borrow
For him a goodly day to morrow
    It was a scene that even the hind
Could not survey with careless mind   30
Although accustomed well to see
Nature in mountain majesty
For every ray the welkin threw
Slept on St. Mary's mirror blue
In blushing glories out of number   35

Like beauty in a mimic slumber
  The Yarrow like a baldrick bright
Upon the vale lay bathed in light
And all her burns and branching rills
Like silver serpents of the hills   40
While far around the eastern heaven
The dark blue mantle of the even
Was softly heaving up the sky
So silent and so solemnly
As if day's fading beauties bland   45
Were shaded by an angel's hand.
    One portion more of mortal prime
A splendid shred of living time
Down in the shades of death was fading
And o'er its bier the pall was spreading   50

SANDY
  Ah Will! here we can look abroad
On all the goodness of our God
We see the heavens benignant smile
On this beloved and favoured isle
Our Maker prompt the land to bless   55
And our hearts glow with thankfulness
But what avail these blessings sent
If by our rulers all misspent?
It greives me more than I can tell
To see the King we loved so well   60
And hero firm whose course sublime
Has been the marvel of our time
Betray the trust in them reposed
Abandon faith, and undisclosed,
To have their perjured measures driven   65
On in the teeth of earth and heaven
Confound them all! For I assever
They're all mansworn and d—— for ever

WILL
  Take time take time, dear neighbour Sandy
Ere with rebellion's birn I brand thee   70
There's such a thing can you not see
As fierce and fell necessity
And here I solemnly protest

I think that all's done for the best
If't will not work as hoped—What then?   75
The senate must annul't again
But glad am I as one approver
That that most sickening plea is over
For ay since I could climb a hill
We have been bothered with that bill   80
Ruin awaited the denial
'Tis fair and just to make the trial

SANDY
    Poor Will! Daft Will! think on the time
When o'er these heights and rocks sublime
Our fathers for the sacred cause   85
Of truth our liberties and laws
From wrath of popish tyrant's slaves
No shelter found but in their graves
Hunted like bandits to the last
Their forms lay bleaching in the blast   90
Till found by shepherds on the waste
With bibles in each bloody breast
And these were all were left to tell
Their names or in what cause they fell
Who thinks of that must think with pain   95
Of setting up that race again
Who, like the devil, let them get
But one small finger in the state
And soon they'll wrench a hole therein
Will let both pope and popery in   100
And the reformed religion must
Once more degraded bite the dust

WILL
The Lord forbid! As I should pray it
I dare not think it far less say it
But wiser men than you or me   105
In this expediency agree
As counterbalance to your clamours
I take the Reverend Doctor Chalmers
Whose heavenly and whose bold appeal
On my conviction placed the seal   110
Thomson and Inglis men of note

Frank Jeffery and Sir Walter Scott
The world more to their judgement looks
Than kings or queens or lords or dukes
When ruling heads like these combine   115
What's to be thought of your's or mine?

SANDY

Of Chalmers I shall say but little
He meddled with a point right kittle
And said what ill became that day
A protestant divine to say   120
The best of men decieved may be
They have been so and so was he
But he'll yet live to change his boast
And see his error to his cost
I grieve for Thomson's dereliction   125
But he's so given to contradiction
That feud and ferment to prolong
He'll take a side he knows is wrong
Jeffery's religious belief
Is something like himself—a brief   130
And though Sir Walter may be steady
He's more than half a pope already
Which I can prove a strick reallity
From something said in old Mortality
But though an angel stood on high   135
Even in yon bright and beauteous sky
And swore with right hand to the heaven
That popery's rights should back be given
I would distrust the dire award
And dread a demon's voice I heard   140

———————————

"See yon—and hold your peace for ever"
Cried startled Will with quake and quiver
And pointed to a dreadful guest
That reared his pale form in the west
Standing upon a frieze of gold   145
He filled the west with human mould
His eye scowled with the gleam of death
As if in sorrow and in wrath
His right hand like a polar ray

Was heaved above the milky way   150
The evening star kithed like a gem
In buckler of his diadem
And altogether such a lightness
Such angel features and such brightness
Never appeared on Scottish sky   155
Or startled shepherd's fearful eye
   Will saw in it the guardian sprite
Of Erin smiling with delight
But Sandy knew the visitant
For angel of the Covenant   160
Rising in wrath with lifted hand
Indignant o'er a guilty land
To swear in language motioned stronger
The Church's time should be no longer
   With beating hearts and bristling hair,   165
Our shepherds left their mountain lair;
For the last moorcock of the fell,
Had mounted from the heather bell,
With rigid wing and crow elate,
And silent sunk beside his mate.   170
Hush'd was the pipe of grey curlew,
And lonely plover's plaintive whew.
The bleating kid had sought its dam,
The ewe cowered down beside the lamb;
And bogles of the darksome cleugh,   175
Put on their robes of deadly hue
The harden'd sinner to belay,
And turn his steps another way;
An eirier scene man never saw,
From the dark cone of Benger-Law.   180
The eastern emerald glimmered high,
The polar bear had oped his eye;
While, worst and dreadfullest by far,
The giant of the western star
Frown'd in his majesty sublime,   185
O'er shadows of the western clime;
Sooth it was time, one's spirit feels,
For our two herds to take their heels!

MOUNT BENGER
May 4, 1829

The Last Stork

By the Ettrick Shepherd

"Yea, the stork in the heaven knoweth her appointed times; and the turtle
and the crane and the swallow observe the time of their coming; but my
people know not the judgment of the Lord."

JEREMIAH, viii.7.

I've heard a tale of olden time,
Of stately Stork of southern clime,
That sail'd the billowy ocean rare,
That waves above the ambient air—
That rolling sea which heaves reclined   5
Above the regions of the wind,
From which descendeth down amain
The drizzly day, the rattling rain,
The motley mists on mountain blue,
And showers of silver-sifted dew.   10
   O'er this grand ocean of the sky,
Our noble Stork had sail'd on high,
With some few hundred thousands more,
From Nile's debased and muddy shore,
And Jordan's stream, held sacred still,   15
That from the springs of Hermon hill
Descends by Mirom's reedy brake,
And lone Tiberias' sultry lake,
To glut the Dead Sea's pregnant weed—
A gorgeous range for storks indeed!   20
And where they still a welcome prove,
As blessings sent from heaven above.
   There had the guests their gathering made,
To shape the dauntless escalade
Of heaven's own arch, and there the host   25
Gather'd from all Arabia's coast;
From Ethiopia's lakes of gloom,
And jungles of the fierce Simoom:
At last, that none might lag behind,
The word was pass'd as day declined,   30

To mount upon the moaning wind.
   As ever you saw the fire-flaughts sweep
From furnace at the midnight deep,
Pouring with fierce and heavenward aim,
Like rapid shreds of living flame,   35
Till, fading in the dark alcove,
They vanish in the fields above;
So rose from Jordan's sullen tide,
And dark Tiberias' sultry side,
To navigate the cloudy spheres,   40
Thousands of milk-white mariners,
All flickering with their dappled wings,
A spiral stream of living things,
Till, far within the ether blue,
They melt in regions of the dew.   45
   Then nought is seen from earth below,
Nor heard but sounds of distant woe,
A howling, shrieking strain on high,
Alongst the stories of the sky;
As if an host of spirits bright   50
From this dire world had ta'en their flight,
Weeping with dread uncertainty,
Where their abode was thence to be,
All heighten'd by the thrilling pain,
That they might ne'er return again.   55
   It brings to mind that evening drear,
The last of Judah's hope or fear,
When Heathens raised the demon yell
Of triumph, and Jerusalem fell;
When the devouring brand of Rome   60
Uplighted Zion's sacred dome,
And told unto the remnant small
Of God's own people, that their thrall
Was then begun that end should never,
Forsaken by their God for ever.   65
Their temple in one smouldering flame,
What more on earth remain'd for them!
Then rush'd the young and old on death,
Sinking beneath the foemen's wrath,
Till even Havock's bloodshot eye   70
Turn'd from the carnage scared and dry;
And Avarice spared the wailing few,

Which Pity had refused to do.
   What thousands of excluded souls
Would leave that night their earthly goals,   75
Mounting the air like flickering flame,
With rapid but unguided aim,
Guided, though all to them unknown,
The path unto the judgment throne!
Think of the air crowded to be   80
With beings of Eternity,
All fearing, hoping, trembling, crying,
Romans and Jews together flying;
How would they feel their race now run,
Of all that they had lost or won,   85
Of old heart-burnings and of strife,
And all their daring deeds of life!
Alas! would every warrior famed,
Or council where a war is framed,
But think of this as madness past,   90
And to what all must come at last,
And then remember seriously
That there's a reckoning still to be!
   But simile now aside I lay,
For similes lead me still astray,   95
And to our migrant hordes repair.
High o'er the columns of the air,
Like fleets of angels on they steer,
With check, with challenge, and with cheer.
The light foam that we see besprent   100
On surface of the firmament,
Yielded before the downy prow
And silken sails of wavy snow,
And a long path of changing hue
Laid open vales of deeper blue,   105
While shepherd of the Alpine reign,
Of Kryman and the Apennine,
Is startled by the wailing cry
Within the bosom of the sky,
That dies upon the northern wind,   110
And gathers, gathers still behind;
In vain he strains his aching sight,
It strays bewilder'd, lost in light,
While, all alongst the empyrean cone,

Thousands of voices, sounding on,   115
Strike the poor hind with terror dumb!—
He deems man's sins have reach'd their sum,
And his last day on earth is come.
      One resting-place, and one alone,
To mankind ever has been known,   120
A little lake on Alpine fell,
Where Zurich meets with Appenzell;
And such a scene as their descent
From out the glowing firmament,
While skies around with echoes rung,   125
No bard hath ever seen or sung;
They come with wild and waving wheel,
Or mazes of the maddening reel,
Pouring like snowballs in a stream,
Or dancing in the solar beam,   130
With shouts all shouts of joy excelling,
Till even the frigid Alps are yelling.
Such scenes were *once* on Scottish plain,
But there shall ne'er be seen again!
      On Scottish plain! who this may trow?   135
What means our bard? he's raving now;
For save the fieldfare's countless band,
Or snowflakes of the northern land,
Of migrant myriads there are none,
And trivial such comparison,   140
With this great southern inundation,—
I hate so groundless an illation.
      Stop, countryman, for I allude
To a more grand similitude.
'Tis known to you, or, if 'tis not,   145
'Tis pity that it were forgot,
That our own grandsires oft have seen,
As daylight faded on the green,
And moonlight with its hues was blending,
The fairy bridallers descending   150
Straight from the moon like living stream
On ladder of her golden beam,
All pure as dewdrops of the even,
And countless as the stars of heaven;
Their tiny faces glowing bright   155
With flashes of a wild delight,

Their little songs of fairy love,
Like music of the spheres above;
And every saraband and ring
As swift as fire-flies on the wing.   160
That was a scene the soul to glad!
Deem not my simile so bad.
    Well, here within that Alpine lake,
Our blithe aërial sailors take
Their pastime with abundant joy,   165
Yet lost no moment of employ;
Tribe after tribe apart was set,
To stock each marsh and minaret,
From Zealand's swamps which oceans lave,
To Wolga's wastes and Dwina's wave,   170
While a small portion, deem'd the best,
Their potent leader thus address'd:
    "Friends, countrymen, and kinsmen mine,
Most noble Storks of sacred line,
It grieves me much that we have lost   175
Our empire upon Britain's coast,
For nought can happen but mischance,
Without our blessed countenance;
And since the day that we forsook her,
Such dire mischances have o'ertook her,   180
By means of blundering, blustering schemers,
Bald turncoats, trimmers, and blasphemers,
That now she stands o'erwhelm'd with horror,
And trembles at the gulf before her;
To ruin's brink driven on by foes,   185
One other push, and down she goes.
Haste, then, her drooping heart to cherish,
I list not church and state should perish.
One single hint of your descent
May total ruin yet prevent."   190
    "Alas! my liege! whate'er betide,"
A stately noble Stork replied,
"There I shall never go for one,
They are all poachers to a man.
Herons, bog-bumpers, and such game,   195
Are prizes rich enough for them;
For they must shoot at every thing,
Be't duke or teal, or kirk or king;

And not one blessed Stork would be
Alive within two days or three.   200
   "The very last time I was there,
Had I not mounted in the air
Above the clouds, and cross'd the main,
I ne'er had seen your grace again.
Two goodly relatives of mine,   205
Brave noble Storks of royal line,
As a secure and shelter'd rest,
On Wharn-cliff built their airy nest;
The squire shot both that night they came,
And sold them at the mart for game   210
At double price of crane or goose,
Swearing they were white heronsheughs.
People that cannot keep unriven
A sacred garb that's to them given,
Deserve no countenance nor grace   215
From canonized and sacred race.
On Sidmouth cliff or Eldon hill
A bird of heaven might venture still,
Or even on Winshiel's lofty bower,
Or dark Newcastle's smoky tower;   220
But even these the spoilers eye—
Leave Britain to her destiny!"
   But one bold Stork, and one alone,
Straight to the British shores has flown,
And the first day he settled there,   225
As roosting on a palace fair,
Rolling his red eye in the ring,
A sporting Bishop broke his wing,
And bore him home, with smiles of joy,
To his beloved cadaverous boy.   230
That Stork's last speech and dying words
Are all that now my tale affords.
   "Woe to this land, so long beloved,
So long by earth and heaven approved,
But favour'd and preserved in vain   235
In bulwark of her rolling main!
For all her precious blessings sent
Are wholly by the roots uprent.
That sin can never be forgiven,
Committed 'gainst the light of Heaven,   240

The spirit's warnings, and the din
Of the small voice that cries within.
    "Instead of birds that wing the sky,
Of bold and independent eye,
Nought can her wisdom cherish now   245
But gull, and grebe, and heronsheugh;
These slabberers, whom God disapproves,
That watch for fishes and for loaves;
Who, for fat puddock, or such thing,
Would pluck the royal eagle's wing,   250
And on a view, however sinister,
Would sell the kirk and hang the minister.
    "Out on them all! I here disburse
To every class my latest curse!
Since they have sacrificed the last   255
Best blessing to their lot was cast;
Meet they should grovel in the mire,
Till quench'd be all their ancient fire!
The last bird of the heavenly race
Here falls, and leaves his vacant place,   260
Which base venality surrounds,
A prey to harpies and to hounds.
    "Farewell, ye vales of Palestine,
Which I shall ne'er behold again;
Ye piles and altars clothed in dust,   265
Wherein I placed my early trust,
And which, with death before my sight,
My spirit turns to with delight!
    "Farewell, ye clouds, which oft I've rent,
Ye foldings of the firmament,   270
Where oft I've view'd the treasures dire
Of hail, of thunder, and of fire,
With reeling shades of hideous form,
The first gyrations of the storm.
    "Farewell, ye wreathes so downy bright,   275
Ye windows of empyreal light,
Through which I've view'd the rolling world
With all her winding dells unfurl'd,
When snowy Alps and streams were seen,
All else appear'd one level green,   280
While glassy lakes would intervene
As mirrors of the heavenly reign,

In which I saw inverted lie
The marbled clouds that clothed the sky,
And dark blue windows, deeply sleeping,   285
Through which a thousand Storks were peeping.
   "Farewell, ye Stars, whose tiny brightness
I've often fann'd with wing of lightness,
Brushing with snowy down the damps
Away from off your gilded lamps,   290
Then with joint shout of thousand yellings,
Which sounded through your sapphire dwellings,
With boom that made you stop your ears,
And shoot like rockets from your spheres,
Frightening almost to parting breath   295
The children of this world beneath;
This last farewell with grief I render;—
One bird of heaven foregoes your splendour!
   "Farewell, thou Moon, whose silver light
Gilds the dim alcove of the night,   300
And when thy lord to rest has gone,
With modest mien ascend'st his throne,
Dispensing far, as queen beseems,
The bounty of thy borrow'd beams!
Beloved moon, there is a bound   305
Of holiness breathes thee around,
A majesty of virgin prime,
A stillness beauteous and sublime,
That, oh! it grieves thy servant's core
That he shall ne'er behold thee more,   310
Nor pilot to his tribe the way
Through regions of thy modest ray!
   "Imperial Sun, so gorgeous bright,
Great source of glory, life, and light,
The Stork's own deity alone,   315
He worships thee—beside thee, none,
For thou endow'st him with the sense
To seek thy milder influence,
Whether in Europe's shadowy woods
Or regions of the tropic floods;   320
Farewell for ever, king of heaven,
Be all my trespasses forgiven!
And now on Britain's sordid line
I leave my curse, but crave not thine.

Forgive them all save the state botchers,   325
Those piteous pedagogues and poachers,
Praters oppress'd with proud proficiency,
Sapience supreme, and self-sufficiency;
Degrading with their yelping bills,
The shepherds on a thousand hills.   330
O blessed Sun, to man in kindness,
Visit them with Assyrian blindness,
That they may grope about for foe,
To tell them whither they should go.
That curse falls on myself—I bow   335
To thee, to death, and darkness now,
And yield my spirit to the giver.—
Thou beauteous world, adieu for ever!"
    Then the fair journeyer of the sky
Crook'd his fair neck, and closed his eye,   340
Stretch'd out his wing with rigid shiver,
His noble heart gave its last quiver;
And the last guest of heaven is gone
That e'er sought grace in Albion.
Woe to the hands so ill directed,   345
That should have such a life protected;
But that dire day of sin and shame,
Of bare-faced brazenness and blame,
When Heaven's vicegerents were forsworn,
The child shall rue that is unborn.   350

MOUNT BENGER
Jan. 21, 1830

Superstition and Grace

An Unearthly Ballad
By the Ettrick Shepherd

There was an auld carle won'd under yon shaw,
His cheek was the clay, and his hair was the snaw;
His brow was as glazed as a winter night,
But mingled with lines of immortal light;
And forth from his livid lips there flew   5
A flame of a lurid murky hue.
But there was a mystery him within
That roused up the twangs and terrors of sin;
And there was a gleide in that auld carle's ee,
That the saint and the sinner baith trembled to see.   10

But, oh! when the moor gat her coverlet gray,
When the gloaming had flaughted the night and the day,
When the craws had flown to the greenwood shaw,
And the kid blett over the Lammer law;
When the dew had laid the valley asteep,   15
And the gowan had fauldit her buds to sleep;
When naething was heard but the merlin's maen,
Oh then that gyre carle was never his lane.
A bonny wee baby sae meek and mild,
Then walked with him in the dowy wild;   20
But, oh! nae pen that ever grew
Could describe that baby's heavenly hue:
Yet all the barmings of sturt and strife,
And weary wailings of morteel life,
Would soon have been hushed to endless peace   25
At ae blink of that baby's face.

Her brow sae fair and her ee sae meek,
And the pale rose-bloom upon her cheek;
Her locks, and the bend of her sweet ee-bree,
And her smile might have wakened the dead to see.   30
Her snood befringed wi' many a gem
Was stown frae the rainbow's brighest hem;
And her rail, mair white than the snowy drift,

Was never woven aneath the lift;
It threw sic a light on the hill and the gair   35
That it showed the wild deer to her lair;
And the brown bird of the moorland fell
Upraised his head from the heather bell,
For he thought that his dawning of love and mirth,
Instead of the heaven was springing from earth;   40
And the fairies waken'd frae their beds of dew,
And they sang a hymn, and that hymn was new.
Oh! Ladies list—for never again
Shalt thou hear sic a wild unearthly strain.
For they sang the night-breeze in a swoon,   45
And they sang the goud locks frae the moon:
They sang the redbreast frae the wood,
And the laverock out o' the marled cloud;
The capperkyle frae the bosky brae,
And the seraphs down frae the milky way;   50
And some wee feres of bloodless birth
Came out o' the worm-holes o' the earth,
And swoof'd sae lightly round the lea,
That they wadna kythe to mortal ee;
While the eldrich sang it rase sae shrill   55
That the waesome tod yooled on the hill:
Oh! Ladies list—for the choral band
Thus hymned the song of the Fairy-land.

Song of the Fairies

Sing! sing! How shall we sing
Round the babe of the Spirits' King?   60
How shall we sing our last adieu,
Baby of life when we sing to you?
Now the little night-burdie may cheip i' the wa',
The plover may whew and the cock may craw;
For the bairny's sleep is sweet and sure,   65
And the maiden's rest is blest and pure,
Through all the links of the Lammer-muir:
Sin our bonny baby was sent frae heaven,
She comes o'ernight with the dew of even;
And when the day-sky buds frae the main,   70
She swaws wi' the dew to heaven again;
But the light shall dawn, and the howlet flee,
The dead shall quake, when the day shall be,

That she shall smile in the gladsome noon,
And sleep and sleep in the light of the moon.   75
Then shall our hallelues wake anew,
With harp and viol and ayril true.
     But well-a-day!
     How shall we say
Our earthly adieu ere we pass away?   80
How shall we hallow this last adieu,
Baby of life when we sing to you?
     Ring! ring!
     Dance and sing,
And on the green broom your garlands hing;   85
Hallow the hopes of this ray of grace,
For sweet is the smile of our baby's face;
And every ghaist of gysand hew
Has melted away in the breeze she drew;
The kelpie may dern in dread and dool,   90
Deep in the howe of his eiry pool;
Gil-moules frae hind the hallan may flee,
Through by the threshold, and through by the key,
And the mermaid moote in the safron sea:
But we are left in the greenwood glen,   95
Because we love the children of men,
Sweetly to sing, and never to rue,
Till now that we hymn our last adieu;
Baby of life we sing it to you!
     Sing! sing!   100
     How shall we sing
Round the babe of the Spirits' King?
Hither the breezes of elfland bring,
Then fairies away—away on the wing!
We now maun flit to a land of bliss,   105
To a land of holy silentness;
To a land where the night-wind never blew,
But thy fair spring shall ever be new;
When the moon shall wake nae mair to wane,
And the cloud and the rainbow baith are gane,   110
In bowers aboon the break o' the day,
We'll sing to our baby for ever and ay.

Then the carle beheld them swoof alang,
And heard the words of their fareweel sang.

They seem'd to ling asklent the wind,   115
And left a pathway of light behind;
But he heard them singing as they flew,
'Baby of life, adieu! adieu!
Baby of grace we sing to you!'

Then the carle he kneeled to that seraph young,   120
And named her with a tremulous tongue;
And the light of God shone on his face
As he looked to Heaven and named her GRACE;
And he barred the day of sorrow and pain
Ever to thrall the world again: 125
Then he clasped his hands and wept full sore,
When he bade her adieu for evermore.

Oh! never was baby's smile so meek
When she felt the tear drop on her cheek;
And never was baby's look so wae   130
When she saw the stern auld carle gae;
But a' his eeless and elfin train,
And a' his ghaists and gyes were gane:
The gleids that gleamed in the darksome shaw,
And his fairies had flown the last of a'.   135
Then the poor auld carle was blithe to flee
Away frae the queen isle of the sea,
And never mair seeks the walks of men,
Unless in the disk of the gloaming glen.*

MOUNT BENGER
May 7th, 1828

* An edition of this ballad was published long ago by some other
name. It is now so entirely altered that only a few lines of the
original remain.

                                                         J.H.

The Witch of the Gray Thorn

By James Hogg the Ettrick Shepherd

"Thou old wrinkled beldam, thou crone of the night,
Come read me my vision and read it aright;
For 'tis said thou hast insight the future to scan
Far onward beyond the existence of man,
And hid'st thee for ever from eye of the day,   5
But rid'st on the night wind, away and away
Over cloud, over valley, on hemlock or reed,
To burrow in churchyards and harrass the dead.
Old beldam declare thee, and give me to wis
If I stand at the side of such being as this?"   10
    "Proud priest of Inchaffery I know thee too well,
Though thus in disguise thou hast come to my cell:
What is it to thee if through darkness I fly,
Like bird to carreer round the skirts of the sky,
Or sail o'er the seas in my shallop of shell   15
To do what the tongue of flesh dares not to tell?
Suffice it, I know what thy vision hath been,
Ere a word I have heard or a sign I have seen;
Besides its high import distinctly I see;
And, priest of Inchaffery, I'll tell it to thee,   20
Not for love or reward, but it troubles me sore
To have one in my presence I scorn and abhor.
    Thou did'st dream of a coronet blazing with gold,
That was hailed by the young and admired by the old;
And thou had'st a longing the thing to obtain,   25
But all thy bold efforts to reach it were vain;
When lo! thine own mitre arose from thy crown,
And mounted aloft whil'st the other sank down;
It mounted and rose in a circle of flame,
'Mid clamours of wonder and shouts of acclaim;   30
The crown into darkness descended apace,
And thine was exalted on high in its place.
Thou saw'st till the red blood ran down in a stream,
Then awakened'st in terror, and all was a dream!
Priest that was thy dream—And thou must—'Tis decreed—   35
Put down the Archbishop, and rise in his stead."

"Thou lie'st thou old hag. With the cunning of hell
Thou lurest me to practice what thou dost foretell;
But there both thy master and thee I'll defy:
Yet that was my vision, I may not deny. 40
Mysterious being, unblest and unshriven!
Pray had'st thou that secret from hell or from heaven?"
    "I had it proud priest from a fountain sublime,
That wells beyond nature, and streams beyond time;
And though from the same source thy warning might come, 45
Yet mine was the essence and thine but the scum.
I heard and I saw what if thou had'st but seen,
A terror thy mortal existence had been,
For thou had'st grown rigid as statue of lead,
A beacon of terror for sinners to dread! 50
Thou think'st thou hast learning, and knowledge inborn,
Proud priest of Inchaffery I laugh them to scorn!
Thou know'st less of nature where spirits roam free,
Than a mole does of heav'n, or a worm does of thee.
    Begone with thy gold, thy ambition, and pride. 55
I have told thee thy vision, and solved it beside.
But dare not to doubt the event I foretel,
The thing is decreed both in heaven and hell
That thou—an arch traitor—must do a good deed,
Put down the Archbishop, and rise in his stead." 60
    Away went the abbot with crosier and cowl,
And visions of grandeur disturbing his soul,
And as he rode on to himself thus he said.
"The counsels of heaven must all be obeyed;
Nor throne, church, nor state can security have, 65
Till that haughty prelate be laid in his grave.
Let that nerve my arm and my warrantise be."
Well said thou good abbot of Inchafferye!
    The Archbishop had plotted too deep in the state;
The nobles were moved 'gainst the man of their hate; 70
The monarch was roused, and pronounced in his wrath
A sentence unseemly, the Archbishop's death!
But that very night that his doom was decreed,
A private assassin accomplished the deed.
The court was amazed—for loud whisperings came 75
Of a deed too unhallowed and horrid to name,
Abroad rushed the rumour, and would not be stem'd;
The murderer is captured, convicted, condemn'd;

Condemn'd to be hung like a dog on a tree.
Who is the assassin?—Pray who may it be?   80
Ha! The worthy good abbot of Inchafferye!
   In darkness and chains the poor abbot is laid,
And soon his death-warrant is to him conveyed;
His hour is announced, but he laughs it to scorn,
And sends an express for the Witch of Gray-Thorn.   85
She came at his call, and though hideous her form
And shrivelled, and crouched, like a crone in a storm,
Yet in her dim eye that was hollowed by time
The joy of a demon was gleaming sublime,
And with a weak laugh 'twixt a scream and a hiss,   90
She cried "Pray great abbot is all come to this?"
   "Where now thy bright omens thou hag of the night?
Come read me this riddle, and read it aright,
So far thou said'st truth—the Archbishop is dead;
Thy bodement confirm—Shall I rise in his stead?"   95
   "Yes, up to the gallows," the beldam replied;
"This day the archbishop had suffered and died;
But headlong on death I have caused thee to run.
Ha-ha! I have conquered, and thou art undone!"
   "Oh had I the hands which these fetters degrade,   100
To sear out thy tongue for the lies it hath made,
I would rend out thy heart with black falsehood so cramm'd
And consign thy old soul, to eternity, damn'd.
May heaven's dread vengeance depart from thee never,
But descend and enthrall thee for ever and ever!"   105
   "Aye curse thou away, to the theme I agree,
Thy curse is worth ten thousand blessings to me.
Ha-ha thou proud priest, I have won! I have won!
Thy course of ambition and cruelty's run.
Thou tortured'st me once, till my nerves were all torn,   110
For crimes I was free of as babe newly born;
'Twas that which compelled me, in hour of despair,
To sell soul and body to the prince of the air,
That great dreadful spirit of power and of pride,
His servant I am, and thy curse I deride.   115
For vengeance I did it, for vengeance alone;
Without that, futurity lurements had none.
I have now had full measure in sight of the sun,
Ha-ha! thou proud priest! I have won! I have won!
   'Tis not thy poor life that my vengeance can tame,   120

It flies to the future, to regions of flame,
To witness exulting th'extreme of thy doom,
And harass thy being 'mid terror and gloom.
Aye, grind thou thy fetters, and fume as thou wilt,
O how I rejoice in thy rage and thy guilt!   125
And more. I have promise may well strike thee dumb,
To be nurse to thy spirit for ages to come;
Think how thou wilt joy that the task shall be mine
To wreck and to tan thee with tortures condign,
O'er cataracts of sulphur, and torrents of flame,   130
And horrors that have not exposure nor name.
Until this vile world of lust and of crime
Have sounded through fire the last trumpet of Time,
Adieu bloody priest, in thy hour of despair,
When thy soul is forthcoming there's *one* shall be there."   135
    The abbot was borne to the scaffold away,
He stretched out his hands and attempted to pray,
But at that dire moment there sounded a knell
Close to his stun'd ear 'twixt a laugh and a yell,
And a voice said aloud that seem'd creaking with hate.   140
"Ha-ha! thou proud priest, it's too late! it's too late!"
He shivered, he shrunk, drop'd the sign, and was hung;
He gasp'd, and he died, and that moment there rung
This sound through the welkin so darksome and dun.
"I have thee! I have thee! I've won! I have won!"   145

ALTRIVE LAKE
March 11th, 1825

A Greek Pastoral

By the Ettrick Shepherd

Where proud Olympus rears his head
As white as the pall of the sheeted dead
And mingling with the clouds that sail
On heaven's pure bosom softly pale
Till men believe that the hoary cloud   5
Is part of the mountain's mighty shroud
While far below in lovely guise
The enchanted vale of Tempe lies
There sat a virgin of peerless fame
Thessallia's sweetest comeliest dame   10
Gazing upon the silver stream
As if in a rapt Elysian dream.
Far far below her glowing eye
Standing on an inverted sky
Where clouds and mountains seem'd to swingle   15
And Ossa with Olympus mingle
She saw a youth of manly hue
In robes of green and azure blue
Of grape of orange and of rose
And every dye the rainbow knows   20
The nodding plumes his temples graced
His sword was girded to his waist
And much that maiden's wonder grew
At a vision so comely and so new
And in her simplicity of heart   25
She ween'd it all the enchanter's art
   As straining her eyes adown the steep
At this loved phantom of the deep
She conjured him to ascend and bless
With look of love his shepherdess   30
And when she beheld him mount the tide
With eagle eye and stately stride
She spread her arms and her bavaroy
And screamed with terror and with joy
   The comely shade approaching still   35
To the surface of the silent rill

Beckoned the maid with courteous grace
And looked her fondly in the face
Till even that look she could not bear
It was so witching and so dear.   40
She turned her eyes back from the flood
And there a Scottish warrior stood
Of noble rank and noble mein
And glittering in his tartans sheen
     She neither fainted screamed nor fled   45
But there she sat astonished
Her eyes o'er his form and features ran
She turn'd to the shadow then the man
Till at last she fixed a look serene
Upon the stranger's manly mein   50
Her ruby lips fell wide apart
High beat her young and guileless heart
Which of itself revealed the tale
By the quiverings of its snowy veil
A living statue feminine   55
A model cast in mould divine
There she reclined enchanted so
She moved not finger eye nor toe
For fear one motion might dispel
The great enchanter's thrilling spell   60
     "Tis all enchantment! Such a grace
Ne'er rayed a human virgin's face!
Tis all enchantment rock and river
May the illusion last for ever!"
Exclaimed the youth "O maiden dear   65
Are such enchantments frequent here?"
     "Yes, very!" said this mould of love
But hand or eye she did not move
         But whispering said
         As if afraid   70
Her breath would melt the comely shade
"Yes, very! This enchanted stream
Has visions raised in maiden's dream
Of lovers' joys, and bowers of bliss,
But never aught so sweet as this.   75
O pass not like fleeting cloud away
Last dear illusion! last for ay!
And tell me, if on earth there dwell

Men suiting woman's love so well?"

YOUTH
"I came from the isle of the evening sun   80
Where the solans roost and the wild deers run
Where the giant oaks have a gnarled form
And the hills are coped with the cloud and the storm
Where the hoar frost gleams on the vallies and brakes
And a cieling of chrystal roofs the lakes   85
And there are warriors in that land
With helm on head and sword in hand
And tens of thousands roving free
All robed and fair as him you see
    I took the field to lead my own   90
Forward to glory and renown
I learned to give the warrior word
I learned to sway the warrior's sword
Till a strange enchantment on me fell
How I came here I cannot tell   95
    There came to the field an old gray man
With a silver beard and a visage wan
And out of the lists he beckoned me
And began with a tale of mystery
Which soon despite of all controul   100
Took captive my surrendered soul
        With a powerful sway
        It rolled away
Till evening dropped her curtain gray
        And the bittern's cry   105
        Was heard on high
And the lamps of glory begemmed the sky
Yet still the amazing tale proceeded
And still I followed and still I heeded
        For darkness or light   110
        The day or the night
        The last or the first
        Or hunger or thirst
To me no motive could impart
It was only the tale that charmed my heart   115
    We posted on till the morning sun
And still the tale was never done
Faster and faster the old man went

Faster and faster I ran intent
That tale of mystery out to hear   120
Till the ocean's roll-call met my ear
For the forest was past and the shore was won
And still the tale was never done
    He took to a boat but said no word
I followed him in of my own accord   125
And spread the canvass to the wind
For I had no power to stay behind
We sailed away and we sailed away
I cannot tell how many a day
But the crimson moon did wax and wane   130
And the stars drop'd blood on the azure main
And still my soul with burning zeal
Lived on the magic of that tale
Till we came to this enchanted river
Then the old gray man was gone for ever   135
He faded like vapour before the sun
And in a moment the tale was done
        And here am I left
        Of all bereft
Except this zone of heavenly weft   140
With the flowers of Paradise inwove
The soft and silken bonds of love.
Art thou the angel of this glade
A peri or a mortal maid?"

MAIDEN
    "It is all enchantment! once on a time   145
I dwelt in a distant eastern clime
O many a thousand miles away
Where our day is night and our night is day
Where beauty of woman is no bliss
And the Tygris flows a stream like this.   150
I was a poor and fatherless child
And my dwelling was in the woodland wild
Where the elves waylaid me out and in
And my mother knew them by their din
And charmed them away from our little cot   155
For her eyes could see them but mine could not
    One summer night which I never can rue
I dreamed a dream that turned out true

I thought I strayed on enchanted ground
Where all was beauty round and round   160
The copse and the flowers were full in bloom
And the breeze was loaden with rich perfume
There I saw two golden butterflies
That shone like the sun in a thousand dyes
And the eyes on their wings that glowed amain   165
Were like the eyes on the peacock's train
     I did my best
     To steal on their rest
As they hung on the cowslip's damask breast
     But my aim they knew   170
     And shyer they grew
And away from flower to flower they flew
I ran I bounded as on wings
For my heart was set on the lovely things
And I called and conjured them to stay   175
But they led me on away, away!
Till they brought me to enchanted ground
When a drousiness my senses bound
And when I sat me down to rest
They came and they fluttered round my breast   180
And when I laid me down to sleep
They lulled me into a slumber deep
And I heard them singing my breast above
A strain that seemed a strain of love
It was sung in a shrill and soothing tone   185
By many voices joined in one

Cradle song of the Elves

  Hush thee! Rest thee harmless dove!
Child of pathos and child of love
     Thy father is laid
     In his cold death bed   190
Where waters encircle the lowly dead
     But his rest is sweet
     In his winding sheet
And his spirit lies at his saviour's feet
Then hush thee rest thee child of bliss   195
Thou flower of the eastern wilderness

Thy mother has waked in her cot of the wild
And has wailed for the loss of her only child
    But the prayer is said
    And the tear is shed   200
And her trust in her God unaltered
    But O if she knew
    Of thy guardians true
And the scenes of bliss that await for you
She would hymn her joys to the throne above   205
Hush thee rest thee child of love

Hush thee! Rest thee fatherless one!
Joy is before thee and joy alone
There is not a fay that haunts the wild
That has power to hurt the orphan child   210
    For the angels of light
    In glory bedight
Are hovering around by day and by night
    A charge being given
    To spirits of heaven   215
That the elves of malice afar be driven
Then hush thee rest thee lovely creature
Till a change is wrought in thy mortal nature

    When I awoke from this dreamless slumber
There were beings around me without number   220
They had human faces of heaven beaming
And wings upon their shoulders streaming
Their eyes had a soft unearthly flame
And their lovely locks were all the same
Their voices like those of children young   225
And their language was not said but sung
I weened myself in the home above
Among beings of happiness and love
    Then they laid me down so lightsome and boon
In a veil that was like a beam of the moon   230
Or a ray of the morning passing fair
And wove in the loom of the gossamere
And they bore me aloft over tower and tree
And over the land and over the sea
There were seven times seven on either side   235

And their dazzling robes streamed far and wide
It was such a sight as man neer saw
Which pencil of heaven alone could draw
If dipped in the morning's glorious dye
Or the gorgeous tints of the evening sky   240
Or in the bright celestial river
The fountain of light that wells for ever
   But whither they bore me and what befel
For the soul that's within me I dare not tell
No language could make you to concieve it   245
And if you did you would not believe it
But after a thousand visions past
This is my resting place at last
These flocks and fields they gave to me
And they crowned me the Queen of Thessally   250
And since that time I must confess
I've no experience had of less
Than perfectest purest happiness
And now I tremble lest love's soft spell
Should break the peace I love so well"   255

YOUTH
   "No, love is the source of all that's sweet
And only for happy beings meet
The bond of creation since time began
That brought the grace of heaven to man.
Let us bathe in its bliss without controul   260
And love with all the heart and soul
For mine are with thee and only thee
Thou Queen of the maidens of Thessally"

MAIDEN
   "If thou could'st love as a virgin can
And not as sordid selfish man   265
     If thy love for me
     From taint were as free
As the evening breeze from the Salon sea
     Or the odours hale
     Of the morning gale   270
Breathed over the flowers of Tempe's vale
And no endearment or embrace
That would raise a blush on a virgin's face

Or a saint's below or a spirit's above
Then I could love! O as I could love!" 275

YOUTH

"Thou art too gentle pure and good
For a lover of earthly flesh and blood
But I will love thee and cherish thee so
As a maiden was never loved here below
     With a heavenly aim 280
     And a holy flame
And an endearment that wants a name
I will lead thee where the breeze is lightest
And where the fountain wells the brightest
Where the nightingale laments the oftest 285
And where the beds of flowers are softest
     There in the glade
     My lovely maid
I will fold within this rainbow plaid
I will press her to my faithful breast 290
And watch her calm and peaceful rest
And o'er each aspiration dear
I will breathe a prayer to mercy's ear
And no embrace or kiss shall be
That a saint in heaven will blush to see" 295

Then the maiden sunk on his manly breast
As the tabernacle of her rest
And as there with closed eyes she lay
She almost sighed her soul away
As she gave her hand to the stranger guest 300
The comely youth of the stormy west
Thus ends my yearly offering bland
The Laureate's lay of the Fairy land*

* See Blackwood's Mag. vol IV pp 528-9

A Sunday Pastoral

By the Ettrick Shepherd

COLIN

Good morning Keatie Fie for shame
To sleep sae lang ye'er sair to blame
Then at your glass to smile an' smirk
An' be the hindmost at the kirk

KATE

Aye, 'tis o'er true—O wae's my heart   5
An' to reprove is weel your part
Your neighbours o' their faults to tell
When ye're sae early there yoursel'

COLIN

Ah cunning Kate! I ken your way
An' darena wrangle w'ye the day   10
For ye're sae tarte when ye begin
Ye lead ane into words o' sin
An' now when we hae met thegither
An' like sae weel to be wi' ither
Let's chat without a' taunts or scorning   15
O' things befitting Sabbath morning
I am o'er late an' sair to blame
But O I've sic a charge at hame

KATE

Nae doubt, nae doubt! 'Tis a' o'er true
Nae body else has aught to do   20
Ilk turn to Colin's hand maun lie
The lasses a' to court forbye

COLIN

Now Kate I canna stand sic joking
There's nought on earth is sae provoking
When weel ye ken I never parl   25
Either to kiss or court or quarrel
Or sit me down to mince or mell

Wi' ony lass except yoursel

KATE
Alas poor lad ye're sair abused then
An' fausely wickedly accused then   30
Sic tales are through the country fleeing
But then the country's ill for leeing
It was nae true that Meg M,Gill
Came greetin to you on the hill?
I heard sic story an' the cause o't.   35
It was nae true? I'm sure it was not?

COLIN
'Tis hard on twall. Good-morning Kate
I hate at preachings to be late
Besides tis sinfu' to get mad
At sic a glib-tongued wicked jad   40

KATE
Colin I'll gang as fast as you
On this fine day an' faster too
Besides I'll chat of what you will
The bible or the papish bill
The statutes of the ancient law   45
Or beauties of queen Bathsheba
Now tell me Colin on your life
What think you o' that winsome wife?

COLIN
Kate ye're a witch—sae haud your tongue
An elf sae wicked yet sae young   50
Was never nursed on mother's knee
What are Bathsheba's faults to me?

KATE
O nought to you! Who said they were?
I only wanted to prefer
Some scripture argument 'bout sin   55
An' chanced with woman to begin.
But Colin, 'tis right strange of you,
Yet I hae noted an' 'tis true,
Whene'er of womenkind I hint

Then up you flie like fire frae flint   60
Frae whilk it weel might understood be
That things are no just as they should be

COLIN

Sweet Kate! wi' that provokin tongue
My heart wi' rage is aften wrung
But when I turn me round an' see   65
The wily twinkle o' your ee
The cherry cheek an' dimpled chin
My heart strings dirl my breast within
Kate—I suspect that chance what may
We'll hardly reach the kirk the day   70
We wad be blamed by matrons dour
Gaun in at sic a daft-like hour
An' some auld maids I ken beside
Wad cast us looks we coudna bide
Let's turn an' up beneath the heuch   75
Of the wild glen o' Gilmanscleuch
We'll spend in nature's green alcove
The day in pure delights of love
Read on our bibles pray bedeen
An' maybe steal a kiss between   80
If there's a blink o' heavenly bliss
On human nature it is this

KATE

Weel Colin I shall not gainsay
A wilfu' man maun hae his way
Since ye propose't an' think nae shame   85
If 'tis a sin ye'll bear the blame
But tell me this; though gay an' braw
War ye gaun to the kirk ava?

COLIN

Whisht Kate! An' speer nae that again
There's maybe mae to blame than ane   90
There are some things 'tween man and maid
Mair natural to be thought than said
But now our resting-place is here
Come to my side my comely dear
Close to my side nor once avert   95

The vision dearest to my heart
Look round you Kate. The scene you see
Is wild as mountain scene can be
Here sit we in a hollow swarth
Scooped from the bosom o' the earth   100
Our palace wall the shaggy fell
Our couch of state the heather bell
The sounding rivulet combined
With music of the mountain wind
The only anthem which we list   105
Our canopy the yielding mist
Yet here within our desert den
Far frae the walks an' eyes of men
Think o' our heavenly Maker's kindness
For a' our sins an' mental blindness   110
Beyond the bliss of kingly bowers
An earthly happiness is our's
   O Keatie when this scene I spy
Imbedded in thy deep blue eye
Like a wee vision of the mind   115
A dream of heaven an' earth combined
My ardent soul is all on flame
With a delight that wants a name
A flame so holy an' divine
An angel's heart might envy mine   120
My own rapt image too I see
As if I stood 'twixt heaven and thee
Forbid it a' ye powers above
An' O forgie this tear of love
For ne'er was vision so complete   125
In window of a soul so sweet

KATE

Colin I like nae sic pathetics
When chaps get into their poetics
They rave on like the winter winds
An' mischief whiles comes i' their minds   130
Sae that I still may haud you dear
An' keep you sober an' sincere
Kneel down upon that purple lea
An' pray to God for you an' me
The path o' grace has a beginning   135

An' praying winna gang wi' sinning
Tis sweet an' comely to express
Our homage in the wilderness
An' train our youthfu' minds away
Frae courting on the Sabbath day   140
    Colin without one other word
Kneeled down upon the lonely sward
His comely face turned to the sky
With ardor in his dark blue eye
And thus unto his God he prayed   145
As near as't can in rhyme be said

COLIN

O thou who dwell'st beyond yon sun
Where the sinful soul can never won
Thou God of all beings on earth that dwell
The angels of heaven an' spirits of hell   150
O wilt thou deign in thy love divine
To list to such a prayer as mine
Not for myself do I crave thine ear
But for one beside than life more dear
And for her sake I heard shall be   155
For a virgin's soul is dear to thee
    Then thou who reared'st yon ample sky
And planted the paradise on high
When the morning stars together sung
And its arch with hymns of angels rung   160
Who placed the sun on his golden throne
His God's vicegerent and his alone
Then clothed the moon in her silver veil
And the little stars in their diamond mail
Who welled the ocean's mighty wave   165
O'er coral beds to roll and rave
And formed these mountains great and small
And the soul of man the last of all
O hear in heaven most graciously
For we had our lives and souls from thee   170
    O thou who laid'st thine infant head
In a manger for thy cradle bed
When the spirits of guilt were moved with awe
And the angels marvelled at what they saw
The babe of heaven hushed to his rest   175

Upon an earthly virgin's breast
Then yield his life upon the tree
And lie in the grave for such as me
O hear us in heaven thou holy one
For in thy merits we trust alone　　　　　　　180
　　Thou spirit of Grace, adored, believed,
Great messenger all unconcieved
Thou THREE in ONE and ONE in THREE
Potent supreme Divinity
As one great God we worship thee　　　　　185
Then hear our prayers whil'st here we live
And when thou hearest Lord forgive
　　We have no earthly thing to crave
We are more than happy with what we have
We have youth and health and love beside　190
And thee for our father and our guide
Thy own blue heavens smiling o'er us
Religion hope and the world before us
And all we can do is to express
Our gratitude and our thankfulness　　　　195
　　One blessing would earthly hope fulfil
If 'tis accordant with thy will
May we two kneeling thee before
Be joined as one for evermore
And that a prospect may remain　　　　　200
Of acting earthly scenes again
May she be as a fruitful vine—

KATE

Stop Colin stop! I cannae join!
Ye may pray for marriage gin ye will
To think of that can do nae ill　　　　　205
Its sinless joys our God will grant them—
We'll pray for bairnies when we want them.
Ye coudna ask for aught that's worse
Than the heaviest portion o' woman's curse

COLIN

Ah my dear Kate! gin ye be spared　　　　210
You'll change your chime on that award
If pure affection's from above
If "love is heaven and heaven is love"

If loveliness concieved may be
Can eye a sight so lovely see   215
As a young comely mother's rest
With sweet babe to her bosom press'd
Its round and chubby cheek laid low
Misshapen on her breist of snow?
Ah Kate! If pure unmingled bliss   220
Be found in life's imperfectness
All love all fondness is outdone
By mother's o'er her first-born son.
That glow is bright, its workings kind,
Calm, chastened, ardent, yet refined.   225
I think—O may I be forgiven—
That nought can lovelier be in heaven
Far less upon the earth below
Me thinks I see the vision now
    What Keatie? Do ye rue our meeting?   230
I think ye're fuffing now an' greeting

KATE
Tuts! What for will ye speak sae queer
Of things unmeet for maiden's ear
I canna bide that stuff sae sensuous
It sounds like something that's licentious   235
Yet these are truths the heart that strike—
Ye may pray for babies gin ye like

COLIN
Ha Keatie! Truth will ay bear sway
An' nature work in hir ain way
For ye are nature's child complete   240
A mountain rose unsoiled an' sweet
A gem the desart that perfumes
A flower that hardly kens it blooms
When we grow auld an' bowed wi' age
We'll make an yearly pilgrimage   245
Unto this wild an' lonely scene
An' greet o'er days lang past an' gane
'Twill mind me of thy guileless heart
Of what remains and what thou wert
And I'll think of a day of bliss   250
And maiden made to love an' kiss

Wha aince gart me the preaching miss
An' waur than that; when her behest
A solemn task had on me press'd,
She flew up wi' a wicked screed   255
An' pat a' praying frae my head

KATE

Here with the tear-drap in my ee
Colin I beg you'll pardon me.
I did amiss 'mang passions rife
But could not help it for my life   260
In my reproof, though scarce ye'll trow,
I was at least sincere as you.
And now I beg of me you'll take
This book, an' keep it for my sake;
It was my honoured father's gift   265
That day when I our cottage left
With bitter grief an' youthfu' dread
In the wide world to earn my bread
"My bairn" quo he "ye're gaun to leave me
I hope through life you'll never grieve me   270
If ever sin your fancy brook
Think of the author of this book
Think how he reads the heart within
An' grieves if you should yield to sin
An' think o' your auld father too   275
An' how his soul yearns over you.
An' O my bairn when I am dead
Cling to this blessed book an' read
Its holy precepts when you may
An' God will give you grace to pray   280
To pray in purity of heart.—
Fareweel my bairn, since we maun part."
   Now Colin as my sole director
My trusted generous protector
Here do I render up to thee   285
The charge of both my book an' me,
And ne'er again, by it I swear,
'Twixt you and heaven to interfere.
Accept dear Colin the propine
An' O forgie the heart that's thine.   290

He took the book an' first he kiss'd
The donor then the volume bless'd
An' hid it in his bosom true
While on his eyelids stood the dew
Then hand in hand they trode the brae   295
That looks o'er Ettricks wildered way
An' parted on the mountain green
Far happier than a king an' queen

The Perilis of Wemyng

Ane moste woeful Tragedye
Compilit be Maister Hougge

I will tell you of ane wonderous taille
   Als euir was tolde be manne,
Or euir wals sung by mynstrel meete
   Sin' this baisse worild beganne:—

It is of ane May, and ane lovelye May,   5
   That dwallit in the Moril Glenne,
The fayrest flower of mortyl fraime,
   But ane deuil amangis the menne;

For nine of them styckit themsellis for lofe,
   And tenne louped in the maine,   10
And seuin-and-threttye brakke their hertis,
   And neuir lofit womyn againe;

For ilk ane trowit sho wals in lofe,
   And ranne wodde for ane whyle—
There wals sickan language in every looke,   15
   And ane speire in every smyle.

And sho had seuinty skoris of yowis,
   That blette o'er daille and downe,
On the bonny braide landes of the Moril Glenne,
   And these beine all hir owne;   20

And sho had stottis and sturdy steris,
   And blythsome kyddis enewe,
That dancit als lychte als glomyng fleeis
   Out through the fallyng dewe;

And this May sho hald ane snow-whytte bulle,   25
   The dreidde of the haille countrye,
And three-and-threttye goode mylke kie,
   To beire him companye;

And sho had geese and gezlyngis too,
    And gainderis of muckil dynne,   30
And peacokkis, with their gawdye trainis,
    And hertis of prydde withinne;

And sho had cokkis with curlit kaimis,
    And hennis full crousse and gladde,
That chanted in her own stacke-yairde,   35
    And cockillit and laidde lyke madde:

But quhaire hir minnye gat all that geare,
    And all that lordlye trimme,
The Lorde in heuin he kennit full weille,
    But naebodye kennit but himme;   40

For sho neuir yeildit to mortyl manne,
    To prynce, nor yet to kynge—
Sho neuir wals given in holye churche,
    Nor wedded with ane rynge.

So all men wiste, and all men sayde;   45
    But the taille wals in sor mistyme,
For ane mayden sho colde hardly bee,
    With ane doughter in beautye's pryme.

But this bonnye May, sho never knewe
    Ane faderis kindlye claime;   50
She nevir wals blessit in holye churche,
    Nor chrystenit in holye naime.

But there sho leevit ane yirdlye flowir
    Of beautye so supreme,
Some fearit sho wals of the mermaidis broode,   55
    Comit out of the sault sea-faeme.

Some sayit sho wals founde in ane fairye rynge,
    And born of the fairye queene;
For there wals ane rainbowe ahynde the mone
    That nychte sho first wals seene.   60

Some sayit her moder wals ane wytche,
    Comit from a farre countrye;

Or ane princesse lofit be ane weirde warlocke
  In a lande beyond the se!

Och, there are doyngis here belowe   65
  That mortyl nefer sholde kenne;
For there are thyngis in this fayre worlde
  Beyond the reche of menne.

Ane thinge moste sure and certainne wals—
  For the bedisman tolde it mee—   70
That the knychte who coft the Moril Glenne
  Nefer spok ane worde but three.

And the maisonis who biggit that wylde ha' housse
  Nefer spoke worde goode nor ill;
They came lyke ane dreime, and passit awaye   75
  Lyke shaddowis ower the hill.

They came lyke ane dreime, and passit awaye
  Whidder no manne colde telle;
But they eated their brede lyke Chrystyan menne,
  And dranke of the krystil welle.   80

And whenever manne sayit worde to them,
  They stayit their speche full sone;
For they shoke their hedis, and raisit their handis,
  And lokit to Hefen abone.

And the ladye came—and there she baide   85
  For mony a lanelye daye;
But whedder sho bred hir bairn to Gode—
  To reade but and to praye—

There wals no man wist, thof all men guessit,
  And guessit with feire and dreide;   90
But O sho grewe ane vyrgin roz,
  To seimlye womanheide:

And no manne colde loke on hir face,
  And eyne, that bemit so cleire;
But feelit ane stang gang throu his herte,   95
  Far sharper than ane speire.

It wals not lyke ane prodde or pang
  That strength colde overwinne,
But lyke ane reide hett gaad of erne
  Reekyng his herte withinne.   100

So that arounde the Moril Glenne
  Our braife yong menne did lye,
With limbis als lydder, and als lythe,
  Als duddis hung oute to drye.

And aye the teris ranne down in streim   105
  Ower chekis rychte woe-begone;
And aye they gaspit, and they gratte,
  And thus maide pyteous moane:—

"Alake that I had ever beene borne,
  Or dandelit on the knee;   110
Or rockit in ane creddil-bedde,
  Benethe ane moderis ee!

"Och! had I dyit before myne cheike
  To woman's breste had layne,
Then had I ne'er for womanis lofe   115
  Endurit this burning payne!

"For lofe is lyke the fyerie flaime
  That quiveris thru the rayne,
And lofe is lyke the pawng of dethe
  That spletis the herte in twayne.   120

"If I had lovit yirdlye thyng,
  Of yirdlye blithesomnesse,
I mochte haif bene belovit agayne,
  And bathit in yirdlye blisse.

"But I haif lovit ane frekyshe faye   125
  Of frowardnesse and synne,
With hefenlye beautye on the faice,
  And herte of ston withynne.

"O, for the glomyng calme of dethe
  To close my mortyl daye—   130

The last benightyng heave of brethe,
   That rendis the soule awaye!"

But wordis gone eiste, and wordis gone weste,
   'Mong high and low degre,
Quhille it wente to the Kynge upon the thronne,   135
   And ane wrothfulle manne wals hee.—

"What!" said the Kynge, "and shall wee sitte
   In sackclothe murnyng sadde,
Quhille all myne leigis of the londe
   For ane yong queine run madde?   140

"Go saddil mee myne mylke-whyte stede,
   Of true Megaira brode;
I will goe and se this wonderous daime,
   And prof hir by the Rode.

"And gif I finde hir elfyne queine,   145
   Or thynge of fairye kynde,
I will byrne hir into ashes smalle,
   And syfte them on the wynde!"

The Kynge hethe chosen four-score knychtis,
   All buskit gallantlye,
And hee is awaye to the Moril Glenne,   150
   Als faste als hee can dre.

And quhan hee came to the Moril Glenne,
   Ane mornynge fayre and cleire,
This lovely May on horsbakke rode,   155
   To hunte the fallowe deire.

Her palfrey wals of snawye hue,
   Ane paille wanyirdlye thynge,
That revellit ower hille and daille
   Lyke birde upon the wynge.   160

Hir skrene wals lyke ane nette of golde,
   That dazzlit als it flew;
Hir mantil wals of the raynbowis reide,
   Hir raille of its bonnye blue.

Ane goldene kembe with dymindis brychte,   165
   Hir semelye vyrgin crowne,
Shone lyke the newe monis laidye lychte
   Ower cludde of awmber browne.

The lychtening that shotte from hir eyne,
   Flyckerit lyke elfin brande;   170
It wals sherper nor the sherpest speire
   In all North Humber Lande.

The hawke that on hir brydel arme
   Outspredde his pinyans blue,
To keipe him steddye on the perche   175
   Als his lovit mystresse flewe,

Although his eyne shone lyke the gleime
   Upon ane saible se,
Yet to the twaine that ower them bemit,
   Comparit they colde not be.   180

Lyke carrye ower the mornyng sone
   That shymmeris to the wynde,
So flewe her lockis upon the gaille,
   And stremit afar behynde.

The Kynge hee whelit him rounde aboute,   185
   And calleth to his menne,
"Yonder sho comis, this weirdlye wytche,
   This spyrit of the glenne!

"Come ranke your mayster up behynde,
   This serpente to belaye;   190
I'll let you heire me put her downe
   In grand polemyck waye."

Swyfte came the mayde ower strath and stron—
   Ne dantonit dame wals shee—
Until the Kynge hir pathe withstode,   195
   In mychte and maijestye.

The vyrgin caste on him ane loke,
   With gaye and gracefulle ayre,

Als on some thynge belowe hir notte,
    That oughte not to haif bene there.   200

The Kynge, whose belte wals lyke to byrste
    With spechis most dyvine,
Now felit ane throbbyng of the herte,
    And quaikyng of the spyne.

And aye he gasped for his brethe,   205
    And gaped in dyre dismaye,
And wavit his airm, and smotte his breste,
    But worde hee colde not saye.

The spankye grewis they scowrit the daille,
    The dunne deire to restrayne;   210
The vyrgin gaif her stede the reyne,
    And followit, mychte and mayne.

"Go brynge hir backe," the Kynge he cryit;
    "This reiferye moste not bee,
Though you sholde bynde hir handis and feite,   215
    Go brynge hir backe to mee."

The deire sho flewe, the garf and grewe
    They followit harde behynde;
The mylk-whyte palfreye brushit the dewe
    Far fleeter nor the wynde.   220

But woe betyde the lordis and knychtis,
    That taiglit in the delle!
For thof with whip and spurre theye plyit,
    Full far behynde theye felle.

They lokit outowre their left shoulderis,   225
    To se quhat they mocht se,
And there the Kynge, in fitte of lofe,
    Lay spurrying on the le.

And aye he batterit with his feite,
    And rowted with dispayre,   230
And pullit the gerse up be the rotis,
    And flang it on the ayre.

"Quhat ailis, quhat ailis myne royale liege?
   Soche grieffe I doo deplore."
"Och I'm bewytchit," the Kynge replyit,   235
   "And gone for evermore!

"Go brynge hir backe—go brynge hir backe—
   Go brynge hir backe to mee;
For I moste either die of lofe,
   Or owne that deire ladye!   240

"That godde of lofe out through myne soule
   Hathe shotte his arrowes keine;
And I am enchanted through the herte,
   The lyvir, and the spleine."

The deire wals slayne; the royale trayne   245
   Then closit the vyrgin rounde,
And then hir fayre and lyllie handis
   Behynde hir backe were bounde.

But who sholde bynde hir wynsome feite?
   That bredde soche stryffe and payne,   250
That sixteen braif and belted knychtis
   Lay gaspyng on the playne.

And quhan sho came before the Kynge,
   Ane yreful caryl wals hee:
Saythe hee, "Dame, you moste be myne lofe,   255
   Or byrne benethe ane tre.

"For I am so sore in lofe with thee,
   I cannot goe nor stande;
And thinks thou nothynge to put downe
   The Kynge of fayre Scotlande?"   260

"No, I can ne'er be lofe to thee,
   Nor any lorde thou haste;
For you are married menne eche one,
   And I ane mayden chaste.

"But here I promiss, and I vow   265
   By Scotlandis Kynge and Crowne,

Who first a widower shall profe,
　　Shall clayme mee als his owne."

The Kynge hath mounted his mylk-whyte stede,—
　　One worde he sayde not more,—   270
And he is awaye from the Moril Glenne,
　　Als ne'er rode kynge before.

He sanke his rowillis to the naife,
　　And scourit the muire and daille,
He helde his bonnette to his heide,   275
　　And louted to the gale,

Till wifis ranne skreighynge to the door,
　　Holdynge their handis on highe;
Theye nefer saw kynge in lofe before,
　　In soche extreimitye.   280

And everye lorde and everye knychte
　　Maide off his several waye,
All gallopynge als they had bene madde,
　　Withoutten stop or staie.

But there wals nefer soche dole and payne   285
　　In any lande befelle;
For there is wyckednesse in manne,
　　That griefeth mee to telle.

There wals one eye, and one alone,
　　Behelde the dedis were done;   290
But the lovelye Queene of fayre Scotlande
　　Ne'er sawe the mornyng sone;

And seuintye-seuin wedded demis,
　　Als fayre as e'er were borne,
The very pryde of all the lande,   295
　　Were corpis befor the morne.

Then there wals noughte but murnynge wedis,
　　And sorrowe, and dismaye;
While buryal met with buryal stille,
　　And jostled by the waye.   300

And graffis were howkyt in grene kyrkyardis,
  And howkyt deipe and wyde;
Quhille bedlaris swairfit for verye toyle,
  The cumlye corpis to hyde.

The graffis, with their unseimlye jawis,   305
  Stode gaipyng daye and nychte
To swallye up the fayre and yonge;—
  It wals ane grefous sychte!

And the bonny May of the Moril Glenne
  Is weipynge in dispayre,   310
For sho saw the hillis of fayre Scotlande
  Colde bee hir home no mayre.

Then there wals chariotis came owernychte,
  Als sylente and als sone
As shaddowe of ane littil cludde   315
  In the wan lychte of the mone.

Some sayde theye came out of the rocke,
  And some out of the se;
And some sayde theye were sent from helle,
  To bryng that fayre ladye.   320

When the day skye beganne to fraime
  The grizelye eistren felle,
And the littil wee batte wals bounde to seike
  His darke and eirye celle,

The fayrest flowir of mortal fraime   325
  Passit from the Moril Glenne;
And ne'er maye soche ane deidlie eye
  Shyne amongis Chrystyan menne!

In seuin chariotis gildit brychte,
  The trayne went owre the felle,   330
All wrappit withynne ane shower of haille;
  Whidder no manne colde telle;

But there was ane shippe in the Firthe of Forthe,
  The lyke ne'er sailit the faeme,

For no manne of hir country knew,
    Hir coloris, or hir naime.   335

Hir maste wals maide of beaten golde,
    Hir sailis of the sylken twyne,
And a thousande pennonis streimyt behynde,
    And tremblit owre the bryne.   340

Als sho laye mirrorit in the mayne,
    It wals ane comelye viewe,
So manye raynbowis rounde hir playit,
    With euery breeze that blewe.

And the hailstone shroude it rattled loude,   345
    Rychte over forde and fenne,
And swathit the flower of the Moril Glenne
    From eyes of sinfulle menne.

And the hailstone shroude it quhelit and rowed,
    Als wan as dethe unshriven,   350
Lyke deidclothe of ane angelle grymme,
    Or wynding sheete of hevin.

It wals ane feirsome sychte to se
    Toylle through the mornyng graye,
And whenever it reachit the comelye shippe,   355
    Sho set saille and awaye.

Sho set hir saille before the gaille,
    Als it beganne to syng,
And sho hevit and rockit doune the tyde,
    Unlyke ane yirthlye thyng.   360

The dolfinis fledde out of hir waye
    Into the crekis of Fyffe,
And the blackgaird seelis they yowlit for dredde,
    And swamme for dethe and lyfe.

And the pellochis snyfterit, puffit, and rowed,   365
    In dreddour sadde to se,
And lyke the rain-drop from the cloudde,
    They shotte alangis the sea;

And they bullerrit into the bayis of Fyffe,
   Als if through terrour blynde,   370
And tossit and tombilit on the strande,
   In greate dismaye of mynde.

But ay the shyppe, the bonnye shyppe,
   Outowre the greene waive flewe,
Swyffte als the solan on the wyng,   375
   Or terrifyit sea-mewe.

No billowe breisted on her prowe,
   Nor levellit on the lee;
Sho semit to sayle upon the ayre,
   And neuer touche the sea.   380

And awaye, and awaye went the bonnye shyppe,
   Whiche manne never more did se;
But whedder sho wente to hefen or helle,
   Wals nefer maide knowne to mee.

MOUNT BENGER
July 5th, 1827

Notes

In the Notes below, page references are followed by line numbers in brackets. Thus 46(50) refers to the text of 'Elen of Reigh' on page 46, and to line 50 of that poem specifically. Where it seems useful to discuss the meaning of particular phrases, this is done in the Notes: single words are dealt with in the Glossary. Quotations from the Bible are from the Authorised King James Version, the translation familiar to Hogg and his contemporaries. For references to the ballads, the edition used is Francis James Child's *English and Scottish Popular Ballads*, 5 vols (Boston and New York, 1882–98), and the item number in Child is given in parentheses after quotations.

The present edition includes the twenty-six poems anthologised by *A Queer Book* (1832), all but two of which had previously appeared in literary periodicals. Information concerning the textual history of individual items, surviving manuscript versions, and the copy-texts chosen for this volume, will be found in the 'Textual Notes' which conclude each entry.

The Wyffe of Ezdel-more

Along with its immediate successor, 'Robyn Reidde', this poem appears to have had no history in the periodicals before its publication in the *Queer Book* of 1832. One possibility is that it was written specially for the collection, in response to William Blackwood's request of 26 February 1831 for some original poems to offset the republished materials (National Library of Scotland [hereafter NLS], MS 30312, pp. 154–55). Another is that Hogg recycled material previously rejected by other journals, and there is plenty of evidence of poems being returned in the later 1820s as too long or eccentric for the annuals.

'The Wyffe' is set in the wild hilly country at the head of Eskdalemuir, some 6 miles south of Hogg's birthplace in Ettrick. More particularly, the witch ('wyffe') of the title has her den in the region of the hill streams which flow into the White Esk from high points such as Ettrick Pen and Phawhope Hill. It was here that Hogg's grandfather, Will Laidlaw of Phaup (Phawhope), had been a shepherd, and Hogg must have heard many stories about the territory as a young boy. In 'Odd Characters', first published in *Blackwood's Edinburgh Magazine* for April 1827, Hogg describes Will o' Phaup as 'the last man of this wild region, who heard, saw, and conversed with the fairies'. 'The shealing at which Will lived all the better part of his life, at Old Upper Phaup, was one of the most lonely and dismal situations that ever was the dwelling of human creatures. [...] It is on the very outskirts of Ettrick Forest, quite out of the range of social intercourse, a fit retirement for lawless banditti, and a genial one for the last retreat of the spirits of the glen' (*The Shepherd's Calendar*, ed. by Douglas S. Mack (Edinburgh: Edinburgh University Press, 1995), p.107). Eskdalemuir also provides the setting for another Hogg tale involving the supernatural, 'The Laird of Cassway', which was first published in the August 1827 number of *Blackwood's* (see *Shepherd's Calendar*, ed. by Mack, pp.179–99).

Two manuscript versions of the poem have been discovered, the bulk of the first amongst the Hogg papers in the Alexander Turnbull Library, Wellington, New Zealand, the second (and later) version in the National Library of Scotland. The presence of the later manuscript among the papers of Andrew Shortreed, whose name as printer appears in the colophon of *A Queer Book* (1832), suggests that it was used at some stage as printer's copy. Both manuscripts show that Hogg wrote the poem in his full 'ancient stile'; indeed, if (as seems likely) its final composition post-dates the initial plans for the *Queer Book*, it would seem that he persisted in this practice virtually to the end. Regardless of Hogg's preference, the original orthography was heavily toned down for the *Queer Book* version—which, until the present edition, represented the only published record of the poem. An essential ingredient in its blend of daft witchcraft, Eastern mystery, transmogrification, and social satire, Hogg's language can now be enjoyed in full by readers for the first time.

FYTTE THE FYRSTE

1(1) Ezdel-more Eskdalemuir in SW Scotland—see also introductory comments above.

2(37) the Lammas tyde 1 August, a Scottish quarter- day. The phrasing of this line matches the opening of the traditional ballad, 'The Battle of Otterbourne': 'It fell about the Lammas tide' (Child 161C).

2(41) the Caldron brae the Muckle Cauldron Burn runs from Ettrick Pen, at the head of Ettrick, in a SE direction towards Eskdalemuir (Ezdel-more). Its banks ('braes') are close to Phawhope, where Hogg's grandfather, Will Laidlaw o' Phaup, had been a shepherd (see introductory comments, above).

2(42) Colle signifying the name of the Laird's hunting dog or 'pointer', rather than a 'collie dog'. Compare Chaucer's 'Nun's Priest's Tale': 'Ran Colle oure dogge, and Talbot and Gerland'.

2(44) the norlan polle the pole star; the image is of the needle of a compass pointing northwards.

2(58) up the penne probably a reference to Ettrick Pen (2269 feet).

3(65) raysit his doghedis the dog-head of a gun is its hammer; when raised the gun is ready for firing.

3(73) Seike deidde a cry to a dog to seek out fallen game.

3(87) Caldron burne see note to line 41.

4(115) Tom Flemon of Blode-hope Bloodhope Burn runs towards Eskdalemuir from a point about a mile SE of Phawhope Hill. Bloodhope is also mentioned as a territorial designation in Hogg's short story 'The Laird of Cassway' (1827) (see *Shepherd's Calendar*, ed. by Mack, p.191). Tom Flemon appears to be a fictional name.

4(116) Phynglande-sheille the present settlement of Fingland lies about 2 miles S of Bloodhope Burn, near the head of the White Esk.

8(247–49) James Glendonnyng [...] Tom Beattye of Meickyldaille surnames with strong West Border associations for Hogg. In his 'Love Adventures of Mr George Cochrane' (1821), the hero wrestles with a Willie Glendinning during his Border adventures. The Beatties feature in several of Hogg's prose stories, including 'The Laird of Cassway' (1827), where 'Tam Beattie o' the Cassway'—'a sportsman, a warrior, and a jovial blade'—is a main protagonist (*Shepherd's Calendar*, ed. by Mack, p.179). In the present case Hogg probably had in mind Thomas Beattie (1736–1827), tenant in Meikledale near Langholm, an authority in folklore and Walter Scott's source for the ballad 'Tamlane'. In another story in the 'Shepherds's Calendar' series, 'Storms' (1819), reference is made to Beattie having lost 72 scores of sheep through bad weather, an event corroborated by Beattie's surviving journal (see Elaine Petrie, 'James Hogg: A Study in the Transition from Folk Tradition to Literature' (unpublished doctoral thesis, University of Stirling, 1980), pp.178, 313–15).

Hogg was also possibly thinking of one or both of the individuals named here in an earlier note to *The Queen's Wake*, which records that: 'There are two farmers still living, who will both make oath that they have wounded several old wives with shot as they were traversing the air in the shapes of moor-fowl and partridges' (4th edn, Edinburgh, 1815, p.345). The transformation of lovers into moor-fowl also features in Hogg's prose story, 'The Hunt of Eildon' (see *The Brownie of Bodsbeck; and other Tales* (1818), vol. II, pp.334–38).

FYTTE THE SECONDE

9(25) mychtie Aral the Aral Sea is in present-day Kazakhstan (E of the Caspian Sea).

10(63) Mamorais isle the Sea of Marmara, with the island of Marmara in it, is in Turkey; it is visible from Istanbul, presumably the site of the spire on which the Witch proceeds to sit.

13(161) elymental power power over the agencies of physical nature, as demonstrated by the wizard Michael Scott in Hogg's *Three Perils of Man* (1822). This contrasts there with the illusionist magic of the Friar (Roger Bacon): see especially vol. II, chapter 3.

13(171) the solanis flychte alluding to the gannet's spectacular dive for fish.

14(208) quhatis to drynke and eitte the enthusiasm for food and drink matches Hogg's account of a party with 'a farmer in Esdale-muir' in 'An Eskdale Anecdote': 'Our libations were certainly carried on to an extremity, but our merriment corresponded therewith' (*Edinburgh Literary Journal*, 25 April 1829, p.337).

FYTTE THE THRYDDE

17(76) goude and sylken cramasye echoing the traditional Scottish ballad, 'Waly, Waly': 'My Love was cled in the black velvet/ And I my sell in cramasie'.

17(87) Black-coom heighte 'Black Knowe' is found on present maps about a mile N of Bloodhope Head; there is also a 'Black Knowe Head' a further 3 miles W, on the other side of Ettrick Water.

19(156) hoodye crowe a type of carrion crow with a 'hood' of black plumage. The crow in folklore is often shunned by other birds owing to its dirty eating habits and reputation for theft. Transformations, sometimes involving the Devil, are also common: see Stith Thompson, *Motif-Index of Folk-Literature*, 6 vols (Copenhagen, 1955–58), D.151.4, G.303.9.9.17. In 'Odd Characters' (1827), part of the 'Shepherd's Calendar' series, daft Jock Amos follows a crow to a suicide's body and calls it 'the deil's messenger'; crows also feature as demons in the Auchtermuchty tale in *The Private Memoirs and Confessions of a Justified Sinner* (1824).

FYTTE THE FOURTHE

24(57) wordis gone eiste [...] weste echoing a key phrase in 'The Laidley Worm of Banborough hill', one of Hogg's mother's ballads: 'But word's gane east an' word's gane west/ An' word's gane o'er the sea/ That the Laidley worm o' Banborough hill/ Would ruin the North countree'. Hogg quoted this with other stanzas in a letter to Sir Cuthbert Sharpe on 9 September 1834 (NLS, MS 1809, fol. 88).

24(61) kyssit the roode intimating a Catholic (pre-Reformation) setting for the poem; a *rood* was a cross or crucifix, often placed at the entrance of a church chancel.

25(97) Sandy the pyper i.e. the sandpiper, a wading bird which inhabits river banks and utters a clear piping note.

28(194) Beneathe the auld rown tre as a precautionary measure. Rowan-trees were regarded as charms against witchcraft and are still common at the doors or gates of houses in Scotland.

28(195) Maryis kyrke probably a reference to St Mary's Church, on the banks of St Mary's Loch, Selkirkshire. The church is no longer visible, but the churchyard remains.

Textual Notes on 'The Wyffe of Ezdel-more'

As stated in the introductory comments above, two manuscript versions of the poem have survived. The first, evidently the earlier draft, is found in MS Papers 42 in the Alexander Turnbull Library, Wellington, New Zealand. Item 34 there consists of seven 4-page booklets (leaf size 21cm x 13cm), paginated by Hogg 3–30 and bearing the watermark G WILMOT/1827. The text is relatively clean, the bulk of alter-ations and insertions appearing in a different pen stroke, as if added at a later point. The missing leaf at the beginning has recently been located in the possession of the Ettrick and Lauderdale Museums Service: this is headed 'The Wyffe of Ezdel-more', and completes this draft of the poem. The second MS version, written on similar paper and with the same watermark, is found in the National Library of Scotland (MS 8997, fols 11–20), as part of the papers of Andrew Shortreed. Only ten of its fifteen leaves have survived, paginated by Hogg [1]–8, 13–16, 19–20, 25–30. It follows the text in Turnbull 34 closely, incorporating nearly all the alterations and insertions there, and is likewise headed 'The Wyffe of Ezdel-more'. Printer's finger marks on some of the leaves, as well as the figure '33' at the point where that page begins in *A Queer Book* (1832), indicate that this manuscript was used at some stage by the compositor.

Comparison between Turnbull 34 and the NLS version suggests a fairly uncom-plicated re-writing of the text, with Hogg occasionally up-pointing phraseology and improving rhyme schemes. The title 'The Wytchis Dirge' is found only in the later version, and in this song alone Hogg can be seen engaging in a process of anglicis-ation, presumably on the basis that it represents an autonomous unit. In the poem as a whole, however, the 'ancient stile' if anything increases in density, and there is no indication that Hogg warranted its widespread destruction in the *Queer Book* of 1832.

The present edition whenever possible follows the text in NLS MS 8997, as Hogg's final version, filling in the gaps left by its incompleteness from Turnbull 34. The areas where the copy-text is Turnbull 34 are: Fytte the Fyrste, line 256 ('For both these blaidis […]) to Fytte the Seconde, line 118 ([…] our trysting tre'); Fytte the Thrydde, line 29 ('Sayis sho "I'll showe […]) to line 96 ([…] yonne sweite morehenne"'); Fytte the Thrydde, line 161 ('Then the wyffe […]) to Fytte the Fourthe, line 28 ([…] soule withynne'). All corrections and insertions found in Turnbull 34 are incorporated in these areas. At various points Hogg's system of speech marks has been repaired, in a way consistent with his general procedure, and in two instances upper case letters at the beginning of lines have been silently supplied. The following emendations have also been made:

FYTTE THE FYRSTE

(l.126)   cheystist]   cheystit (manuscript)

(l.177)   Adieu—Adieu]   Adieu!—Adieu (manuscript)

(l.186)   valleys]   valleyis (manuscript)

(l.186)   dew descends]   dewe descendis (manuscript)

(l.187)   Where the glaring sunbeam never blends]   Quhare the glairyng sonne beime neuer blendis (manuscript)

(l.188)   gloaming dims the dell]   gloamyng dimis the delle (manuscript)

(l.189)   stillness]   stilness (manuscript)

(l.197)   spirit's]   spirit s (manuscript)

(l.209)   forced to earth's]   forced from earth's (manuscript) ['to' as in Turnbull 34 and *Queer Book* 1832]

FYTTE THE SECONDE

(l.5)   hadde]   hade (manuscript) [In the manuscript Hogg has first written 'halde', and then deleted the 'l', presumably to avoid repetition with 'helde' in the following line; 'hade' is not a form found elsewhere in the poem, so is here emended to 'hadde'.]

(l.71)   drovis]   dovis (manuscript) [Hogg's hand is extremely compressed at this point; *Queer Book* 1832 has 'droves'.]

(l.93)   I'll go wayling]   I'll wayling (manuscript) ['go' as in *Queer Book* 1832]

(l.194)   on mee?]   on mee (manuscript)

FYTTE THE THRYDDE

(l.216)   unto]   nto (manuscript)

FYTTE THE FOURTHE

(l.86)   stynte]   styynte (manuscript) [Turnbull 34 and *Queer Book* 1832 stynte]

(l.91)   caime in his]   caime his (manuscript) ['in' as in Turnbull 34 and *Queer Book* 1832]

(l.207)   quhan hir voyce]   quhan voyce (manuscript) ['hir' as in Turnbull 34; *Queer Book* 1832 has 'her']

Robyn Reidde

As with its predecessor, no direct evidence about the composition of 'Robyn Reidde' has been discovered, and there is a strong possibility that it was written specially for the *Queer Book* project. The name of the hero suggests two main components in the poem's genesis: the Robin Hood ballads; and the Border 'reiving' ballads—Reid is a name connected with the English Border, especially in the region of Otterburn. Several key Border ballads, such as 'Jamie Telfer in the Fair Dodhead', were known by Hogg from recitation well before publication in Walter Scott's *Minstrelsy of the Scottish Border* (1802–03), and their presence can be felt throughout the poem. Hogg's presentation of his hero also reflects the more comic vein found in ballads such as 'Dick o' the Cow', another *Minstrelsy* item, in which an 'innocent fule' strikes back after his cattle are stolen.

The preoccupation with games of skill—wrestling, archery and fencing—relates most obviously to a later phase in Hogg's life, when he played a leading part in the formation of the St Ronan's Border Club. At the first Border Games organised by the Club, held at Innerleithen in September 1827, wrestling was one of the main events, and remained so at the main annual meetings held in July 1828 and 1829. Archery formed part of a contest held at the end of October 1830, involving the St Ronan's Bowmen; according to a report in the *Edinburgh Weekly Journal* on 3 November, 'The shooting was excellent, and Mr Boyd [...] had one arrow in the very centre of the bull's-eye'. On 17 March 1831 a special preliminary games was held at Yarrow, close to Hogg's home, and the 'Rules' for this meeting, in Hogg's hand, have survived in the Alexander Turnbull Library, New Zealand. Rule 5 reads: 'Every wrestler to do his best and no sham wrestles which are quite unfair for others and those who gain a sham wrestle to be turned from the ring' (MS Papers 42, Item 5). This is echoed in Jocke Dickson's protest, 'that wals not fayre', on being overcome by the superior skill of Robyn Reidde (Fytte the Fyrste, line 189). It is noticeable that the Yarrow Games took place only three weeks after Blackwood, on 26 February 1831, had pointed out the need for fresh materials to introduce the *Queer Book*.

FYTTE THE FYRSTE

29(17–18) Wallace [...] Robyn Brusse Sir William Wallace (1272?–1305), the patriot; and Robert the Bruce (1274–1329), later Robert I of Scotland: heroes of the Scottish wars of Independence.

29(19) Will Skarlette and lyttil Johne leading figures in the Robin Hood legend and ballads.

29(21–22) Adam Belle [...] Cloudesslee between them form the title of the popular broadside ballad, 'Adam Bell, Clim of the Clough, and William of Cloudesly' (Child 116).

30(37) lord Douglasse the powerful Douglas family once held the Wardenship of the Scottish West and Middle Marches in perpetuity, but their influence diminished in the 16th century.

30(37) Jedde forest Jed Forest, near Jedburgh in Roxburghshire, a favourite rendezvous for Scottish armies before making assaults on England.

30(38) the laddis of Liddiesdaille Liddesdale, a valley in S Roxburghshire, was inhabited by two of the most prominent Border clans, the Elliots and Armstrongs, whose exploits are recorded in some of the best-known Border ballads. Walter Scott's early expeditions to Liddesdale played a crucial part in the development of his *Minstrelsy of the Scottish Border* (1802–03).

30(39) lord Scrope Henry Scrope, of Bolton (1534–92), was English Warden of the West March from 1563 until his death; he was succeeded by his son, Thomas (1567?–1609), who held the office up to the union of the crowns in 1603. The latter, sometimes distinguished as 'young Scrope', was the unlucky victim of the raid described in the ballad 'Kinmont Willie'. See also note to line 218, below.

30(39) Dyrdan waiste Dirdan [Darden] Burn flows towards the River Coquet, about 6 miles NE of Otterburn, some 15 miles from the border with Scotland; the land round it, in the English Middle March, was known as Dirdan Waste.

30(40) settle the Border maille meetings between English and Scottish Wardens on days of truce were used to settle disputes between the inhabitants of the two countries, and such an event appears to be envisaged here.

30(59) Tynedaille [...] Bewcastil key areas of (respectively) the English Middle and West Marches. Tynedale was frequently involved in Border raids and a centre for English reivers; Bewcastle Waste, protected by a fort, was the main area through which Liddesale raids passed into England.

30(60) merrye Carlysle with its Castle and Cathedral, Carlisle was the main administrative centre on the English Borders.

31(63–64) James Stewarde [...] Harry Toudder James V of Scotland (though James IV is a possibility) and Henry VIII of England.

33(161–62) Reidde [...] Northumberlande the Reids were most commonly found in Redesdale, Northumberland, in the region of Otterburn.

35(218) His motelye foole to bee echoing the comic ballad, 'Dick o' the Cow', especially stanza 10: 'Now Dickie's gane to the gude Lord Scroope,/ And I wat a dreirie fule was he'. Its hero, according to Scott, 'from the privileged insolence which he assumes, seems to have been Lord Scroope's jester' (*Minstrelsy of the Scottish Border*, ed. by T.F. Henderson, 4 vols (Edinburgh, 1902), II, 77, 71).

FYTTE THE SECONDE

35(1) St Edmundis fayre the shrine of St Edmund, the last king of East Anglia (died *c.* 870), made Bury St Edmunds (Suffolk) an important place of pilgrimage in the middle ages.

37(54) Sant George's heidde St George, the patron saint of England.

37(57) scallopit cowlle a cloak and hood, as worn by monks, with a border patterned in the shape of a scallop shell.

FYTTE THE THRYDDE

38(1) Newcastle placing this part of the poem in Northumberland, close to the Eastern Border with Scotland.

39(28) at kyrke style a stile or narrow entrance to a churchyard, common as a meeting-place and where announcements were made.

39(29) good lord Piercy the Percies were the most powerful family on the Eastern

English March, comparable in influence to the Scottish Douglasses, their trad-
itional enemies. The most celebrated 'Lord Percy', Hotspur (son of the first
earl of Northumberland), opposes the Earl of Douglas in 'The Battle of Otter-
bourne', a version of which was compiled by Hogg for Walter Scott (see *Minst-
relsy*, I, 283–85).

41(103) clinkum clankum a ringing noise, as of a bell or (as suggested here) the
clash of swords.

42(139) passado lunge and fense technical terms in fencing: a thrust with one foot
advanced; a sudden advance; a movement of defence.

43(151–53) kyng James [...] Langhame [...] Douglasse James V of Scotland
banished the Douglas family from Scotland, having escaped from their custody as
a youth. James was also active in the pacification of the Borders, and it was near
Langholm in Dumfriesshire that he executed the border reiver, Johnie Arm-
strong, the hero of the well-known ballad of that name. In a number of his stories
Hogg shows an awareness of the Stuart policy to reduce the power of the nobility.

Textual Notes on 'Robyn Reidde'
The manuscript history of this poem parallels that of its predecessor, with drafts
surviving in the Turnbull Library, New Zealand, and in the National Library of
Scotland. Item 37 in Turnbull MS Papers 42 consists of five 4-page booklets (leaf size
21cm x 13cm), paginated by Hogg [1–3], 4–18, and bearing the watermark G
WILMOT/1827. No header is found, and the present 'Fytte' structure is absent,
though the text itself covers the whole span of the poem. A number of alterations
and insertions there appear to be written in a different pen stroke from the main text,
suggesting that Hogg later revised this draft in preparation for another. NLS MS
8997 includes a fragment (fols 21–22) of a later MS version, representing slightly
more than a third of the complete poem. It comprises a single large sheet (42cm x
26cm) with one quarter missing, paginated by Hogg [1]–2, and bearing an identical
watermark to Item 37 in Turnbull. Though it is again untitled at the beginning, the
presence later of the heading 'Fytte the Seconde' indicates that Hogg was by now
planning a sub-division of the poem in that way. Almost without fail the text
incorporates the revisions found in Turnbull 37, corroborating the view that the
latter is a preparatory draft. The survival of the NLS fragment in the papers of
Andrew Shortreed, the *Queer Book*'s printer, leaves little doubt it was used in
producing the printed version.

    The present edition follows the NLS fragment, as Hogg's final version, turning to
the Turnbull 37 to supply the areas of missing text. NLS MS 8997, fols 21–22, thus
provides copy-text for the following sections of the poem: Fytte the Fyrste, line 1 to
104 (' [...] greye gose wyng'); Fytte the Fyrste, line 145 ('"Tell mee thyne naime
[...]) to 174 ([...] at one thyng'); Fytte the Fyrste, line 213 ('Now Robyn Reidde
the sporte [...]) to Fytte the Seconde, line 56 ([...] quhille I bee deidde'"). When
Turnbull 37 is used all revisions and alterations there are incorporated, with the
result that the present text is less of a hybrid than might be imagined, and readers are
unlikely to sense any differences between sections. Since neither manuscript supplies
a title, the *Queer Book*'s 'Robin Reid' is adopted, though with orthography changed
to match the predominant form in the NLS fragment and Hogg's consistent practice
in Turnbull 37. The sub-headings 'Fytte the Fyrste' and 'Fytte the Thrydde' are also
added, positioned as in the *Queer Book* of 1832, but spelt in the form found in the final
MS of 'The Wyffe of Ezdel-more'. Quotation marks are silently supplied where
Hogg's (normally efficient) system breaks down. One initial letter is raised at the
beginning of a line, and on a few occasions letters lost at the edge of the page have
been restored. Additionally the following emendations have been made:

FYTTE THE FYRSTE
(l.11) blewe]   bewe (manuscript)
(l.41) Reidde]   Reidd (manuscript)·
(l.81) beardless]   beardess (manuscript)
(l.109) skille—seye]   skille seye (manuscript)
(l.155) to anye]   too anye (manuscript) ['to' as in Turnbull 37 and *Queer Book* 1832]
(l.213) Reidde]   Reidd (manuscript)

FYTTE THE SECONDE
(l.1) St Edmundis fayre comis]   St Edmundis comis (manuscript) ['fayre' as in Turnbull 37; *Queer Book* 1832 has 'fair']
(l.73) monke!"]   monke" (manuscript)

FYTTE THE THRYDDE
(l.79) also]   aslo (manuscript)
(l.93) lystes]   lyste (manuscript) [*Queer Book* 1832 lists]
(l.136) to and fro]   too and fro (manuscript)

Elen of Reigh

This poem first appeared as the lead item in a special double issue of *Blackwood's Edinburgh Magazine* for September 1829 (vol. 26, pp.[271]–277). A postscript to Blackwood's letter to Hogg on 8 August suggests that this positioning was a conscious decision on his part: 'I have commenced my first No with Elen of Reith [*sic*]. It is very beautiful indeed' (Turnbull MS Papers 42, Item 76). Certainly Hogg had submitted the poem in his most positive manner: 'I hope you will acknowledge *Elen of Reigh* as my masterpiece Kilmeny not excepted and though it has been hurriedly written I shall be much disappointed if you do not' (NLS, MS 4024, fol. 297). There is perhaps more than a touch of disingenousness here, however, since Hogg had already sent a version of the poem to S.C. Hall, editor of *The Amulet*. This is evident from Hall's letter to Hogg of 25 June: 'The poem Ellen Reigh is also I think most splendid & powerful—but I preferred the "tale of the Martyrs" as embodying a more distinct story' (NLS, MS 2245, fol. 148). Hall returned the unwanted poem with his letter of 25 June, and it would seem that Hogg rewrote it for *Blackwood's* in July.

Hogg's likening of the poem to 'Kilmeny' (1813)—his most celebrated single poem—is echoed by D.M. Moir in a letter to Blackwood on 17 August 1829: 'Elen of Reigh is a highly poetical vision, but deficient in reality. It is of the Kilmeny genus, but comes not up to that Paradisiacal apparition—It is very beautiful nevertheless' (NLS, MS 4025, fol. 200). Both poems depict virginal girls entering a more 'paradisiacal' state. Kilmeny's mysterious return ('Where gat you that joup o' the lilly scheen?/ That bonny snood of the birk sae green?/ And these roses, the fairest that ever were seen?') is paralleled, for instance, by Elen of Reigh's appearance in death: 'Around her temples and brow so fair,/ White roses were twined in her auburn hair;/ All bound with a birch and holly band' (lines 356–58). A religious meaning is perhaps implicit in the title of the present poem—with 'Reigh' representing a form of the Gaelic word (*righ, ree*) for King or God.

The twin heroines of 'Elen of Reigh', Maria Gray and Elen, also appear to have a firm biographical source. Hogg's two nieces by marriage, Mary and Janet Gray, stayed for several months with the Hogg family in 1828 before following their parents to India. On 27 August Hogg wrote to his wife, who had accompanied them to Edinburgh, regretting that he would be unable to see them off: 'My great desire was to see my two dear girls on shipboard and see how they were accommodated and under whose care but now harvest having come on and not one of my summer bargains sold it is out of my power to get to Liverpool but perhaps it may yet be in my power to see them before leaving Scotland. I inclose Mary the few verses I promised her and am sorry I have not had the opportunity of inserting it in her Album and to Jannet I send an inscription to be bound in with a copy of The Queen's Wake' (Turnbull MS Papers 42, folder 75).

46(50) Visions to dream of, not to tell echoing S.T. Coleridge's 'Christabel', Part I (1797, published 1816), line 253 ('A sight to dream of, not to tell!'). A similar allusion is found at line 109 of 'Love's Jubilee'.

46(59) Will nothing serve, but beauteous women? Hogg's fondness for describing pretty girls was an object of satire in the 'Noctes Ambrosianae' series in *Blackwood's Edinburgh Magazine*.

47(102) But human life is like a river the following set-piece echoes Burns's 'Tam o' Shanter', lines 59–66 ('But pleasures are like poppies spread [...] '), and more generally Psalm 90.

51(234) Glen-Reigh an imaginary location, though with a hint of Hogg's own territory. Compare Hogg's reference to 'Mr Anderson of Eltrive, (Ault-Righ, *the King's burn)*' in *Confessions of a Justified Sinner* (1824), p.369: this, of course, is both Hogg's own home (Altrive) and the farm where in the novel Robert Wringhim spends his last days.

51(240) Maria Gray Aged eighteen the inscription imagined by Hogg is similar to those found on gravestones belonging to his own family in Ettrick churchyard. Hogg's youngest daughter, born in August 1831, was christened Mary Gray Hogg [later Mrs Garden].

54(355) sweetest odours reminiscent of the 'odour of sanctity' said to have been exhaled by saints after their death.

54(358) birch and holly commonly associated with heaven in traditional songs and ballads. The Christian symbolism of holly is apparent in the song 'The Holly and the Ivy'; and in the ballad 'The Wife of Usher's Well', the wife's (drowned) sons return briefly from Paradise wearing 'hats [...] o the birk'. (Child 79A).

54(363) in your deaths you were not divided echoing David's lament for Saul and Jonathan in 2 Samuel 1.23 ('and in their death they were not divided').

Textual Notes on 'Elen of Reigh'

A complete draft of the poem can be pieced together from Items 33 and 51 in MS Papers 42 in the Alexander Turnbull Library, New Zealand. Each item consists of a 4-page booklet, without watermarks, and the text continues between the two in a similar pen stroke, indicative of uninterrupted composition. In this draft the heroine is named as 'Gillian of Lea', 'Lea' itself in the earliest stages having been altered from what appears to be 'Gree'. The text is crammed in both directions on the pages—a space-saving device common in Hogg's earliest drafts—and the set-piece comparing life to a river (lines 102–13) is found as an addendum at a later point. In the circumstances, it seems probable that Hogg wrote up fresh copies when submitting to S.C. Hall and Blackwood (see introductory comments, above).

Even so, the text is substantially the same as that which appeared in *Blackwood's Edinburgh Magazine*, where the main contribution by the compositors was probably the addition of standard punctuation. More punctuation was supplied by the *Queer Book* of 1832, which also made a number of grammatical adjustments (e.g. 'were' for 'was' at line 179), while committing one clear error by printing 'either' instead of 'ether' (line 205). In two cases, however, misreadings in *Blackwood's* appear to be corrected, and Hogg's involvement at some point is not an impossibility.

A slightly altered version of 'Maria Gray' (lines 278–309) featured as 'Mary Gray' in *Songs, by the Ettrick Shepherd* (1831), pp.296–97. The manuscript of this version is in the National Library of Scotland (MS 3112, fol. 281), and the pagination by Hogg (203–04) indicates that it originally belonged to a sequence of autograph materials prepared for *Songs*, a large section of which survives in NLS, MS 4805. 'Mary Gray. A Ballad' (NLS, Acc 8432) is a different poem, similar to that in Stirling University Library, MS 25, Box 1 (1), which was printed by the University of Stirling Bibliographical Society in 1981.

The present text is reprinted from *Blackwood's*, with the following emendations:
(l.240)   Gray Aged eighteen"]   Gray—aged eighteen," (*Blackwood's*) [Turnbull 33 Gray Aged eighteen"]
(l.251)   death]   death— (*Blackwood's*)
(l.255)   Time]   time (*Blackwood's*) [Turnbull 33 Time]
(l.269)   loneliest]   loveliest (*Blackwood's*) [Turnbull 33 and *Queer Book* 1832 loneliest]
(l.270)   dingly]   dingy (*Blackwood's*) [Turnbull 33 and *Queer Book* 1832 dingly]
(l.308)   free—]   free, (*Blackwood's*) [dash as in 'Mary Gray' in *Songs* (1831), p.297]

The Goode Manne of Allowa

This ballad was first published in the November 1828 issue of *Blackwood's Edinburgh Magazine*, vol. 24, pp.561–69. It was sent to Blackwood on 8 October 1828: 'I inclose you *the Goode Manne of Allowa* of which I hope you will approve' (NLS, MS 4021, fol. 282). Blackwood acknowledged it promptly on 11 October 1828: '"The Goode Manne of Alloa" I have not had time to read more than three or four verses of, and I am sure it is good' (NLS, MS 30311, p.73).

As with other Hogg ballads in *Blackwood's*, there are elements of the traditional ballad and more contemporary verse. The sea-bed discovery of the wreck and its main occupant ('And there wals laide ane royall maide') offers a kind of imaginative extension of the last stanza in 'Sir Patrick Spence' ('And thair lies guid Sir Patrick Spence,/ Wi the Scots lords at his feit'). There are also possibly traces of another marine ballad, 'The Mermaid of Galloway' from R.H. Cromek's *Remains of Nithsdale and Galloway Song* (London, 1810), where the mermaid of the title absconds with a young bridegroom: 'She faulded him i' her lilie arms,/ An' left her pearlie kame;/ His fleecy locks trailed owre the sand/ As she took the white sea-faem' (p.242). Hogg later recalled his 'sensations of delight' on first hearing the poem, and his suspicion that Allan Cunningham was 'author of all that was beautiful in the work' (*Memoir of the Author's Life* and *Familiar Anecdotes of Sir Walter Scott*, ed. by Douglas S. Mack (Edinburgh and London: Scottish Academic Press, 1972), p.73). In the sheer comic impetus of the 'Goode Manne'—the tremendous ride on a grey horse, and dangerous confrontation with the supernatural—it is difficult not to sense a tribute to Burns's narrative masterpiece 'Tam o' Shanter' (1791). Hogg's comic vein also invites comparison with the mock-epic style employed by William Tennant, most famously in *Anster Fair* (1812), which shares a setting on the north bank of the Forth with the 'Goode Manne', while also incorporating its own mermaids (see Canto IV).

It is also possible that the setting of the poem stemmed partly from Hogg's association with Tennant, a native of Fife and teacher at Dollar Academy from 1819. In a letter of 27 June 1829 Tennant wrote in the most friendly terms inviting Hogg to stay with him: 'I think you would find some pleasure in visiting again your Alloa friends, to say nothing of the happiness we should have in seeing you here' (NLS, MS 2245, fol. 151). Hogg's Alloa circle had developed through his friendship with Alexander Bald, a merchant in Alloa, Hogg becoming 'a frequent visitor' at the Bald home. The tone of the relationship is evident in a letter to Mrs Bald on 18 June 1816: 'my heart cleaves a good deal to Alloa. There is a warmth of friendship in your circle of friends towards me, which I have noted with delight' (see Mrs Garden, *Memorials of James Hogg*, 3rd edn (Paisley, 1904), pp.65, 71). It is not unlikely that some of poem's satire had a special meaning for Hogg's good friends in Alloa.

56(39) taike them wyngis and flye Proverbs 23.5 ('for riches certainly make themselves wings; they fly away as an eagle toward heaven').

57(91–92) Grenoke Banke [...] Bank of fair Scotlande two leading Scottish commercial banks of the period. The Greenock Banking Company was founded in 1785, and eventually amalgamated with the Western Bank of Scotland in 1842. On Sunday, 9 March 1828, it suffered from a spectacular robbery carried out by two London burglars, using false keys, who made off with booty worth more than £34,000. The Bank of Scotland, founded in 1695, was based in Edinburgh.

59(132) Deffane glenne Glendevon in the Ochil Hills, through which the river Devon flows before joining the Forth near Alloa.

60(191) Mackintoshis patent wairre Charles MacIntosh (1766–1843), inventor of the raincoat, patented his waterproof fabric in 1823.

61(229) whyte hass-bane echoing the ballad, 'The Twa Corbies': 'Ye'll sit on his white hause-bane,/ And I'll pike out his bonny blue een'.

61(230) hollande serke a woman's shift or chemise made from linen originally imported from the province of Holland in the Netherlands.

62(233) pullit out his knyffe a similar incident occurs in *The Pilgrims of the Sun* (1815), where the greedy Monk of Lindeen tries to take the rings from Mary Lee's corpse, in that case re-animating her body: 'He drew a knife from his baldrick gray,/ To cut the rings and fingers away' (Part Fourth).

64(315) oulde Kilrose Culross in Fife, lower down the Forth than Alloa; a Royal Burgh since 1588, it still preserves many buildings from the 17th century, when it was equivalent in size and importance to Glasgow.

65(363–64) on Allowais fertylle holmis [...] died no record of a stranding of whales in March, as indicated by Hogg's footnote, has been traced. However *The Stirling Journal* for 20 October 1825 records that 'on Saturday last' a number of whales visited the Forth, fifteen being stranded near Alloa and killed. 'When cut up they were found to have a very great deal of excellent blubber, which is now under the process of being converted into oil.' Cambus, as mentioned in Hogg's footnote, is a village at the confluence of the river Devon with the Forth, about 2 miles W of Alloa.

67(397) tryit him in the fyre see 1 Peter 1.7.

67(416) ane nedilis ee as in Matthew 19.24.

Textual Notes on 'The Goode Manne of Allowa'
While no manuscript of the text used by *Blackwood's Edinburgh Magazine* has been discovered, an earlier draft version survives in MS Papers 42 in the Alexander Turnbull Library, New Zealand. Item 46 consists of two 4-page booklets, with an 1815 watermark. The text contains an unusually large number of alterations, and the presence of different inks points to several stages of intervention. Some of the place names differ from those in *Blackwood's*: at line 132 Hogg's own 'Mont-Benger Glenne' appears rather than 'Deffane glenne'; the 'goode manne' lands on 'the Lowthen [Lothian] shorre' instead of 'the shoris of Fyffe' (line 313), alarming 'the foemen of Doonbarre' rather than 'the goode men of Kilrose' (line 325). Interestingly the first two stanzas of the published version are found on the verso of the second booklet: this, of course, includes the crucial third and fourth lines, concentrating the poem's geography on the northern bank of the Forth.

The eradication of Hogg's 'ancient stile' by the *Queer Book* of 1832 has a particularly destructive effect in the case of this poem, dissipating much of its vitality and unsettling the quirky mixture of humour and Henrysonian moralism. A facsimile of the text as it originally appeared in *Blackwood's* was published in *Altrive Chapbooks*, no. 3 (September 1986), pp.96–105, with an Editorial Note by Douglas S. Mack. The present edition also follows *Blackwood's*, but the stanza at lines 229–32 has been reinstated from Turnbull 46, largely on the grounds that its physically direct and bathetic imagery might have led to censorship. Punctuation consistent with that used by *Blackwood's* has been supplied in this instance; and closing quotation marks have been added at line 104 to repair an obvious deficiency. Other emendations made to the *Blackwood's* copy-text are as follows:

(l.17) ochone!" [...] manne,] ochone," [...] manne! (*Blackwood's*)

(l.59) streikit] striekit (*Blackwood's*) [Turnbull 46 and *Queer Book* 1832 streikit]

(l.165) ronne] rome (*Blackwood's*) [Turnbull 46 ronne; *Queer Book* 1832 run]

(l.227) heid] heid, (*Blackwood's*)

Jock Johnstone the Tinkler

'Jock Johnstone' was first published in *Blackwood's Edinburgh Magazine* for February 1829 (vol. 25, pp.173–78). William Blackwood refers to its acceptance 'last month' in a letter of 28 February 1829, his adviser D.M. Moir having previously commended 'Hogg's Ballad' as a 'good and spirited one' at the end of January (NLS, MS 30311, p.219; MS 4025, fol. 180).

Hogg was on familiar ground in the traditional ballad style, and here one senses a particular affinity with *The Mountain Bard* (1807), his early collection of original ballads. The poem is set in Hogg's own territory, the journey undertaken at the start proceeding from a point close to his birthplace in Ettrick, through the hills, towards St Mary's Loch in the Yarrow valley. The heroic part played by the 'tinkler'—indicating an itinerant tinsmith, and, in geographical context, almost certainly a gypsy—also recalls one of Hogg's earliest poems, 'Geordie Fa's Dirge', in his *Scottish Pastorals* (1801), where the exploits of a celebrated 'fiddling tinkler' are directly associated with Annandale in Dumfriesshire: 'Arm'd wi' a pleugh-staff, fer out-bye,/ Twa men wi' swords, he gart them lie./ His doughty deeds on Annan river/ [...] I oft hae heard him tell wi' pleasure' (lines 37–39, 42). In the present poem, the 'tinkler' turns out to be no ordinary Johnstone, but Lord of Annandale. Before this revelation, however, the worsting of the haughty Lord Douglas allows a good deal of 'plebeian' fun and deflation, similar in kind to the exploits in 'Robyn Reidde', and linking both poems thematically with other comic ballads by Hogg in the 1820s.

69(1) Yoke-burn Ford the Yoke Burn runs towards Ettrick Water from its source about 2 miles N of Ettrick Church.

69(14) St Mary's fane referring to St Mary's Church, now only visible as a churchyard, above St Mary's Loch. Hogg's use of *fane* ('temple') matches Scott's in *The Lord of the Isles* (1815): 'To old Iona's holy fane' (Canto IV, stanza x).

69(19) Douglas according to Hogg's 'Statistics of Selkirkshire', the powerful Douglas family controlled revenues in Ettrick Forest 'for the space of 200 years', before the intervention of James IV in 1503 (*Transactions of the Highland Society of Scotland*, 9 (1832), 290–91).

69(24) winna [...] ride wi' thee a traditional form of words, echoing for example the 'reiving' ballad, 'Jamie Telfer in the Fair Dodhead': 'Them that winna ride for Telfer's kye,/ Let them never look i the face o me' (Child 190A).

69(25) the Shepherd cleuch Shepherdscleuch is close to the Yoke Burn (see note to line 1), between Ettrick and St Mary's Loch.

69(26) Corsecleuch burn enters the Loch of the Lowes from the SE, close to its junction with the larger St Mary's Loch.

70(31) the Earl of Ross though mainly associated with Northern Scotland, the Ross family at one time held lands in the ancient counties of Dumfries and Wigton. William, seventh Earl of Ross, having made over his estate in 1370 to the female line, was succeeded by Euphemia, Countess of Ross—an event which might have caught Hogg's eye (see Sir Robert Douglas, *The Peerage of Scotland*, rev. by John Philip Wood, 2 vols (Edinburgh, 1813), II, 413).

70(45) to St Mary's kirk to St Mary's Church, above St Mary's Loch, after a journey through the hills from the Ettrick to Yarrow valley.

71(70) beauteous Harriet of Thirlestane Thirlestane Tower was situated on the opposite side of Ettrick Water from Gamescleuch, about a mile NE from Hogg's birthplace. A tragic event there forms the subject of Hogg's earlier ballad, 'Thirlestane', in *The Mountain Bard* (1807). The epithet 'beauteous' perhaps recalls the legendary figure of Mary Scott, the Fair Maid of Yarrow, a descendant of the Scotts of Thirlestane.

72(115) brave Lord James Douglas perhaps identifying the protagonist as Robert Bruce's renowned companion, Sir James Douglas (1286?–1330). If so, Hogg is markedly less reverential than some other contemporary writers, notably Walter Scott, who presents Douglas as a figure of heroic proportions in his last published tale, *Castle Dangerous* (1832).

73(163) salmon wriggling on a spear alluding to the traditional method of fishing for salmon, described elsewhere by Hogg as 'leistering' (see *Memoir of the Author's Life*, ed. by Mack, p.64).

74(196) Henderland a farm near the mouth of Megget Water, which flows into St Mary's Loch about a mile below the site of St Mary's Church.

75(207) Lord of Annandale the Johnstones of Annandale were a powerful family on the Western Border of Scotland, especially in the 14th and 15th centuries. Sir John de Johnston's valour in an engagement with the English at Solway in 1378 is described in Wyntoun's *Cronykil of Scotland*; while Sir Adam Johnston of Johnston helped put down the rebellion of the Douglasses against James II in 1455 (see Douglas, *Peerage of Scotland*, I, 70–71).

Textual Notes on 'Jock Johnstone the Tinkler'
An early draft version of the ballad survives in the Turnbull Papers (Item 32). This consists of a 4-page booklet, with the watermark BOOTH/1826, and begins with the 15th stanza of the poem as found in *Blackwood's*—the earlier stanzas presumably having been written on a separate leaf. As is usual with Hogg's earliest drafts, the text appears in both directions on the page, the few alterations visible apparently having been made at the same stage of composition. Hogg would then have prepared a fair copy for Blackwood, taking the opportunity to make a number of minor verbal adjustments in the process. Collation between Item 32 and *Blackwood's* indicates the original ballad terminology entered the Magazine relatively unscathed. Some of Hogg's more 'archaic' terms, however, were later standardised by the *Queer Book* of 1832, which also added further punctuation and raised initial letters in the case of words such as 'tinkler'.

The present edition reprints the text in *Blackwood's*, with the following emendations:
(l.31) lord]   lord, (*Blackwood's*)
(l.91) care,"]   care, (*Blackwood's*)
(l.94) brooks."]   brooks". (*Blackwood's*)
(l.108) prinkling]   trinkling (*Blackwood's*) [Turnbull 32 prinkling]
(l.174) steed,]   steed (*Blackwood's*)

(l.220) to-day."]   to-day. (*Blackwood's*)

A Lay of the Martyrs
Originally published in *The Amulet* for 1830, pp.145–54, this was the first poem
featured in the *Queer Book* to have an origin in the annuals rather than in *Blackwood's
Edinburgh Magazine*. On 8 April 1829 S.C. Hall, the *Amulet*'s editor, had invited 'a
prose tale and a poem from you at your earliest convenience' (NLS, MS 2245, fol.
144). Hogg not only acted expeditiously, but also heeded Hall's tacit warning about
the need for respectability in a religious publication. Two poems were offered, an
early version of 'Elen of Reigh' and 'A Lay of the Martyrs'. Hall's letter of 25 June
1829 indicates that proofs of the latter had already been seen by Hogg: 'I have to
apologise for so long delaying my reply to your most welcome communications—"a
tale of Pentland" & "a tale of the Martyrs" I have printed in the Amulet, and duly
received the corrected proofs from you' (NLS, MS 2245, fol. 148).
     From childhood Hogg had heard stories about the persecution of the Covenanters
in later 17th-century Scotland, and his first published novel, *The Brownie of Bodsbeck*
(1818), drew heavily on family traditions in Ettrick. As a shepherd and farmer in
the Nithsdale region *c*. 1805–09, he would also have come into contact with tales
about atrocities committed by the Royalist forces in SW Scotland. Locations men-
tioned early in the 'Lay' connect its events with the wild mountainous country of
Upper Nithsdale, to the east of Sanquhar (itself a centre of Covenanting resistance).
Another probable source is Robert Wodrow's *The History of the Sufferings of the Church
of Scotland* (1721–22), which Hogg knew intimately. More particularly, the incidents
in the poem could stem from Wodrow's account of the Enterkin Pass Rescue, in July
1684, an ambush which led to the release of a number of Covenanting prisoners and
ultimately to the execution of three participants in the Edinburgh Grassmarket the
following December. The harassing of the country about Enterkin after the incident
is described in some detail by Wodrow, and it seems likely that the poem's events in
part reflect this situation.
     The ballad was well suited for *The Amulet*, whose devout female readership would
have identified with the Covenanters' plight, especially as seen from the vantage
point of its two women speakers.
77(3) Wanlock-head in Upper Nithsdale, about 5 miles NE of Sanquhar; Wan-
     lockhead was a busy lead-mining community in the 19th century.
77(4) Louther brae the Lowther Hills range between Dumfriesshire and Lanark-
     shire; Green Lowther (2403 feet) and Lowther Hill (2377 feet), the two highest
     points, overlook the village of Wanlockhead from the SE.
77(13) Enterkin the Enterkin Burn runs for about 6 miles from a point close to
     Wanlockhead, entering the River Nith at Enterkinfoot; it was once used as a
     route between Dumfries and Edinburgh. For the the Enterkin Pass Rescue in
     1684, see introductory comments above.
77(14–15) dens o' the Ballybough [...] howes o' the Ganna linn neither place
     name has been identified, but the kind of hiding-place indicated matches
     Wodrow's account of Graham of Claverhouse's visit to the region in the after-
     math of the Enterkin Pass Rescue: 'Wonderful were the preservations of the
     persecuted about this time. The soldiers frequently got their clothes and cloaks,
     and yet missed themselves. They would have gone by the mouths of the caves and
     dens in which they were lurking, and the dogs would snook and smell about the
     stones under which they hid, and yet they remained undiscovered' (*History of the
     Sufferings of the Church of Scotland*, 4 vols (Glasgow, 1836–38), IV, 174).
79(68) say how I liked him now echoing the words allegedly spoken by Graham of
     Claverhouse to the wife of John Brown after her husband's summary execution:

'Claverhouse said to his Wife, What thinkest thou of thy Husband now, Woman? She said, I thought ever much good of him, and as much now as ever' (Patrick Walker, *Some Remarkable Passages in the Life and Death of Mr. Alexander Peden* (1724), p.75).

81(133) the popish duke either the Duke of Lauderdale (1616–1682), Secretary of Scottish Affairs from 1660 to 1680; or the Duke of York, who took up residence at the Palace of Holyroodhouse in November 1679, briefly acting as Royal Commissioner in Scotland before his accession as James VII and II in 1685. The cupidity of Hogg's 'duke' best fits Lauderdale; 'popish', on the other hand, more obviously relates to the Duke of York, a professed Roman Catholic, who installed a Catholic chapel at Holyrood.

81(145) down the bow probably the Nether Bow, Edinburgh's eastern entrance. The journey envisaged appears to be up the Canongate from Holyrood, through the Netherbow Port (gate), and down to the Grassmarket—the place of execution—at the foot of the Castle.

82(187) right hand hang beside his cheek compare Wodrow's account of the execution of the preachers John Kid and John King in 1679: 'Their heads were cut off, and their right hands, and affixed upon the Netherbow-port of Edinburgh' (*History of the Church of Scotland*, III, 136). The practice of diplaying both the heads and hands of executed Covenanters features in two influential novels of Hogg's period, Scott's *Tale of Old Mortality* (1816) and John Galt's *Ringan Gilhaize* (1823).

83(227) never yet laid that burden on echoing Psalm 55.22 ('Cast thy burden upon the Lord, and he shall sustain thee').

Textual Notes on 'A Lay of the Martyrs'
The present text is based on Item 63 in MS Papers 42 in the Turnbull Library, Wellington, New Zealand. With a full header at the beginning, it bears all the marks of a final manuscript copy by Hogg. The poem is written in double columns on both sides of a single sheet (*c.* 42cm x 26cm; watermark G WILMOT/1827), in a similar pen stroke, and virtually without alteration. At the top another hand has written in pencil the legend 'Amulet', and the presence of printer's ink marks also points to this having been the copy used for setting in London. An earlier MS version also survives in the Turnbull collection. Item 40 consists of a 4-page booklet (leaf size 23cm x 18cm), bearing an 1825 watermark, and its packed pages are characteristic of Hogg's early drafts. Collation shows quite a few local changes between items 40 and 63, perhaps the result of the poem having been laid aside for a while previous to its writing up for *The Amulet*.

If Hogg did receive and return proofs, he can only have given them cursory attention. Deteriorations in *The Amulet* printed version include: the transference from Marley (as found in both Turnbull drafts) to Morley Reid; the interpretation of 'goodman' as 'good man'—most obtrusive among several anglicisations; and the disruption of Hogg's upper case 'C' when the Royalist 'captain' is being directly addressed. *The Amulet* also supplied standard punctuation, a process furthered by the *Queer Book* of 1832, which introduced a more complex system of speech marks.

The present text reproduces Hogg's final (unpunctuated) manuscript version, as found in Turnbull Item 63, with only the following alterations: the provision of speech marks at lines 113 and 228; the insertion of two commas in line 143; and the raising of 'god' to 'God' at line 226. 'Edinburgh' is also preferred to 'Edenburgh' at line 125, where the manuscript is ambiguous.

A Cameronian Ballad

This ballad featured in *The Amulet* for 1831 (pp.173–80), and, as with 'A Lay of the Martyrs' in the previous number, its focus on two female speakers was well calculated to appeal to *The Amulet*'s readership. A more complex situation is nevertheless found in the juxtaposition of the religious/class antagonism shown by the Cameronian Janet with the more pragmatic and humane values of her aristocratical lady. The Cameronians, so named after their leader Richard Cameron (d. 1680), steadfastly refused to accept secular authority in religious matters, and this, together with their denial of good works as a means of salvation, is reflected in Janet's readiness to accept her husband's death at the battle of Bothwell Bridge in 1679 as a martyrdom. Her patroness, in contrast, observes both spiritual and material priorities ('The better you are in either state,/ The less shall I repine'), and intervenes to rescue John Carr from the field of slaughter. While Hogg characteristically allows both attitudes to stand, a softening is sensed in Janet's later responses, while the poem as a whole expresses a wider conviction that compassion is what matters, not the cause, and that good is possible on both sides. In this respect, Hogg manages to satisfy the expectations of a contemporary religious readership without losing hold of his own values.

84(15) Earlston either the Covenanter William Gordon of Earlstoun (1614–1679), or his son, Alexander Gordon of Earlstoun (1650–1726). The death of William Earlstoun at Bothwell Bridge is described by Wodrow in the following terms: 'that excellent person, William Gordon of Earlston, who was coming up to the western forces, was killed by the English dragoons, who behaved but very cowardly at the bridge. [...] And, as if the death of so good a man had not been expiation enough for this crime, his lady had her jointure seized, her house spoiled, and many horses and cattle taken from her' (*History of the Church of Scotland*, 4 vols (Glasgow, 1836–38), III, 108). Alexander, who was at the battle and escaped his pursuers by dressing in women's clothes, is identified by Walter Scott as the 'brave Earlstoun' of the Covenanting ballad 'The Battle of Bothwell Bridge', published in his *Minstrelsy of the Scottish Border* (1802–3), perhaps from the recitation of Hogg's mother (see Elaine Petrie, 'James Hogg: A Study in the Transition from Folk Tradition to Literature' (unpublished doctoral thesis, University of Stirling, 1980), p.305). Alexander's wife, Janet (d. 1696), shared much of her husband's imprisonment after his eventual capture. Earlstoun Castle is about 2 miles N of St John's Town of Dalry, Kirkcudbrightshire, in SW Scotland.

86(94) best o' this warld's breed i.e. the best of those who are not the people of the Covenant.

86(95) your liefu lane all by yourself; solitary.

87(119) o' the water o' Clyde i.e. from the River Clyde, over which the Royalist forces forced their passage to secure victory at Bothwell Bridge.

Textual Notes on 'A Cameronian Ballad'

In addition to *The Amulet* for 1831, 'A Cameronian Ballad' appeared in another contemporary journal, *The Annual Register, or A View of the History, Politics, and Literature, of the year 1830* (London, 1831), pp.529–32. A superficial reading of dates might suggest that the *Annual Register* contains the earlier version. But whereas the *Register* was offering a *restrospective* view of public events, and must have been published after 1830, the *Amulet* (as a keepsake for the following year) would have been ready for sale well in time for Christmas 1830. Collation between the two texts suggests that the *Annual Register* version was almost certainly taken from the *Amulet*. Scots terms are anglicised on at least 30 occasions ('wha' to 'who', 'sae' to 'so' etc.);

more tellingly still, 'your leel goodman' in line 1 becomes 'your leel, good man', and later 'the water o' Clyde' (i.e. the river) is changed to 'the waters o' Clyde'. The *Annual Register* also regularised stanza structure by placing the whole poem in eight-line stanzas, unlike the *Amulet* which includes six quatrains among its octets. The *Queer Book* of 1832—which used *The Amulet* for its copy-text—then divided the whole poem into quatrains. The title also became 'Bothwell Brigg', and a number of routine adjustments were made (e.g. the raising of 'ladye' to 'Ladye'). A few substantive changes (such as the substitution of 'Earlston' for 'Earylton') appear to correct misreadings of the original manuscript.

The present text is based on *The Amulet* for 1831, the earliest version known to have survived. It nevertheless follows the *Queer Book* of 1832 in placing the poem in quatrains, largely on the grounds that no fully consistent pattern can be discerned in the *Amulet*'s mixture of octets and quatrains (it is not impossible that Hogg's crowding of stanzas in the manuscript was the original source of confusion). The following emendations have also been made:

(l.10)   rules]   rubs (*Amulet*) [*Queer Book* 1832 rules]
(l.15)   Earlston]   Earlyton (*Amulet*)
(l.60)   break.]   break; (*Amulet*)
(l.64)   thy life and mine]   my life and thine (*Amulet*) [This emendation follows the wording found in the *Annual Register* (1831), which, though not authorial, offers the best solution to the awkwardness of the *Amulet* text at this point.]
(l.95)   liefu]   liefe (*Amulet*) [*Queer Book* 1832 leifou]
(l.115)   sackless]   sachless (*Amulet*)
(l.127)   bled]   bled, (*Amulet*)
(l.137)   land]   land, (*Amulet*)
(l.139)   hand, [...] night]   hand [...] night, (*Amulet*)
(l.144)   yoursels]   yoursel's (*Amulet*)
(l.158)   trow] traw (*Amulet*)

The Carle of Invertime

This poem first appeared in the 1829 number of *The Anniversary* (pp.100–07), the short-lived annual edited by Hogg's friend and fellow-poet Allan Cunningham, who had written to Hogg on 6 March 1828 soliciting a contribution: 'I can afford to pay at the rate of something like a pound per page and five or eight pages from your pen in your happy manner will be of much service to me. See a Vision for me or dream a dream—converse with a spirit or do what you please. I have little room for my work is a varied one and the pages will hold some 30 or 34 lines each' (NLS, MS 2245, fol. 114). From the evidence of the poem in *The Anniversary* Hogg obliged on several counts. 'The Carle' is cast in the visionary, 'Kilmeny' style Cunningham must have been hoping for; and the idea that Hogg is here operating as a poet of the first rank is reinforced by its attribution to 'the author of The Queen's Wake'. Furthermore, in length the poem seems tailor-made to suit Cunningham's requirements—its 204 lines taking up less than eight of the *The Anniversary*'s pages. Cunningham expressed his pleasure in a letter to Hogg on 26 May 1828: 'Your poem is excellent' (NLS, MS 2245, fol. 120).

Hogg's subject-matter also meshed neatly with the topic of 'Time' which Cunningham's Preface announced as a running theme in the collection. In imaginative scope 'The Carle' is reminiscent of larger 'philosophical' poems by Hogg, notably *The Pilgrims of the Sun* (1815). Its Christian allegory, the leading of the 'old gray wife' by Hope towards Eternity, is also similiar in some respects to Christiana's pilgrimage with Mercy in Part II of Bunyan's *Pilgrim's Progress*.

90(4) Gudeman of Invertime *Gudeman* was sometimes applied specifically to the keeper of a jail (e.g. 'the Gudeman of the Tolbuith'). *Inver*, as a prefix in place names, usually means a confluence of streams or the mouth of a river: hence 'Inver Time', at the junction or gateway of time.

92(78) true Faith, sweet Charity the speaker is Hope, so the passage echoes 1 Corinthians 13.13 ('And now abideth faith, hope, charity, these three; but the greatest of these is charity').

94(166) vale of death Psalm 23.4.

Textual Notes on 'The Carle of Invertime'
No manuscript of the poem, as published in *The Anniversary*, survives. However, a fragment of another version is held in the National Library of Scotland (MS 9634, fols 3–4). This consists of two leaves, paginated by Hogg 5, [6], 7, 8, and covers an area approximating line 110 to the end of the poem. The clean script and presence of an end inscription ('Mount-Benger/ March 29th 1828') both indicate that it was intended as a final draft. Collation against the *Anniversary* text reveals large areas of rewriting, and a more obtrusive religious dimension in the NLS version (which ends with the chorus 'Halleluiah'). One explanation is that Hogg rewrote the poem to order; another, that Cunningham made his own changes owing to pressure of space. The *Queer Book* of 1832, in following the *Anniversary* text, made a number of formal changes, including the creation of fresh lines to show double rhymes at lines 67, 69, 77, 79, 109, 111, 145, 147—a characteristic also evident in the NLS fragment.

The present edition of 'The Carle of Invertime' is reprinted from the *Anniversary* of 1829. A 'new' verse paragraph is created at line 195, through indentation and spacing, matching the *Queer Book* of 1832 and NLS MS fragment. Additionally, the following emendations have been made:

(l.152)   the sole]   thy sole (*Anniversary*) ['the' as in MS 9634 and *Queer Book* 1832]
(l.196)   Time]   time (*Anniversary*) [MS 9634 Time]
(l.202)   Eternity back to Time]   eternity back to time (*Anniversary*) [MS 9634 and *Queer Book* 1832 Eternity back to Time]

The Lairde of Lonne
'The Lairde of Lonne' first appeared in *Blackwood's Edinburgh Magazine* for April 1830 (vol. 27, pp.571–77), having been sent to Blackwood with an air of confidence on 12 February 1830: 'At your request I send "the Laird of Lonne" which I hope you will think in my best old stile' (MLS, MS 4027, fol. 180). Blackwood's preference for ballads was well-known to Hogg, and the poem brought a favourable response in a letter of 27 March 1830: 'Your Laird of Lonne is excellent and will be much liked' (NLS, MS 30311, p.556).

'Lonne' is apparently a fictional designation, though its (verbal) proximity to Lorn in Argyllshire helps give a Highlandish air to the eponymous Laird. The main events in the ballad are set in Berwickshire, in SE Scotland, and Hogg's end note points to a source in the genealogy of the Home family. The worsting of the swaggering Laird by the Knight of Home, in the guise of a beggar, matches similar deflations in 'Robyn Reidde' and 'Jock Johnstone the Tinkler'. Such upsets evidently appealed to the *Blackwood's* readership, while arguably allowing a vent for more 'plebeian' feelings on Hogg's part.

96(17) the Mers the Merse, an area in the south of Scotland, close to the East March.

96(24) lynkit at hir quheele worked vigorously at her spinning wheel.

97(36) alle wals nevir golde that shonne proverbial: 'All that glisters is not gold'.

97(41) Landale gaite see note to Hogg's end note, below.

97(57) keikit bye glanced (or peeped) aside.

98(77) the Lorde of Marche the Border Warden; in this context, most probably the Warden of the Scottish East March.

98(86) Whitfielde, and Kelle, and Halsyngtonne Kello and Halsington are both Berwickshire locations, listed as part of the possessions of the Home family in Sir Robert Douglas's *The Peerage of Scotland* (see 2nd edn, 2 vols, Edinburgh, 1813, I, 732). No 'Whitfield' belonging to the Homes has been located, though 'The great Earl of Whitfield' features in the ballad 'Hobie Noble' (Child 189).

100(158) let the skaithe go with the skorne matching the proverbial expression 'Scorn comes commonly with scathe'.

102(203) hayre helterre halter made out of animal hair. In Hogg's 'A Few Remarkable Adventures of Sir Simon Brodie' the Marquis of Montrose, masquerading as a groom, is likewise seen 'riding on a sorry jade and leading a gallant steed with a hair halter' (*Tales of the Wars of Montrose* (1835), vol. II, pp.169–70).

102(204) sonke of strae a straw cushion, used as a substitute for a saddle. Compare Scott's description of the pony belonging to 'Old Mortality' (Robert Paterson): 'It was harnessed in the most simple manner, with a [...] hair tether, or halter, and a *sunk*, or cushion of straw, instead of bridle and saddle' (*The Tale of Old Mortality*, ed. by Douglas S. Mack (Edinburgh: Edinburgh University Press, 1993), p.9).

104(296) Quhatis to be wonne at womanis hande In his 'Familiar Anecdotes of Scott', Hogg quotes the lines 'Nought's to be won at woman's hand/ Unless ye gie her a' the plea', when describing his accession to his wife's proposal that they make a spur-of-the-moment visit to Scott in his Edinburgh lodgings (see *Memoir of the Author's Life*, ed. by Mack, p.115).

104(299–300) Knychte of Home [...] Border boundis the Home family, one of the most powerful in SE Scotland, usually held the Wardenship of the Scottish East March. See also following note.

105(note) Hogg's details match the account of Sir Alexander Home of Home (succ. 1456) in Sir Robert Douglas's *The Peerage of Scotland*: 'He married, first, Mariota, daughter and heiress of Landals of Landals, in Berwickshire' (2nd edn, 2 vols (Edinburgh, 1813), I, 733).

Textual Notes on ' The Lairde of Lonne'
An earlier draft, containing the whole poem minus one stanza, is found in Items 53 and 47 in Turnbull MS Papers 42. The absence of significant alteration suggests a fairly spontaneous first composition, preparatory to writing out a fresh copy for Blackwood. Collation against the text in *Blackwood's Edinburgh Magazine* discloses mainly local alterations, most noticeably the substitition of the more Highland-sounding 'M'Killum' and 'Gilfillane' for 'the Lyndsay' and 'the Douglass' at lines 5 and 6—though 'Lowrie of the Lonne' is in place from the start. With the *Queer Book* of 1832 the spelling of Lonne was changed to Lun, and much of Hogg's 'ancient stile' disappeared. The present text is reprinted from *Blackwood's*, with the following emendations:

(l.86)   Halsyngtonne;]   Halsyngtonne (*Blackwood's*)
(l.202) beiste]   beigle (*Blackwood's*) [Turnbull 47 beste; *Queer Book* 1832 beast]
(l.213) heifit]   keipit (*Blackwood's*) [Turnbull 47 hefit; *Queer Book* 1832 heaved]

Ringan and May
'Ringan and May' was first published in *Blackwood's Edinburgh Magazine* for June 1825, vol. 17, pp.712–14, followed immediately by 'The Witch of the Gray Thorn',

another *Queer Book* poem. No information directly relating to its submission has been discovered, notwithstanding the noticeably earlier date of 14 March 1825 which appears in the end inscriptions of both the *Blackwood's* version and the only surviving autograph manuscript. D.M. Moir, writing as Blackwood's literary confidant, much preferred this poem to its companion in the Magazine: 'I like the first best as it has more of his peculiar wild natural touches than the other' (NLS, MS 4015, fol. 88).

Certainly Hogg here allows full vent to his 'ancient stile', writing consciously after the fashion of the medieval Scottish 'makars'. More particularly, the dialogue between Ringan and May follows Robert Henryson's 'Robene and Makyne' in depicting an attempted seduction in a pastoral rustic mode. The language of the poem also mixes Henrysonian terms (e.g. 'baisse' in the sense of morally despicable) with phrases more recognisably Hogg's own ('the streimmers of hevin'; 'duste and droulle'; 'leifu [lovely] charmis'). Such a hybrid 'ancient stile' undoubtedly allowed Hogg to be more daring in sexual terms: in fact, the two phases of the laveroke's (lark's) song are interpretable as paralleling courtship followed by consummation. Similarly, the poem's imagery moves freely between physical and spiritual planes, the bird's flight joyously linking the 'dewye yirde' and 'yettis of hevin', resulting in one of Hogg's most fluent explorations of the relationship between earthly and heavenly love.

Textual Notes on 'Ringan and May'
A full autograph manuscript of the poem, clearly that used as printer's copy by *Blackwood's Edinburgh Magazine*, is held in the Beinecke Library at Yale University (Osborn Files, 18.19). It consists of two leaves, paginated by Hogg [1]–4 and perhaps once conjugate, each measuring *c.* 23cm x 19cm without visible watermarks. Both show signs of folding, and printer's marks are also evident. Across the top of the first page, in Blackwood's hand, are the words 'Bourgeois across the page'—the first term referring to the fount size to be used in printing. The presence of a full header is typical of Hogg's final drafts; and the text is punctuated in a way which seems to invite a straightforward transference into print.

In the main the *Blackwood's* version follows Hogg's text accurately, though a more standardised punctuation tends to obscure the distinction between lines relatively free of marks (such as those describing the lark's unimpeded flight) and those with a more halting rhythm (as in the listing of inferior birds). On seven occasions spellings which match English forms are changed to Scots, after the regulation vernacular forms of Hogg's day. Apart from a few other minor variations (e.g. a tendency to change 'y' to 'i'), Hogg's 'ancient stile' was nevertheless largely retained.

With the *Queer Book* of 1832, however, the poem underwent a full-scale de-antiquation. Rhetorical gaps left by the pruning of end forms invited the addition of new words at three points: 'that burdye' became 'that wee burd' at line 10; at line 19 'heire our straynis' was replaced by 'hear how our strains'; and 'quhen my love had warbelit' (line 53) expanded to 'when my love Ringan had warbled'. A further tier of punctuation was also added, with an influx of commas within lines, and the layout of the poem became significantly different—the original linear model, matching the alliterative tradition, being broken up into a series of stanzas ranging from four to fourteen lines. One victim in the move towards a more conventional 'lyric' form was the important break between lines 52 and 53, marked in both the manuscript and *Blackwood's* versions by asterisks. A more detailed description of the manuscript and printed versions will be found in P.D. Garside, 'Notes on Editing James Hogg's "Ringan and May"', *The Bibliotheck*, 16 (1989), 40–53.

The present text of 'Ringan and May' is based on the Beinecke manuscript at Yale. Single quotation marks however have been preferred to Hogg's original double marks to signify speech within speech, with fresh single marks being silently added in three instances. Additionally the following emendations have been made, with a view to completing Hogg's punctuation and regularising the beginning of speech utterances.

(l.13) sayis, "My]   sayis "my (manuscript)
(l.32) hevin.]   hevin (manuscript)
(l.59) I, "He]   I "he (manuscript)
(l.60) yirde;]   yirde (manuscript)
(l.84) said, "My]   said "My (manuscript)

The Grousome Caryl
First published in *Blackwood's Edinburgh Magazine* for January 1825 (vol. 17, pp.78–85), this poem represents the earliest item in the *Queer Book* of 1832 in terms of initial date of publication. Hogg apparently submitted it to Blackwood on 5 January 1825: 'I send you a notable ballad for Maga take care and don't lose it' (NLS, MS 4012, fol. 179). Blackwood's response of 22 January offers an early glimpse of his uncertainty about Hogg's 'ancient stile', but otherwise was entirely complimentary: ' [...] at no period whatever was the Scots language so written But this does not signify—it is capital English & good poetry' (NLS, MS 30308, p.43).

The poem is set in Moffat Dale, between St Mary's Loch and the town of Moffat, and contains a number of specific references to place names and topographical features. Its action involves two journeys up Moffat Water towards the Grey Mare's Tail, a spectacular waterfall and well-known beauty spot: the first by the fearsome giant ('grousome caryl') of the title, the second by the pursuing Lord of Annandale. This pass linked the Yarrow valley with the more densely populated areas in SW Scotland, and Hogg must have trodden through it on numerous occasions. The story offers a legendary explanation for an ancient earthwork about 400 yards from the Grey Mare's Tail, close to the junction of Tail Burn and Moffat Water. In a note to his earlier ballad, 'Mess John' (1807), Hogg had given an account both of the waterfall and its close neighbour: 'Immediately below it, in the straitest part of that narrow pass which leads from Annandale into Yarrow, a small strong entrenchment is visible. It is called by the country people *The Giant's trench*. It is of the form of an octave, and is defended behind a bank' (*The Mountain Bard* (Edinburgh, 1807), p.90). The same site, overgrown with bracken and pointing in the direction of St Mary's Loch, can still be found much as Hogg described it.

110(17) **Craigyeburn** Craigieburn is a settlement about 2 miles E of the centre of Moffat, at the junction of the Craigie Burn and Moffat Water. 'The bonny Lass of Craigyburn' features in Hogg's ballad, 'Mess John', in *The Mountain Bard* (1807).

110(19) **Saddil-Yoke** Saddle Yoke (2412 feet) is a hill on the left-hand bank of Moffat Water, going upstream from Moffat towards St Mary's Loch.

111(35) **Carryfron Gans** Carrifran Gans, a steep ridge about a mile NE of Saddle Yoke, further towards the Grey Mare's Tail.

112(69) **the Greye-Meris Linne** the Grey Mare's Tail, a spectacular 200-foot waterfall.

112(71) **ane holle lyke bendyd bowe** an ancient trench in the shape of bow can still be seen close to the foot of Tail Burn, pointing up Moffat Water in the direction of St Mary's Loch.

112(75) **Straung-Cleuche Linne** a stream running through Strang Cleuch falls into Moffat Water about 800 yards NE of Tailburn Bridge.

112(76) **Raken Guille** Raking Gill joins Moffat Water about another 600 yards upstream from Strang Cleuch (see note above).

112(91) **worde is gone easte [...] weste** a familiar ballad phrase (see note to 'The

Wyffe of Ezdel-more', Fytte the Fourthe, line 57).

112(92) From Yarrawe unto the Ae i.e. from Yarrow Valley to the Water of Ae, a tributary of the Annan.

112(93) Lord of Annerdaille the Johnstones of Annandale were one of the most powerful families on the West Scottish Border (see also note to line 207 of 'Jock Johnstone the Tinkler', above).

112(94) Lochess Lochwood Tower, about 6 miles S of Moffat, was the chief fortress of the Johnstone clan in Annandale.

113(101) wale wychte menne a common ballad phrase, 'the best and bravest men'.

113(107) Hunter-Heck Hunterheck is a small settlement just outside Moffat, approaching Moffat Dale.

113(119–23) Jowler [...] German [...] Harper names for hunting dogs; the first also appears in Canto the First of Hogg's *Mador of the Moor* (1816): 'One hound alone had crossed the dreary height,/ The deep-toned Jowler, ever staunch and true'.

113(127) wairnynge note signal to begin.

114(133) Selcothe Burne Selcoth Burn flows into Moffat Water about 2 miles upstream from Craigieburn, further towards the Grey Mare's Tail.

115(170) hill of Turnberrye Upper and Nether Tarnberry overlook the Grey Mare's Tail from the SW.

117(256) yew-tree in the original *Blackwood's* version this reads as 'bay-tree', the leaves of which traditionally formed hero's laurels, though no evidence has been found of bay wood being used for the manufacture of bows. In the *Queer Book* of 1832, 'bay-tree' is altered to 'yew tree', a favoured material in the middle ages.

118(273) Peele-Knowe not identified by name, though current O.S. maps show a Watch Knowe about 1 mile to NE of Tail Burn.

118(293) Gyantis Trensche [...] Gyantis Grave two names traditionally given to the earthworks below the Grey Mare's Tail. On current O.S. maps the site is marked as *Giant's Grave*.

118(295) Jamis, our nobil Kyng almost a generic figure in Hogg, though here probably with more than a touch of James IV, in whose reign 'fairies, brownies, and witches, were at the rifest in Scotland' (see 'Mary Burnet', in *The Shepherd's Calendar*, ed. by Mack, p.212).

119(303) Bodisbecke Bodesbeck farm is about 4 miles from the Grey Mare's Tail, in the direction of Moffat. The same location features in Hogg's novel, *The Brownie of Bodsbeck* (1818).

119(312) hoddye-crawis carrion crows with a 'hood' of black plumage. For the association of crows with the devil in folklore and by Hogg, see note to 'The Wyffe of Ezdel-more', Fytte the Thrydde, line 156.

119(319–21) Annerdaille [...] Nythe [...] Gallowaye proceeding westwards over Annandale, Nithsdale, and Galloway (the gateway to Ireland).

119(322) worste helle mock-derogatory comments against Galloway are something of a running joke in Hogg. Compare, e.g., 'Tam Craik's Tale' in *The Three Perils of Man* (1822): 'The only rational hope concerning it is, that, as it is a sort of butt-end of the creation, it will perhaps sink in the ocean, and mankind will be rid of it' (vol. II, p.319).

Textual Notes on 'The Grousome Caryl'

No manuscript of this ballad has been located, so that the version in *Blackwood's Edinburgh Magazine* of January 1825 represents the first known state of the poem. Blackwood's willingness to overlook Hogg's 'orthography', as expressed in his letter of 22 January 1825, indicates that the original 'ancient stile' was allowed to stand, attention being limited to such matters as punctuation. In the *Queer Book* of 1832, however, standardisation extended far beyond accidentals, with Hogg's archaic terms surviving only in isolated pockets.

The present edition reprints the *Blackwood's* text, with the following emendations:
(l.56)   eldrischlye]   erdlischlye (*Blackwood's*)
(l.102)   neide,]   neide. (*Blackwood's*)
(l.111)   blode-hundis,]   blode-hundis (*Blackwood's*)
(l.151)   snorit,]   snorit (*Blackwood's*)
(l.180)   thryve]   shwyve (*Blackwood's*) [*Queer Book* 1832 thrive]
(l.256)   yew-tree]   bay-tree (*Blackwood's*) [*Queer Book* 1832 yew tree]
(l.279)   there]   then (*Blackwood's*) [*Queer Book* 1832 there]
(l.285)   saye,]   saye (*Blackwood's*)

Love's Jubilee
First published in *The Literary Souvenir* for 1826 (pp.121–27), 'Love's Jubilee' is the earliest among those *Queer Book* poems which were derived from the new annuals. Hogg submitted it to the editor Alaric A. Watts on 2 February 1825, shortly after having received a complimentary copy of the 1825 number: 'I [...] have written rather a happy poem for the next Souvenir which I send with a promise that it shall not appear in any other work for a year at least after its appearance in your work. I have no copy, not a scrap, you have the first and last and therefore if you do not publish take care and do not lose it' (NLS, MS 1002, fol. 102).

Both the date of Hogg's letter and the end inscription of the published version suggest that the poem was actually completed at Candlemas [2 February], one of the Scottish quarter-days and the Feast of the Purification of the Virgin Mary. The candles burned then have an origin in the Roman festival for Februa, the mother of Mars; and in Scotland the day before Candlemas was dedicated to St Bride, the successor to a Celtic goddess of the same name—the Day of Bride being the old Celtic festival of spring. The poem's dialogue between supernatural Spirits, with their respective male and female charges, is also reminiscent of traditional representations of Mars and Venus; while tone and imagery both evoke, without ever exactly paralleling, Shakespeare's *A Midsummer Night's Dream*. In a letter of 16 February 1826, Allan Cunningham praised the piece as being in his friend's 'happiest' manner: 'it is pure and graceful, warm yet delicate and we have nought in the language to compare to it save Kilmeny. In other portions of verse you have been equalled and sometimes surpassed, but in scenes which are neither on earth nor wholly removed from it—where fairies speak and spiritual creatures act, you are unrivalled' (NLS, MS 2245, fol. 90). In its *Queer Book* context, 'Love's Jubilee' links with several other items (e.g. 'Ringan and May') which explore the relationship between physical and spiritual love.

120(6) star of love the planet Venus; often called the 'evening star', because it is the first to show at nightfall.

121(37) yon twin stars possibly referring to Castor and Pollux, twin stars in the constellation of Gemini.

121(70) sweet wood-reef *woodruff* is a low growing herb, with clusters of small white flowers and sweet-scented leaves; often, as here, descriptively called 'sweet wood-ruff'.

121(71) wabron leaf the plantain-leaf. Compare John Leyden, 'Scenes of Infancy' (1803): 'The wabret leaf, that by the pathway grew,/ The wild-briar rose, of pale and blushful hue'. Leyden in a note observes that 'WABRET, or WABRON, a word of Saxon origin, is the common name for the plantain-leaf in Teviotdale'

(*Works* (1858), p.128, 128n).

122(90) celestial bow the rainbow.

123(109) An eve to dream of—not to tell compare S.T. Coleridge, 'Christabel', Part I, line 253 ('A sight to dream of, not to tell!'). In the *Queer Book* of 1832 this line and its repetition at line 143 are placed in quotation marks, effectively acknowledging the allusion.

Textual Notes on 'Love's Jubilee'

No manuscript of the poem apparently survives, and it is not improbable that the only copy was destroyed in London after printing. The present edition follows the text in the *Literary Souvenir*, in preference to the more formal version in the 1832 *Queer Book*, except for the two following emendations where the *Queer Book* punctuation is preferred:

(l.107) spell] spell, (*Literary Souvenir*)
(l.108) be, by] be by (*Literary Souvenir*)

Ane Rychte Gude and Preytious Ballande

This ballad first appeared, under its present title, in *Blackwood's Edinburgh Magazine* for August 1828 (vol. 24, pp.177–83). No correspondence relating to its composition has been found, though the end inscription in *Blackwood's* suggests a submission to the Magazine early in July 1828 (the same inscription appears in the manuscript sent to Blackwood, though 'July 9th' there replaces another date, scarcely decipherable, but perhaps 'June 8th'). For the *Queer Book* of 1832, where sweeping alterations to Hogg's 'ancient stile' were made, the title was changed to 'The Spirit of the Glen'.

As the original title indicates, the poem is written in the traditional ballad style and employs a number of key ballad phrases and strategies. Its narrative displays a trinary organisation common in oral story-telling, with the young heroine facing temptation in three encounters (brownie, witch, youth), while the poem itself is divisible into three sections (beginning/temptation/conclusion). Marjorie's return to the guiding arms of the dominie (schoolmaster), bringing the story full circle, underlines Hogg's moral point about the superiority of domestic virtue to the sexual snares and vanity of the world.

125(3) maike a form of the Scots word *mak* or *make*, denoting a 'match', 'image' or 'resemblance'. A similar use of the term to suggest a supernatural presence is found in Hogg's earlier poem, 'Kilmeny', lines 52-56 (see *Selected Poems*, ed. by Douglas S. Mack (Oxford: Clarendon Press, 1970), pp.34, 162).

127(71) eske and snaike *ask* or *esk* is a common name for the newt in Scotland, and is sometimes also used to describe the lizard. Its association here with the snake matches a tendency to class the *ask* among the venomous animals, an idea encouraged by the similarity of the word to *asp*.

127(72) wounde hir heile echoes Genesis 3.15.

127(93) floryde Eden rose not identified, but almost certainly a species of wild rose found in Hogg's territory (or, possibly, the similarly biblically-named Rose of Sharon).

128(110) droichel manne dwarf, i.e. the Brownie mentioned by name in the next quatrain.

129(157–58) gowne of sylke [...] cramasye traditional sexual snares, as in the Scottish ballad 'Waly, Waly'.

133(294) the teire blyndit hir ee a form of words commonly found in the ballads, as in 'Mary Hamilton': 'But whan she cam down the Cannongate/ The tear blinded her ee' (Child 173A).

Textual Notes on 'Ane Rychte Gude and Preytious Ballande'

The manuscript used by *Blackwood's Edinburgh Magazine* survives among the Blackwood Papers in the National Library of Scotland (MS 4805, fols 3–7). It consists of five large-size sheets (31cm x 19cm), paginated by Hogg [1]–9, and is complete with a full header and end inscription. The absence of significant alteration suggests that Hogg wrote from an earlier draft, though no other MS versions have been located. Apart from occasional question marks and a rudimentary system of speech marks, the text is largely unpunctuated. There are signs of printer's thumb marks on fol. 3, and the top of the first page carries the instruction 'Bourgeois across the page' with William Blackwood's initials (for the significance of this, see 'Textual Notes on "Ringan and May"'). Collation against the text in *Blackwood's* shows that Hogg's orthography survived mostly unscathed, with the compositor(s) mainly attending to punctuation. However a significant mistake is found in the third line, where Hogg's 'maike' was transformed into a 'snaike', presumably as a result of misreading and/or unfamiliarity with the term. This error was corrected by the *Queer Book* of 1832; but generally the new version dissipated much of the original mystery and excitement of the poem by eradicating Hogg's 'ancient stile'.

The present edition adopts the NLS manuscript as copy-text. At various points, however, gaps in Hogg's system of speech marks are silently repaired; lower case initial letters at the beginning of lines or speeches are also raised on five occasions, and question marks have been supplied at lines 80, 180, 186 and 248. A few other guiding marks have been added, which are recorded below, together with two emendations which attempt to correct verbal slips by Hogg in the manuscript:

(l.61)   Yes, there is ane,]   Yes there is ane (manuscript)
(l.85)   virtue,]   virtue (manuscript)
(l.159) hir necke]   his necke (manuscript) [*Queer Book* 1832 her]
(l.201) (for […] hee)]   for […] hee (manuscript)
(l.346) Neer]   Near (manuscript) [*Blackwood's* Nere; *Queer Book* 1832 Ne'er]

Jocke Taittis Expeditioune till Hell

'I have only been able to insert Jocke Taitte in this No.', William Blackwood told Hogg on 26 August 1830, and the item duly appeared in *Blackwood's Edinburgh Magazine* for September 1830 (vol. 28, pp.512–17). Hogg had submitted his ballad, and other material, with a letter to Blackwood dated 13 August: 'I send you other three pieces in order that you may always have it in your power to select the best' (NLS, MS 4027, fol. 190). While Blackwood's reply of 26 August expressed dissatisfaction with one of the other items sent, 'A Sunday Pastoral', no reservations stood in the way of 'Jocke Taittis', for which Hogg was sent immediate payment: 'I enclose you four notes for Jocke Taitte who is a glorious fellow' (Turnbull MS Papers 42, Item 77).

Compared with the more challenging 'Sunday Pastoral', Hogg's presentation of his shepherd protagonist in familiar comic mode offered little to disturb readers of the Magazine. Jocke's visit to Hell, like that of the hero in his earlier poem 'Connel of Dee' (1820), is a voyage of moral discovery, in which the promiscuousness of high society is seen as non-fulfilling and self-destructive. Like its immediate predecessor in this collection, the ballad comes full circle, bringing its protagonist home more appreciative of a natural existence and with a broader moral awareness.

136(19) bullet heide i.e. a head round like a bullet, though just possibly here with something of the sense of 'pig-headed' too.

137(35) starre of lofe the planet Venus, the earliest star and one of the brightest seen.

137(45) myne collye true a shepherd's collie dog, in addition to being indispensable for his work, would have been as close to him as any other creature.

137(52) woulde raither haif gone myselle inadvertently inviting the Devil's appearance, as in the proverb 'Talk of the devil, and he is sure to appear'.

137(59) the muckil deille the Devil, Satan.

138(77) Gil-Moullis name for the Devil. Compare 'A Witch's Chant', reprinted from Hogg's play 'All-Hallow Eve' (1817), in *Songs, by the Ettrick Shepherd* (Edinburgh, 1831): 'Come from the earth, the air, or the sea,/ Great Gil-Moules, I cry to thee!' (p.138).

140(150) tirlyt at the pynne made a noise on the gate for admittance. An old ballad phrase, evident for example in 'Prince Robert' (Child 87A): 'O he has run to Darlinton,/ And tirled at the pin'.

141(194) kaille out throughe the reike proverbial, to receive one's just deserts.

Textual Notes on 'Jocke Taittis Expeditioune till Hell'

No record has been found of the manuscript sent by Hogg to *Blackwood's Edinburgh Magazine* in August 1830. However, an earlier draft of the poem survives in the Turnbull Library, New Zealand. Item 27 in MS Papers 42 consists of a 4-page booklet, with an '1826' watermark, and has text crowded in both directions on the page. Unlike most early drafts by Hogg it carries a title at the head, though this is in a darker pen stroke than the main body of text and appears to have been added at a later point. In the same ink, too, the first line has been altered from 'There wals ane lad sat on ane hille' to its present form. Since no mention of 'Jocke Taitte' is found elsewhere in this version, it seems likely that Hogg decided on a specific name for his shepherd when taking up the poem again for rewriting. The first three stanzas are found in an even earlier state on the last page of a similar booklet in the Turnbull collection (Item 23), which also contains an early draft of 'A Sunday Pastoral'.

The present edition is based on the printed text in *Blackwood's*. At lines 209–16, however, it restores two stanzas from Item 27 in the Turnbull Library, largely on the grounds that their sexual explicitness might have led to suppression. Punctuation has been supplied here to match the normal Magazine procedure. At lines 193 and 195 dashes disguising the identities of 'the Lord of—' and 'chieftaine of M—' in *Blackwood's* are expanded to 'the Lord of F—' and 'chieftaine of M,Nab', the forms found in Turnbull 27. Additionally, the following emendations seek to correct two probable misreadings and one lapse in punctuation.

(l.6) bothe] bathe (*Blackwood's*) [Turnbull 27 both]

(l.30) espye;] espye (*Blackwood's*)

(l.205) allaye] alloye (*Blackwood's*) [Turnbull 27 allaye]

A Bard's Address to his Youngest Daughter

The subject of this poem is Harriet Sidney Hogg, Hogg's fourth child and third daughter. Though 1828 has been given as her date of birth, some family sources indicate that 1827 is the correct year, a dating corroborated by a letter of William Blackwood's to Hogg on 29 December 1827: 'I had almost forgot to offer Mrs Blackwood's congratulations and my own to Mrs Hogg & you. We hope she and the little stranger are doing well' (NLS, MS 2245, fol. 110). The original manuscript version, on which the present edition is based, is remarkably similar in tone to Hogg's letters to his wife in Edinburgh, during the summer of 1828, when Harriet was being treated for a deformed foot. 'Kiss Maggy and Harriet for their dear papa. I wakened this morning saying, "dear, dear, sweet Harriet." I had been dreaming that she had a fever' (quoted in Mrs Garden, *Memorials of James Hogg*, 3rd edn (Paisley, 1904), p.178).

The poem was first published in *Friendship's Offering* (1830), an annual conducted by Hogg's fellow-Scotsman, Thomas Pringle. For details of this version, which appeared as 'by the Ettrick Shepherd', and for further alterations which took place in the *Queer Book* of 1832, see 'Textual Notes' below.

144(13) Maggy Hogg's second daughter, Margaret, born nearly three years before Harriet, on 18 January 1825.

145(34) Let little children come to me Jesus's words, 'Suffer the little children to come unto me', as given in Mark 10.14 and Luke 18.16.

145(39–42) Thy very name [...] extremitye Harriet was named after Harriet, Duchess of Buccleuch (1773–1814), daughter of 1st Viscount Sydney. Hogg is apparently alluding to her dying wish that he should receive the farm at Altrive Lake. The Duke's letter of gift of 26 January 1815, however, points to a general influence on the Duchess's part rather than to any specific death-bed request (NLS, MS 2245, fol. 13).

145(49) for grandam's sake Hogg's mother, Margaret Laidlaw Hogg, had died in 1813.

145(51) her who left thee late Hogg's mother-in-law, Mrs Janet Phillips, who lived with the Hogg family at Mount Benger 1827/8 shortly before her death.

145(54) Jessy [...] James the two eldest Hogg children.

Textual Notes on 'A Bard's Address to his Youngest Daughter'
Hogg's original manuscript, on which the present text is based, forms part of MS Papers 42 in the Alexander Turnbull Library, New Zealand. Item 62 consists of a single unpaginated leaf, unfolded and with cut edges. An embossed stamp, consisting of a crown and the words 'BATH' underneath, appears at the top left hand corner. On the recto is an untitled poem of three stanzas, which first appeared as 'A Scots Sang' in the *Edinburgh Literary Journal*, 17 January 1829, p.140. Overleaf is found a full version of 'A Bard's Address', under its present title, with the text continuing in two additional columns across the right-hand margin. Apart from the replacement of 'sweet' by 'mild' in the second line, and the alteration of 'mixest' to 'minglest' at line 18, there are no verbal changes—consistent with a fairly spontaneous composition on Hogg's part.

No record of the manuscript sent to Thomas Pringle for *Friendship's Offering* has been discovered. Collation of the version there against Item 62 reveals a number of disparities, with Hogg's more intimate terms being made more formal and impersonal throughout, and the omission of a whole section claiming kisses in the name of Harriet's various relations (see lines 49–58 in the present text). To some degree, this is consistent with the transference from a private to a public mode, and it is not implausible that Hogg himself restructured the poem with this in mind. Another possibility is that cuts were made to make space in the periodical itself—the poem ends exactly at the foot of page 314. Writing on 1 June 1831, Pringle was still insistent that contributions should be kept to 'about a page or a couple of pages each' (Turnbull Library, MS Papers 42, Item 81).

The *Queer Book* of 1832 followed the text in *Friendship's Offering*, though a large insertion paralleling the 'lost' MS passage indicates strongly that Hogg at some point intervened to supply a perceived deficiency. This appears after the present line 34, and reads as follows:

> And now, sweet child, one boon I crave,—
> And pout not, for that boon I'll have,—
> One kiss I ask for grandam's sake,
> Who never saw thy tiny make;
> And one for her who left us late,
> Laid low, but not forgotten yet;
> And thy sweet mother, too, the nearest

> To thee and me, the kindest, dearest,—
> Thou sacred, blest memorial,
> When I kiss thee, I kiss them all! (p.241)

Almost certainly Hogg was working from his memory of the earlier version, which appears to have been current for a good while in his family. A fragment headed 'The original manuscript of a Bard's address to his youngest daughter', in the hand of Harriet herself (Mrs Robert Gilkison), is found in NLS MS 1870 (fol. 23). This matches the first column written across the right-hand margin of Turnbull 62, incorporating the passage omitted from *Friendship's Offering* and imperfectly reinstated in the *Queer Book* of 1832.

A version of the Turnbull MS has already been printed in David Groves's edition of Hogg's *Selected Poems and Songs* (Edinburgh: Scottish Academic Press, 1986), but with some misreadings occurring in the process. Punctuational marks were also added by Groves at strategic points. The present edition eschews all editorial interference, apart from the raising of four initial letters in the title, the provision of spaces between verse paragraphs, and the addition of two commas in line 69 where the reader might otherwise stumble.

Johnne Graimis Eckspeditioun till Heuin

First published in *Blackwood's Edinburgh Magazine* for April 1831 (vol. 29, pp.641–44), this poem was the most recent of the periodical items anthologised by the *Queer Book* of 1832. Hogg first mentioned it to Blackwood in a letter of 8 October 1830: 'I have nothing else quite new except "Johnnie Graimis expeditioune tille heuin" which I am sure you will not like' (NLS, MS 4027, fol. 196). The title next surfaces on 15 March 1831, when the *Queer Book* was being actively planned: 'I send you what I conceive to be a very original ballad I wrote both it and John Graham intentionally for Maga but you may put them where you think them most advantageous to me' (NLS, MS 4029, fols 251–52). On 17 March Blackwood announced that the poem would be placed in the immediately imminent number of the Magazine. A postscript to the same letter records a visit by the Duke of Buccleuch: 'Some of your MS. of Johnne Graime was lying on my desk. I did not fail to show it to his Grace' (NLS, MS 30312, p.164).

Two elements probably lay behind Hogg's hesitancy in submitting 'Johnne Graimis'. Firstly, the poem is in a relatively complex stanzaic form (ababcccb) and employs 'archaic' terminology to the full. Secondly, it touches on some of Hogg's more radical concerns, Johnne Graime's spiritual pride contrasting unfavourably with the sincere Christian feelings shown by a female penitent. The situation echoes the parable of the pharisee and the publican in the temple (Luke 18.10–15), while strongly implying that full redemption is available to the sexually 'fallen' woman. This non-productive 'eckspeditioun' to Heaven offers a kind of companion-piece to Jocke Taitte's journey of self-discovery to Hell, though in the *Queer Book* of 1832 the correspondence was obscured by a change of title to 'The Miser's Warning'—itself, perhaps, a means of camouflaging the very recent appearance of the poem in the periodicals.

147(15) wrong sowe be the eirre proverbial: 'To take the wrong sow by the ear'.

148(36) To all Eternitye the view of Eternity expressed in this stanza is similar to that in Hogg's long poem, *The Pilgrims of the Sun* (1815).

149(83) lost sheippe as in the parable of the lost sheep (Luke 15.1–7).

149(86) vice's wydde and weitlesse waye 'for wide is the gate, and broad is the way, that leadeth to destruction, and many there be which go in thereat' (Matthew 7.13). The image is also similar to Bunyan's way of Destruction, open and undemanding, in *Pilgrim's Progress*.

Textual Notes on 'Johnne Graimis Eckspeditioun till Heuin'

This poem went through several drafts before being sent to Blackwood for pub-
lication. The Turnbull Library, New Zealand, holds two early manuscript versions.
Item 50 in MS Papers 42 consists of an unheaded single leaf, with the watermark G
WILMOT/1827 partly visible, and contains seven stanzas of the poem, matching
the present stanzas 1–4, 6–8. The first line locates the habitation of the main
protagonist ('There livit ane man into Dalgryce'), a designation which is preserved
in the later and complete draft found in Item 29. This is written on a full-size sheet (*c.*
38cm x 24cm), and has the watermark A COWAN & SON/1829. With a full
header, and paginated by Hogg [1]–2, this might represent the version Hogg had in
readiness early in October 1830. The bulk of the manuscript used as copy by
Blackwood's Edinburgh Magazine survives in the Blackwood Papers in the National
Library of Scotland (MS 4805, fol. 20). Written on similar paper to Turnbull 29 and
incorporating revisions made in its predecessor, there are clear signs of its having at
one stage been cut into slips and then reassembled through a process of lamination.
As a result of the loss of one of these slips, the top right-hand corner of the
manuscript is missing. Another interesting feature is that the stanzas are numbered
consecutively from 1 to 24, apparently in Hogg's hand, while there are traces in
pencil of the names of compositors on different slips.

The *Blackwood's* compositors followed Hogg's text with a measure of accuracy,
adding standard punctuation and slightly normalising some idiosyncratic-seeming
spellings. With the *Queer Book* of 1832, however, a more thoroughgoing adoption of
English forms significantly altered the tenor of the poem.

The present text is based on the manuscript in the National Library of Scotland,
with Turnbull 29 supplying those areas of text missing through its incompleteness
(lines 53–69, 113–28). Quotation marks are silently added where Hogg's own
system breaks down, and question marks have been introduced at lines 18, 20, 28,
60, 64. Additionally, the following emendations have been made.

(l.37)   rysis]   ryis (manuscript)
(l.41)   primmyt his mou]   primmyt hi (manuscript) [Turnbull 29 here supplies a
    deficiency caused by a hole in the NLS MS; 'his mou' is also found in *Blackwood's*
    and *Queer Book* 1832.]
(l.125)   to repentance]   too repentance (manuscript)
(l.170)   donne]   doune (manuscript) [Turnbull 29 and *Blackwood's* donne]
(l.179)   grone—]   grone (manuscript)

St. Mary of the Lows

'St. Mary of the Lows' first appeared in the *Forget Me Not* for 1829 (pp.25–29). This
was the oldest of the London annuals, having been established in 1823, and the
numbers from 1827 were edited by Frederic Shoberl. Hogg first sent material on 1
April 1827, having received a complimentary copy from its publisher, Ackerman:
'I have written the romantic stories &c accompanying this solely for your work and
request of you to show them to Mr Shoberl without loss of time' (NLS, MS 8887, fols
36–37). Though no evidence about the present contribution has apparently
survived, most probably it was written and submitted at a later point during the
early months of 1828. Hogg's combination of two current reflective modes, the
churchyard meditation and romantic expression of grief over a lost love, was well
directed at Shoberl's popular and relatively eclectic literary miscellany.

St Mary's Churchyard is located on a hill side on the northern bank of St Mary's
Loch, in the Yarrow Valley, and affords spectacular views over the loch, which at
its southern point connects with the smaller Loch of the Lowes. The church burial
ground, which served local farming communities, was still in use in Hogg's day. An

earlier note by Hogg to his ballad 'Mess John' (1807) suggests that remnants of the original Chapel or Church also survived: 'The ruins of St Mary's Chapel are still visible, in a wild scene on the banks of the lake of that name [...] The chapel is, in some ancient records, called *The Maiden Kirk*, and, in others, *The Kirk of Saint Mary of the Lowes*' (*The Mountain Bard*, (Edinburgh, 1807), p.86). By projecting a feudal origin, the poem effectively offers a historical panorama of Ettrick Forest: from its early days as a royal hunting-ground, through border conflict and civil strife, to a new domestic calm marked by the advent of sheep-farming. The graveyard (somewhat fancifully) is depicted as mingling pre-Reformation warriors and Presbyterian martyrs, while elements of both the Catholic and Protestant creeds are traceable in Hogg's closing reflections on the premature death of an unnamed woman.

153(10) hallow'd soil echoing Walter Scott's lines in the Introduction to the 2nd Canto of *Marmion* (1808): 'Yet still, beneath the hallow'd soil,/ The peasant rests him from his toil'. Hogg heard Scott recite his description of St Mary's Loch from the proofs of *Marmion* before its publication (see *Memoir of the Author's Life*, ed. by Mack, p.111). His own version noticeably extends the social and historical range of those buried in the churchyard.

153(18) hunted as the osprey's brood the osprey, which feeds on fish, was hunted down as a pest in country districts. Here Hogg likens its plight to that of the Covenanters when persecuted in the 17th century.

153(24) low graves the graves of the Covenanters were often marked by very small stones, owing to the circumstances of their burial after summary execution. St Mary's churchyard contains a number of rough slabs without visible inscription, but there is no evidence to connect these with the Covenanters. Several examples, however, can be found in nearby Ettrick churchyard.

153(25) the last of all the race Walter Grieve, minister of the reformed presbyterian synod, who died on 7 March 1822 aged 75 years. His son, John Grieve, helped support Hogg in Edinburgh and was one of his closest friends. For details of surviving monuments to the Grieve family, see 'St. Mary's Kirkyard, Yarrow', *Transactions of the Hawick Archaeological Society* (1964), p.49.

154(41) forest bowmen alluding to Ettrick Forest once having been a royal hunting-ground. Compare Hogg's 'Statistics of Selkirkshire': 'The forest of Ettrick continued a hunting station of the kings of Scotland from the days of Alexander the Third to those of Queen Mary Stuart, who was the last sovereign that visited it' (*Prize-Essays and Transactions of the Highland Society of Scotland*, 9 (1832), 290).

154(46) Scotts, and Kerrs, and Pringles of these leading clan names on the Scottish Border, only that of Scott can be found in St Mary's churchyard.

154(65) here lies one the young woman addressed is probably a fictional creation.

Textual Notes on 'St. Mary of the Lows'
No manuscript of this poem has been discovered, and it is not unlikely that the copy sent to London was destroyed after printing. Nonetheless there is reason to believe that the text in the *Forget Me Not* represents a reasonably fair version. When first sending contributions on 1 April 1827, Hogg had made a point of asking for proofs; and he still enjoyed good relations with Shoberl ('the only editor this year who has aught from my pen') as late as 4 June 1831.

The *Queer Book* of 1832 introduced a number of minor changes in accidentals, its main verbal alteration being the substitution of 'Border' for 'forest' at line 41 (arguably diminishing the focus on Ettrick Forest at this point). More remarkably, it left out the final stanza of the original poem altogether, ending with the penultimate stanza at the foot of a page (p.256). Although it is tempting to conclude space was a

factor—procedure would have demanded a whole page for the remaining verse—
the failure of the normally punctilious printer to provide a concluding mark is more
indicative of a production error.

The present edition reprints the text from the *Forget Me Not* for 1829, without
alteration.

The Origin of the Fairies

This relatively long narrative poem was first published in *Blackwood's Edinburgh
Magazine* for August 1830 (vol. 28, pp.209–17). Blackwood communicated his
decision to include it, ahead of other material by Hogg, in a letter of 31 July 1830:
'[...] I could only make room for your fairies' (NLS, MS 30312, p.59). The end
inscription in the Magazine version indicates that it had not been long out of Hogg's
hands.

The story combines two elements common in fairy lore: the enticement of an
adult male into fairyland; and sexual intercourse between a fairy and a human,
bringing problematical results. Hogg also introduces one of his favourite themes, the
disappearance of the fairies from Scotland, the later stages of the poem associating
this with religious and civil strife in the 17th century.

157(12) Dumblane the town of Dunblane, an ancient cathedral city in Perthshire,
about 6 miles N of Stirling; 'Dumblane' is an alternative spelling.

157(15) light green and the yellow colours traditionally associated with the
fairies.

161(173) a tale of truth should aye be told echoing a number of proverbs about
truth-telling, though no exact parallel has been found.

161(197) star of love Venus.

162(228) seven pure beings seven is a mystical number in folklore.

166(377) weird sisters more commonly three in number, as in the case of the
witches in *Macbeth*: 'The Weird Sisters hand in hand' (I.3.30). Also associated
with the Classical Three Fates, and with the Scandinavian Norns, they are
usually depicted as foretelling or controlling the destiny of human beings.

168(459) the psalms and the prayers of the Covenanters in the 17th century,
compelled to worship in hiding. Though Hogg appears to identify religious
discord as a main cause of the fairy exodus, this has also been associated with a
new intolerance towards superstition after the Reformation. A similar theme
underlies Richard Corbet's 'A Proper New Ballad, Intituled the Fairies' Fare-
well' (1647), which connects the disappearance of the English fairies with the
Puritans in the reigns of Elizabeth I and James I.

168(461) hunters of men i.e. Royalist persecutors of the Covenanters.

Textual Notes on 'The Origin of the Fairies'

The manuscript used as printer's copy by *Blackwood's Edinburgh Magazine* has not
been discovered. The larger part of an earlier draft, however, survives in the Turn-
bull Library, New Zealand. Item 28 in MS Papers 42 consists of a 4-page booklet,
with an '1815' watermark identical to that found in Item 46 (an early draft of 'The
Goode Manne of Allowa'). Like Item 46, the text is packed tightly on its pages
and has the multiple alterations of a rough working draft. Noticeably this lacks
the preamble of the printed version, and its opening line introduces the 'laird of
Falstane' rather than 'Knight of Dumblane' ('The laird of Falstane is a hunting
gone'). At certain points, especially when the narrator speculates what his own
reaction might have been, this draft is noticeably more direct in sexual terms than
the published version. In fact, a process of self-censorship can already be seen in the

striking out of the following lines, which must have been rewritten at a later point (compare lines 128–31):

I think if I had the dizziness felt
I would have gripped her by the belt
And since a fall there needs should be
To have brought the fair maid down with me
Goodness be thanked, that I was spared
From being that day in the place of the laird!

Turnbull 28 is incomplete, the text reaching only as far as line 359 of the published poem, a subsequent booklet or leaf having presumably been lost.

One clear presentational difference between the Turnbull draft and *Blackwood's* is found in the latter's use of line spaces to divide the text at certain points. Two of these seem to be fairly arbitrary, and it is not impossible that the compositor(s) acted independently in an effort to alleviate the visual density of Hogg's couplets. The *Queer Book* of 1832 took the process further by creating a space between each verse paragraph (this helps 'expand' the poem to no less than 23 pages). Collation between the two printed texts reveals mostly punctuational variants, though two verbal changes by the *Queer Book* appear to correct misreadings of the manuscript.

The present edition reprints the *Blackwood's* text, but the spaces between verse paragraphs at lines 131/2 and 171/2 have been removed, leaving the main narrative to run without break between lines 12 and 413. Indentations are introduced at lines 106 and 234, to form 'new' verse paragraphs, as in Turnbull 28. The following emendations have also been made:

(l.57) sward;] sward, (*Blackwood's*)
(l.144) felt, beneath] felt beneath (*Blackwood's*)
(l.154) beside] bride [*Queer Book* 1832 beside]
(l.171) better.] better (*Blackwood's*)
(l.184) morn] morn, (*Blackwood's*)
(l.313) within!] within, (*Blackwood's*)
(l.374) said the] said, the (*Blackwood's*)
(l.394) all,] all (*Blackwood's*)
(l.410) play'd, with] play'd with (*Blackwood's*)
(l.417) leave] have [*Queer Book* 1832 leave]

A Highland Eclogue

This poem was first published in *The Gem* for 1830 (pp.194–200), a literary annual edited by Thomas Hood, whose first number a year earlier had included items by Scott, Keats, and John Clare. Hood had originally written to Hogg on 22 April 1828 asking for contributions: 'It is my *earnest* wish to see you numbered with the Contributors who grace my list' (NLS, MS 2245, fol. 116).

The particular history of the poem, which has some of the characteristics of a rough sketch, is unknown. A number of details point to an imaginative overlap with the tragic Highland events of the last volume of *The Three Perils of Woman* (1823). In the present case, however, divisions are healed through two positive factors: human good sense, which insists on the setting of preconditions before marriage; and the benign influence of religion, seen from the broadest vantage point.

170(2) Mary of Moy Moy is about 8 miles SE of Inverness, and Moy Hall was the seat of Mackintosh, Chief of the Clan Chattan. It was here that an attempt was made by government forces to capture Prince Charles Edward, a few weeks before the battle of Culloden in 1746; this was foiled by the suspicions of Lady Anne Mackintosh and the intervention of a handful of Jacobites led by the Moy blacksmith. In *The Three Perils of Woman* (1823), Lady Mackintosh features as

Lady Balmillo and the blacksmith becomes Peter Gow, one of Hogg's central characters. For Hogg's use of Mary as a name for his young heroines, see Douglas S. Mack, 'Hogg and the Blessed Virgin Mary', *Studies in Hogg and his World*, 3 (1992), 68–75.

170(26)Allan of Borlan-dale Borlan-dale has not been identified, though there is a similarity to Borrodale, in the Western Highlands, where Charles Edward first landed on the mainland of Scotland, leaving again from the same place in 1746. The name Allan of Borlan-dale also echoes that of the young Highlander, Diarmid M'Ion of Boroland, the main male romantic figure in the first two volumes of *The Three Perils of Woman*.

172(76) Sky the Island of Skye, in the Inner Hebrides.

173(115) schedule-deed gerent a *deed* in Scots law refers to a formal written instrument setting out the terms and conditions of an agreement, while in Hogg's day *schedule* normally referred to a deed recounting an action of legal significance; *gerent* is not a term of legal significance, and one suspects that Hogg is largely improvising his legal terminology.

174(154) the dark and the bright indicative of the lights and shadows of Scottish life, which Hogg had made his theme in *The Three Perils of Woman*.

Textual Notes on 'A Highland Eclogue'

Though no manuscript has been found, the relatively free punctuation in *The Gem*, together with the survival there of several idiosyncratic spellings, suggests a fairly uncomplicated transcription of the poem on its first printing. For the *Queer Book* of 1832, the title was changed to 'Allan of Dale', introducing a hint of the Allan-a-dale of the Robin Hood ballads (as well as of Scott's recent *Ivanhoe* (1820)) which is arguably inappropriate to the poem as a whole. The *Queer Book* also endeavoured to standardise grammar and orthography (e.g. 'knelt' for 'kneeled' (l.21) and 'indictment' for 'inditement' (l.119)), in the process taking the poem further away from Hogg's original text.

The present text is reprinted, without alteration, from *The Gem* for 1830.

Will and Sandy

This topical poem first appeared in *Blackwood's Edinburgh Magazine* for June 1829 (vol. 25, pp.748–51). It was sent by Hogg to Robert Blackwood on 4 May 1829: 'I herewith send you a prose and a poetical article for the next Maga at your father's request' (NLS, MS 4024, fol. 290). The prose item was probably 'Sound Morality', published in the same number, which also involves a dialogue between two Scottish shepherds. Writing to William Blackwood on 23 May, D.M. Moir expressed a preference for 'Will and Sandy': 'His poem is much better, and although unequal contains a great quantity of splendid poetical imagery' (NLS, MS 4025, fol. 190).

Through its use of pastoral dialogue, 'Will and Sandy' can be linked with some of the earliest poems in Hogg's career, notably 'Dusty, or, Watie an' Geordie's Review of Politics' (1801), in which two shepherds discuss contemporary issues. Striking resemblances are also found in 'Will and Davy, A Scotch Pastoral', first published in *The Spy*, no. 22 (26 January 1811), pp.175–76. In a similar setting ('Where Yarrow pours her silver billow [...] '), Davy upholds the joy of nature as a counter to Will's forebodings of public disaster. At one point in 'Dusty' (line 85ff.) legislation brought about by William Pitt the Younger for the religious toleration of Catholics becomes the focus of attention ('For sen they past the Papish bill,/ Frae ae mischief they've run t'nother,/ An' neer had luck i' ane nor other'). In 'Will and Sandy' the central issue is the Catholic Emancipation Bill, which was debated at packed meetings in Edinburgh during March 1829 before being carried the following month.

Blackwood's itself became deeply involved in the debate, with two articles in the number for April 1829 censuring the Duke of Wellington for bringing in the measure (see vol. 25, pp.401–11, 503–24).

As in earlier dialogues Hogg allows the contrary views of the two shepherds to stand freely, without apparent authorial intervention. In another topical poem, 'Aughteen Hunder an' Twenty-Nine' (*Edinburgh Literary Journal*, 26 December 1829, pp.432–33), he appears almost to relish the discomfiting of the Protestant opposition ('Now lat the cocks o' Calvin craw,/ Their kaims are croppit sairly'), while ending on a more personal and humanist note ('For thou hast brought an angel sweet/ Unto the Braes o' Yarrow').

175(5) enlightened martyrs Covenanting preachers in the 17th century. Especially famous for his prophecies was Alexander Peden (1626?–1686), who is supposed to have foreseen the terrors of the French Revolution. No particular prophecy relating to 1829 has been found, but Hogg possibly was aware that the Battle of Bothwell Bridge had been fought 150 years before the present Catholic Emancipation Act.

175(7) isle adjacent Ireland, whose dominantly Catholic population made it central to the issue of extending civil rights.

175(18) Mount-Benger's lofty height Mountbenger Law (1770 feet), overlooking the Yarrow Valley (and Hogg's current home at Mount Benger) from the north.

175(20) Meggat-dale through which Megget Water runs, entering St Mary's Loch about 6 miles SW of Mountbenger Law.

175(34) St. Mary's mirror i.e. the surface of St Mary's Loch, Selkirkshire.

176(37) Yarrow Yarrow Water, flowing between St Mary's Loch and Selkirk.

176(60–61) King [...] hero George IV (d. 1830); and the Duke of Wellington, then Prime Minister.

177(80) that bill the Catholic Emancipation Bill (10 Geo. IV, c. 7), which threw open to Roman Catholics most civil and military offices, a recurrent issue in British politics since the Irish Act of Union of 1800.

177(87) popish tyrant's slaves alluding to the Royalist attempts to suppress the Covenanters in the 17th century; James VII and II, the last reigning Stuart in the male line, openly espoused Catholicism.

177(97–98) devil [...] one small finger compare Hogg's 'The Witches of Traquair' (1828), where Colin Hyslop remembers his father's pious warning: 'My father tauld me, that if I aince let the Deil get his little finger into *ane* o' my transactions, he wad soon hae his haill hand into them a'' (*Shepherd's Calendar*, ed. by Mack, p.224).

177(108) Chalmers Thomas Chalmers (1780–1847), Professor of Divinity at Edinburgh from 1828, and a leader of Presbyterian opinion. Chalmers had argued against opposing Catholic Emancipation at meetings held in Edinburgh on 14 March and 1 April 1829. 'It is not because I hold Popery to be innocent that I want the removal of these disabilities; but because I hold, that if these were taken out of the way, she would be tenfold more assailable' (*The Speech Delivered by the Rev. Dr. Chalmers [...] March 14, 1829 on the Subject of the Roman Catholic Claims* (Southampton, 1829), p.7).

177(111) Thomson Andrew Mitchell Thomson, D.D. (1779–1831), Minister of St George's Church, Edinburgh from 1814, and an influential voice in the Church of Scotland. A letter by him, in favour of Catholic Emancipation, was read out at the meeting held in Edinburgh on 14 March 1829.

177(111) Inglis John Inglis, D.D. (1763–1834), Minister of Greyfriars' Church, Edinburgh, another leading figure in the Church of Scotland.

178(112) Frank Jeffery Francis Jeffrey (1773–1850), editor of the *Edinburgh Review*,

and soon to be Lord Advocate on the return of the Whigs to power in 1830.
Jeffrey was one of the speakers, alongside Chalmers, at the pro-Catholic meeting
held in Edinburgh on 14 March 1829. The spelling of his name as 'Jeffery' is a
consistent feature in Hogg's writing (see *Memoir of the Author's Life*, ed. by Mack,
pp.26–27).

178(112) Sir Walter Scott somewhat reluctantly accepted the need for Catholic
Emancipation early in 1829. See, e.g., his Journal entry for 9 March 1829, after a
meeting with fellow Edinburgh Tories: 'we subscribed [...] with a slight alter-
ation affirming that it was our desire not to have intermeddled had not the Anti
Catholics pursued that course. And so the Whigs and we are embarkd in the
same boat' (*The Journal of Sir Walter Scott*, ed. by W.E.K. Anderson (Oxford:
Clarendon Press, 1972), pp.530–31).

178(130) a brief potentially a double pun, on Jeffrey's handling of legal writs
(briefs) as an advocate and on his diminutive stature (barely 5 feet).

178(132) more than half a pope already though brought up as a Presbyterian,
Scott appears to have considered himself in later life as a member of the Episcopal
Church of Scotland.

178(134) something said in old Mortality Presbyterians in Scotland had been
outraged at the sympathy apparently shown to the Episcopalian position in
Scott's *Old Mortality* (1816), set during the Covenanting period. Hogg had earlier
disputed with Scott the accuracy of the novel in relation to his own *Brownie of
Bodsbeck* (1818): 'in no one instance have I recorded in The Brownie that which is
not true an' that's mair than you can say of your tale o' Auld Mortality'
(*Anecdotes of Sir W. Scott*, ed. by Douglas S. Mack (Edinburgh: Scottish
Academic Press, 1983), p.48).

178(144) pale form in the west in Hogg's *The Royal Jubilee: A Scottish Mask* (1822),
various spirits meet in Holyrood Park to honour George IV's visit to Scotland,
including the Genius of the West, who is depicted as a grim old Covenanter. Such
a figure, warning of disaster, appears to be imagined here by Sandy.

179(151) evening star Venus.

179(158) Erin a poetical name for Ireland.

179(180) Benger-Law see note to line 18.

179(182) polar bear the constellation Ursa Major, known as the Great Bear.

179(184) giant of the western star perhaps referring to constellation Orion,
traditionally figured as a giant hunter.

Textual Notes on 'Will and Sandy'

The manuscript used as copy by *Blackwood's Edinburgh Magazine* survives in the
National Library of Scotland (MS 4805, fol. 8). It consists of a single sheet (*c.* 26cm x
22cm), paginated by Hogg [1]–2, and without visible watermark. There are signs of
this having been cut into slips, so compositors could work simultaneously, and then
reassembled. The manuscript is incomplete, ending at line 164, the final verse
paragraph presumably having been written on another leaf since lost. The text is
thinly punctuated, the full apparatus in the Magazine evidently being the work of
the compositors. Hogg's orthography was also standardised in *Blackwood's* (e.g.
'grieves' for 'greives' and 'Jeffrey' for 'Jeffery'), while at line 70 Hogg's 'birn'
(meaning a brand) was misread as 'birr' ('rebellion's birr'). Interestingly the *Queer
Book* of 1832 restored 'birn'; but in most other respects it distanced the poem further
from its MS state—the insertion of spaces between verse paragraphs adding a 'lyric'
air at odds with the original context. In preserving the end inscription usual
procedure was not followed, no doubt in an effort to retain the sense of a once
topical poem.

The present edition uses the manuscript as primary copy-text, supplying the missing section of the poem from the *Blackwood's* printed version. Inevitably this introduces an element of unevenness at line 165, and comparison between the two sections will show the extent to which Hogg's manuscript was regularised when transformed into print. It is unlikely that readers alive to the poem's rhythms will have difficulty in following syntax up to this point, but as a basic guide question marks have been added at lines 58, 75, and 116. A misplaced quotation mark has also been repositioned; and one initial letter at the beginning of a line is silently raised. In addition, the following emendations have been made:

(l.11)   mountain, moor, and]   mountain moor and (manuscript)
(l.13)   may—]   may (manuscript)
(l.64)   undisclosed,]   undisclosed (manuscript)

The Last Stork

This is another topical poem, concerned with Catholic Emancipation, and, more broadly, the plight of the administration at a time of increasing Whig pressure for Reform. It was first published in *Blackwood's Edinburgh Magazine* for February 1830 (vol. 27, pp.217–22), when deep divisions threatened Tory unity. William Blackwood on 9 January 1830 expressed his preference for the poem's imaginative, as opposed to satirical, qualities: 'In this N^o I have your Stork, which is a beautiful & spirited Poem, though as I told you it wants something to make it more direct and applicable as a Satire on the late Papist measure' (NLS, MS 30311, p.485). Yet Hogg would have been acutely aware that his contribution was directed at a Tory journal deeply involved in the debate, and his letter to Blackwood of 4 January (NLS, MS 4027, fols 178–79) shows that he had read the January 1830 number with great interest. One article there, by 'One of the Old School' [David Robinson], fulminates against the low quality of current political life: 'To the prevailing faction of public men, official and otherwise, all distinctions between right and wrong, purity and guilt, are destroyed' (vol. 27, p.45). Another, on 'The Effects of Variations in the Currency', pictured the Ministry as 'beset on the one hand by economists, and on the other by the stock-jobbers, and the money-lenders', adding that 'nothing short of a determined and united movement on the part of the agriculturists, can nullify the intrigues and importunities of these persevering parties' (vol. 27, p.71). High Tory opinions of this kind are clearly reflected—and perhaps, to a degree, satirised—in Hogg's own tirade against the spirit of the times.

There is a possibility that Hogg might have heard a story about a pair of storks roosting on the roof of St Giles' Cathedral in Edinburgh. This is recorded in Book 15 of *Scotichronicon* as occurring in 1416:

> In the same year a pair of birds called storks came to Scotland and nested on [the belfry of] the church of St Giles in Edinburgh. They stayed there for part of the year, but where they went afterwards is unknown. They give the greatest care to their offspring, as Pliny says, to the extent that while they are carefully looking after their nests, they continously cast their soft feathers while lying down. But no less extraordinary devotion is shown by the chicks to their mothers, for however long the mothers have spent on the training of their young, they are supported by the chicks for as long. Hence the stork is called the affectionate bird. (ed. by D.E.R. Watt, vol. 8 (1987), p.87).

As this passage suggests, the reputation of the stork for faithfulness was well established in Classical times. It also has a Biblical origin, the Hebrew name for stork signifying pity or mercy, presumably because of the loyalty shown between nesting birds. The poem's motto is taken from the prophet Jeremiah's upbraiding of the Jews for their foolishness and impenitency, part of a larger diatribe which foretells the destruction of Jerusalem by Nebuchadnezzar. The density of Biblical allusion, particularly in the later stages, is reminiscent of the 'Chaldee Manuscript' published in *Blackwood's* in 1817.

180(16) Hermon hill a mountain on the border between Lebanon and Syria, believed by some authorities to be Mount Sion of the Old Testament; most notable of its numerous streams are three that feed the Jordan river.

180(17) Mirom's reedy brake probably referring to 'the waters of Merom', as in Joshua 11.5.

180(18) Tiberias' sultry lake i.e. Lake Tiberias (the Sea of Galilee).

180(28) fierce Simoom the 'simoom' is a hot and suffocating sand-wind which sweeps across African and Asiatic deserts at intervals during the spring and summer.

181(56–59) that evening drear [...] Jerusalem fell i.e. the taking of Jerusalem by the Roman general (later emperor) Titus, in A.D. 70, when the temple was destroyed and the city razed.

181(61) Zion's sacred dome Zion was one of the sacred hills of Jerusalem, on which the city of David was built, and which became the centre of Jewish life and worship.

182(107) Kryman and the Apennine the Crimean mountains (Crimea is called 'Krym' in Russian); and the Apennine Mountains in Italy.

183(122) Appenzell Swiss town and canton, about 50 miles E of Zurich, close to the present border with Austria.

183(138) snowflakes of the northern land the snow-bunting, called in Scots the 'snowflake' or 'snawfleck': a small Arctic bird which visits Britain in the winter.

183(147) our own grandsires such as Hogg's grandfather, Will Laidlaw of Phaup, reputedly the last man in Scotland to converse with the fairies (see Hogg's 'Odd Characters' in *The Shepherd's Calendar*, ed. by Mack, p.107).

183(152) ladder of her golden beam like Jacob's ladder in Genesis 28.12.

184(170) Wolga's wastes and Dwina's wave the Volga and the Dvina, Russian rivers.

184(198) duke or teal *duke* most obviously relates to the Duke of Wellington, the current Prime Minister, though the Scots pronunciation of 'duck' as 'duke' almost certainly involves an element of punning; the *teal* (itself close to the Scots *deil*, devil) is the smallest form of common duck.

185(208) Wharn-cliff possibly referring to Glenwhargen Craig, about 5 miles S of Sanquhar, which rises sheer from the road to a height of 1000 feet. Hogg had lived near there while working as shepherd and farming in Nithsdale *c.* 1807–10, when the local landlord was the notorious Duke of Queensberry ('Old Q'). There are also Wharncliffe Crags about 6 miles NW of Sheffield, affording extensive views.

185(217) Sidmouth cliff spectacular red cliffs in South Devon; but probably also alluding to Henry Addington (1757–1844), 1st Viscount Sidmouth, a veteran Tory and Home Secretary from 1812 to 1822.

185(217) Eldon hill Eldon Hill is in county Durham, about 2 miles SE of Bishop Auckland. John Scott, 1st Earl of Eldon (1751–1838), had been Lord Chancellor from 1801–6 and 1807–27, and was a prominent Tory opponent of the Cabinet's liberal policy with regard to Catholic Emancipation. Perhaps Hogg also has in mind here the Eildon hills, a striking landmark near Walter Scott's home at Abbotsford.

185(219) Winshiel's lofty bower not identified, though there is a Winshields in co. Durham.

185(220) Newcastle's smoky tower another conjunction of place and title appears to be intended: Henry Pelham Fiennes Pelham (1785–1851), 4th Duke of Newcastle, was a prominent opponent of Reform.

185(239) That sin can never be forgiven of blaspheming against the Holy Ghost, as in Mark 3.29 and Luke 12.10.

186(242) small voice see 1 Kings 19.12.

186(248) fishes and for loaves Matthew 14.17–21.

187(322) trespasses forgiven echoing the Lord's Prayer.

188(332) Assyrian blindness as in Elisha's prayer to the Lord in 2 Kings 6.18; the temporary blinding of the Syrian army allows them to be led away.

Textual Notes on 'The Last Stork'

An earlier draft of this poem survives in MS Papers 42 in the Turnbull Library, New Zealand. Item 25 consists of two 4-page booklets, the second and smaller of which is watermarked G WILMOT/1827. This ends at line 280 of the published version, but the remainder of the text is found in another booklet in the Turnbull Library (Item 18). Interestingly Hogg begins the poem in his 'ancient stile', before shifting to more conventional couplets after some 30 lines; at a later point he also replaced his original title, 'Ane pastoral of the Swamp', by writing the present title above it. The first booklet is apparently dated at the head 'Jnr. 5—7', which is consistent with a fairly rapid first composition early in 1830.

The present text is reprinted from *Blackwood's Edinburgh Magazine*, as the earliest record of Hogg's final version. Indentations have been introduced at lines 74, 201 and 253 on the authority of Turnbull 25, and the following emendations have also been made:

(motto) viii.7.] viii.7, (*Blackwood's*)
(l.39) Tiberias'] Tyberias' (*Blackwood's*)
(l.44) Till, far] Till far (*Blackwood's*)
(l.83) flying;] flying, (*Blackwood's*)
(l.106) shepherd] shepherds (*Blackwood's*) [*Queer Book* 1832 shepherd]
(l.108) Is startled] Are startled (*Blackwood's*) [*Queer Book* 1832 Is startled]
(l.221) spoilers] spoiler's (*Blackwood's*)
(l.252) minister.] minister; (*Blackwood's*)

Superstition and Grace

This poem first appeared in *The Bijou* for 1829 (pp.129–34), an eclectic literary annual, edited by William Fraser, whose first issue in the previous year had included items by J.G. Lockhart, Coleridge, Southey, and Hogg himself. While no correspondence with Fraser has apparently survived, there is little reason to doubt that 'Superstition and Grace' was submitted in May 1828 as its end inscription suggests. Hogg's end note points to another version being published long ago and now much altered, but here there is reason to suspect an element of disingenuousness. In subject matter and much of its wording the present poem derives directly from 'The Gyre Caryl', written in Hogg's 'ancient stile', which appeared in the *Poetical Works of James Hogg*, 4 vols (Edinburgh, 1822), II, 167–78. The latter's positioning in *Poetical Works* also indicates that it was once conceived as part of a larger project to be titled *Midsummer Night Dreams*. For further information on this scheme, which occupied Hogg in about 1814, see *Selected Poems and Songs*, ed. by Groves, pp.211–12.

189(14) Lammer law Lammer Law (1773 feet), Lothian, a peak in the Lammermuir Hills, 4 miles S of Gifford.

189(18) gyre carle supernatural being.

190(67) Lammer-muir i.e. the hilly moorland country in SE Scotland.

191(92) Gil-moules name for the Devil. See also note to 'Jocke Taittis Expeditioune till Hell', line 77.

192(137) queen isle of the sea Britain. In describing the banishing of older forms of superstition, this poem overlaps with accounts of the departure of the fairies from Scotland in 'The Origin of the Fairies' and 'The Last Stork'.

Textual Notes on 'Superstition and Grace'
No manuscript of the poem first published in the *Bijou* has been found, nor of the 'The Gyre Caryl' on which it is so closely based. Collation of the printed texts, however, shows how Hogg thinned out much of his original 'ancient stile', transposed certain passages, and also removed some of the more arcane chants in the earlier poem. Another interesting difference, reflecting perhaps the organs of publication in view, is the substitution of 'Ladies' for 'lordyngs' as a form of address to the reader. The extent to which the *Bijou* editor was aware of being offered a recycled poem is unclear. Even as late as the 1838–40 *Poetical Works of the Ettrick Shepherd*, published by Blackie and Son, the two poems were presented as if autonomous works (vol. II, pp.93–98, 141–45).

The present text is based on the *Bijou* of 1829, as the version of the poem nearest to Hogg's original manuscript. However, the printer in London appears to have had some difficulty in reading Hogg's hand, especially when confronted with Scots terms. The *Queer Book* worked hard to correct errors of this nature, but some of its solutions appear to be based on guesswork, and more than once 'The Gyre Caryl' of the 1822 *Poetical Works* proves to be a better guide. The following emendations seek to correct misreadings and faulty punctuation by the *Bijou* printer.

(l.16) fauldit]   faulelit (*Bijou*) [*Poetical Works* 1822 fauldit; *Queer Book* 1832 faul't]
(l.21) grew]   grew, (*Bijou*)
(l.37) fell]   fell, (*Bijou*)
(l.38) bell,]   bell. (*Bijou*)
(l.42) sang]   sung (*Bijou*) [*Poetical Works* 1822 and *Queer Book* 1832 sang]
(l.51) feres]   fires (*Bijou*) [*Poetical Works* 1822 and *Queer Book* 1832 feres]
(l.55) rase]   rage (*Bijou*) [*Poetical Works* 1822 rase]
(l.57) list—for the choral band]   list for the choral band, (*Bijou*)
(l.67) Lammer-muir]   lammer-muir (*Bijou*)
(l.71) heaven]   Heaven (*Bijou*)
(l.73) quake,]   quake (*Bijou*)
(l.77) viol and ayril]   viol ayril (*Bijou*) [*Poetical Works* 1822 vele and ayril; *Queer Book* 1832 viol, and ayril]
(l.83) Ring! ring!]   King! king! (*Bijou*) [*Poetical Works* 1822 Ryng! ryng!; *Queer Book* 1832 Ring! Ring!]
(l.98) adieu;]   adieu (*Bijou*)
(l.102) Spirits' King]   spirits' king (*Bijou*)
(l.115) asklent]   artlent (*Bijou*) [*Poetical Works* 1822 and *Queer Book* 1832 asklent]
(l.124) pain]   pain, (*Bijou*)

The Witch of the Gray Thorn

'The Witch of the Gray Thorn' first appeared in *Blackwood's Edinburgh Magazine* for June 1825 (vol. 17, pp.714–16), placed immediately after 'Ringan and May', another *Queer Book* poem. No direct evidence about its submission to the Magazine has been discovered, though the end inscription of 11 March 1825 indicates a composition several months before publication.

In its Gothic fatalism, use of dramatic couplets, and medieval ambience, 'The Witch' is reminiscent of 'The Abbot McKinnon', the last and one of the most powerful poems in *The Queen's Wake* (1813). The tempting of the present Abbot by a prophecy which proves true, but leads to his ruin, also brings to mind the double-edged promises made by the witches in *Macbeth*. By focusing on the temptation of a religious person to murder and damnation Hogg likewise touches on some of the leading issues in his *Private Memoirs and Confessions of a Justified Sinner* (1824).

193(11) priest of Inchaffery the ruins of Inchaffray Abbey, an Augustinian foundation, are about 6 miles E of Crieff, on Tayside. Established in 1200 by Gilbert, Earl of Strathearn, it featured prominently in Scottish history in the Middle Ages.

194(54) a mole does of heav'n echoing the wizard, Michael Scott, in *The Three Perils of Man* (1822): 'No more than the mole that grovelleth beneath the sward' (vol. II, p.109).

195(113) the prince of the air the Devil.

195(119) I have won! similar to Gil-Martin's 'Ah, hell has it' at the murder of George Colwan in *Confessions of a Justified Sinner* (1824), p.118.

196(133) through fire the last trumpet of Time see Matthew 24.31 and Revelation 20.15.

Textual Notes on 'The Witch of the Gray Thorn'
An autograph version of the poem, evidently that used by *Blackwood's Edinburgh Magazine*, survives in the Turnbull Library, New Zealand (MS Papers 42). Item 17, comprising a large 4-page booklet (*c.* 39cm x 24cm) watermarked SMITH & ALLNUTT/1821, contains two poems in Hogg's hand, 'The Anti-burgher in Love' and the present poem. The first has been crossed out in pencil, but above 'The Witch' William Blackwood has written 'Bourgeois across the page'—an instruction about print size and layout, similar to that found on the manuscript of 'Ringan and May'. Hogg's text is virtually without alteration, apart from the transposition of two couplets at lines 128–31; it is also fully punctuated, as if inviting a straightforward transference into print.

Comparison with the text in *Blackwood's* shows a number of alterations, verbal and punctuational. Several word changes appear to result from misreading: 'picture' for 'future' (line 3); 'Mad' for 'Proud' (11); 'swells' for 'wells' (44); 'crane' for 'crone' (87); 'hallowed' for 'hollowed' (88); 'tease' for 'tan' (129). Additional punctuation was introduced, with a large influx of commas within lines. Nearly all these changes were incorporated in the *Queer Book* of 1832, which also added a greater degree of formality (e.g. through the raising of initial capital letters to create 'Priest' and 'Heaven'). The *Queer Book* version also inexplicably omits lines 102–03.

The present edition follows the manuscript in the Turnbull Library, without verbal alteration. Hogg's idiosyncratic spellings are preserved, and at line 45 the last letter in 'come', obscured in the gutter, has been added with a comma. Of the following emendations, the last three attempt to mend an instability caused by Hogg's imperfectly executed transposition of couplets in the manuscript:

(l.67) be."] be" (manuscript)
(l.112) despair,] despair (manuscript)
(l.131) name.] name (manuscript)
(l.132) crime] crime, (manuscript)
(l.133) Time,] Time. (manuscript)

A Greek Pastoral
'A Greek Pastoral' was sent to William Blackwood on 6 April 1830: 'I inclose you herewith two poems of very different characters and as different from the laird of Lonne I like to give them every variety' (NLS, MS 4027, fol. 181). Blackwood responded favourably on 17 April 1830: 'I have been much delighted with your

Greek Pastoral, and the First Sermon. They will appear in this N°, (MS 30310, p.577). In the event, only the present poem appeared in *Blackwood's Edinburgh Magazine* for May 1830 (vol. 27, pp.766–71), 'The First Sermon' being delayed until the following number.

In one important respect, 'A Greek Pastoral' was specifically aimed at *Blackwood's*. At the end of his manuscript Hogg placed a reference to an article in the February 1819 number by John Wilson, then co-editor, titled 'Observations on the Poetry of the Agricultural and that of the Pastoral Districts of Scotland, illustrated by a Comparative View of the Genius of Burns and the Ettrick Shepherd' (vol. 4, pp.521–29), in which Wilson had placed Hogg on a footing with his renowned predecessor. The following passage was reproduced in full as a footnote to the poem when printed in *Blackwood's*:

> We have to remind such of our readers as are well acquainted with the poetry of the Ettrick Shepherd, that to feel the full power of his genius, we must go with him
> 'Beyond this visible diurnal sphere,'
> and walk through the shadowy world of the imagination. It is here, where Burns was weakest, that he is most strong. The airy beings, that to the impassioned soul of Burns seemed cold—bloodless—and unattractive—rise up in an irresistible loveliness in their own silent domains, before the dreamy fancy of the gentle-hearted Shepherd. The still green beauty of the pastoral hills and vales where he passed his youth, inspired him with ever-brooding visions of fairy-land—till, as he lay musing in his lonely sheiling, the world of fantasy seemed, in the clear depths of his imagination, a lovelier reflection of that nature—like the hills and heavens more softly shining in the water of his native lake. Whenever he treats of fairy-land, his language insensibly becomes, as it were, soft, wild, and aerial—we could almost think that we heard the voice of one of the fairy-folk. Still and serene images seem to rise up with the wild music of the versification—and the poet deludes us, for the time, into an unquestioning and satisfied belief in the existence of 'those green realms of bliss' of which he himself seems to be a native minstrel.

> In the department of pure poetry, the Ettrick Shepherd has, among his own countrymen at least, no competitor. He is the poet laureate of the Court of Faëry—and we have only to hope he will at least sing an annual song as the tenure by which he holds his deserved honours.

By offering the present poem as his 'yearly offering bland' (line 302), Hogg is responding in kind as 'poet laureate of the Court of Faëry'. But behind the blandness lies a sharper barb. Hogg's self-assertion needs to be seen in the context of his increasing suspicion early in 1830 that Wilson was blocking his entry into the Magazine. Moreover, Hogg had become convinced that the presentation of himself as the buffoon-like 'Shepherd' in the 'Noctes Ambrosianae' series had been a decisive factor in his failure to gain a grant from the Royal Society of Literature. The point is made explicitly in his letter to Blackwood of 6 April 1830, enclosing the poem: 'Every churchman voted against me on the ground of my dissipation as described in the *Noctes* and neither denied by myself nor any friend publicly' (NLS, MS 4027, fol. 181). Behind this, too, lay Hogg's longer-standing anxiety about being patronised by the classically-educated Wilson and Lockhart. Yet there is evidence that he had acquired a working knowledge of Classical literature when living in Edinburgh, especially through his friendship with James Gray of the High School. As well as showing a familiarity with the landscape and legends of ancient Greece, 'A Greek Pastoral' asserts the value of the author's own genius, equating the Scottish and Greek poetic traditions through the meeting of the Thessalian maid and Hogg's archetypal Highland youth.

197(1) Olympus mountain in northern Greece; in Greek mythology the home of the Gods, and commonly associated with the Muses.

197(8) vale of Tempe a valley renowned for its beauty, between Mount Olympus and Mount Ossa in northern Greece.

197(10) Thessallia's sweetest comeliest dame Thessaly is the largest division of Greece, in the NE of the country, and bounded on the N by the range of mountains which ends at the Aegean Sea with Mount Olympus. It was considered a centre of magic and the supernatural.

197(16) Ossa Mount Ossa, the largest peak facing Olympus.

199(80) isle of the evening sun i.e. Britain, in the far West; or perhaps, more specifically, one of the Western Isles. The following lines are strongly Ossianic in character.

199(97) silver beard similar to the 'long grey beard' of S.T. Coleridge's Ancient Mariner—like the Wedding Guest in Coleridge's poem, Hogg's Highlander is enchanted by the old man's 'tale of mystery'. The imagery of the sea journey which follows also matches in some respects the Mariner's voyage.

200(144) peri supernatural being in Persian mythology: originally represented as malignant in character, but subsequently as more benign and endowed with grace and beauty. There is no etymological connection with the term 'fairy', though commentators in Hogg's time were inclined to see one.

200(150) Tygris the river Tigris, in present-day Iraq.

201(159) enchanted ground a term used in romance to describe territory that was subject to a magician. The 'enchanted ground' in *Pilgrim's Progress* is a strange country in which the pilgrims become drowsy.

203(268) Salon sea not identified by name, but presumably the sea facing Thessaly.

204(note) for the specific passage cited and its relevance to the poem, see introductory comments above.

Textual Notes on 'A Greek Pastoral'

The final manuscript of this poem survives intact in the Blackwood Papers in the National Library of Scotland (MS 4805, fols 9–13), paginated by Hogg [1]–10. The watermark (A COWAN & SON/1829) is the same as that in Hogg's letter of 6 April 1830, enclosing the poem, and there are clear signs of the sheets having been folded into a package. An earlier draft of the poem is found in Items 52 and 70, MS Papers 42, in the Turnbull Library, New Zealand. This has a different ending from the couplet in the final version ('And thus concludes my fairy tale/ Of Pireus' stream and Tempe's vale/ The fair enthusiast still their boast/ And the warrior from the Grecian host'). It also lacks the end reference to Wilson's article, indicating the decision to add a personal nuance came later.

Comparison between the final MS version and the text in *Blackwood's* shows a number of verbal changes, all of which seem to derive from misreading ('winsome' for 'crimson' at line 130, 'bands' instead of 'bonds' at line 142, and 'buds' for 'beds' at line 286). The *Queer Book* of 1832 largely followed *Blackwood's*, with only a few changes in punctuation and spelling, while removing Hogg's end reference and the long extract printed as a footnote by the Magazine.

The present edition uses the manuscript in the National Library of Scotland as copy-text. At line 9, however, a seemingly unnecessary indentation has been removed. Speech marks have also been added at lines 255, 256, 263, 264, 275 and 276, in keeping with Hogg's practice earlier in the manuscript. No attempt has been made to supply full punctuation, though some marks have been supplied to complete Hogg's own punctuation or as a basic guide for the reader. These are recorded below, with other emendations.

(l.10) Thessallia's]   Thessallia (manuscript) [Turnbull 52 and *Queer Book* 1832
    Thessallia's]
(l.12) dream.]   dream (manuscript)
(l.40) dear.]   dear (manuscript)
(l.62) face!]   face (manuscript)
(l.67) Yes, very]   Yes very (manuscript)
(l.74) bliss,]   bliss (manuscript)
(l.75) this.]   this (manuscript)
(l.142) love.]   love (manuscript)
(l.144) peri or a mortal]   perie or mortal (manuscript) [Turnbull 52 peri or a
    mortal; 'peri' and 'a' also in *Blackwood's* and *Queer Book* 1832]
(l.150) this.]   this (manuscript)
(l.207) one!]   one (manuscript)
(l.256) No, love]   No love (manuscript)
(l.259) man.]   man (manuscript)
(l.268) Salon]   Sulon (manuscript) [Turnbull 52 and *Queer Book* 1832 Salon]
(l.303) Laureate's]   Laureate s (manuscript)

A Sunday Pastoral

This version of 'A Sunday Pastoral' was first published in *Blackwood's Edinburgh Magazine* for November 1830 (vol. 28, pp.737–41). The poem had initially been sent to William Blackwood on 13 August 1830, along with 'Jocke Taittis Expeditioune till Hell' and another (unidentified) piece. Replying on 26 August, Blackwood regretted that only 'Jocke Taitte' could be inserted in the September number of the Magazine, and asked Hogg to reconsider the Pastoral:

> There are some as fine and sublime passages in it as any you ever wrote, but alas there is a mixture of what would I fear be considered as low and not in good taste—the ludicrous mixed with solemn and fine religious feeling. [...] My idea is that with very little alteration you could make it a fine picture of rural and innocent love softened and elevated by high devotional feeling. (Turnbull Library, New Zealand, MS Papers 42, Item 77).

Hogg's first reaction, in his letter of 1 September 1830, was one of defiance: 'the Pastoral shall never be materially altered while I live the mixture of love and religion in it can only be objectionable to those who are ignorant of the pastoral life.' On 8 October, however, he told Blackwood that he had drafted a new version: 'I have re-written the Sunday Pastoral with some additions but no material alterations'. Hogg then apparently waited until 20 October before sending a new manuscript, by which time he was heavily involved in preparations for the recently-proposed *Songs, by the Ettrick Shepherd* (1831) (NLS, MS 4027, fols 192, 196, 198). A fuller account of the different versions of the poem, and their composition, is given under 'Textual Notes' below.

'A Sunday Pastoral' combines elements of Classical pastoralism with the Scottish vernacular tradition. It is also filled with biblical allusions: most obviously in Colin's prayer (lines 147–202), which evokes Psalm 65:5–7 as well as the creation in Genesis 1. Notwithstanding Blackwood's intervention, Hogg still manages to explore the relation between sexual and spiritual experience in a daring and innovative fashion, and the message that God is found in Nature as well as in Church remains intact, in spite of a more conventional moral conclusion.

206(44) **the papish bill** the Catholic Emancipation Act of 1829. An earlier
    'Papish bill' features in one of Hogg's earliest poems, also a pastoral dialogue,
    'Dusty, or, Watie an' Geordie's Review of Politics; an Eclogue'—see *James Hogg:*

Scottish Pastorals, ed. by Elaine Petrie (Stirling: Stirling University Press, 1988), pp. 5, 44–45.

206(45) statutes of the ancient law i.e. the Jewish law as expounded in the early books of the Old Testament.

206(46) Bathsheba was seen bathing by King David and became pregnant by him (2 Samuel 11.2–5). Kate's jibes play on the scandalous nature of the liaison, Bathsheba's already being married, and the illegitimacy of the conception. Pregnancy out of wedlock was common in rural Scotland in the period, as the records of many a Kirk Session show; the poem also comes close hereabouts to Hogg's own fathering of illegitimate children (at least two in the period 1805–10).

207(76) Gilmanscleuch a settlement along Ettrick water, about 3 miles SE of Hogg's farm at Altrive. The lines here echo Hogg's ballad, 'Gilmanscleuch', first published in *The Mountain Bard* (1807): 'In Gilmanscleuch, beneath the heuch,/ My fathers lang did dwell'.

209(159) When the morning stars together sung Job 38.7 ('When the morning stars sang together').

210(202) fruitful vine 'Thy wife shall be as a fruitful vine by the sides of thine house', one of the blessings granted to the God-fearing in Psalm 128.

210(209) woman's curse 'in sorrow thou shalt bring forth children', as decreed by God after the Fall in Genesis 3.16.

210(213) love is heaven and heaven is love an allusion to Walter Scott's *The Lay of the Last Minstrel* (1805), Canto III, stanza ii ('For love is heaven, and heaven is love').

211(242) A gem the desart that perfumes compare Thomas Gray's 'Elegy Written in a Country Churchyard', lines 53–56.

213(296) Ettricks wildered way again placing the poem firmly in Ettrick, close to Hogg's birthplace and his present home at Altrive.

Textual Notes on 'A Sunday Pastoral'

The manuscript used as copy by *Blackwood's Edinburgh Magazine* is in the Blackwood Papers in the National Library of Scotland (MS 4805, fols 16–17). It consists of two large sheets (*c.* 38cm x 24cm), bearing the watermark A COWAN & SON/1829, and the poem is written virtually without alteration in double columns down three pages. Each sheet shows signs of having been cut into four sections, presumably to facilitate setting, and then reassembled through a process of lamination.

The survival of two earlier manuscripts in the Turnbull Library, New Zealand, makes it possible to give a fuller account of the history of the poem. Item 23 in MS Papers 42 has all the marks of an early draft: the text is written on the first three pages of a 4-page booklet, with Hogg maximising space by writing downwards then in sideways columns, and a similar pen stroke indicates a spontaneous composition in one sitting. This draft ends with the triplet found at lines 250–52 in the present text. Item 56 consists of one large leaf, identical in dimensions and watermarking to the MS in the National Library of Scotland, with a smaller leaf (*c.* 24cm x 12cm) glued at the bottom. With its formal heading, and carefully written double columns, the first leaf follows Hogg's normal practice in preparing copy for publication, and the presence of fold marks also encourages the view that this was the manuscript sent to (and rejected by) Blackwood in August 1830. Some uncertainty surrounds the smaller leaf, where a single column covers each side, but the most probable explanation is that Hogg decided to extend the poem after its return. Noticeably the script after line 252 (where Item 23 had finished) is in a darker ink, and contains a much larger number of alterations—some passages replaced by insertions remain undeleted—as if Hogg was preparing for a new version. What is added here is essentially the same as the conclusion found in the NLS/*Blackwood's* version, where Kate recalls her father's injunction to heed the Bible. This ending very likely represents the most significant of the 'additions' mentioned by Hogg in his letter to Blackwood on 8 October 1830. In effect, Hogg wrote two 'final' versions of 'A Sunday Pastoral'. A text based on Turnbull Item 56, edited by Peter Garside, has been published in *Studies in Hogg and his World*, 4 (1993), 94–108.

Collation of the manuscript version in the National Library of Scotland against the text in *Blackwood's* suggests a fairly straightforward transference into print, apart from the provision of standard punctuation: the most prominent substantive change ('mortal' for 'mental' at line 110) probably originated from misreading. Interestingly, the *Queer Book* of 1832 restored 'mental'; but in other respects (e.g. through the spacing out of paragraphs) the poem became further removed from its original pastoral style. One final intervention by the author is worth recording. In 1835 Hogg presented a book, made up from running copy of the *Queer Book* sent to him in London by Blackwood, to Charles Marshall, the schoolmaster at Mount Benger. The book ends abruptly at p.352, with line 154 of 'A Sunday Pastoral', but Hogg continues the poem in his own hand on a blank leaf at the end, reproducing lines 155–56 and 171–80 of the published text verbatim but without punctuation. This volume is now in the possession of the University of Stirling Library.

The present edition uses the manuscript in the National Library of Scotland as copy-text. Question marks are added at lines 48, 52 and 230, and the following emendations have also been made:

(l.1)   Good morning]   Goodmorning (manuscript)
(l.139) An']   An (manuscript)
(l.181) Grace, adored, believed,]   Grace adored believed (manuscript)
(l.219) Misshapen]   Mishapen (manuscript)
(l.225) refined.]   refined (manuscript)
(l.235) that's]   that s (manuscript)
(l.263) And now I]   And I now I (manuscript)
(l.287) again, by it I swear,]   again; by it I swear (manuscript)

The Perilis of Wemyng

This ballad first appeared in *Blackwood's Edinburgh Magazine* for August 1827 (vol. 22, pp.214–21). It was submitted to Blackwood on 5 July 1827: 'I [...] have stretched a point for all my throng to write you rather a good ballad off hand' (NLS, MS 4019, fol. 193). Blackwood responded in like spirit on 14 July, stating that 'the Ballad is capital' (MS 30310, p.182). The circle of approval was completed by D.M. Moir's observation to Blackwood on 21 July that the contribution contained 'a great deal of imagination—a wonderful deal' (MS 4020, fol. 29).

Like 'The Goode Manne of Allowa', this poem offers a successful blending of the traditional ballad, Burns's humour and pace, and the Coleridgean supernatural. Its title, which is reminiscent of Hogg's *Three Perils of Woman* (1823), has an element of ambiguity about it, since 'perils' are interpretable as being both caused and suffered by women. With the *Queer Book* of 1832 it was changed to the more descriptive 'May of the Moril Glen'. This is one of the few *Queer Book* poems to have attracted modern critical interest (see Alexander Scott's 'Hogg's *May of the Moril Glen*', in *Scottish Literary News*, 3:1 (1973), 9–16). The poem has also been reprinted from *Blackwood's* in *Longer Scottish Poems*, ed. by Thomas Crawford *et al*, 2 vols (Edinburgh: Scottish Academic Press, 1987), II, 329–40.

214(5) ane lovelye May 'A May, in old Scottish ballads and romances, denotes a
     young lady, or a maiden, somewhat above the lower class' (Hogg's note to *Mador*

of the Moor, Canto Second).

214(6) Moril Glenne evidently a fictional place; 'moril' is interpretable as Hogg's 'ancient' spelling of 'moral'.

215(57) fairye rynge ring of darker grass, caused by the extra nitrogen released by fungus; in folklore, a place where fairies meet and where they can be seen by mortals.

218(142) Megaira brode perhaps alluding to Megara, a city in ancient Greece, though no connection with the breeding of horses has been discovered.

219(192) grand polemyck waye reminiscent of James VI of Scotland, whose pedantic intellectualism had recently featured in Scott's novel, *The Fortunes of Nigel* (1822).

223(329) seuin chariotis seven is a mystical number.

224(337) maste wals maide of beaten golde echoing the traditional ballad, 'The Demon Lover': 'But the sails were o the taffetie,/ And the masts o the beaten gold' (Child 243F).

224(362) the crekis of Fyffe i.e. the narrow inlets on the northern bank of the Firth of Forth.

Textual Notes on 'The Perilis of Wemyng'

Very little is known about the composition of the work. In sending his manuscript to Blackwood on 5 July 1827, Hogg suggested that his nephew Robert might 'attend to the spelling for I have written it so hurriedly that it is not even spelled in my own way' (NLS MS 4019, fol. 193); but whether any intervention of this kind took place is uncertain. In addition to changing the title, the *Queer Book* of 1832 obliterated much of Hogg's 'ancient stile', turning the poem into a more trite and conventional ballad. The present edition reprints the text in *Blackwood's* without emendation.

Glossary

THIS Glossary sets out to provide a convenient guide to the Scots, English and other words in *A Queer Book* which may be unfamiliar to some readers. An effort has been made to include most orthographical variants, except for cases where the only difference lies in the addition of a final 'e', in which case the shorter version is normally entered (*goud* rather than *goude*, *laverock* rather than *laverocke*). The Glossary concentrates on single words only, and guidance on expressions, phrases and idioms involving more than one word will be found in the Notes.

In interpreting Hogg's mock-antique Scots, it is important to remember that 'quh-' stands for 'wh-' and '-it' for '-ed'; and that plurals can be given as '-is' rather than '-s'. Words that appear unfamiliar primarily as a result of Hogg's 'ancient' spelling, such as *haldockis* ('haddocks') and *veetalis* ('vitals'), are generally not included in the Glossary. Readers wishing to make a serious study of Hogg's Scots should consult *The Concise Scots Dictionary*, ed. by Mairi Robinson (Aberdeen: Aberdeen University Press, 1985), and *The Scottish National Dictionary*, ed. by William Grant and David Murison.

abone, aboon: above
ae: one
aglee: awry
ahynde: behind
als: as
an: if
aneath, anethe: beneath
asklent: aslant
asperre: apart
aumouss: alms, food or money given in charity
ava: at all
avyse: advice
ay, aye: still; always
ayril: meaning uncertain, but possibly signifying a musical air

bagnio: a brothel
baigel: to proceed slowly as if fatigued
bairn: a child
baisse: base, low; morally despicable
baldrick: a girdle, a belt
ballande, ballant: a ballad
banne: to curse
barmings: yeast formed on a fermenting liquor
bauke: a crossbeam
bavaroy: a kind of cloak
bawbee: a halfpenny

bedeen: together
bedlar: a gravedigger
begoude: began
beilde: protection, shelter
beldam: an old woman; a hag
ben, benne: inside; towards the inner part of a house
bente: a moor; open country
beryl: a transparent precious stone of yellowish green colour
bestedde: beset
bigg: to build
birn: a brand of ownership on an animal
blee: a blow
bleyter: the bittern
bleze: a blaze
blink, blynke: to blink, to look fondly at; a glance, a gleam, a moment
bluther: to make a bubbling noise
boardly, bordlye: burly, stalwart
bog-bumper: the bittern
bogle: a ghost, a phantom
bore: a hole, a crevice
borrelis: bore-holes
bosky: bushy, full of thickets
boudlye: bandy
bound, bounne: a boundary
bountith: a bounty, a gift
boustrous: rough, coarse

bouzely, bowzelly: bushy, shaggy

brae: a hill; a bank

braid: broad, extensive

braw: fine, splendid in dress

bree: the brow

brekis: breeks, trousers

brent: smooth, unwrinkled

brigg: a bridge

brock: the badger; also used contemptuously of a person

broostle: a sudden movement forward

brownie: a goblin or evil spirit

bruckle: brittle

bruike: to brook, put up with; to enjoy the possession of

buller: to gurgle, to rush noisily

burdlye: see under 'boardly'

busk: to equip, to dress oneself

but: outside of

but an, but and: as well as, and also

but and benne: in both the inner and outer parts

byrsis: bristles

capperkyle: the wood-grouse

carle, caryl: a man, a fellow; an old man

carrye: clouds in motion

cauldryffe: chilly, cheerless

cayne: see under 'kane'

chack: to chatter, to make a clicking noise

cheenye: china plate

cheip: to chirp

chirle: a chirp, a warble

claw: to scratch

cleide: to clothe

cleuch, cleugh: a narrow glen

cloack: to brood, to hatch

clout, cloutte: to patch, to mend; a rag, a piece of cloth

cloutt: to strike, to slap

cludde, clude: a cloud

coft: bought

cooffe: a fool, a simpleton

corbye (craw/crowe): the raven

cracke: to gossip, to brag

cramasie, cramasye: crimson cloth

craw: to crow; the crow, the rook

crombe-clothe: a cloth laid under tables to help keep the carpet clean

cropp: the craw of a bird

crousse: lively, spirited

cushat: the wood-pigeon

dab: to peck

dad: to dash, to strike heavily

dang: knocked, struck

dantonit: intimidated

dawtyit: beloved, cherished

deidclothe: a shroud

deil, deille: devil

dejeune, dejune: the first meal of the morning

deraye: disorder, uproar

dern: to hide

descryve: to describe

dike: a field wall

dirl: to tingle, to vibrate

disk: dusk

dobye: having spikes, prickly

dochte: would

dole: grief, pain

domonie, domonye: a schoolmaster

dool: grief, distress

dowe: a dove; term of endearment for a sweetheart

downae: am unwilling to

dowy: sad, dismal

drammock: a mixture of raw oatmeal and cold water

dre: to endure, to suffer

dreddour: fear, apprehension

dreep, dreip: to drip; to drop slowly

droulle: in phrase 'duste and droulle', dust and ashes

droye: cold, damp

duddis: clothes

duddye: ragged, tattered

dufflit: duffled, coarsely matted

duffye: soft, spongy

dynnle: to roll, to vibrate

ee: eye

een, einne: eyes

egill: the eagle

eilde: old age

eistren: eastern

eke: also

eldern: elderly

eldrich, eldrisch: wierd, unearthly

eldron: old

ell: a measure of length originally taken from the forearm

elwand: a measuring rod, one ell long

ely: to disappear
emerant: emerald
eneuch, enewe: enough
erne: iron
eske: the newt; the lizard
este: a nest
ether: the adder
everilke: every
eyne: see under 'een'

fadge: a loaf of bread
faeme: foam
fain, fayne: willing, content; gladly
falchion, falshown: a short broadsword
fane: a temple
fauld: to fold, to enclose
fay: a fairy
feidde: enmity, hostility
feint (a): a strong negative—never a, devil a ('feint' is a Scots form of the English 'fiend')
fere: a companion, a mate; a dwarf
ferlye: to wonder, to marvel
fieldfare: a species of thrush
fire-flaught: a flash of lightning
flaitte: to wrangle, to scold
flaught: to weave, to intertwine
fle, flee: to fly; a fly
flegge: a fright, a scare
flewe: the chaps (cheeks) of a hound
fogge: moss
forbye: besides
fould: see under 'fauld'
fyer-flaught: see under 'fire-flaught'

gaad: a goad, an iron rod
gair: a strip of green grass on a hillside
gairlye: greedy, covetous
gaite: see under 'gate'
gang: to go
ganne: the mouth
gar: to make; to cause
garf: meaning uncertain
gate: a way, a course
gay an': very
geare, geire: gear, possessions
gerse: grass
geyte: mad, insane
gif: to give
gif, gin: if
girn: to grin
glacher: to glower, to stare intensely

glaiffe, glaive: a glove
glamour, glaumorye: witchcraft, enchantment
gledde: the kite; the buzzard
gledge: to squint, to give a sideways glance
gleid: a spark, a glimmer
glittye: slimy, slippery
gloaming, glomyng: twilight
gloff: a shock, a scare
glymit: glanced, squinted
gobe: a bird's beak
goodman: a husband; the head of an establishment
goodwife: the female head of a household
gorcock: the red grouse cock
goud, gowd: gold
goustye: ghastly, eerie
gowan: the daisy
graen: to groan
grebe: a freshwater diving bird
greet: to weep
grewe: a greyhound
gudeman: see under 'goodman'
guest: a ghost
gurly: stormy, surly
gyrn: see under 'girn'
gysand: dry, shrivelled

hackerit: cracked, wrinkled
hadder: see under 'hedder'
haffatis: the face, the temples
haflins: half, almost
hagg: a marshy hollow in a moor
haill: whole; in a healthy state
haille: hail; small shot, pellets
hald: had
hallan: an inner wall, erected between the door and the fireplace
haslet: the guts, the entrails
hass-bane: the collar-bone
haunk: to fasten with a loop
hawis: hawthorn berries
hedder: heather
hedder cowe: a tuft or twig of heather
herd: a shepherd; a herdsman
herrounsheugh, heronshu: the heron
herry: to plunder, to lay waste
herytage: inheritance, property
heuch, heugh: the steep slopes of a hill
hind: behind
hind, hynde: a farm-servant; a youth; a

peasant

holm, houm: a stretch of low-lying ground by a river

houffe: a shelter; a public house

hough: the thigh

houke, howck, howk: to dig; to hew

howe: a hollow

howlet: the owl

ilk, ilka, ilkan: each; every

illfaurd: ugly, unbecoming

inditement: composition; a formal written charge in law

irne: iron

izel: a burnt-out cinder

jaulke: to trifle, to dally

jaw: to dash, to splash

jink, jynk: to move nimbly, to dodge

kaille: cabbage soup

kairle: see under 'carle'

kane: payment (often rent) in kind; a penalty, a reckoning

kebbuck: a whole cheese

keik: to peep, to glance

kelpie: a water demon

kembe: to comb; a comb

kente: a staff, a pole

keppyt: caught

keude: hare-brained, deranged

keuste: tossed

kie: cattle

kith: see under 'kythe'

kittle: puzzling, tricky

knabbe: to strike, to knock

knolle: a stroke, a blow

knowe: a knoll, a small hill

knowe heidde: a hilltop

kye: see under 'kie'

kythe: to show, to display; to appear

laine, lane: alone; by herself/himself/myself/yourself

langsyne: long ago

laverock, laveroke: the skylark

lea, le: a meadow; open grassland

lee: to lie, tell lies

leel, leille: loyal

leifu: lovely

leirre: learning, skill

leman, lemanne: a lover, a paramour

leuin, levin: lightning

liefu: solitary

lift: the sky

ling: to swing along

linn: a waterfall; a tumbling burn in a gorge; a ravine

linty: the linnet

locker: to curl, to bend

locker: the ranunculus (most commonly, the buttercup)

lone: a cattle track, pasture ground

losel: a scoundrel, a loafer

loun, lowne: a rogue, a rascal

loup: to leap

lout: to stoop, to bend

low: a loch, a lake

lugg: the ear

lychtsome: pleasant, carefree

lydder: sluggish, slack

lyfte: see under 'lift'

lymmer: a loose woman, a whore

lyng: heather

lynk: to trip along; to work vigorously (at)

lynne: see under 'linn'

maen: a moan

maene: a (horse's) mane

maike, make: a figure, a form; a resemblance

maille: rent, tribute

marled: marbled, mottled

maskis: a mastiff

maun: must

may: a maiden, a young lady

meide, meidde: a reward

melle: to speak, to converse

menzie: a household, a retinue

merk: a sum of money equal to two thirds of a pound

merl: the blackbird

messan: a small dog; a mongrel

mickle: see under 'muckil'

minnye: a mother

mistyme: inconsistent

modderit: confused, dazed

moote: to moult; to decay slowly

mou: the mouth

moudiwort, moudy: the mole

moulde: earth, soil

muckil, muckle: large, big; much

myresnyppe: the common snipe

naife: the navel
neifuit: clasped, shovelled with the hand
nicher, nycher: to whinny; to snicker
noisome: noisy; harmful
nolt-herde: a cowherd
nor: than
norlan: northern

ochon, ohon: alas! oh!
or: before
oussen, owssen: oxen
ouzel: the blackbird

partan: the common crab
pawkye: shrewd, lively
peaseweippe: the peewit
pelloch: the porpoise
pirl: to twist, to curl
plashy: watery, sodden
plevir, pliver: the plover
pocke: a bag, a pouch
poutt: a chick, a young game bird
powe: the head
powhood: a tadpole
powlderit: dusty
prinkle: to tingle, to prickle
propine, propyne: a gift, a reward
ptarmigand: the ptarmigan (a
    mountain-dwelling grouse)
puddock: the frog
pykit: pointed, spiked

quaiffe: a coif, a close-fitting cap
quean, queine: a young woman; a hussy
quhille: till

rackle: to fasten up with a chain
rail, raille: a woman's short-sleeved
    mantle, a bodice
raire: to roar; a roar
rampaugent: disorderly, riotous
rath: early; eager
reard: to roar, make a loud noise
reek, reike: to smoke; smoke
refit: robbed
reide: advice, council; red
reiferye: robbery
reive: to rob; to take away
rokelaye: a kind of short cloak
ronkilit: wrinkled
row: to roll, to wrap
rowill: spiked wheel on a spur

rowt: to shout, to bellow
rung: a stout stick

sackless: innocent, inoffensive
sair: sore; severely, very much
sanct: to vanish
saraband: a slow Spanish dance
sark: a shirt; a woman's shift or chemise
scraughe: a loud cry, a scream
scrowe: a crowd, a commotion
sea-mawe, sea-mewe: the seagull
sennil: seldom
serke: see under 'sark'
seye: to try, to attempt
shaw: a wood, a thicket
sheille: a hut for shepherds; a small
    house, hovel
shillpha: the chaffinch
shole: a shovel
sic: such
siccan, sickan: such, of such a kind
siller: silver
skaith: hurt, injury
skelloche: a scream, a shriek
skelp: to strike; a blow
skimmer: to shimmer; to move rapidly
skirl: to scream, cry out with fear or pain
skraich, skraigh, skreigh: to screech
skreigh: first light, the crack of dawn
skrene: a veil
skyffat: a sharp hard blow
sloate: the track of an animal
smudge: to smirk
snell: hard, severe
snocker, snockir: to snort; a snort
snok: to sniff, to scent out
snood: a ribbon for tying hair
snool: to subdue; to cringe; to humiliate
snork: to snort
snowflake: the snow bunting
snyfter: to snort; a snort
solan: the gannet
sonke: a straw cushion
soome: to swim
spang: to stride vigorously, to bound
spankye: frisky, dashing
speer: to ask, to beg
spurr: to kick, to scratch
stang: to sting; a sting, an acute pain
stawit: glutted, satiated
stend, stenne: to leap, to bound; a leap, a
    bound; high, alert

sterne: a star

stevin: a loud outcry, a din

storm-cock: the missel-thrush

storte: trouble, strife

stott: a bullock

stounne: a stunning blow

stoure: dust, dust in motion

stoure: grim, stern

stown: stolen

strath: a river valley

strauchle: to walk laboriously, or with difficulty

streik: to stretch

stron: a headland or promontory

sturt: trouble, disquiet

styck: to stab

styme: a tiny amount, a jot

stynte: the stint (a small marsh bird)

sunket: a titbit

swaird: sward, the green turf

swairf: to faint

swaw: to swing, to sway

swoof: to make a rustling or murmuring sound

swyth: quick! away!

syne: thereupon

taed: the toad

taigle: to linger

tawse: a whip, a strap

teal: a small freshwater duck

teene, teine: harm, hurt; sorrow, grief

teipe: a type, a representation

thof: though

thole: to endure, to suffer

throppil, throppyl: the throat

thumbikins: a thumbscrew

tidder: the other (of two)

till: to; until

timeous: timely, fitting

tinkler: an itinerant tinsmith; a gypsy

tod: a fox

tome: empty

torfel: to toss or tumble about

toune: a farm, an estate

tout: to toot; a toot, a trumpeting noise

touzel, touzil: to tousle, to fondle

tow: a rope

towzlye: dishevelled, ruffled

trammis: legs

tryste: an appointed meeeting, a rendezvous

twall: twelve o'clock

tyrelit: stripped

unchancye: unlucky, ill-fated

unco: very, exceedingly

unfarrante: rude, unsophisticated

upsettying: haughty, presumptuous

wae: woe; grieved, sorrowful

waf, waif: to wave, to flap

waikryffe: restless, lightly sleeping

waire: to spend, to waste

wale: the pick, the choice; hand-picked

wallet: a pedlar's pack, a travelling pack

wanne: see under 'win'

wanyerthlye, wanyirdlye: unearthly

warlocke: a male witch

wauff: see under 'waf'

weapanshawe: a muster of men in arms

weare, weir: war, combat; warlike qualities

weathergalle: an atmospheric appearance (e.g. an imperfect rainbow or mock sun) regarded as a portent of bad weather

weirde: strange, uncanny; destiny, one's particular fate

weirdly: magical, sinister

weitlesse: witless

welder: a wether, a male sheep (especially a castrated ram)

wemyng: women

whaisk: to wheeze, to gasp for breath

whew: to whistle; a whistle

whig, whigamore: slang names for a Covenanter

whiles: sometimes

whilly-whaup: the curlew

whilly-whewe: a melody, an air

whilom: while

whush: a stir, a commotion

wife: see under 'wyffe'

win: to gain; to reach; to deliver (a blow); to harvest

wis: to know

witch-bell: the harebell, *Campanula rotundifolia*

wo worth: woe betide, a curse on

wodde, wode: mad, crazy

won: to dwell

won, wonne: see under 'win'

wow: wow! gee!

wrethe: a bank of snow
wudde: see under 'wodde'
wychte: a wight, a person
wychte: valiant, courageous
wyffe: wife; a woman; in formations such as 'weird wyffe' also signifying a witch
wythershynne: the wrong way round, in a contrary direction to

yaud: an (old) horse
yaup: to cry shrilly, to scream

yerke: to jerk, to bind tightly; a blow, a slap
yerm: to complain, to whine
yestreinne: yesterday evening
yette: a gate
yettlin: an article made of cast-iron
yird, yirth: the earth
yont: along, beyond
yool, yowl: to howl, to wail
youffe, yuff: to bark
yowe: a ewe
yowte: a bellow